Married to the man sh... the mother of two ado... other an artist. Susanne loves everything romantic and pretty, so her home is brimming with romance novels, movies and shoes. With her interest in all things medical, her career has ... in the dental field and the medical world in different ...—and now Susanne has taken that love into writing Mills ... on Medical Romance.

...il Gordon loves to write about the fascinating ...nation of medicine and romance from her home in a ...ire village. She is active in local affairs, and is even ... upon to write the script for the annual village ...ime! Her eldest son is a hospital manager, and helps ...l her medical research. As part of a close-knit family, ...nsures having two of her sons living close by, and the ...he not too far away. This also gives her the added ...e of being able to watch her delightful grandchildren ... up.

...Heaton first started writing romance at school, and ...ke her stories in to show her friends, scrawled in a big ...ler, with plenty of crossings out. She dreamt of ... herself, and after knowing her husband-to-be for ...ee weeks shocked her parents by accepting his ... proposal. After four children—including a set of ...nd fifteen years of trying to get published, she finally ...'The Call'! Now she lives on Hayling Island and, ...'s not busy as a First Responder, creates her stories ...g along the wonderful Hampshire coastline with her ..., muttering to herself and scaring the locals.

...ouisa on Twitter, @louisaheaton, on Facebook, ...eatonAuthor, or on her website, louisaheaton.com.

Winter Wonderland Wishes

SUSANNE HAMPTON
ABIGAIL GORDON
LOUISA HEATON

MILLS & BOON

First Published in Great Britain 2018
by Mills & Boon, an imprint of HarperCollins*Publishers*
1 London Bridge Street, London, SE1 9GF

WINTER WONDERLAND WISHES © 2018 Harlequin Books S. A.

A Mummy to Make Christmas © 2015 Susanne Panagaris
His Christmas Bride-to-Be © 2015 Abigail Gordon
A Father This Christmas? © 2015 Louisa Heaton

ISBN: 978-0-263-27470-7

1218

MIX
Paper from
responsible sources
FSC® C007454

This book is produced from independently certified FSC™ paper to ensure responsible forest management.

For more information visit: www.harpercollins.co.uk/green

Printed and bound in Spain
by CPI, Barcelona

A MUMMY TO MAKE CHRISTMAS

SUSANNE HAMPTON

As I was putting the final touches to this book I was given the news that my amazing editor Charlotte was moving along her career pathway and would no longer be working with me. So this will be my final dedication to her and my last written recognition of her guidance, patience, much needed honesty and unwavering belief in my work. However, what I have learnt from her over the last five books will travel with me on my writing journey, so in many ways all of my books and writing success in the future will be a dedication to Charlotte Mursell.

Thank you, Charlotte.

CHAPTER ONE

DR HEATH ROLLINS momentarily looked away from the emails on his laptop computer, across the living room of the family home, to see his father sitting by the lace dressed bay window in his favourite armchair. With the mid-morning sunlight streaming into the room, he was intently reading the paper. Heath smiled a bittersweet smile as his gaze roamed to the old oversized chair, upholstered in green and blue tartan. It was a piece of furniture his mother had tried to have re-covered or removed from their home for many years but Ken Rollins had been adamant that it stayed. And stayed exactly as it was. It was a Clan Sutherland tartan, of the Highland Clans of Scotland, Heath would hear his father tell his mother, and it had direct links to the maternal side of his family. She would tell him that family connections or not, it was an extremely unattractive chair that looked out of place in their new French provincial decor. Frankly, it was hideous and it just didn't belong.

His mother and father had argued about very little except that chair. But, unlike all those years ago, now his father was stuck in that now slightly worn chair for hours on end, his leg elevated and his knee freshly dressed after surgery. And there were no more arguments about the chair as Heath's mother had passed away twenty years ago.

Heath then caught sight of his own suitcases, stacked against the hall wall, with the airline tags still intact. He would shortly be taking them to the room that would be his for the next month. His attention returned to the email he was drafting to the Washington-based podiatric surgeon travelling to Australia to work with his father. As he perused her résumé to find an email address, he couldn't help but notice her impressive qualifications and certifications. A quizzical frown dressed his brow as he wondered why she had chosen to relocate to Adelaide and consult at his father's practice. Then he dropped that line of thought. It was not his concern.

'I hope you don't mind the last-minute change in plans, Dr Phoebe Johnson,' he muttered as he pressed 'send' on the keyboard, hoping that even if she had turned off her computer she would receive the notification via her mobile phone. 'It looks like you'll be working with me not my father. At least until he's back on his feet again.'

Phoebe Johnson had switched off her cell phone an hour earlier. There was no point in having it on as there was only one person who would try to reach her and she would go to any lengths to avoid another conversation with her mother.

Unfortunately her mother had found her.

'Why on earth are you leaving Washington? It's been over three months since you postponed the wedding, Phoebe. It's time you set a new date.'

'I *cancelled* the wedding, Mother. I didn't postpone it.'

Completely dumbfounded, and shaking her head, Phoebe stood on the steps of her rented brownstone apartment, her online printed boarding pass and her passport both gripped in one leather-gloved hand while the other searched for keys in her oversized handbag. The second of her matching tweed suitcases was balanced precariously by her feet, and her heavy woollen coat was buttoned up against the icy December wind that was howling down the narrow car-lined street.

She found her keys and, aware that the meter was running on the double-parked cab, hurriedly locked the front door. She was in no mood for another confrontation and frustrated that at the eleventh hour it was happening again. Her mind was made up. She was not looking back.

'How can you work things out if you go rushing off to another country? Surely you've punished Giles enough for his indiscretion?' her mother continued, not at all deterred by anything Phoebe had said, nor by her imminent travel plans. 'I'm certain he's learnt his lesson.'

Phoebe tugged down her knitted hat, at risk of blowing away in a chilly gust, then made her way down the snow-speckled steps with her last suitcase and handed it to the cab driver, who had been tapping his foot impatiently on the kerb.

'It isn't a punishment, Mother. I ended it. I gave the ring back, returned the wedding presents and told Giles that I never want to see him again. It's about as final as it gets. And I've thought this through until I've gone almost mad. You don't seem to understand—I no longer love Giles and I don't want to see him again. *Ever*. To be honest, I'm surprised that after everything he's put me through you'd want him to have any part in my life.'

She paused as she looked long and hard at her mother, completely bemused that they saw the situation so very differently.

'He's not the man for me. I don't know if there even *is* a man for me, but right now I'm not looking. I want to put all my energy into my work and I refuse to waste another second on Giles.'

With that said, Phoebe headed to the waiting cab. The

headlights of the oncoming traffic were reflected on the icy road as night began to fall.

'That seems so harsh. He really does regret his behaviour. His mother told me so over our bridge game yesterday,' her mother continued as she followed Phoebe, her pace picking up with each step. 'Please see reason, Phoebe. Giles is committed to making it up to you. He's apparently not at all his usual jovial, outgoing self at the moment. He's taken the postponement very seriously. Esme said he's quite sullen, and that's not like him. She thinks he's turned over a new, more responsible leaf. He's sown his last wild oat.'

She placed her gloved hand over Phoebe's as her daughter reached for the door handle of the cab. Stepping closer, she dropped her voice almost to a whisper.

'Darling, you could do worse. Giles is so very handsome—and let's not forget his family tree. His ancestors arrived on the *Mayflower.*'

Phoebe rolled her eyes in horror that her perfectly coiffed mother, dressed in her favourite New York designer's latest winter collection, was pulling out both the looks *and* the ancestry cards. She watched the driver close the trunk, walk to his door and climb inside.

Pulling her hand free, she responded in an equally low voice. 'Let me see... My sulking but extremely good-looking ex-fiancé, with his impeccable lineage, is apparently committed to me but isn't averse to sleeping with other women. Please, Mother, let's not try to paint him as something he isn't. I don't think he is capable of loving anyone but himself, and I don't believe for a minute that he's turned over a new leaf. And, frankly, I don't care. He ruined any chance of us being husband and wife when he chose to cheat on me.'

She kissed her mother goodbye and climbed into the

cab, then dropped the window to hear the last of her mother's not so wise words.

'Darling, as your grandmother always said, every man is entitled to one big mistake in life.'

'He slept with both of my bridesmaids the weekend before our wedding—that's not one big mistake...that's two enormous, deal-breaking mistakes!' Phoebe's voice was no longer soft or controlled and she didn't mind if the cab driver heard. Her frustration had limited her ability to care.

'If you want to be *technical*, it's two....but couldn't you see fit to consider it Giles's one weekend of poor judgement and call it the same mistake?'

The cab pulled away and Phoebe slumped back into the cold leather seat. Over the rattling of the engine she heard her mother's parting words.

'Darling, don't forget—Christmas is a time for forgiveness.'

Phoebe was abruptly stirred from her unpleasant recollection of the pointless argument that had occurred less than twenty-four hours previously. An impeccably groomed flight attendant was standing beside her seat, accompanied by a young girl in a lime-green sweater and matching pants, with a mass of golden curls, a red headband and a big smile. Everything about her was a little too bright for Phoebe at the end of a long-haul flight.

The little helper reached across to Phoebe with a basket of cellophane-wrapped candy. 'If you chew something it will stop your ears getting blocked when we land. Would you like one?'

Phoebe wasn't sure what she wanted, but politely smiled and accepted a sweet. She would never hurt a child's feelings. She had no idea what Phoebe had been put through, and she envied her innocence just a little. The young girl had no idea that boys grew into cads.

'Thank you,' she said, and as the pair moved on to the next passenger Phoebe unwrapped the candy and slipped it into her mouth.

She wasn't sure of anything. She should be a happily married woman back from an eight-week honeymoon in Europe, but instead she was a single woman about to arrive in the land Down Under. And this trip was probably the first of many she would make on her own.

Midway over the Pacific Ocean she had looked out of her tiny window into complete darkness. It had represented her life…the huge unknown.

The very thought of ever trusting a man again was ludicrous. She would more than likely see out her days as a spinster, she'd told herself as she had flicked through the choices of inflight entertainment when the rest of the passengers had been sound asleep. Her head had been much too busy thinking about things that she knew she couldn't change, and her thoughts had been as unrelenting as they'd been painful.

All men were the same—well, except for her father, she had reminded herself, as she'd realised there was nothing she'd wanted to watch on her personal screen and pulled down her satin night mask to try and shut out the world. He was one of the last decent men and then they broke the mould.

Susy, her best friend since junior college, who had left Washington two years previously to work as a barrister for the Crown Prosecution Service in London, agreed with her. She had sworn off relationships after her last disastrous rendezvous three months prior.

Men were not worth the effort or the heartbreak, the two friends had decided over a late-night international call before Phoebe's flight. They'd both eaten copious amounts of ice cream in different time zones as they'd commiserated. Susy had been devouring her feel-good salted caramel treat after returning home from a long day in court, while Phoebe had been scraping the melted remnants of her cookies and cream ice cream at just past midnight, Washington time.

'They're just not worth it,' Susy had said into the phone as she'd dropped her empty bowl and spoon on the coffee table, kicked off her shoes and reached for a throw.

'Absolutely not worth even a second of our time,' Phoebe had agreed. 'They are full of baloney—and I'm not talking about the good Italian mortadella. I'm talking the cheap and nasty supermarket kind of baloney.'

'My sentiments exactly.'

'Men and women shouldn't even be on the same planet.'

'Not even the same universe,' Susy had replied, reaching for the bowl of luxury candies her mother had sent over for her recent birthday. She'd still been suffering from post-break-up sugar cravings. 'I think the entire male race should be banished. Except for your dad, though, Phoebs—John's a real sweetie, so he can stay. Mine hasn't called since my birthday, so he can take a jet to another planet for a while with the rest of them.'

Not long after their decision to relocate the earth's male population Phoebe had felt her eyes getting heavy and had said goodnight to her friend. She was glad she had such a wonderful friend, but very sad that they had both been hurt by callous men. She had no clue why they had both been dealt bad men cards, but she was resolute that it would never happen again.

Because neither of them would ever date again.

From that day forward it would be all about their careers.

The plane dropped altitude to land. The sun was up and Phoebe looked from the window to see varied-sized squares of brown and green crops making a patchwork quilt of the undulating landscape. It was nothing like landing in Washington, where she lived, or New York, where she had undertaken her medical studies. Australia couldn't be further from either, in distance or in landscape, and for that reason she couldn't be more relieved.

She was a little anxious, but she was a big girl, she kept reminding herself. It would be a healing adventure. A time to bury the past and focus on furthering her career in podiatric surgery. And time away from her mother. As much as Phoebe loved her, she doubted she would miss her while she was still clearly on Team Giles.

Phoebe did, however, have a strong bond with her father John, and would miss him and their long chats about local and world politics, theology, and to which particular rat species Giles belonged. Susy was right—her father *was* one of the last good men. Over the years he had taught Phoebe to seek out answers, to find her path and not to be afraid to experience life and the joys the world had to offer. He had told her always to demand in return the same good manners and consideration that she gave to others, and most importantly to smile… even if her heart was breaking. There were always others far worse off.

And, much to the chagrin of his wife, John had agreed that time away from Washington and the wedding debacle was the best idea for Phoebe.

'We are now commencing our descent into Adelaide. Please ensure your tray table is secured and your seat is in the upright position. We will be landing in fifteen minutes and you will be disembarking at gate twenty-three. The current time in Adelaide is eleven-thirty. Your luggage will be available for collection on Carousel Five. Adelaide is experiencing a heatwave and expecting an extremely hot forty-three degrees for the fifth day in a row. For our overseas passengers, that's a hundred and nine degrees Fahrenheit—so shorts and T-shirts would be the order of the week, since the hot spell is not ending for another few days! We hope you enjoyed your flight and will choose to fly with us in the future.'

Phoebe rested back in her seat and her mind drifted back to the snow-covered streets of Washington that she had left behind. And to her cheating fiancé and quite possibly the world's worst bridesmaids... She thought of her position at the university hospital...and of how, after the flight attendant's announcement, she might quite possibly die of heat stroke on her first day in a new country...

Fifteen minutes later, a disembarked and ever so slightly dishevelled Phoebe looked around the sea of strangers waiting with her in line at Customs and questioned herself for heading to a country where she didn't know a soul. But then reason reminded her that the alternative would be crazier.

Staying with the very charismatic but totally insincere Giles. Accepting his pathetic 'last fling' excuse and her mother's unrelenting need to defend his abominable behaviour due to his impressive family tree... Giles's womanising would have his notable ancestors with their seventeenth-century Pilgrim morals turning in their graves.

She shook her head as she moved one step closer to the booth where a stern-looking official was scrutinising the passports of the very weary long-haul travellers wanting to enter the country.

Despite her stomach churning with nerves at the prospect of being so far from home, particularly at Christmas, she knew she had done the right thing. Remaining in her home town wasn't an option as the two families were joined at the hip, and that closeness wasn't allowing her to heal and move on. Thanksgiving had gone a long way to proving her right, with both families and a supposedly contrite Giles gathering and expecting her to join them. She'd refused, but she had known immediately that Christmas gatherings would be no different.

If she'd stayed it would have given her mother a glimmer of hope that she would rekindle her relationship with Giles. That an ensuing wedding of the year in Washington might be on the cards again, and that the wedding planner would once again ask Phoebe's father to check the diary of the Vice-President to ensure he could attend.

In Phoebe's mind there was absolutely no chance that she would wed a man who had been unfaithful. She couldn't turn the other cheek and ignore his indiscretions. It was the twenty-first century and she had choices. She wanted to be a man's equal partner in life. That was what she needed and if she never found it then she would not take second best. She would rather spend her life alone.

For better or worse with Giles would mean Phoebe always hoping his behaviour would get better, but knowing he'd more than likely get worse. The further away she stepped from her ex-fiancé the more she suspected he had done her a huge favour by showing his true nature before the wedding. No doubt, she surmised, having a wife who wouldn't ruffle feathers but would instead add value to his reputation by having her own medical career, and whose father was a Presidential advisor, had all been part of Giles' political game plan.

It had become painfully clear once she'd broken up with him that Giles had manipulated her for his own benefit. She thought she had fallen in love, but now she wasn't so sure. Perhaps it had been a little rushed, and she'd been caught up in the idea of happily-ever-after once the wedding momentum had started. All of her friends except for Susy were engaged or married and it had seemed a natural progression.

The wedding had been set up so quickly by her mother who, along with Washington's most popular wedding planner, had had everything moving at the speed of light.

Susy had accepted the role of her maid of honour, and the two young women had been excited about seeing each other after so long, but the day before she'd been due to fly out Susy had called and broken disappointing news. She was unable to leave London as the jury had not returned the verdict on a very prolonged case. In her own words, she'd said she'd have to miss the wedding of her best friend in the world in order to see some bad guys locked away for a very long time in an English prison.

Deflated and disappointed, Phoebe had understood, but it had left her with only two distant cousins in her bridal party. She had agreed to include the young women, who were both twice removed on her mother's side of the family, because she had been secure in the knowledge that Susy would be beside her for the days leading up to her wedding and with her at the altar of the Cathedral Church of Saint Peter and Saint Paul.

She barely knew the girls. She hadn't seen them in over five years and from what she had heard they were party girls who were living on the west coast and their antics in social media were a constant source of embarrassment to their respective families.

It had been decided that it was time they returned to Washington and settled down. They were both single and in their early twenties, and the families' combined strategy had been to use the wedding as their wayward daughters' entrée into the right circles. They'd hoped that a society wedding would help the girls meet potential husbands and leave their wild life behind them.

Unfortunately that had never happened. They'd flown in a few days before the final dress fittings and managed to ruin Phoebe's life in the process.

Looking back, Phoebe realised that everything about that day had been wrong, but at the time she hadn't been able to step back far enough to see it for what it really was. But now she could. The three months since the scheduled wedding day that never happened had given her time to see Giles for the man he was. Controlling, calculating and ambitious. There was nothing wrong with ambition, but, fuelled by his other character flaws and good looks, it made for a man who would do whatever he wanted, whenever he wanted—and apparently with whomever he wanted. A misogynist, with a lot of family money and connections.

Phoebe would be eternally grateful to the best man, Adrian, who had delivered the bad news the day before their nuptials. She appreciated that it had been a difficult call for him, but knew he had spent a number of months working closely as a political intern with her father and respected him enormously. Adrian had told Phoebe that he cared too much for her and her family to stand by and let Giles hurt her. He'd broken the boys' club rules and she knew he would no doubt pay the price with his peers. She also knew that her father would do his best to support him, but Adrian was not motivated by professional gain and that made his act even more admirable. Honesty in the political arena was rare, and Phoebe and her father were both grateful.

Phoebe's head was spinning as she was finally called up to one of the immigration booths. She dragged her hand luggage behind her and handed over her passport. Then, with everything in order, her visa was stamped and she was waved through to collect her luggage.

'Enjoy your stay, Miss Johnson.'

Phoebe's lips curved slightly. It was an attempt at a smile but she was still not sure how she felt and whether she had just made another of life's bad calls—a huge error she would live to regret almost as much as accepting the first date with Giles and, six short months later, his proposal in the opulent wood-panelled and chandelier-filled dining room of that five star hotel in Washington.

The ring was a spectacular four-carat diamond, set in platinum, and it had been served on a silver platter along-side her *crème brûlée* dessert. A single strategically placed violin had played as Giles had fallen to one knee. But it had only been a fleeting kiss on the forehead he'd given her when she'd agreed to be his wife.

It hadn't been a passionate relationship, but she had still believed their life together could be perfect. He wasn't one to show public displays of affection and she had accepted that. In hindsight, she suspected he preferred to look around at all the enamoured faces in the room rather than at hers. He had enjoyed the attention the proposal had focused on him. In person and in the media.

As she shuffled through the airport to collect her checked baggage Phoebe drew a deep breath and thought about the irony of his reticence in showing any public display of affection with her while enjoying very *private* displays of affection with other women. And she felt sure there had been more than the two she knew about. It was all about appearances. And what happened behind closed doors seemed inconsequential to him.

She shuddered with the thought of how close she'd come to being his wife. And the lies that would have been the foundation of their marriage.

No matter what lay ahead, her life *had* to be better than that.

CHAPTER TWO

THE MOMENT PHOEBE saw the sign *'Welcome to Adelaide'* she decided she would quiet her doubts. There was no room for second-guessing herself. She was already in her new home. *This is it,* she said to herself silently as she collected her luggage and then made her way to the cab rank. *No turning back now.*

The airport was only twenty minutes from the centre of town, where she would be living. The town she would call home for six months. Six months in which she hoped to sort out her life, her head, and if possible her heart—and forget about the man who had seduced her bridesmaids.

'You were supposed to meet potential husbands—not hump the groom!' she muttered under her breath.

Phoebe noticed the cab driver staring at her strangely in the rear vision mirror. His eyes widened. She realised that her muttering must have been audible to him and she bit her lip and looked out of the window in silence.

Phoebe paid the driver, giving him a generous tip. She had been told it was not necessary in Australia, but it was second nature. He placed her suitcases on the pavement and tucked the fare into his pocket. She was left standing in the heat.

It was a dry heat, like the Nevada desert, and it engulfed her like a hot blanket dropped from the sky. She was grateful that she had changed on the two-hour stopover in Auckland, and was now wearing a light cotton sundress and flat sandals. She lugged her heavy suitcases, one at a time, up the steps to the quaint single-fronted sandstone townhouse that she prayed had air-conditioning. The suitcases were so heavy it would have cost a small fortune in excess baggage if her father hadn't insisted on paying for her first class flight.

On Phoebe's personal budget, post hand-beaded wedding dress, along with the purchase of the maid of honour's and the bridesmaids' dresses, beautifully crafted designer heels for four, three pearl thank-you bracelets and half of a non-refundable European honeymoon, she could only have managed a premium economy flight. But she'd been so desperate to leave Washington for the furthest place that came to mind she would have rowed to Australia just to get away from the drama of the cancelled wedding and her desolate mother.

Phoebe drew another laboured breath. A week ago she'd known little of Adelaide, save the international bike race and the tennis that took over the city in January. Her career as a podiatric surgeon specialising in sports-related conditions made her aware of most large-scale sporting events worldwide. She hoped that her skills would be utilised in Adelaide, a city ten thousand miles from home. She was there with no clear plan for the future. She did, however, have a job.

Her father had been wonderful. It was fortunate for Phoebe that his role at the White House gave him the knowledge and connections to assist her, which meant that her application to practise in Australia had been fast-tracked. She met all of the criteria, and her credentials were impeccable, so approval had been granted.

She'd had the option of a small practice in Adelaide

or a much larger practice in Melbourne that focused entirely on elite sportsmen and women. While the second option was her dream job, it was still a few weeks off being secured, and Phoebe had liked the idea of leaving town immediately. She had also done some research around the sole practitioner, Dr Ken Rollins, a podiatric surgeon in his early sixties with an inner-city practice and the need for an associate for six months. The position sounded perfect. His research papers were particularly interesting and Phoebe looked forward to working with him.

So she was more than happy with her decision. They were two very different opportunities, but she felt confident she had made the right choice.

Opening the door to her leased townhouse was heavenly. It was like opening a refrigerator. The air-conditioning was on high and the blinds were half closed, giving a calm ambience to the space. There was a large basket of fruit and assorted nibbles on the kitchen bench. Her father, no doubt, she mused.

She dropped her bags, closed the front door and wandered around the house for a moment before she found the bedroom and flung herself across the bed. Embarrassed at remembering what she'd said to herself in the cab, she kicked off her shoes and then reminded herself that the driver would have witnessed far worse than a jet-lagged passenger's mutterings. The pillow was so cool and soft against her face as she closed her heavy eyes. Exhaustion finally got the better of her and she fell into a deep unexpected sleep.

It was nearly four hours before Phoebe stirred from her unplanned afternoon nap. Her rumbling stomach had woken her and she remembered the basket she had spied on her arrival. The fruit was delicious, and she had opened the refrigerator door to find sparkling water, assorted juices, a cold seafood platter, two small salads and half a dozen single serve yoghurt tubs.

Thanks, Dad.

She smiled. She knew her father must have called the landlord and arranged for the house to be stocked. She knew, despite what she said, that he felt to blame for the way everything had turned out as *he* had introduced to her young, 'going places' political intern fiancé.

John Johnson had thought Giles was a focussed young man with a huge career ahead of him and he'd had no hesitation in introducing him to Phoebe. He'd been polite, astute, with no apparent skeletons in the closet, and from a well-respected Washington family. But they had all been hoodwinked.

There was no way that John could have foreseen the disaster. And he had done everything in his power to get her away from the situation when it had turned ugly. Phoebe would never blame him for anything.

After eating, Phoebe showered and sent her father a text message to let him know she was safe and sound and to thank him for everything he had arranged. Then she raised the air-conditioning temperature enough to ensure that she didn't freeze during the night before setting the alarm on her phone and climbing back into bed.

She just wanted to be fresh and not suffering the effects of jet-lag.

Eight hours later, as Phoebe lifted the blinds and looked across the Adelaide parklands, she felt refreshed. She had never flown such a distance and had expected to be exhausted, but she was feeling better than she had in months. It was as if a weight had been lifted from her shoulders.

The view from her bedroom window was picturesque. The morning sun lit up the large pinkish-grey gum trees towering over the beautifully manicured gardens. The flowers were in bloom in the garden's beds and it was like a pastel rainbow. It was a new beginning.

She reached for her phone and took a snapshot, sent it to her father in a quick text, then headed for the shower. She wasn't about to be late for her first day on the job. She wanted to get there early and learn the ropes before the patients arrived. Working with an older, more experienced specialist would be a learning experience for Phoebe, and she was excited by the prospect. It would keep her mind off everything she had been through.

Ken Rollins's papers focussed on his holistic and conservative approach in treating lower limb conditions, using a variety of modalities such as gait retraining, orthotic therapy, dry needling and exercise modification. Phoebe had printed the most recent before she'd left Washington and she'd read it on her flight over. He would be a great mentor.

It was going to be a much-needed change and Phoebe couldn't be more optimistic. After all, she had heard Adelaide was the place to raise children or retire, and it had the highest aging population of any other capital city, so she assumed there would be a lower than average population of single men. Single, arrogant, self-serving men, all incapable of remaining faithful. There truly couldn't be a better city in the world for her at that moment, but for the fact that she knew she would miss Christmas with her family. It was her favourite time of year. But it was the price she had to pay for her sanity.

As Phoebe stepped out of her house half an hour later the heat of the day was already building. She felt glad she had chosen a simple cream skirt that skimmed her knees, a black and cream striped blouse and black patent Mary Jane kitten heels with a slingback, so she didn't need to wear stockings. Her shoulder-length chestnut hair was pulled into a high ponytail and she had applied tinted sunscreen, a light lip gloss and some mascara.

She hoped the practice rooms would be as cool as her townhouse. Her previous address at this time of the year was freezing cold at best and icy on bad days. She knew she wouldn't cope in the heat for too long, but felt confident that the inner-city practice would be cool as a cucumber.

Unfortunately, as she discovered five minutes later, she couldn't have been more wrong. The air-conditioning at the practice had been working overtime during the heat-wave. Phoebe had arrived when the city had been swel-tering for close to a week. The infrastructure of the old building was buckling and clearly the air-conditioning had been the first thing to succumb. It was like a sauna as she entered, and she wondered if it wasn't cooler outside than inside the old building.

A bell above the door had chimed as she'd walked in but the waiting room was empty and it appeared no one had heard her enter. Standing alone in the uncomfortable, stifling air she felt sure that in minutes she would be re-duced to a melting mess. Not a great first impression, she surmised as she looked around anxiously, all the while hoping that Ken Rollins would appear at any minute and take her into the air-conditioned section of the practice. There *had* to be an air-conditioned part.

Then, in the distance, she heard a noise and saw a very tall male figure walking down the corridor towards her. She blinked as she saw that he was bare to the waist with a white hand towel around his neck. She pinned her hopes on the fact this man was working on the air-conditioning and that he was good at his job, because she was wilting quickly. And she doubted her more senior boss would enjoy working in these conditions either.

She couldn't help but notice as he drew near that the man was wearing dress pants and highly polished shoes. Although nothing covered his very chiselled, sweat-dampened chest.

'I'm looking for Dr Ken Rollins. I'm Dr Phoebe Johnson from Washington.'

'*You're* Phoebe Johnson?' the man said, with a look of surprise on his handsome face and doubt colouring his deep voice.

'Yes, I am. Did he tell you I was arriving?'

The man wiped his forehead and then his hands on the towel he was carrying, then stretched out his free hand. 'I'm Heath Rollins, Ken's son, and I've been expecting you.'

His voice was sonorous and austere. And the frown on Phoebe's face did little to mask her confusion. *Why on earth was he expecting her and why was he half naked?*

'So are you here to repair the air-conditioning for your father?'

'Not exactly. I'm attempting to repair the air-con, but I'm not a repairman—not even close as you can tell by how hot it still is in here. I'm a podiatric surgeon from Sydney.'

Phoebe was more confused than ever. Why did Ken Rollins have his *podiatric surgeon* son trying to fix the air-conditioning unit? And why wasn't Ken there to meet her?

'Is your father in with patients already?' she asked as she looked around her surroundings, hoping that the older surgeon would suddenly appear and clear up the confusion. And bring his son a shirt so he could cover up.

'No, he's not…'

'Is he running late?'

'No he's not,' he replied without any hint of emotion in his reply. 'I'm actually standing in for him for the next four weeks.'

Phoebe quickly realised as she shook his hand that the man standing before her was potentially her new boss. She took a few steps back from the very warm handshake and looked warily at him. She had signed on to work with *Ken* Rollins. *This* Dr Rollins was definitely not in his sixties. *Disastrous*, was the first thought that came to her mind. The second thought, as she looked at his lightly tanned physique, was not in any way ladylike and nothing she wanted to be considering with this man. Or *any* man, now that she had sworn off the species. It was not what she needed. In fact this was close to a catastrophe.

She had envisaged an older, established and experienced mentor to work closely with for five days a week over the next six months. This was supposed to be a professional development opportunity. And the man standing before her stripped to the waist was anything but professional development. He was not what she wanted and nor did she have the capacity to deal with him either. With the combination of Heath Rollins's half-naked physique and the heat in the room Phoebe knew she had stepped into the fire—literally.

'Where exactly *is* your father?' she asked. 'And why are you stepping in for him?'

As she spoke she was doing her best not to be distracted by his very toned body or his equally gorgeous eyes. But it was a struggle, and she faced the prospect that the cruel hand of the universe had just replaced her playboy fiancé with someone even more handsome, if a comparison was to be made. And she had to work with him until almost the middle of the following year. Six long months.

She settled her eyes on the stubble-covered cleft in his chin, then moved them to his soft full lips, framed by dimples and slightly smiling, and then finally she looked up and discovered his brilliant blue eyes.

She had to admit that he was a very different type from

Giles. This man had more cowboy good-looks, while Giles
was the Wall Street slick type. But she didn't want *any*
type of good-looking and she was far from happy with
the arrangement. Good-looking men were all the same,
and a long-haul trip to the other side of the world only to
find that fate had ordered her another one was not what
she had wanted.

Suddenly she felt a little dizzy. The heat was closing in
by the minute. She mopped her forehead with a tissue as
she reached for a seat and promptly sat down with a sigh.
Her plans had gone terribly awry and the added lack of air-
conditioning made it unbearable. This was nothing close
to the first day she had planned in her mind.

'I sent you an email outlining the changes,' he said, his
lean fingers rubbing his chin. 'You shouldn't be surprised.'

'What email?' she managed as she looked around for
something to use as a fan and grabbed a magazine, which
she moved frantically through the air in front of her face
in the hope that it would cool her down.

'The one that clearly explained my father was in an
accident two days ago, fractured his patella and had to
undergo surgery, so you'll be working alongside me until
he returns.'

'So he's coming back?' she asked, with a little relief
colouring her voice. 'When, exactly?'

'In about a month, if his rehabilitation goes as planned.
It wasn't a complete reconstruction, so he should be back
on deck a lot sooner than after a full recon.'

Phoebe nodded and bit the inside of her cheek as she
considered his response. At least it was four weeks, not
six months. She felt a little better about the time frame
but the confirmation that Heath was going to be her boss,
for however short or long a time, was still not news she
needed to hear.

She kept her improvised fan moving through the thick air, trying to bring some relief to the situation. Against the oppressive heat it was little use; against news of the working arrangements it was no use at all. For the next four weeks she would be working with a man too handsome for his own good and definitely for the good of all the women who fell victim to his charm. But, thinking of what she had just escaped, she knew she would never fall for a man like Heath. Not that she was on the market for anyone anyway.

She loosened the belt cinched at her waist to allow her to breathe a little more easily in the mugginess that was wrapping around her.

'You're looking extremely pale,' he said, with something she thought sounded like a level of concern. 'I'll get a glass of water for you.'

Phoebe swayed to and fro in her seat, watching as Heath crossed back to her with a plastic cup he had filled from the water cooler. She took a few sips, then shakily handed him back the cup. Just as the polished wooden floor became a checked pattern that surged towards her in waves. As she fought the swirling focus that made her feel more disorientated by the minute, she wondered why any of this had happened to her.

Was there any way she could escape the heat? Why did Ken have to wreck his knee *now*? Why did she have to work with *this* man for the next few weeks?

Suddenly there were no more questions. The stifling heat finally claimed her. And Dr Phoebe Johnson fainted into Heath's strong arms.

CHAPTER THREE

'GOOD, YOU'RE BACK with us.'

Phoebe heard the deep timbre of a male voice very close, and when she opened her eyes she realised just how close. She was facing some well-defined and very naked male abdominal muscles, only inches away from her. Her brow formed a frown as she realised she recognised the distinctly Australian accent. It was her temporary boss—and in her direct line of vision was his bare tanned stomach.

Still lying down, she attempted to let her eyes roam her surroundings—until she was finally forced to look up and see Heath looking down at her. She couldn't read his expression. He wasn't frowning, but nor was he smiling. His look was serious. Concerned. And the concern appeared genuine. She discovered her resting place was an examination table. And soon realised there was a cool towel on her forehead and that a portable fan was stirring the heavy air and moving the fine wisps of hair that had escaped from her ponytail.

'She's lucky you were there to catch her. Sorry—I stepped out to get a cool drink and missed her.'

Phoebe heard a second voice. It belonged to a female but she couldn't see anyone from her vantage point. It made sense to her, even in her disorientated state, that for him to have set so much in place so quickly, such as the cool towel and the fan, he had to have had some assistance.

'I must apologise, Phoebe. I'd hoped to have the air-con up and running before you arrived,' Heath said, in a serious, professional tone that belied his appearance. He looked more like a private dancer than a stoic doctor. 'I'm not surprised you passed out. Aussie summers can be tough if you're not used to them.'

Phoebe was so embarrassed when she realised what had happened. She stirred from her horizontal position, but still felt light-headed so didn't attempt to sit completely upright immediately. But while she slowly moved she remembered a little of the conversation they had shared—including the news he had imparted to her. *You'll be working along-side me.* Silently she begged the universe to tell her it wasn't true.

The last thing she needed was a man like Heath. She needed to be thinking about her career as a podiatric sur-geon and she wanted to be taught by an experienced older practitioner. This new arrangement was not a dynamic she had even considered as a possibility when she'd agreed to work in Adelaide. She'd thought it would be six months of respite. An emotionally healing time packaged as a work-ing sabbatical.

'Here's some water,' the young woman said as she stepped into view, and she handed Heath a glass with a plastic concertina straw. 'It's not too cold.'

Phoebe squinted as she tried to focus. The woman looked to be in her mid-twenties. Blonde, quite tall, very pretty, with a lovely smile. Phoebe suddenly felt Heath's strong arm lift her upright, yet there was no warmth in the way he held her. It was as if she was an inanimate object.

'Hold on to your cold compress and sip this,' he said as he curved the straw to meet her lips.

He held the drink steady with one hand while the other still supported her. His bedside manner she would have described as 'reserved' at best.

Phoebe held the cold towel in place as she slowly sucked the water through the straw and felt immediately better for it. But the sight of her skirt no longer demurely skimming her knees did not make her feel good at all. Most of her legs were bare, for the world and Dr Heath Rollins to see, and she was horrified.

'I've had enough, thank you,' she said as she moved her mouth away from the drink and then, struggling to keep the towel on her head, she tried to lift her bottom slightly and release the hem of the skirt.

There was little covered at all. Fainting and baring parts of her anatomy that should be saved for the beach, or more intimate encounters, was definitely *not* a great start to this already less than desirable working relationship. She had secured the job purely on her references, and now she could only guess what he was thinking as she reached down to gain some dignity.

'Here—let me help you.'

His hands lifted her gently and with ease. Her heartbeat suddenly increased with the unexpected touch of his hands on her bare skin. Suddenly she did not feel like an inanimate object. And this time her giddiness wasn't from the heat of the room. His closeness while he held her up made the job of adjusting her clothing difficult. She finally wriggled the skirt into place and swung her legs around, subtly encouraging Heath to release her and step back.

Clearing her throat, and raising her chin a little defensively, Phoebe looked at Heath as if he were almost the perpetrator of the incident. 'How exactly—?' she began and then paused for a moment. 'How did I get here? I don't remember leaving the reception area. I do remember feeling very hot, then light-headed, but where was I when I fainted?'

'You passed out on a chair in the waiting room, and I carried you in here and put you on your side. You were out for less than a minute. As soon as your head was level with your body you came to.'

The way he spoke was quite clinical and detached, but she still managed to feel uneasy at the mental picture of him scooping her up in his arms and carrying her to the examination bed with little or no effort.

Her eyes briefly scanned his firefighter physique before she blinked and turned away. Ken Rollins would be back before she knew it, she told herself. Then all would be right in her world again. This was just a hiccup in her plans. And if Heath's attitude was anything to go by she had nothing to worry about. His body might have been created for sin but his manner certainly hadn't.

'Thank you. I'm sorry I created such a fuss.' Her tone quickly mimicked his coolness.

'These things happen, but you seem fine now,' he said as he stepped back further and turned to face the other woman.

'Tilly, you can finish up. I think we're fine here. Thanks for cancelling the next two days' patients. The air-con should be repaired by Thursday. You can pick up the twins from childcare early and stay home for a couple of days.'

'Are you sure, Heath? I can come in and do some accounts and general office catch-up work tomorrow.'

'No,' he replied firmly, wiping his brow with the back of his hand. 'It's like a sauna today and it will be worse tomorrow. It's a health and safety issue to be working in these conditions.'

'All right—have it your way,' Tilly said as she reached over and kissed him on the cheek. 'See you at home tonight, then. Oh, and Dr Johnson? I hope you feel better soon.'

'Thank you, but please call me Phoebe.'

Phoebe looked down at the young woman's hand as she left the room and saw a wedding band and stunning solitaire diamond. They were married. And they had twins. Of course they did. They were perfect for each other. Two stunning blonde Aussies, sun-kissed and fabulous. She could only guess how gorgeous their children would be.

Phoebe wondered if she had read Heath incorrectly. Perhaps he *wasn't* a Giles clone. Perhaps he was an austere but loving husband who just happened to be very good-looking and in Phoebe's still emotionally raw state that had incorrectly translated to him being a potential cad. All good-looking men had been tarnished by Giles. And she had clearly been scarred.

She suddenly felt very self-conscious, and a little sad at her own ability to jump to conclusions. Perhaps all men were not the same... Just the one she had chosen. And Susy's recent choice too.

Moving awkwardly on the examination table, she tried to inch her skirt down further to cover her knees.

He shook his head. 'You don't have to rush to cover up. I'm not looking at your legs, if that's what you're worried about.'

Phoebe felt instantly embarrassed. She began fidgeting nervously and smoothing the rest of her clothes into place, and then tidying her hair in an attempt to gain composure without saying a word. There was nothing that came to mind that wouldn't make her appear even sillier and more self-conscious, so she stayed silent.

Heath watched the way she was fussing. He found her behaviour so far from the image he had created in his mind of a podiatric surgeon from Washington with impeccable references, who was triple board certified in surgery, orthopaedics, and primary podiatric medicine. She was also a Fellow of the American College of Foot and Ankle Surgeons, the American Academy of Podiatric Sports Medicine and the American College of Foot & Ankle Orthopaedics & Medicine. All of those qualifications had had him picturing someone very different. He'd thought she would be brimming with confidence, more than a little aloof. And definitely nowhere near as pretty.

Dr Phoebe Johnson had taken Heath by surprise...

Phoebe's blood pressure had slowly returned to normal and she felt more steady physically.

'So, what would you like me to do? I guess if you've cancelled the patients there's probably no point me being here. I can take some patient notes back to my house and read over them.'

She looked around and ascertained where she was in relation to the front door and the reception area, where she assumed her bag would be, and headed in that direction. His wife, she assumed, had already left.

'There's definitely no point you staying here, and to be honest your first two days' patients are post-op and quite straightforward,' he told her as he followed her out to where her bag was resting by a chair. 'Here is probably the worst place to be. We don't want a repeat performance.'

The waiting room and reception area was even hotter as it faced the glare of the morning sun on the huge glass panes.

'If you're sure I can't do anything here, then I'll see you on Thursday.'

She reached for the front door and he stepped closer to her to hold the door open. Her face looked angelic, and he was intrigued by her. He momentarily wondered why, with all her experience and qualifications, she wanted to work in Adelaide, of all places? Suddenly he felt curious. She was just nothing like he had imagined. He could work out most people, and he prided himself on being able to know what made them tick. But not her. Not yet.

When he'd glanced over her résumé in search of her contact details he had worried that she would not find the practice enough of a challenge, with her interests and her extensive experience in sports podiatry, but then had conceded that she had made her professional choice and it was none of his concern. And if she did grow bored and move on before the six months were up—again, it was not his concern. He wouldn't be there long enough for it to have any impact on him. His father could find a replacement if she did.

'Okay, I'll see you on Thursday.'

'Yes. I'll see you then,' Phoebe responded as she walked past him into a wall of warm, dry air.

She wasn't sure if it was warmer outside than in, but it felt less humid—although she quickly realised neither was particularly pleasant. It was still early, but the pavement held the heat from the day before and she could tell it would be blisteringly hot in a few hours.

'I hope you find a way to stay cool.'

Without much emotion in his voice, but clearly being polite, he said, 'I think I'll take my son to the pool later on today. Maybe you should hit the beach or a pool—there's quite a few around. There are some indoor ones too. Oscar's looking forward to finding some other children to play with.' Before he turned to walk inside he added, 'I hope you find a way to stay cool too.'

Phoebe stopped in her tracks. 'I thought you and your wife had twins?' she called back to him from the bottom step, with a curious frown dressing her brow.

'No, my sister Tilly has twin girls, but they're only two

and a half years old. Oscar's five,' he told her, with a little more animation. 'Tilly's like a mother to Oscar while we're in town, and it's been good for him since it's just the two of us the rest of the time. I'm sure as they grow up the cousins will all be great friends, but right now Oscar really doesn't find them much fun at all.'

He looked back at Phoebe with an expression she couldn't quite make out as he paused in the doorway, as if he was thinking something through before he spoke.

Phoebe turned to leave.

'It's ridiculously hot out there,' he remarked, catching her attention. 'If you have time perhaps we could pop round to the corner café and grab a cool drink. I wouldn't want you fainting on the way home. I can answer any questions you have about the practice.'

Phoebe could see he was a very serious man—nothing like Giles, with his smooth flirtatious manner. But there was something about Heath that made her curious. She reminded herself that she would never be interested in him in any way romantically, but with his demeanour she didn't flag him as a threat to her reborn virginal status. And she did want to know about the running of the practice so she decided to accept his invitation. He was her boss after all.

'I have time.'

Phoebe had decided on the quick walk to the café that she did not want to discuss her personal life and that she would not enquire about his. She knew enough. He was Ken Rollins's son. He was filling in for a month, and he was the single father of a five-year-old boy. That was more than enough. Whether he was divorced or had never been married was none of her business and immaterial.

She wasn't going to be spending enough time with Heath for his personal life to matter. Four weeks would pass quickly and then he and his son would be gone. She wasn't sure if she would ever even meet the boy. It wasn't as if a medical practice dealing with feet would be the most interesting place for a child to visit, she mused, so their paths might never cross.

'Thank you,' she said as she stepped inside the wonderfully cool and thankfully not too densely populated coffee shop.

'They make a nice iced coffee,' Heath told her as they made their way to a corner table and he placed his laptop containing patient notes beside him. 'It's barista coffee, and they add ice-cold milk and whipped cream. They do it well.'

'Sounds perfect—but perhaps hold the cream.'

'Looking after your heart?' he enquired as he pulled out the chair for her.

In more ways than one, she thought.

It was a surprise to Phoebe how easy she found it to talk with Heath. While he was still reserved, and borderline frosty, he was attentive and engaged in their discussion. He asked about her work at the hospital in Washington and their conversation was far from stilted, due to their mutual love of their specialty. With Giles, she had not spoken much about her work as he hadn't seemed to understand it and nor had he wanted to. It had been plain that he wasn't interested and he'd never pretended to care. It had been all about *his* career aspirations and how they could achieve them together.

'I've seen your résumé—it's impressive, but definitely geared towards sports podiatry. My father's practice is predominately general patient load along with the occasional sportsman or woman—not the focus I assume you're accustomed to. How do you think you will adjust to that?'

'Sports podiatry is a passion of mine. I've been working in a fantastic unit within a large teaching hospital, where we offer a full spectrum of services for the athlete—including physical therapy and surgery, with an emphasis on biomechanics. My focus outside of essential surgical intervention was primarily on orthotic treatment directed to correct structural deficiency and muscular imbalance. But in general my goal is to return any patient, regardless of their profession, to their maximum level of function and allow them to re-engage in an active life.'

Heath agreed with all she was saying, but added, 'I understand—I just hope you don't begin to feel that this practice is not what you signed up for.'

'No, I love what I do—and feet are feet, no matter what the owners of them do.'

Heath found her answer amusing, but he didn't smile. He rarely did, and those moments were saved for his son. And there was still that unanswered question...

'So tell me, Phoebe, if you love the hospital back in your hometown, you enjoy your work and your colleagues, why did you want to leave?'

Phoebe nervously took a sip of the icy drink. It was rich and flavoursome, just as good as he had promised...and she was stalling. 'I needed a break from Washington,' she finally responded.

'A Caribbean cruise or skiing in Aspen would have been easier than relocating to the other side of the world. And if you were looking for alternative employers I'm sure there must be loads of options for someone of your calibre in the US. It's a big country.'

'I wanted more than a quick vacation or a new employer. It was time for a sea change.'

'Like I said, there are a lot of places that would fit that

bill on your own continent—and I'm sure with a lot less red tape than it must have taken for you to work Down Under.'

'I suppose,' she said nonchalantly, trying to deflect his interest in her reasons for being there, which did not seem to be abating easily with anything she said.

It wasn't the Spanish Inquisition, but it felt close. Phoebe did not want to go into the details of her failed engagement to Giles. Nor her desperate need to escape from him and her mother to a place neither would find her. And there was no way he would ever hear from her the tale of the bridesmaids from hell bedding the groom. It was all too humiliating. And still too raw.

Heath was her temporary boss and he would be leaving once his father's knee had healed. The less he knew the better. In fact the less everyone in the city knew about her the better.

'Your father's interest in harnessing the power of biomechanics and advanced medical technology to challenge convention and his ensuing breakthrough results were huge draw cards for me to come and work with him. And I wanted to know more about his collaborative approach to co-morbidities. Your father wrote a great paper on the subject of the co-operative approach to treating systemic problems.'

Heath sensed there was more, but he took her cue to leave the subject alone. He appreciated she had a right to her privacy on certain matters. Just as he did to his own. And there was no need for him to know too much, he reminded himself, as they would be working together for a relatively short time and then he would be leaving. Theirs would be a brief working relationship. Nothing more.

But, stepping momentarily away from being her very temporary boss, he had to admit Phoebe was undeniably beautiful.

Phoebe shifted awkwardly in her seat, not sure if Heath had accepted her response and they could move on. Unaware that her glass was empty, she casually took another sip through her straw. Suddenly the loudest slurp she had ever heard rang out. To Phoebe's horror, apparently it was the loudest the people at an adjacent table had ever heard too, as they shot her a curious stare.

The sound echoed around the café. Phoebe's eyes rolled with embarrassment. Only half an hour before she had passed out in his arms, revealed far too much of her legs, and now her manners were more befitting a preschooler. She wanted to find an inconspicuous hole and slink inside. Heath had such a serious demeanour she could only imagine what he was thinking. It was, without doubt, the worst first day on the job of anyone—ever.

'I told you they make the best iced coffee. There's never enough in my glass either,' Heath said, his mouth almost forming a smile.

It was the first time, in the hour or so since they'd met, that she had seen him show anything even vaguely like a smile. And it was the most gorgeous almost-smile she had ever seen. Her heart unexpectedly skipped a beat.

Giles would have been mortified, she thought. He would have shot her a glare that told her she had embarrassed him. His body language would have reminded her that it was unladylike without saying a word. She would have felt his displeasure while those around would have had no idea. But Heath didn't appear to react that way, and it surprised her. Apparently in his eyes it was *not* cringeworthy behaviour—or if he thought it was he certainly masked it well.

She felt her embarrassment slowly dissipate. Maybe it wasn't the worst day ever after all. And that was confirmed when he continued the conversation as if nothing had happened.

'So, how do you see this working arrangement? Are you happy to split your time with taking half of my father's post-operative patients and the remainder to be new patients, along with a surgical roster?'

'That sounds great to me. I'm fairly flexible—not a hard and fast rules kind of woman—so we can just see how it all works out, and if we need to move around within those parameters we can discuss it as it unfolds.'

Heath didn't feel the same way at all. 'You'll learn quickly that I'm a rules kind of a man. I live by a number of them, and if I set something up then I like to stick by it. So I'd rather we made up our minds and set up now the way it will play out.'

'I guess…' Phoebe replied, a little taken aback by his rigid stance on their working arrangements. She had heard that Australian people were laid-back. Heath didn't fit that bill at all. 'But in my opinion most situations have both a teething period and a grey area. There's generally room to manoeuvre and move around with some degree of compromise if you're willing to look for it.'

'Not with me. Once I've made a decision, it's rare that I'll shift my viewpoint. In fact it would take something extraordinary to make me change my mind.'

While she appreciated Heath's honesty upfront, she thought she would pity whoever lived with him if they got the bathroom roster wrong. 'Well, then, since it's only for a month let's go with your way. You undoubtedly know the practice and the patient load better than I do, so I'm happy to carve it in stone right now if that's how it's done around here.'

Heath appreciated her wit, but made no retort.

An hour later they were still at the café. Once they had agreed to their working arrangements Heath had dropped all other lines of questioning and given Phoebe the low-down on the city she would call home for a few months.

Despite the ease with which they spoke, Heath had still not had his questions answered about Phoebe's motives for relocating. But he did know she was a lot more adaptable than he was. It made him curious, although he didn't verbalise it.

With her academic record the surgical world was quite literally her oyster. There would be few, if any, practices or teaching facilities that would not welcome her into their fold with open arms. There was no ring on her finger, but he would not be arrogant enough to assume that there was no man in her life. If there was then he too must be as adaptable as Phoebe, and willing to compromise and let her travel to the other side of the world for work. *He* was not that type of man.

'Adelaide is very quiet, I assume?' she asked as she relaxed back into her chair and admired the artwork on the café walls.

'Yes—a little too relaxed in pace for me. It's very different from Sydney, which I prefer. I grew up here, but moved to Sydney about ten years ago when I finished my internship. I was offered a position on the east coast and I took it.'

'I'd like to see Sydney one day, but I think Adelaide will be lovely for the next six months.'

'Adelaide's like a very large country town,' Heath replied. 'And that's the reason I never stay too long.'

'A large country town suits me. It isn't the size of the town but more the attitude of the people that matters.'

Heath watched Phoebe as she studied the eclectic collection of watercolour paintings and charcoal sketches on the wall. She was smiling as she looked at the work of novice artists and he could see her appreciation of the pieces. There was no sign of the big town superiority that he had thought she might display, and she didn't launch into a spiel about comparisons with Washington, as he had expected.

'That's what my father keeps telling me when I try to get him to relocate to Sydney. He won't budge. He likes the growing medical research sector in Adelaide, even if it's a small city by comparison.'

'From all reports he's one of the finest podiatric surgeons in the southern hemisphere. I look forward to meeting him when he's up to it.' While Heath had not enquired more about her reasons for relocating, to cement that line of questioning shut she added, 'Your father's work is revolutionary in its simplicity, and I respect his conservative approach of proceeding, where possible, with surgery as the second not the first option. His expertise in soft tissue manipulation and trigger point therapy is impressive. A lot of practitioners routinely go for surgery, but your father is quite the opposite, preferring to view his patients through a holistic filter and follow a slightly more protracted but less invasive treatment plan.'

Heath could see that his father's work had made quite an impression on Phoebe. 'I hope you're not disappointed that you'll be working with me. It's like ordering Chinese takeout and having pizza arrive on your doorstep.'

Phoebe liked his quirky analogy, although it seemed at odds with his less than lighthearted nature. He was far from a poor second, and she silently admitted that pizza was a favourite of hers. Heath was charming and knowledgeable, and his reserved demeanour was a pleasant change.

Although his rigid viewpoint might possibly test her reserves of patience in the long term, she was very much looking forward to working with him in the short term.

She doubted he would disappoint on any level, but professional was the only level she was interested in exploring.

Heath considered the woman sitting opposite him for a moment. She was a highly regarded surgeon in their mutual field, but there was a mixture of strength and frailty to her. It was as if she was hiding, or running away from something. And he wasn't sure *why* he wanted to work her out, except that it was as if she was second-guessing herself on some level. He had no idea why she would.

Heath knew that she was an only child, that her father was a Presidential advisor and her mother a Washington socialite, and that she'd spent her high school years at a prestigious private school in Washington. She had openly chatted about that. He also knew that she had graduated top of her class from her studies at the New York College of Podiatric Medicine, and had done her three-year residency at the university hospital.

It would appear she had the makings of someone who could be quite consumed with their own self-importance, but she wasn't. She was, he'd realised quickly, very humble—because Heath knew of her Dux status from his father, not from her. Phoebe hadn't brought it up. It was a huge honour and she was omitting it from her abbreviated life story over morning coffee.

In that way she was not unlike his wife, Natasha—a former model and fashion designer who had also been very humble about the accolades she'd been given both on and off the runway.

Natasha had not been at all what Heath had imagined a model would be like the night he'd met her at a fundraising event. He'd been thirty and she only twenty-three. After a whirlwind courtship they'd married, and Natasha had fallen pregnant soon afterwards. They'd both been so excited and looking forward to growing their family.

Heath had come to learn that she worked actively and tirelessly for many causes—including one to support research into a cure for the disease that had eventually claimed her life. And from that day, Heath's purpose in life—his only focus outside of his work—had been raising their beautiful little boy, Oscar, who had been given life by the only woman Heath had ever loved.

And nothing and no one would ever come between them.

Not his work and not a woman.

It was a promise he'd made to himself five years earlier. The day he lost his wife. The day he'd walked away from the hospital without her and realised he would never again hold her in his arms or wake next to her in the bed they had shared. He'd vowed that day that he would dedicate his life to being the kind of father to their son that Natasha would have wanted.

And he would never wake with another woman in his arms.

He had been true to both promises.

Oddly, sitting with Phoebe, he felt almost comfortable, more at ease than in a long time, and he suspected their mutual professional interests had a lot to do with that. He couldn't remember the last time he had spoken in depth to a woman about his chosen career and engaged in a meaningful conversation. He had taken lovers over the years, but nothing more than a shared night. He left before dawn, and conversation was at the bottom of the list of his needs on those occasions.

'I'd better let you go and I'll head back to the practice and sort out the air-con, or we'll have melted patients for the next few months,' Heath told her in a matter-of-fact tone as he stood. 'It's only December, and both January and February are hotter months in general.'

Phoebe was taken aback by the way Heath ended their time together. He had invited her to go for a drink and now he was excusing himself quite abruptly. Not that she minded at all. In fact she was relieved, as it gave him no further opportunity to quiz her about her personal life.

'You mean hotter than this?' Phoebe asked.

'Not hotter, but hot for longer stretches.'

Phoebe shrugged. 'Well, then, I *really* hope you get the air-conditioner working.'

He paid the tab and walked Phoebe to the door and then out into the street. His body language was stiff and distant again. Any hint of being relaxed had evaporated.

'I'll see you in a few days. Take some downtime to recover from your trip and I'll see you on Thursday morning at eight. If you get a chance, try to head to the beach or a pool. It will do you the world of good.'

Phoebe nodded. 'Okay, thanks—maybe I will.' She walked away, then suddenly turned around and called out. 'Heath, we never discussed Thursday's patients.'

Heath turned back and looked at Phoebe for the longest moment, then glanced at the laptop tucked loosely under his arm. 'We didn't, didn't we?'

CHAPTER FOUR

'Daddy!'

Heath was welcomed home by tiny arms that wrapped around his knees and hugged him ferociously. He bent down and returned the hug before he picked up his son in his strong arms and swung him around like a carousel ride. Oscar was his reason for living. He had been the beacon of hope during his darkest days. Heath would never let Oscar down. No matter what the future held, he would be his son's anchor through life. He was the only thing that brought a smile to Heath's face and love to an otherwise broken heart.

'How's my favourite little man?' he asked, kissing his tiny son's chubby cheek.

'I'm good, Daddy.'

Heath lowered him to the ground, then sat on the sofa. Oscar climbed up next to him.

'Can we go to the pool tomorrow—can we, please?'

Heath considered his son for a moment. He had his mother's deep brown eyes and he was the apple of his father's. There was nothing Heath wouldn't do for him, but he did like to have fun and tease him a little sometimes.

'I thought you hated the pool? You distinctly told me the other day that you never, *ever* wanted to go swimming again. You said that you would rather eat live worms than go to a swimming pool!'

'Don't be silly, Daddy. I *loooooove* the pool!'

Heath picked Oscar up and put him on his lap and held him tightly. 'Then it looks like tomorrow we're off to the pool, my little man.'

Phoebe enjoyed a lazy sleep-in the next day. It would end, she knew, when the air-conditioning at the practice was repaired, so she made the most of it. Then she had a quick shower, put on shorts, sandals and a T-shirt, and went out to buy a newspaper. While she enjoyed a light breakfast she planned on reading local stories of interest and about the issues affecting the town she would call home for the near future.

When she arrived home there was a delivery man on her doorstep, holding a medium-sized box, which she signed for and carried into the kitchen.

She discovered it was filled with Christmas gifts. All wrapped in colourful paper and equally pretty ribbons. And every one had her name on it.

She rang her father, but it went to voicemail. 'Hi, Dad. I know you're probably busy, but thank you so much for my gifts. By the way, how did you get the presents here the very day after I arrived?'

A few minutes later, as she was putting the presents away in her wardrobe, she received a text message.

I posted them a week before you left. Hope you like them. PS I would have been in trouble if you'd cancelled the trip! Xxx

Although she would miss her family, knowing they were only a call or a text away made her feel less lonely.

After breakfast and a thorough read of the newspaper, in a small cobblestoned patio area that had an outdoor table setting for two under a pergola covered in grape vines, Phoebe felt even more positive about her temporary stay in Australia. She was actually enjoying this time to herself, and she decided after completing the crossword and finishing her freshly squeezed orange juice that Heath's suggestion of spending some time swimming wouldn't be so bad.

She could do with some sun. A long, relaxing swim at the beach or in a pool was just what the doctor ordered. With no preference, but also no idea where to go, she looked up some local beaches and public pools on the internet.

The beach, she discovered, would mean a thirty-minute tram trip to Glenelg, or there was a pool about a ten-minute cab ride away in Burnside. She opted for the pool.

Searching in her suitcase, she found her floral bikini, sarong and sunblock. She slipped on the bikini, stepped into her denim shorts and popped a white T-shirt over the top. Then, with a good book, a towel, a wide-brimmed hat and a bottle of water in her beach bag, she called for a cab.

Phoebe had found a perfect spot on the lawn area, adjacent to a huge shade cloth and overlooking the pool. She surmised the sun would get intense later, and she would shift into the shade, but she wanted to enjoy a few minutes of the warm rays and assist her vitamin D intake.

The pool was picturesque, with huge gum trees and parklands surrounding the fenced area. There were quite a few families and some small groups of young mothers with babies enjoying the peaceful ambience of the late morning. Children were laughing and splashing in the crystal water of the wading pool and more serious swimmers were head down, doing lengths of the main pool.

Phoebe had spread out her large blue towel and set up camp. She had spied the fruit in the refrigerator before she'd left home, so she had packed an apple and some strawberries in with her water. Slipping out of her shorts and T-shirt, and putting her hair up atop her head, she strode across the lawn and climbed into the water for a long, relaxing swim.

She was right—it was just what the doctor had ordered. Quite literally.

She lay on her back, lapping the pool slowly and looking up at the stunning blue sky through the filter of her sunglasses. Her worries seemed to dissipate—not completely, but more than she had imagined they would when she had alighted from the plane just a day earlier.

Fifteen minutes later she climbed from the pool and dried herself off with her sun-warmed towel before she spread it out and sat down. With her sarong beside her, in case she needed to cover up, she put on her floppy straw hat, pulled out her book and flipped the lid on her sunblock. She thought of how if she was back in Washington she would be trying to get the ice off her windscreen—instead she was about to cover herself in sunscreen. Perhaps there was justice in the world—or at least a little compensation in the form of sunshine.

She poured a little lotion into her palm and began to rub it over her shoulders.

'Phoebe?'

Phoebe spun around to see Heath standing so tall he was blocking the sun. His chest was bare and his low-slung black swimming trunks left little to her imagination. Beside him was the cutest little boy, with the same blond tousled hair, dinosaur-patterned swim trunks, and a very cheeky smile. But very different eyes. While Heath's were the most vivid blue, his son's huge, twinkling eyes were a stunning deep brown.

'Hello, Heath,' she managed, a little shocked to find him in front of her, and a little more shocked by how gorgeous he looked in even less clothing than the day before.

'I didn't expect to see you here. I didn't think you'd actually take my advice about getting some sun and a swim.'

'It sounded like a good idea,' she replied, trying not to show how embarrassed she felt in choosing the same outdoor pool as Heath. He had described the city as a large country town, but now she wondered how small Adelaide was to have found them in the same place. 'And I do need to get some vitamin D.'

As she said it Phoebe realised she was wearing only a string bikini, and suddenly felt very self-conscious. She hadn't thought twice about it with the other pool guests, as she didn't know them, but for some reason she felt more exposed in front of Heath. She wanted to reach for her sarong and bring it up to her neck, but realised how silly she would appear.

Heath sensed that Phoebe was feeling awkward in that very brief and very stunning bikini. He had witnessed her discomfiture the previous day, when she had been so intent on tugging her skirt into place. But suddenly his eyes just naturally began to roam her body. Every curve was perfect, he thought, before he quickly slipped on his sunglasses, then turned his attention back to his son. Where it had to stay.

'Oscar.' Heath began ruffling the little boy's hair with his hand. 'This is Phoebe—she'll be working with me for the next month, while Grandpa gets better.'

'Hello, Phoebe,' the little boy responded. 'You're pretty—like Aunty Tilly.'

Phoebe felt herself blush. 'Thank you, Oscar, that is a very nice thing to say.'

'It's the truth,' he replied. 'My kindy teacher isn't as pretty as you, but she can sing really well. Can you sing?'

'No, I'm afraid I can't.'

'That's okay. Don't feel bad. My grandpa can't sing either—he tries in the shower, but it sounds terrible and the dog next door barks. He barks a *lot*. I don't know if Daddy can sing. I've never heard him try to sing. Even when there's Christmas carols he never sings along.'

'That's because my voice is worse than Grandpa's,' Heath added, knowing his inability to sing Christmas carols had nothing to do with the quality of his voice. There was much more to it than that. 'It's best I don't try or the dog next door might run away.'

'You're silly, Daddy. The dog can't open the gate.'

Phoebe smiled at their happy banter. It was the first time she had seen a full smile from Heath. The other time there had been only the hint of a smile. She thought he should do it more often.

'Can I go in the pool now? Can I? Can I? Please, Daddy?' Oscar's words became faster and louder as they came rushing out.

'Sure can.' Heath said, eager to move away from Phoebe in her skimpy bathing suit. 'I hope you enjoy your time here today, Phoebe,' he added before he took his son's hand. 'If you need anything we're not too far away.'

'Thanks, I'm sure I will be just fine.'

Heath positioned his sunglasses on the top of his head, nodded in Phoebe's direction and then reached for his son's hand and walked towards the water's edge.

Phoebe suddenly felt a little shiver run all over her body. She ignored it. She had no intention of asking Heath for anything or paying any attention to her body's inappropriate reaction to her boss. It was her hormones, simply out of sorts after the emotional rollercoaster of the last few months, she decided. Perhaps jet-lag was playing a part too.

She had worked with some very attractive medics over the years and he was just another one—nothing more, she thought as she reached for her book. Once Heath Rollins exited from the practice she would never see him again. And that was how she wanted her life to remain. No men and all about her career.

Heath loved being with his son. He always gave him one hundred per cent of his attention when they were together. Oscar was his reason for getting up every day, although he never let the little boy feel that pressure or carry that load. He didn't want his family to attempt to change that dynamic or to question his reasons for still being alone five years after Natasha's death. His choices were no one else's business. He would cover for his father at the practice and then return to Sydney, where he and Oscar would live life the way he wanted. With no interference or futile attempts at matchmaking.

Heath knew that no woman would ever replace Natasha. And, even more than that, he thought every day of how Natasha had been denied the joy of watching her child grow into a man. Some days were harder than others. The sadness, the guilt, the emptiness... Aside from Oscar, Heath's work was his saviour. It was a distraction that gave him purpose.

But today he felt as if someone else was pulling his thoughts away momentarily. Someone who was not only academically and professionally astute, and beautiful from head to toe, but whose humility appeared genuine. But, he reminded himself as he took Oscar to the bigger pool for a father-son swimming lesson, he barely knew her and he was happy with his life just the way it was. He had Oscar and he had his career and that had been enough for him for five years.

He slipped small brightly coloured goggles over his son's eyes and held him securely, encouraging him to take big strokes and put his head under the water, and he didn't look back in Phoebe's direction. Not once.

Despite her best efforts, Phoebe couldn't concentrate on her book. Initially she thought it was tiredness that made her read and reread the same sentence until there was no point continuing. But then she realised it was curiosity, or something like it, that drew her to glance back at Heath and his son. Through her sunglasses Phoebe could see how the two were incredibly close, and the love between them was palpable. Heath looked to be the perfect father, and watching them made Phoebe smile just a little.

She had never thought too much about having children. She'd assumed she would, and had looked forward to being a mother one day, but it hadn't been a driving force in her life. Unlike some of her friends, who had set a date by which they wanted to have the picket fence and three children, Phoebe liked to live her life as it unfolded and had never been one to over-plan. She had spent so long studying, achieving her career goals through long hours at the hospital and in surgery, and then she had got caught up in the wedding...

She blinked away memories that needed to be forgotten and decided, sitting on her damp towel in the sticky heat and looking up at the towering gum trees, that this would be the day she packed them away for good. The pain, the disappointment and the humiliation had no place in her life. She didn't know what did have a place exactly, but the sadness seemed to be fading in the warmth of the Australian sun and Phoebe finally felt good about life. Three months in the same cold town hadn't helped, but the distance and the glorious summer weather appeared to be working. Her decision to set sail was one she felt a little surer she would not regret.

With her mind wandering, she hadn't noticed the two handsome men walking towards her. Both dripping wet, they stood at the bottom of her towel and she came back to the present with a jolt. But a very pleasant one.

'I hope we didn't scare you. You looked like you were a million miles away.'

'About ten thousand, to be exact.'

'You're homesick for Washington already?' Heath asked, almost hoping she would confirm his thoughts and tell him she was planning on returning immediately to the US. That would be fortuitous news for him, because he had a gut feeling that Phoebe's presence might bring complications into his otherwise contained life.

'Not at all,' she replied honestly and, being completely clueless to his hopes, she had lightness in her voice. 'I was just thinking about how lucky I am to be melting rather than freezing.'

'If you were a chocolate bar you wouldn't say that!' Oscar told her with a big smile, before he scampered back to the wading pool and signalled to his father to follow.

Phoebe watched Oscar run in and out of the pool for the best part of an hour, and she found it difficult not to occasionally look at Heath, who stood watch over his son. She walked to the far end of the pool, as she didn't want to infringe on Heath and Oscar's time together. He was a single father, who no doubt worked long hours like most medical professionals, so their time together as father and son was precious. She was surprised that a man who said he didn't like to compromise certainly appeared to let his son make the rules.

Sitting on the pool edge, she dangled her legs into the water and thought for the first time in her life she had no future plans. Past these next six months in Adelaide she had no clue where she would go. Perhaps back to Washington—perhaps not. There was a newfound security in having no security in place. Nothing set in stone. And no one to let her down since she only had herself to rely upon. No man to break her heart and shatter her dreams. She had a temporary job and an income and that was all she really needed for the time being.

Phoebe Johnson was finally sailing her own ship and she liked it. She hoped that in this town, so far from everyone she knew, she might possibly find herself. But not for a very long time did she want to share her heart, her bed or potentially her future with a man—if indeed she ever did.

She pulled her legs out of the water and headed back to her towel, where she ate her apple and her strawberries and then felt her stomach rumble. It was time to go back to her house for lunch, she decided, and began to pack up her belongings. Heath and Oscar were lying in the shade, eating ice cream, so she waved and quietly headed out to the main road. She planned on hailing a passing cab.

After five minutes, with no sign of any passing cabs, she reached into her bag to dial for one.

'Daddy, look—there's Phoebe. Is she waiting for her daddy to pick her up?'

'I don't think so, Oscar. She just arrived in town and her father lives in another country a long way from here.'

'Then we need to take her home. That would be a nice thing to do.'

Although part of him knew extending an invitation to

share a ride home was close to the last thing he should do, given his desire to stay away from Phoebe when she had so little clothing on, Heath knew it was the right thing to do. Phoebe knew no one, and she was stranded at the pool after she'd taken him up on his suggestion. She had at least now put shorts on.

There was only one thing to do, he knew, as he took Oscar's hand and walked slowly over to Phoebe.

'Can we offer you a ride home?'

Phoebe had accepted the ride back to her home with a still mostly serious Heath and his very excited and happy little boy. She assumed Oscar had inherited his outgoing personality from his mother. The conversation came predominantly from the back seat, where Oscar was recalling his swimming prowess, until they drew near to her house.

'I'm here on the left—well, I think I am,' she said, then paused as she questioned the accuracy of her directions. 'I tried to notice the way the cab driver took me and reverse it in my head.'

'It's two down on the right, actually. I have your address,' he told her as he ignored her directions and kept driving. 'I noted it from your personal records, which were transferred with the immigration form. It's listed as your residence for the next six months.'

Phoebe could sense he was being a little condescending, and while he wasn't exactly rude she still didn't take kindly to it. She had only been in the country two days, and she thought even to be in the close vicinity of her new home was quite good. She doubted *he'd* do any better if the tables were turned and he was dropped into Washington.

'Well, maybe it was transcribed incorrectly and maybe it was the street you just passed—on the *left*.'

Heath sensed she was being petulant and he found it

almost amusing. He had grown up in Adelaide and knew the street she was referring to was home to a food market and some restaurants—not houses.

'Fine, then I'm happy to turn around and drop you back in the street you think is yours.'

Phoebe knew he had called her bluff, and on such a hot day he had won.

'No, let's do it your way and see if you're right.'

'Let's.'

'You sound like Aunty Tilly and Uncle Paul,' Oscar suddenly announced from the back seat. 'They talk like that all the time, but in the end Aunty Tilly always wins.'

Heath froze, and so did Phoebe. Heath knew he was talking about his sister and brother-in-law—a married couple—and that Phoebe would suspect as much. They both went silent, and the rest of the short trip was dedicated to Oscar's chatter about the pool.

It wasn't long before Phoebe found herself waving good-bye and thanking her travelling companions before making her way inside her house. Oscar's comment still resonated with her long after she'd closed the front door. *They'd sounded like a married couple bickering.*

Initially, looking over at her handsome, almost brooding chauffeur, with his wet hair slicked back and his shirt buttoned low over his lightly tanned chest, she'd felt herself wondering what might have been had they met under different circumstances...before she had been hurt so terribly by Giles.

But as she tried to forget that heartbreak she couldn't deny that her heart beat a little faster being so close to Heath. His nearness had made her play self-consciously with loose wisps of her hair and swallow nervously more than once as she had looked away from his direction and to the scenery outside of the car during the trip home.

But she wasn't interested in men and particularly not pompous men who took enjoyment in proving they were right. And romance only brought anguish into her life, she reminded herself. After Oscar's bombshell she'd realised she had to step back. Right away from any contact with Heath outside of work arrangements, she decided as she dropped her bag of wet things into the laundry.

Pushing the child's observation out of her mind, Phoebe made some lunch. What could Oscar really know about married couples? Nothing, she told herself, and decided to call her father. It was late in Washington, but he had left a message on her phone so she knew he was still awake.

'So, what do you think of Adelaide?'

Phoebe wasn't sure what to tell her father. She hadn't seen much of the city, save for the airport, a coffee shop, a stifling hot podiatric practice and of course the pool, so her experience was limited. Her view of the parklands was lovely, but she had kept inside a small radius since arriving so thought she wasn't yet placed to give a great evaluation. And when it came to the people of Adelaide she had spoken to the customs official, her cab drivers, Heath, Oscar and momentarily Tilly.

Not really enough to gauge a whole town, she thought. Immigration had been pleasant, the cab drivers were polite, Tilly seemed sweet, Oscar was cute—and then there was Heath. She really didn't want to spend time thinking about him. Particularly after Oscar's comment.

She was confused, but pushed thoughts of him to the back of her mind. He was a conundrum that she wasn't sure she cared to solve. It could be another woman's problem, she decided. One good-looking man had already taken too much of her time and energy with no reward. And she was definitely not looking for a replacement. No matter how handsome.

'It's super-hot,' she finally replied.

'That's it?' Her father laughed heartily. 'You fly to the other side of the world and all you can tell me about the city is that it's super-hot? Wouldn't want *you* to be the only witness for the prosecution any time soon.'

Phoebe realised how vague it had sounded, and she also knew she didn't need to have her guard up. Her father knew the worst that had happened.

'I met Dr Rollins, and the practice is great, but the air-conditioning has broken down so we just had coffee yesterday, and today I went for a swim since I have the day off while it gets repaired.'

'So Ken Rollins is a good man? Do you think you'll enjoy working with him?'

Phoebe drew breath. She wished she could answer in the affirmative to both questions but she couldn't. She hadn't met Ken.

'Ken's undergone emergency knee surgery, so his son is looking after the practice.'

'It's fortunate for him that he has a son to take over,' her father replied, then added thoughtfully, 'But I know you were looking forward to working with Ken after you read his papers. I hope you're not disappointed?'

It was the second time she had been asked that question. And her answer still stood. She wasn't disappointed. Confused about the man, and definitely not interested beyond their working relationship, but not disappointed.

'Working with Heath will be a learning experience.'

'I hope you enjoy it, then,' he told his daughter.

'I hope so too, and if nothing else I've got a few months of warm weather ahead,' she said, trying to remind herself of the only benefit she should be considering.

'Try feeling sorry for your father. I'll be shovelling snow at some ungodly hour in the morning. Perhaps you should get some sleep, sweetie. Your flight would have been tax-ing, and the high temperatures will add to that.'

'It was a little tiring, but I think…' Phoebe paused as she heard the beeping of a text message come through. 'Can you hold for one minute, Dad? I think I got a message…'

'Sure, honey.'

Phoebe pulled the phone away from her ear and saw a number she didn't know. She recognised it as local and read the message.

Phoebe, it's Tilly. I know it's late notice, but would you be free for dinner tonight around seven at my place? Dad will be here and he'd love to meet you. And I would love to chat properly. Heath can pick you up.

An invitation to have dinner with the family was some-thing Phoebe hadn't expected and she felt her errant heart race a little with the prospect of seeing Heath again. She knew it was crazy but her response to seeing him again made it obvious she may have a battle ahead. It clearly wasn't going to be as easy as telling herself the facts. She couldn't look out of a car window and ignore her reac-tion. She had to look inside of herself and face the fact that Heath was awakening feelings that she thought she had packed away when she had decided to focus on her ca-reer. Suddenly butterflies began to quicken in her stomach.

She didn't answer the text immediately as she quickly made plans in her head. She couldn't decline as that would be rude. And she wanted to meet Ken. With her breath-ing still a little strained, she resolved to get a taxi there on the pretext of saving Heath the trip—when she was only too aware it was to avoid the closeness of him in the con-fines of his car.

'I'm back,' she said, trying to concentrate once again on the conversation with her father. 'How's Mother?'

'She's fine. At her yoga class and then off to have a manicure, I think—or maybe it's to have her hair done. I can't remember. My day's been taken up with a new healthcare bill that the President wants to pass through Congress. It's a struggle, but you know me, I'm always up for a challenge.'

'Always—and you're so good at it.'

'Thanks, but the apple didn't fall too far from the tree. Look at you. Going to the other side of the world after what you've been through is quite the challenge too.'

'Hardly going to change the world here—and you did all the work. I really do appreciate you arranging everything. The house is wonderful, and it's stocked for a hungry army. Thank you so much.'

'You are more than welcome—but, speaking of an army, I'd better go, honey,' her father cut in. 'Urgent briefing with the Secretary of Defence at six a.m. tomorrow, so I'd better get some sleep before I head out in the wee hours of the morning with salt and a shovel to clear the driveway.'

'Okay, Dad. Love you.'

'Back at you—and I hope you have fun, whatever you do.'

Phoebe went into her room and collapsed into the softness of her bed, dropping the mobile phone beside her. She decided to take a shower and think logically about the invitation before rushing in. Perhaps she should decline and meet Ken another time. Perhaps she should avoid Heath in a social situation. Keep it purely professional the way it should be. Stepping under tepid water, Phoebe washed her hair, and by the time she had rinsed out the conditioner she had come to the conclusion that she had to stop overthinking the situation.

Oscar's remark had thrown her, and Heath's attitude had been a little patronizing, but he was right—he had known the way to her home. And she hadn't. Perhaps she had been a little defensive for no reason other than to push him away.

Her head was spinning and it wasn't the heat. Her house was wonderfully cool.

'Get a grip, Phoebe Johnson. Stop creating false drama where there is none. Heath Rollins is not interested in you. It's dinner with Ken's family and that's it. Almost business. And Oscar was way off the mark. He's only a child, and no judge of what married couples *really* sound like. You have nothing to worry about. Heath Rollins is not looking for love any more than you.'

So she accepted the invitation...with the proviso that she would catch a cab.

CHAPTER FIVE

'PHOEBE SEEMS LOVELY,' Tilly said as she placed a large bowl of homemade potato salad on the dining table, where Heath, Oscar, Ken, her husband Paul and her two daughters were seated, waiting for Phoebe to arrive.

Heath watched as Paul, a tall man with an athletic build, by trade an engineer who directed huge construction teams, struggled to keep his tiny girls from climbing down from their booster chairs and heading back to their toys. He was clearly losing the battle, and one of them took off across the room, so he surrendered and set the girls up with a picnic blanket on the floor, added some toys and invited Oscar to join them.

Tilly was a wonderful cook, who never liked to see anyone leave hungry, so she had grilled a selection of chicken shashlik, vegetable patties and gourmet sausages from her local butcher, along with her famous potato salad and a Greek salad.

'Can someone please remind me why she's coming to dinner? She's here to work—not join family gatherings, surely?'

'It's called being hospitable to a stranger in town, Heath. And she's lovely, as I said.'

'Yes, she's nice.' Oscar seconded his aunt's opinion of

Phoebe as he stood up and strained to reach for a slice of bread from the table.

Smiling, his grandfather slid the plate closer to him to make the task easier.

'You met her too, Oscar?' Tilly asked as she brought cold drinks to the table.

'Yes, at the pool,' Oscar responded as he sat down with his twin cousins again, a big slice of bread in his hand. 'And we drove her home and she and Daddy talked a lot.'

'So you all went to the pool together, then?' Tilly addressed her question to Heath, her eyes smiling.

'I took Oscar to the Burnside pool and Phoebe happened to be there,' he responded defensively.

He had experienced more than a few attempts by his sister to matchmake over the years, and he intended to quash this attempt immediately. He wasn't buying into her supposedly casual conversation that would no doubt lead to something more like an interrogation over his love-life if he allowed it.

'So, of all the pools in Adelaide, a woman who knows nothing of Adelaide just happened to choose that one?'

Heath's silence was his answer.

'So everyone has met the doctor I hired except me?' Ken asked. 'Well, at least I'll get to meet her tonight and judge for myself.'

'*I* haven't met her yet,' Paul said. 'But then I didn't know you'd even hired anyone—I thought Heath was filling in for you.'

'He is. But the practice is growing, and I needed help, and Dr Phoebe Johnson was highly recommended. I had made arrangements for her to work with me before the accident. From all accounts she's a brilliant young podiatric surgeon looking for a change of scenery, so I jumped at the chance. Pardon the pun,' he said as he looked down at his bandaged knee.

'Very pretty too,' Tilly remarked.

'I hadn't heard that part, but it never hurts to have a pretty doctor in the practice,' said the older Dr Rollins. 'So, Heath, do you think you two will get along?'

Heath considered the question and answered in his usual guarded tones. 'I've read her transcripts and she has an impressive record—and the reports from the Washington hospital are great. We chatted yesterday morning at the café for a while, and she seems suited to the role.'

'Yesterday morning? You mean you took her out after she fainted? Quick work, Heath. I'm impressed,' said Tilly.

'Phoebe fainted? Is she okay?' Ken asked.

'I didn't *take her out*—we had a cool drink to talk about work and, yes, Dad, Phoebe's fine. The heat just got to her but I'm sure we won't have a repeat once the air-con is up and running again. You might like to consider renovating the building in the not too distant future.'

He'd added that to change an obvious subject direction that he didn't like.

'I could do you a rebuild,' Paul chipped in. 'Bulldoze and start again. Prime real estate there, and I've been saying for years the old building has had its day.'

Ken looked stony-faced at his son-in-law, to end that line of conversation, and then turned back to Heath. 'So, when my newest employee is conscious and upright, *is* she pretty?'

Heath looked around the table and realised they were all poised for his reply. 'Yes, she's pretty.'

Tilly smiled a self-satisfied smile, while Ken nodded to himself and Paul winked at his wife.

Heath saw the looks they gave each other and lowered his voice so that Oscar wouldn't hear the adults' conversation. 'Just because I made mention of Phoebe's appearance, don't think for a minute that I'm interested in her. It was a response to a direct question. Don't try and set us up. I don't need anyone in my life, and if you try anything you'll be short one staff member. *Me*. I'll be on a plane back to Sydney faster than you can blink. Neither Oscar or I need anyone else in our lives.'

'Are you sure about that?' Tilly asked with a brazen look.

'Yes. You know how I feel. It's been just Oscar and me for the last five years. No woman has come into our lives.'

'I know, but now Phoebe has. And you've already broken one of your unbreakable rules with her. *No woman shall meet your son*. Well, she has and he seems to like her.'

Just then the doorbell rang, and Heath stood up and walked briskly past the Christmas tree that Tilly had decorated that morning. It was the second time he had walked past it that evening, and both times he had looked at it only briefly and then looked away without making mention of it. He was still not able to face Christmas and all the trimmings. He doubted he ever would again. There was nothing that could make him enjoy the holiday season. He had tried and failed. Christmas was just too painful.

As he opened the door Oscar ran over to join him.

'Hello, Phoebe!' Oscar called out excitedly before Heath had a chance to greet her. 'Aunty Tilly has cooked lots of food, so I hope you're hungry.'

'Hello, Oscar,' she replied, and smiled at his toothy grin and cheeky smile before he ran off, allowing her to lift her gaze to greet Heath. 'Hello.'

Heath drew a deep breath. Phoebe looked gorgeous. She wore a deep blue halter dress. Her skin was pale against the fabric and looked like delicate porcelain, and her hair

was falling in soft curls around her shoulders. Her beauty
was not lost on him.

'Hi, Phoebe—come in.'

He moved back from the doorway and as she stepped
inside he couldn't help but notice as she brushed past him
that the back of her dress was cut low and revealed even
more of her bare skin. His pulse instantly, and against his
will, picked up speed.

'Phoebe,' Tilly said as she opened her arms to greet her
dinner guest. 'So lovely you could make it. It's only casual,
but I thought you could meet Dad and chat over a bite to
eat since he was feeling a little left out.'

'It's my pleasure—thank you so much for inviting me,'
she said, and then, spying the huge Christmas tree, she
couldn't help but comment. 'That is a *gorgeous* tree, Tilly.
Christmas truly is my favourite time of year.'

The two women walked into the dining room and on
their way Phoebe gave her hostess some chocolates she had
brought as a thank-you gift. Heath followed, and after hearing the Christmas comment realised that he and Phoebe
had less in common than he'd first thought. She was a professional woman, and he had hoped she wouldn't be the
nostalgic type. Apparently, he'd been wrong.

He couldn't deny to himself that Phoebe was stunning,
and in that dress desirable, but he wasn't looking for a
woman to share his life the way his family thought he
should. And one night with Phoebe in his bed wouldn't
work any way he looked at it. It would only complicate
his life on so many levels, and that was something he
didn't need.

As they entered the dining room, Ken was chatting
with Paul.

'The simple joy of enjoying a pale ale any time I like
is my compensation for not being able to operate. But be-

lieve me, I would prefer to have the use of my gammy knee than to be sitting around all day,' Ken said, then paused as he caught sight of Phoebe. 'Please excuse my bad manners and not standing to meet you,' he continued with an outstretched hand. 'I'm Ken Rollins, and you must be Dr Phoebe Johnson.'

Phoebe stepped closer to Ken and met his handshake. 'Yes, I'm Phoebe, and I'm very happy to finally meet you.'

Ken was impressed with the grip in her handshake. 'For a slender woman you have a strong handshake. But then you're a surgeon, so a strong and steady grip is a prerequisite for our shared field of medicine.'

Phoebe wasn't sure how to react, so she smiled.

'Please—sit down, I didn't mean to embarrass you. And sit next to *me*. I want to hear everything about you that wasn't written down on your incredibly impressive résumé. I'm sure there's lots to know.'

'Fire away,' she managed to return as she took her seat at the table, hoping his questions would be broad enough to avoid the awkward moments in her recent history.

Tilly began handing the platters of food around and soon everyone was filling their plates, while Paul put the children's food on their picnic blanket for them to share, then returned to join the adults.

'So why Adelaide?' Ken asked as he took a serving of Greek salad, ensuring there was plenty of feta cheese and olives on his plate.

'The chance to work with you,' Phoebe replied. 'I read your most recent paper on improvements to prescribed orthotic devices to control motion and position of the leg during locomotion and I think your work is outstanding. The chance to have you mentor me was too good to pass up.'

'Well, I must say that is lovely to hear, and I look

forward to working with you once my knee is tickety-boo again,' he told her, with a hint of pride in his expression. 'So tell me about your family. I picked up from our correspondence that your father works at the White House.'

Ken reached for another shashlik and held the plate so that Phoebe could take one as well.

'Yes, he's an advisor to the President. He's been in the world of politics for over nineteen years. He was in international banking before that.'

'And you weren't tempted to follow him into the political arena?' Heath cut in.

'Not at all. You see, you're right—it's an arena, and that's why I wouldn't do it. Sometimes it's great, but at other times it seems like a fight to the death. I'd rather be repairing bodies than ripping apart political opponents and their policies.'

'Touché,' Ken replied with a huge smile.

'Still, it must be an interesting lifestyle,' Tilly commented. 'Do you visit the White House often?'

'Now and then. But my place is the other side of town, nearer to the hospital. I just hear about it when I visit or call my parents.'

'I suppose it would be a little like the emergency department of a hospital—with everyone rushing frantically and everything code blue,' Tilly replied.

Phoebe smiled at her. 'You're not too far wrong with that analogy. It's like everything needs to be delivered or decided yesterday. I would most certainly go mad. My father, however, loves a challenge—he sees the big picture and the changes that need to be made for the disadvantaged and most particularly those with intergenerational problems.'

'And your mother? What does she do?' Ken asked between bites.

'Anything and everything social. Fundraising committees, women's political auxiliaries—pretty much anything that she believes helps with my father's career. Along with her bridge club.'

'So why did you choose medicine?' Ken asked. 'With a father in politics and, for want of a better word, a socialite mother, why did you choose to specialise in podiatric surgery?'

'My best friend Susy's mother had an accident driving us to school when I was fourteen…' Phoebe began.

Feeling a little parched from answering all the questions, took a sip of her cold drink before she continued.

'Anyway, she broke her heel and I was there when the paramedics took her by ambulance to the hospital. Susy and I had both been strapped in the back of the car and didn't suffer even a scratch. I visited her mother in hospital a few times with Susy, and I became curious and started asking the nurses questions. Then one day her podiatric surgeon came in. I asked him all about the operation and he went into great detail with me and that was it. I knew what I wanted to do with my life.'

'I'm impressed that you knew at such a young age—'

'I think that we should let poor Phoebe eat,' Tilly cut in. 'She's been grilled and she's passed with flying colours, Dad, so now she gets fed and watered.'

They all smiled, and then chatted about themselves so Phoebe could enjoy the delicious dinner Tilly had prepared and also get to know the family.

Everyone but Heath told her something about themselves and their lives. Heath stayed quiet, and Phoebe noticed his jaw clench more than a few times as they talked about Oscar as a baby. It was obvious to Phoebe that it had been a difficult time for him. But why exactly she wasn't sure, and they all clearly avoided the topic of Oscar's mother.

'Do you want to look at the stars?' Oscar suddenly asked Phoebe as she sat waiting for Heath to bring a drink out to the patio, where everyone had moved after dinner to enjoy the balmy evening.

'Do you have a telescope?'

'No, but we can lie on the grass and look up and see them. That's one of my favourite things to do at night. Grandpa knows lots about stars.'

Phoebe thought it was a lovely idea, and very sweet of Oscar to extend the invitation for her to join him. She stepped out of her shoes and followed him to a patch of lawn just near the patio, where they both lay down on the grass and looked up at the stars twinkling in the ebony sky. The cool ground beneath her bare skin felt wonderful.

'That's the saucepan. Can you see it? You have to draw a line between the big star—up there—and the others—just there—and it looks like a saucepan,' he said, pointing his tiny finger straight up in the air. 'And it has a handle too.'

'I can see it,' she responded as she looked to where he pointed.

They both lay staring at the perfect night sky and Oscar talked with lightning speed about everything his grandfather had told him. Phoebe was impressed with all he had retained, and his interest in astronomy.

'Perhaps you might grow up and study the stars,' she said. 'That would make you an astronomer.'

'I think I might visit them instead.'

'So you want to be an astronaut?'

'Yes. That would be more fun than just looking at them.'

Heath stood in the doorway to the patio and looked out

at the two of them, lying in the dark on the lawn, talking. He had no idea what they were saying but he could hear their animated chatter. He felt a tug at his heart, thinking that his wife had missed out on doing just that. And that Oscar had missed out on those important long talks with his mother.

They had both been cheated. And even though his pain lessened with every passing year he wondered if Oscar's would grow as he realised what he had lost.

"You know, Phoebe's nothing like I imagined,' Ken said softly when he saw Heath in the doorway with Phoebe's drink.

Heath agreed with his father's sentiments but he would not let him know. He wouldn't let any family member know, for fear of them trying to make a spark ignite between them. He had found her to be sweet when they'd first met, sexy at the pool, and looking at her now, lying beside his son, he was discovering she was apparently maternal—but that wasn't a combination he wanted. He preferred sexy with no strings attached, for one-night stands that could never break his heart. Or impact on his son.

'I think we should probably get going,' he said to his father. 'I need to get Oscar to bed—and you as well, Dad.'

'Don't fuss about getting me to bed, son,' Ken told him as he watched Oscar and Phoebe. 'I'm quite enjoying the company and I'm not that old yet. But, having said that, I imagine young Oscar might be getting tired after a day out.'

'Let him spend the night with us,' Tilly offered as she stepped outside and was pleasantly surprised to see her nephew relaxing on the lawn with Phoebe. 'Then we can get up early and have a swim before it gets hot. I think he's a little lonely over at Dad's. I can do some things with him that you—'

'That I can't do because they are things only a mother can do?'

'No, Heath. Not even close,' Tilly replied in a gentle tone. 'You're doing an amazing job with Oscar. He's adorable and polite and I love him to bits—you know that. But it's hard with you working long hours, and Dad can't do anything while he's laid up, so I thought I'd help out and do something fun while you're stepping in for Dad. Stop being so hard on yourself.'

'I'm not being hard—I'm a realist, and I think Oscar is out of his routine over here. He probably misses his nanny and preschool. Once he gets back to Sydney he'll be fine again.'

'I'm sure you're right. But in the meantime let me have him for a day.'

'Tilly's enjoying having you both in Adelaide,' Paul added. 'And I'm sure she wants to make the most of it. It doesn't happen often enough.'

'Absolutely,' Tilly agreed. 'Check with Oscar and see if he's up for it...'

'Up for what?' Oscar and Phoebe had left their observation spot on the lawn and walked up quietly without the others noticing.

'A sleepover and a day with us tomorrow.'

'Sure am—then I can go swimming with Aunty Tilly in the morning. Can I, Daddy, *please*?'

'Well, I guess the decision has been made,' Heath said, not having expected Oscar to jump at the idea of a sleepover so quickly. He'd thought they were joined at the hip, but perhaps that tie was loosening. And maybe he did need to let Tilly mother him now and then.

'Do you want to sleep over too, Phoebe? And Daddy could too?'

Heath's eyes widened in surprise at Oscar's invitation to both of them.

Phoebe smiled. 'That's very kind of you, but I have to go home to my own bed and my pyjamas.'

'I sleep in my T-shirt and jocks in summer,' Oscar cut in, with a serious tone in his little voice. 'You could do the same.'

They all smiled at Oscar's matter-of-fact response— well, everyone bar Heath. He was still thinking about the void in his son's life that was becoming more and more obvious. It was one that he'd thought he had managed to fill.

'Perhaps another time,' Phoebe said politely, thinking that there was no way she would be stripping down to her underwear for a sleepover with Heath.

Tilly tried not to laugh as she hugged her nephew and, looking at his food-stained T-shirt, she directed a request to Heath. 'Could you drop off some fresh clothes tomorrow morning in case we want to go out?'

Still deep in thought, he responded, 'Sure—as long as you're sure it's not too much trouble for him to stay?'

'Not at all,' Tilly said as she picked up Oscar and put him on her lap. 'Early-morning swim for you and me, Oscar—and, Phoebe, if you're not doing anything please come over and join us for a swim.'

Phoebe was surprised at how warm and welcoming the family was, and was very quickly feeling at home, but she declined, thinking that perhaps the offer was Tilly just being courteous.

Heath looked at his sister and then back at Phoebe without saying a word, then he kissed his son goodnight and walked out to the car. He was glad Phoebe had not accepted. She was becoming too close to his family too quickly. And starting to get under his skin a little too. He understood why she was a perfect fit for his family, with her down-to-earth personality, quick wit and sense of fun. He was also very aware that those same traits combined with her beauty were making her far too desirable to him. And he didn't like it.

She could leave at any minute, and that wouldn't be fair to Oscar. He didn't want him to grow close to a person who would walk away. He needed to protect his son from that pain. And, more than that, he didn't want their life to change.

'I will see you in the morning,' he called out before he drove away, with his father and Phoebe in the car.

The sun was setting as the three of them drove through the city to Phoebe's home. Each one was thinking about the same thing. How quickly and naturally Phoebe was seeming to fit into their lives. Ken was thrilled; Phoebe was surprised—Heath was more worried than he had been in a very long time...

CHAPTER SIX

HEATH WOKE AT four and lay staring out his window to the dark sky that was softly lit by a haze-covered moon. He knew the warm air outside would be heavy and still. He rolled onto his back and lifted his arms above his head and thought back over the previous two days, since Phoebe had fallen into his arms.

He didn't want to be thinking about her—and especially not at four in the morning, lying in bed—but her face wouldn't leave his mind. When Phoebe had been close to him—close enough for him to smell the scent that rested delicately on her skin and close enough to see the sparkle in her beautiful green eyes—he had struggled to remember why he didn't want a woman in his life on any permanent basis.

But that was something he had to remember. Particularly now.

His life had begun to change since he'd arrived back in Adelaide.

He had worried for a little while that the life he had built with his son, just the two of them, might not be enough for Oscar one day. And he feared now that that day was almost upon him. But he didn't want to lose control. Once before he had lost control of a situation—lost his wife and almost lost his mind. He wouldn't let it happen again. He needed to remain in control and not blindly accept change.

And he couldn't accept Phoebe as the catalyst for that change.

He was more than concerned after seeing how comfortable the family had been with her. It was moving too fast for him. He had to put the brakes on the level of intimacy he thought they were all building with her. It needed to stop immediately. The air-conditioning repairman had notified him that the work was completed at the practice and while there were no patients booked in until the next day, he would send Phoebe a message just after nine and ask her to call into the practice to go over the patient notes. That would serve his purpose.

He needed to remind her why she was there—and it wasn't to grow close to any member of his family, and particularly not his son. It was a relationship he didn't want to see develop and risk it being torn apart when they headed back to Sydney and Phoebe headed back to her home country.

Phoebe woke early, picked up the paper and was halfway through the crossword when she got the call just after eight.

'Hi, Phoebe—it's Tilly. Would you like to jump in a cab and have breakfast by the pool with us? I'd pick you up, but by the time I load the diaper gang you could already be here.'

'I'm not sure…' She hesitated to accept the invitation. 'This is your time with Oscar. I don't want to infringe on that.'

'Nonsense. I would love to chat to another adult. Away from the surgery my days are filled with nursery rhymes and potty-training, and Oscar could do with another set of eyes on him while he's in the pool. It is hard with three of them, and my stomach is in a knot trying to keep a watch over them all. At their age it's a bit like herding cats.'

'Well, if you're sure I can help, I'd love to.'

'It's settled, then,' Tilly said. "See you soon—and don't forget your swimsuit.'

Half an hour later Phoebe was alighting from a cab at Tilly's home and a very happy little boy was opening the front door before she'd even reached the doorbell. He was wearing his swimsuit, dry flippers and goggles on the top of his head.

'Hi, Phoebe! Have you got your bathers?'

'Bathers?' she asked as she walked up the paved entrance towards him.

'He means swimsuit,' Tilly said as she invited Phoebe inside. 'In Australia we call a swimsuit bathers. You'll get used to our funny expressions soon enough.'

Phoebe smiled at her hostess, then turned her attention to Oscar, 'Yes, I have my bathers—so I hope you're wanting to swim, because in this weather *I* do!'

Phoebe didn't hear the three text messages from Heath because she was splashing in the pool with his son, and Melissa and Jasmine were excitedly screaming from the sidelines behind the child-safe fence, blocking out all other sounds. Oscar's floating armbands were in place but Phoebe didn't let him go for even a second. They'd had a lovely morning, stopping only for some juice and freshly cut fruit, after which Oscar walked Phoebe around the garden, collecting insects in his bug catcher.

'I only keep them for a few hours, then I let them go back to their daddies...and their mummies. I think some of them have mummies too.'

'I'm sure some of them have both, and some just have

a mummy or a daddy,' Phoebe said, then fell silent as he continued walking, collecting and talking.

Oscar suddenly seemed very deep in thought for a five-year-old, and it worried Phoebe a little.

'My mummy died when I was very little.'

Phoebe felt herself stiffen as he delivered this news. 'I'm sorry to hear that, Oscar.' She paused to gain some composure as her heart went out to the little boy. 'I'm sure she's looking over you every day.'

Phoebe had not considered the prospect that Heath might be a widower. She wasn't sure why it hadn't occurred to her, but now she knew it did go part way to explaining why he was such a serious man, who appeared only to lighten up around his son. Losing his wife and the mother of his child would have been a life-altering tragedy.

'I was very little. I couldn't talk or walk and I don't remember her. But I know her name was—'

'Hello, you two.'

Heath's deep voice suddenly called from the back door, interrupting their conversation and making them both turn abruptly.

Phoebe felt her stomach drop. Then it lifted, and then spun as her heart fluttered nervously. She'd thought she had her reactions to Heath under control, but suddenly she discovered she didn't.

But she had to.

Somehow.

'Hello, Daddy!'

'Hi, Heath.'

Heath quickly crossed to them and dropped to his knees. 'I'm sorry, Oscar, but I'm going to have to take Phoebe to work with me.'

'But we're having *fun*, Daddy, and I want her to stay. She showed me how to swim like a bug and...'

'Swim like a bug?' Heath asked, turning to Phoebe with a curious look on his face.

'The butterfly stroke,' Phoebe said as she looked at this man whom she now knew had suffered the tragedy of losing his wife. It did put a different filter on the way she saw him, but she didn't want him to know that. He seemed too stoic to want pity—in fact she suspected pity would drive him into a darker place.

Despite what she now knew she didn't want it to colour her feelings towards him. She wasn't looking for love and he was obviously still grieving. Although she *was* grateful for the insight, as she would understand his motives a little better and make their working relationship easier. She just had to get her emotions under control. And he was dressed again, as he had been the night before, so it made it easier to concentrate.

'How did you know I was here?' she asked, trying to mask how sad she felt for them both. And how equally drawn she was to the father and son.

'Well, you didn't answer your phone, so on the off-chance that my sister had convinced you to visit I called her and she said you were swimming with Oscar. Unfortunately I'll have to cut that short and ask you to head back to the surgery with me.'

'Like this?' She looked down at her swimsuit covered by a sarong. She had chosen not to wear her bikini that day, and had slipped the one-piece swimsuit under her sarong before she'd left her house. 'But if the air-conditioning isn't running maybe this is the right thing to be wearing.' She tried to be lighthearted. Friendly. At ease. Everything she wasn't feeling.

Heath had tried not to look at her body, but he couldn't help but notice how stunning she looked. He definitely

didn't want to be alone with her at the practice in the outfit she was barely wearing.

'Perhaps not,' he replied, trying to avert his eyes from
her petite curves. 'I can drop you home to change, if you'd
like.'

A little while later, after a quick stop at her house for a
change of clothes, they sat reading through the patient
notes in the cool surgery. The newly repaired and effi-
ciently running air-conditioner was working perfectly, but
Phoebe had the distinct feeling that this activity wasn't
really essential. They were straightforward records that
could easily have been read through prior to her meeting
with each patient.

She wondered if it wasn't so much her being at the practice that was important but perhaps more her *not* being
at Tilly's house with Oscar. She wasn't sure why but she
said nothing, and continued to concentrate for the next
two hours on the records that Heath was explaining in
great detail.

Occasionally she would glance at the man across from
her. His chiselled jaw, with a light covering of stubble, was
tense. There was no half-smile. She realised there was no
chance of a full smile and she knew why. Despite her resolve to keep it professional, still she felt her heart pick up
speed a little when their eyes met by accident. And at that
time, they both paused for only a moment in silence. She
didn't know how he was feeling or what he was thinking
but there was something Heath was keeping to himself.

And she suspected it was his heart.

Finally she left to go home. It was a short walk, and she
wanted the time to clear her head. She now knew that
Heath was still suffering from the loss of his wife and al-

though she also knew that Oscar had been little when his mother had died she wasn't sure exactly how long ago it had happened. Three years? Four years? Even five?

But there was one other thing she knew. Heath must have loved his wife very much, and if it had been half as much as he clearly loved Oscar then, although her life had been cut short, his wife had been a very lucky woman to have known that deep a love and commitment. It was something that Phoebe knew she had never experienced. And probably never would.

'Why don't you guys move here permanently?' Tilly asked, sitting down and pouring herself a cold soft drink after dropping Oscar back at her father's later that day. Paul had arrived at her home to mind the twins for a little while. 'I adore Oscar, and I'd love Mels and Jazzy to grow up with their big cousin to keep the boys at bay. I think it makes complete sense.'

'My thoughts exactly,' Ken agreed, while admiring the stunning violet and red hues of the setting sun. The lighting provided a canvas for the silhouettes of the towering gum trees that surrounded his home and the scent of eucalyptus floated in the night air.

But Heath didn't notice anything. He could still remember the scent of Phoebe, sitting so close to him at work, could see her beautiful face, and nothing he did was successful at pushing those images from his mind. He could vaguely hear the mutterings of his father and his sister, but none of it registered. His mind was consumed by thoughts of Phoebe and he felt uneasy. Her sweetness. Her sincerity. She had stumbled into his world and into his arms quite literally, and for some inexplicable reason he couldn't shake her from his thoughts. But he wouldn't break another rule. He had to ignore this fleeting infatuation.

Heath came back to the conversation to see two sets of eyes on him, seeking answers. He didn't like the fact that a family inquisition was developing on the back porch because there was another one going on in his mind and one was more than enough to endure. Two would certainly send him crazy.

'The air-con is now working and that's all that matters. Let's leave it at that. Phoebe is a surgeon, in town to meet the terms of her employment contract. And, by the way, Tilly, she can't be your babysitter.'

'My babysitter? That's a little unfair. She knows no one, and she was alone in her house, and I thought she'd enjoy a swim and a chat. And, FYI, Oscar totally commandeered her for the better part of two hours and that was not my plan—it was his.'

'Well, I'm here only until Dad's knee mends. End of story. So I hope Oscar doesn't get comfortable with the current arrangements. It's all only temporary.'

With that Heath stood up and went inside to find his son. Reading him a story was always a highlight of his day, but that night it would also serve as his avenue of respite from the barrage of questions about Phoebe.

And for a short while it might also silence those inside his head.

'I like Phoebe,' Oscar told his father as he went to turn out the light. 'She's neat.'

'As in tidy?'

'Daddy, you're being *silly*. Not tidy. She's fun—and she makes you happy too.'

Heath was taken aback by his son's words. 'What do you mean by that?'

'Well, I saw you smile. You don't smile very much. I always thought you were sad, but now that Phoebe comes over you're happy more. That makes me happy too. It's almost like we're a family—like Aunty Tilly and Uncle Paul.'

Phoebe called London after she'd eaten her takeaway dinner. She wanted to chat with Susy and hoped with the time difference that while it was evening in Adelaide she would catch her young barrister friend before she left in the morning for court in London.

'Phoebs, how are you?'

'I'm great—how are you, Susy? And how's work? Anything interesting that you can talk about?'

'I'll put you on loud speaker—trying to finish my makeup before I rush out the door.'

'If it's not a good time I'll try another day,' Phoebe said as she rested back into the three soft white pillows on her bed.

The ceiling fan was moving the air above her and Phoebe had opened a window on the approaching darkness. She knew she would be in air-conditioning all of the next day and she wanted to sleep with fresh air, even if it *was* a little warm.

'No, I'm good to talk. Nothing to report. There was a guilty verdict in the grand theft case, which I was thrilled about, and today I'm selecting the jury for a new IT case. Possession of data with intent to commit a serious offence. Same old, same old.' Susy laughed. 'I *do* love my job. We've been securing a high percentage of convictions lately, so it makes it all worthwhile. Unfortunately there's never a shortage of bad guys needing to be put away. But let's forget about me—how are you on your adventure Down Under?'

'It's hot—melting hot, to be accurate.'

'Well, I don't feel even a teeny bit sorry for you, if that's what you're hoping for. I spent last night in my Welling-

tons, overcoat and scarf, shovelling snow off my car in case
I need it in an emergency. I'll take the Underground into
London again today. So, my sister from another mother,
stop complaining—'cos while you're over there, getting a
suntan, I'm warding off frostbite!'

Both women laughed.

Then Susy's voice became momentarily stern. 'Seriously, Phoebs, has the creep left you alone? And your
mother—is she finally coming to terms with the fact that
Niles won't be a member of the family?'

'It's Giles...'

'I know...but I prefer to disrespect him at every opportunity, and forgetting his name is a start.'

'I promise he's out of the picture completely. Mother
is still not convinced, but I've given up on telling her that
cheating is a deal-breaker.'

'Absolutely,' Susy agreed, in her prosecuting barrister
tone. 'Guilty, charged and dumped. I do wish there was
a way to lock him *and* those tarts away. Pity there's no
legal avenue to put the lot of them behind bars and throw
away the key.'

'In a perfect world there would be, but I'm trying not
to think about him any more. Just onwards and upwards.
I'm starting work tomorrow with...Heath.' Phoebe stumbled over his name.

'I thought you were working with Ken Rollins? Who's
Heath?'

'His son, actually. Ken needed emergency knee reconstruction. His son's a podiatric surgeon too, so he's stepped
in to help out for the next few weeks.'

'I hope you're not disappointed? I know you were really excited to be working with Ken.'

This was now the third time she had been asked and
still her answer remained the same. Disappointed, no...

confused, yes…and now she was feeling a little melancholy about what had made Heath the man he was.

'I was looking forward to working with Ken, but I'm sure Heath will be an equally good operator.'

'So good to hear you back to your old optimistic self, Phoebs. I'd love to chat and hear all about Heath, but I have to dash. The Underground waits for no one,' Susy said. 'Hope sonny-boy is not too nerdy or dull—but it's only for a few weeks. Talk tomorrow. I'll call you.'

With that, Suzy hung up.

Nerdy? *I wish…* Dull? *Not in anyone's book.* In fact she had to admit that Heath seemed perfect…if a little battle worn.

Heath arrived at the practice early the next morning. He had a surgical list beginning at one, with two post-operative patients and two new patients in the morning. Phoebe's day was light—three morning patients and two in the afternoon. Heath had arranged it that way to allow her to settle in.

Generally December was not busy, as most patients delayed non-urgent treatment, particularly surgery, until after the busy holiday season. By the time her patient numbers increased Heath knew he would be back in Sydney and his father would be back on deck.

'Good morning,' Tilly greeted her brother as she dropped her bag behind the desk. 'Loving the cool air in here.'

'It's great, isn't it? Not sure the landlord will be thrilled when he sees the invoice, but it's worth every penny.'

'*Dad* owns the building. *He's* the landlord.'

Heath laughed. 'Yes—and hopefully I'll be back in Sydney when he gets the bill in the mail. I had it completely overhauled and replaced the motor.'

'I think he can cover it.'

'Not sure about that, since he has the most expensive receptionist in the country.'

Tilly rolled her eyes and smiled. 'You're in fine form today, Heath. Be nice to your sister or I'll walk out—and then you'll be lost without my administrative wizardry.'

Heath headed back to his consulting room, and on the way checked that everything had been prepared for Phoebe. Her patient list was all in order. He had set up her log-in details for the computer and given her access to the database with the patient notes. The room was spotless. Although he refused to admit it to himself, he wanted to impress her.

'Hi, Phoebe,' Heath heard his sister say cheerily from the other end of the practice.

'Hi, Tilly,' Phoebe replied. She stepped inside, feeling apprehensive and nervous, as if it was the first day at school. 'It's a lot cooler than a couple of days ago in here.'

'Hopefully we can avoid doctors and patients fainting,' Heath said as he walked briskly down the corridor and into the waiting room.

'Good morning, Heath.'

'I'll show you to your consulting room.'

Phoebe could sense that he had slipped back into his cool demeanour again, but he wasn't quite as cold and she did not take it personally.

'I'll try not to faint on the way,' she said, in an attempt to lighten the mood.

Heath smirked, but because he was leading the way Phoebe didn't see. Her view was his broad shoulders, slim hips and the long stride he was taking. And, despite not wanting to notice, it was the best damn view she had seen in days. In fact the last time she had seen anything so impressive was in the very same man at the pool.

* * *

'Nancy Wilson?' Phoebe called into the waiting room.

A young woman stood up and followed Phoebe into her consulting room, hobbling a little and clearly in pain.

Phoebe closed the door. 'Let me introduce myself, Nancy. I'm Dr Phoebe Johnson and I've stepped in to help Dr Ken Rollins for the next few months. Please take a seat.' Phoebe had briefly read the patient's notes and was aware of her medical history of chronic heel pain. 'I see you have undergone some reconstructive treatments with Dr Rollins.'

'Yes, but it hasn't made a permanent improvement.'

'I see. Did you find any of them had long-lasting benefits? I know it was more invasive, but was the plasma therapy successful from your perspective? Or did you prefer the low-intensity shock wave treatment?'

'Both were good—but only short term. I'm an ice skater. I hope to compete for Australia in Switzerland in nine months, so I need to be back on my feet and out of pain to train in Europe and then compete. At the moment it feels like there's a pebble in my left shoe when I walk. On really bad days it's like a shard of glass.'

'They are common descriptions of the problem. Please come over to the examination table and I'll have a look,' Phoebe said, and assisted the young woman to the narrow table against the far wall. She moved a small step into place with her foot to help Nancy climb up onto the bed. 'I appreciate you've tried the conservative approach, and to be honest, Nancy, sometimes after all else fails there's no choice but to choose corrective surgical treatment.'

Phoebe eased the soft boot and sock from the woman's left foot and then, slipping on surgical gloves, began her examination. Although the conservative restorative treatments to increase blood flow and break up scar tissue had assisted temporarily with pain management, Phoebe decided that surgery was the only option.

'Unfortunately your plantar fasciitis has not improved with past treatments, and your ice skating training has, according to your notes, been compromised for a number of months now.'

'Yes, I do train, but only for short periods, and then I require ice, cortisone, and when all else fails codeine to manage the pain—and then I lie in bed for hours some days.'

'Heavy doses of pain relief or cortisone are not long-term options for anyone, but particularly not at your age, Nancy. Nor is being incapacitated in bed an option for an athlete. Your condition is almost epidemic in the United States, with one in ten people suffering from varying degrees of heel pain from scar tissue, and it appears this approach is no longer viable for you, considering your lifestyle. We'll need to proceed to the next level on your treatment plan, so you can move forward with your career.'

'Surgery is fine by me. I just want to get it over and finished and get back on my feet—literally.'

Phoebe gently put the sock and soft boot back on the young woman and helped her down from the examination table. She explained the risks of surgery, confirmed that Nancy was in general good health and a suitable patient for surgery, and then walked her out to the front desk for Tilly to make the hospital arrangements and for Nancy to sign the consent forms.

Heath had just seen off his first patient for the day, and was at the reception desk checking up on a late arrival.

'Were you part of the medical team assisting the disabled athletes at the international games last year?' Nancy asked Phoebe as they waited for Tilly to check the surgical roster at the Eastern Memorial, where Phoebe would be operating.

'Yes, I was—but how did you know? The games weren't held in Australia.'

'My older brother Jason's a weightlifter. He lives in Detroit with his wife and baby daughter,' Nancy continued as she offered Tilly her credit card for the consultation payment. 'He suffers from congenital amputation of his left leg below the knee, and he had a similar issue to me with his right heel the night before his heat. I remember he told me about a consultation he had with Dr Phoebe Johnson, the podiatric surgeon with the American team. Once I heard your accent I assumed that there couldn't be two of you in the same specialty.'

'No—not that I'm aware of anyway,' Phoebe replied as she finished signing the notes so Tilly could book surgery the following week. She turned back to Nancy. 'Being involved with the teams was a wonderful experience. Can you please give my best to Jason? If I remember correctly he won a medal—was it silver?'

'Yes, and he was thrilled to win it. He swore that if it wasn't for you and the treatment you provided to alleviate the pain he would have pulled out and wasted almost four years of training.'

Heath walked back to his office, unavoidably impressed with this experience that Phoebe had kept close to her chest and not put on her CV. She was even more unforthcoming than him!

He wondered what else he didn't know about his temporary associate. And he still wondered if this small inner-city practice would prove enough of a challenge for her...

The morning was steady, and by lunchtime Heath was preparing to leave for his afternoon surgical list at the Eastern Memorial. Aware that Phoebe's last patient for the morning had left, he knocked on the open door of Phoebe's consulting room.

'Come in, Tilly.'

Heath paused. 'It's not Tilly.'

Phoebe turned from her computer screen, where she was reading through the notes for her first afternoon patient.

'Sorry, Heath—come in.'

With only fifteen minutes before he had to leave for the hospital, he wanted to catch up and see how her morning had progressed. And he just wanted to see her but couldn't admit that even to himself.

Before he had a chance to open his mouth, Tilly knocked on the door.

'This time it has to be Tilly,' Phoebe remarked as she watched Heath cross his arms across his broad chest.

'Yep, you're running out of alternative suspects now.'

Phoebe smiled, then asked Tilly to join them.

'Sorry to interrupt, Phoebe, but your afternoon patients have both cancelled due to the extreme weather,' Tilly told her. 'So it looks like you've got the afternoon off.'

'Oh, no. That's disappointing,' Phoebe said, slumping into her chair and not masking her feelings. 'I feel so guilty, being here and doing nothing.' She had a strong work ethic and that made sitting around seem a complete waste of time for her and a waste of money for the practice. 'I've had more time off since I arrived than I've worked.'

Heath considered her for a moment and then came up with a suggestion. 'I have an idea to appease your misguided sense of guilt. Why don't you assist me in Theatre over at the Eastern Memorial this afternoon? I have three on the surgical list and I could do with an extra set of hands—but we'd need to leave immediately.'

Phoebe sat bolt-upright and answered with an unhesitating, 'Yes!' as she reached for her bag. 'Let's go...I'm all yours.'

Heath nodded, but his body abruptly reminded him that if his life had played out differently and Phoebe really was *all his* there would be far more pleasurable things he would do with her that afternoon.

CHAPTER SEVEN

THE SCRUB NURSE greeted Heath as he prepared for the first patient.

'Abby, we have Phoebe Johnson, a podiatric surgeon from Washington, joining us this afternoon,' Heath announced as he turned off the tap with his foot and shook the water from his hands into the scrub room trough.

'Hi, Phoebe, welcome aboard.'

'Pleased to meet you, Abby.'

Phoebe slipped her freshly scrubbed hands inside some surgical gloves. Her long dark hair was in a flat bun and neatly secured inside a floral cap, and like the other two she was already dressed in sterile blue scrubs. They entered the theatre just as the patient was drifting off under anaesthesia.

'So, today's patient is a thirty-five-year-old professional skateboarder. He's here for a lateral ankle ligament reconstruction. The ankle has not responded to non-surgical treatment and has been unstable for over six months,' Heath informed the surgical team, including two observing third-year medical students as he began marking the stained sterile area. 'Would you like to lead on this one, Phoebe?'

Phoebe was both flattered and pleased to be asked.

Heath was a complex man, but a man who treated her as his equal, not only in words but in actions.

Quietly she declined. 'I'd prefer to assist today. We can switch it around another time, perhaps.'

'Certainly.' Heath looked over his surgical mask at Phoebe for slightly longer than required before he averted his eyes back to the patient. 'I routinely use the modified Brostrom procedure.' He confidently made a J-shaped incision over the outside of the patient's left ankle with his scalpel, identified the ankle ligaments and began the process of tightening them, using anchors that he placed on to the fibula bone.

Phoebe appreciated the way he led the students through the procedure by describing the steps clearly and precisely.

'I'm stitching other tissue over the repaired ligaments to further strengthen the repair,' he said as he continued, with Phoebe holding the incision open with forceps.

Phoebe had done many of these operations over the years. 'That looks great, Heath. Very clean and tidy. I've had a few when I've needed to use tendons to replace the ligaments. I've woven a tendon into the bones around the ankle and held it in place with stitches, and occasionally a screw in the bone. I've utilised a patient's own hamstring tendon before. But it made it a much longer operation as I had to take the hamstring tendon through a separate incision on the inside part of the knee.'

Heath nodded in agreement. 'On more than one occasion I've needed to use a cadaver tendon and had to weave it into the fibula bone. There's many ways to solve a problem like this, and as we know each has its merits.'

Phoebe and Heath worked together as if they had been operating as a team for years—or at the very least months. Their effortless collaboration would be deceptive to any external observers, who might not think that this was their first time together in the operating theatre. Phoebe was able to pre-empt Heath's next move, and neither of them could deny their natural synchronisation.

'That went well.'

Phoebe nodded her agreement with Heath's statement as they scrubbed in for the second operation. Each was exceptionally happy with how well they'd worked together but not wanting to state the obvious.

They made a great team.

The afternoon progressed well, with the other two patients' procedures completed successfully and on time. Phoebe felt a great deal of satisfaction working with such a skilful surgeon as Heath. His dexterity and knowledge in the field was second to none and, while she was confident in her own abilities, she felt there was still much she could learn from him.

After only a short time in the operating theatre with Heath she could see that he had a level of skill that must come close to his father's. The knowledge Heath had casually and without ceremony imparted to her already was amazing, and she was excited for the next few weeks until he left for Sydney.

'I really hope we can do this again.' The words rushed from her lips with unbridled honesty as she removed her surgical gloves and cap.

Heath watched as her long dark hair tumbled free and fell over her shoulders. In the harsh theatre lights she still looked gorgeous, and he knew that in any lighting her stunning smile and sparkling eyes would bring a glow to the room.

'I'd like that,' he said, and again kept his eyes focused on her for a little longer than a casual glance.

Phoebe flinched and felt something tug at her heart.

Was it pity for the man? Or desire? She wasn't sure, but there was something stirring inside.

'Would you like to grab some dinner? My way to say thank you for assisting in there this afternoon.'

Heath had surprised himself with the invitation, but he enjoyed spending time with Phoebe and it seemed a natural progression for the day. They had a professional connection, and he told himself it was nothing more than a dinner invitation to a colleague.

'I'll have to go out and eat anyway. Oscar will be eating at Tilly's, and Dad will more than likely defrost a TV dinner, so I will need to pick up something or eat alone at a restaurant. You'll be doing me a favour by sharing a table with me.'

'If you put it that way…' she replied.

'That's settled, then,' Heath said as he left to change into his street clothes. 'As you know, I have your address, so what say I pick you up at seven?'

'Sounds perfect.'

'I'll put Oscar to bed early, since last night was a late one for him, then you and I can have a nice dinner somewhere—maybe even in the foothills. I'll show you something of Adelaide. It should be a little cooler out tonight, so I'll find a good alfresco restaurant.'

Phoebe walked into the female change room. There were two other young doctors also changing from their scrubs to day clothes, but they didn't notice Phoebe and continued their conversation.

'Did you know he's back in town?' an attractive redhead asked the other woman. 'He's been here for a week already.'

'The doctor with the *no second date* rule?' the blonde doctor replied as she ran a brush though her short bobbed hair, then put it back on the shelf and closed her locker. 'Yes, I heard he came back last week and that he's here for a month.'

'I wonder how many hearts he'll break in that time, with his hard and fast rules. And don't forget the *never meet his son* rule. There was another one too, but I can't think of it now.'

'I think it's to *leave before the sun comes up*.'

'That's right. Pity he's so damned gorgeous—if he wasn't he'd never get away with it.'

They both slammed shut their lockers. 'But despite all that he doesn't hide the rules. I hear he's upfront with all the women he intends to bed. They all know what they're getting into and not one has ever met his precious son. Dr Rollins is a player, but he's an honest one.'

Almost two hours later there was a knock on Phoebe's front door.

Thank God, she thought as she sprayed a light fragrance on her neck and wrists, that this wasn't really a date. It had the makings of a date, and to others observing it might even look like a date, but to Phoebe it most certainly *wasn't* a date. She wasn't ready for anything close to a date. And after what she'd heard in the locker room she never would be. They would only ever be friends— because she had already met his son, so clearly he wasn't thinking about bedding her.

Deep in thought, she smoothed her hands over her long white summer dress as she made her way from her room. The halter-style dress, cinched at the waist by a thin gold belt, was made of soft cotton that flowed as she moved. She wore simple flat gold sandals to match. Her hair fell in silky curls around her bare shoulders.

'Hi, Phoebe,' Heath greeted her as she opened the door.

'Hi, Heath. Let me grab my bag and I'll be right with you.' She picked up her purse and keys and locked the door behind her as they left.

'It's a little cooler this evening, like I predicted, so I've left the top down to enjoy the fresh air on the drive but if you'd prefer I can put it up again.'

Phoebe looked past him to see his silver convertible sports car parked by her front gate. Then her gaze quickly returned to him. His white T-shirt was snug across his toned chest and he wore khaki trousers. A single, handsome medic with a sports car would be every woman's dream. But not hers—not after what she'd heard.

She reached into her purse for a hair tie. 'You can leave the top down,' she said and she pulled her hair into a high ponytail.

Heath had to remind himself that he was doing the right thing and providing dinner for a colleague who had done a great job in Theatre that afternoon. And not that she was a woman whose company he was very much beginning to enjoy.

'So, I thought we'd head up to Hahndorf for dinner. It's a German town in the Adelaide Hills.'

'Sounds lovely,' she said as they walked to his car.

Heath held open the car door and, after lifting the flowing hem of her dress safely inside, closed and patted it, as if he had secured precious cargo. It did not go unnoticed by Phoebe and it made her feel torn—almost like jumping back out and telling him that it was a mistake and she wasn't hungry.

The car suddenly felt a little like a sports version of a fairytale carriage, and she was *not* looking for Prince Charming—and by reputation he was far from that gallant. But he was in the car and the engine was running before she could muster an excuse.

'Hahndorf—is that how you say it?'

'Yes,' he said, and moments later had pulled away from the kerb and into the traffic. 'It's about twenty minutes up the freeway. Something different—I hope you like it.'

As he said this he turned momentarily to see Phoebe look back at him with her warm brown eyes. She was a conundrum. He sensed so many layers to the woman who sat beside him, and one layer appeared to be a lack of trust. He wondered why. What had caused Phoebe to be outwardly happy and yet as distant as himself on a personal level?

Except around his son. She seemed to let her guard down around him very easily.

Had her heart been broken? he wondered as he entered the freeway and picked up speed.

The drive in the warm evening air was wonderful and their chatter was intermittent as Phoebe admired the scenery of the foothills.

'It was a pity you didn't bring our work to Tilly's the other morning. We could have gone over the patient notes by the pool,' Phoebe suddenly announced as he slowed a little to take the turn-off to Hahndorf.

Guilt slammed into Heath. 'I thought it would be easier at the office,' he said, clearing his throat. He had to keep it simple, when in fact it was so far from that.

Phoebe surveyed the scenery, dotted with massive gum trees that enveloped them as they drove into the quaint town. This evening would be a no-strings-attached walk in the park—or in this case a walk in a German town.

'I'm looking forward to visiting this town and to eating authentic German cuisine. I've never had the opportunity to travel to Germany—or the time, to be honest—so this is my chance to sample it.'

Heath pulled into a restaurant car park. The breeze had

picked up but there were no rain clouds, so he left the top of his car down. 'There are great reviews about the food here, although I've not been. Tilly says it's very nice.'

Heath looked down at his watch. Their dinner reservation was not until seven forty-five, so they had fifteen minutes to spare.

'Would you like to walk for a few minutes? Take in the sights of the town? It's not quite the size of New York, so fifteen minutes should have it covered.'

Phoebe turned to catch what she thought was a smile from Heath.

They walked along the narrow footpath and stepped inside the small antiquity shops still open for the tourist trade and window-shopped at those that had closed.

Heath was enjoying the time with Phoebe.

'I think we can head back to the restaurant, if you're ready,' he told her as they stepped from a bric-a-brac shop where Phoebe had been admiring the vintage hand-embroidered tablecloths and runners. 'The sauerkraut is probably primed to go.'

Phoebe laughed and followed his lead to the casual eatery, where the *maître d'* showed them to a table outside and provided them with menus. There were lights strung up high across the alfresco dining area, and their small table had a lovely street view. She felt more relaxed the more she thought of Heath as a colleague. A very handsome colleague, who bedded other women but would never bed her.

'I love that all the speciality dishes are served with creamy mustard potato bake, sauerkraut, red wine sauce and German mustard. It seems so authentic. Hahndorf really is Adelaide's little Germany,' Phoebe said as she looked over the menu.

Heath ordered a crisp white wine and some iced water while Phoebe tried to focus on the menu. It all looked wonderful, and there was a varied selection within the list of traditional German fare. Her mouth twisted a little from side to side as she carefully considered her options. Her finger softly tapped her bottom lip as she weighed up her decision.

Heath fell a little further under the spell she didn't know she was casting—one he was finding it almost futile to ignore.

'I think...' She paused to reread, and then continued. 'I think I would like the smoked Kassler chops, please.'

'Sounds great. I'll go with the Schweinshaxe—crispy skin pork hock is a favourite of mine.'

With that he signalled the waiter and placed their order. The waiter returned moments later with the drinks, before leaving them alone again.

Phoebe was staring at the people walking by and at the cars slowly moving down the single-lane road that meandered through the town. She was thinking about Washington, covered in snow, while she was enjoying a balmy evening in the foothills on the other side of the world.

'A penny for your thoughts?'

'It will cost you a quarter.'

'A quarter of what?'

'A quarter of a dollar.'

Heath rubbed the cleft in his chin and considered her terms. 'Tell me honestly—are your thoughts right now worth twenty-five cents?'

'I guess unless you pay up you'll never know,' Phoebe returned with a cheeky smile.

Heath decided to call her bluff and, reaching for his wallet, found a twenty-cent and a five-cent coin. He placed both on the table and pushed them towards her with lean strong fingers. 'Well, your thoughts are officially mine now.'

'I was thinking about Washington...'

'International thoughts are always more expensive, so I can see why there was a price-hike from a penny to twenty-five cents,' he teased. 'So go on.'

Phoebe bit the inside of her lip. 'That's it.'

'That's it?'

'Yep. I'm afraid you probably didn't get your money's worth after all,' Phoebe said with her head at a tilt. 'It was always going to be a gamble. When the stakes are high and you play big...sometimes you lose.'

Heath's lips curved a little at her response. He suddenly had the feeling that spending time with Phoebe would never be a loss.

'That was delicious—thank you so much.'

'You're most welcome,' he replied as they made their way along the now darkened street.

Street lamps lit their way, but the sky was dark and dotted with sparkling stars. The breeze had picked up a little over the almost two hours they had spent eating and conversing, but it was refreshing, not cold, and it carried along with it the gentle wafts of eucalyptus and other native bushes.

Phoebe filled her lungs with the beautiful fresh air. Both had purposely steered the conversation away from their personal lives and discussed issues aligned to their careers.

'We can head to my father's home, if you like, to have a coffee with him.' Heath wanted to prolong his time with Phoebe, but in a way that was safe for both of them.

'Isn't it a bit late to be calling on your father?' she asked as they left the freeway and headed towards the city residence.

'My father is a night owl. He has been for many years. He was always the last to bed. I remember coming home in the early hours of the morning sometimes, maybe from a pub crawl with uni friends, and he would still be up reading.'

'And your mother didn't mind?'

Heath drew a shallow breath. Although it had been a long time since his mother had died he still felt the loss.

'My mother was killed in a light plane crash returning from Kangaroo Island. She was a social worker and had been over there consulting about issues with the high rate of school truancy. She was working on strategies to keep the children on the island engaged, and she called my father just before she boarded, very excited with the outcome. She told him that they had made significant progress and that she would tell him all about it when she arrived home. The plane went down ten minutes after take-off from Kingscote, in bad weather that had come in quickly.'

'I'm so sorry to hear that.' Phoebe's hand instinctively covered her mouth for a moment. She felt her heart sink with the news he had just broken. That meant he had lost two women he had loved. That was a heavy burden to carry for any man.

'How old were you at the time, Heath?'

'Sixteen—so it will be twenty years this July since she was killed.'

The desolate expression on Phoebe's face told Heath how she was feeling. She knew she had no words that could capture the depth of his sadness so she didn't try to speak.

'I think, to be honest, he has no reason to go to bed early any more. There's no one waiting so he stays up late—unless he has an early surgery roster…then he goes to bed at a reasonable hour.'

'And he's never wanted to remarry?'

'No. He and my mother were soul mates. He didn't think he would find that again, so he never looked.'

'That's sad. There might have been someone just perfect...' Phoebe replied—then realised that she was overstepping the mark, by commenting about someone else's love-life when her own had been a disaster, and stopped.

'Perhaps. But he's never recovered from losing my mother. Some people never do. They just can't move on.'

Phoebe wondered if Heath was the same as his father. Cut from the same cloth and faithful to the woman he had lost. Never having healed enough to be with someone else.

They travelled along in silence after that, until Heath pulled up at the front of the beautiful old sandstone villa that his father had called home for so many years, and where he was staying for just a few weeks. Standard white roses, eight bushes on each side, lined the pathway.

Someone must have been watering them in the extreme weather, Phoebe mused as she walked past them, tempted to touch the perfect white petals. Their delicate perfume hung in the night air. The front porch light was on and the home had a welcoming feel to it. It was as if there was a woman still living there, Phoebe thought as she made her way to the front door with Heath.

He unlocked it and they both stepped inside.

'Hi, Dad, we're home. I hope you're decent. I have Phoebe with me, and you don't need to scare her in your underwear, or worse.'

Phoebe felt a smile coming on at the humour in his greeting and it lifted her spirits. She looked around and was very taken by the beautiful stained glass around the door of the softly lit entrance hall. And she felt comforted by the lighthearted side of their father-son relationship. It was not unlike the way she related to her own father. The warmth, respect and humorous rapport were very similar.

'I'm outside on the patio.'

Heath dropped his keys onto the antique hall stand and

then led the way down the long hallway, through the huge country-style kitchen, complete with pots and pans overhanging the marble cooking island, to the back veranda. From what she could see of the house in the dim lighting it was pristine, and she wondered if it was the work of Ken or if perhaps he had a cleaning service to keep it looking so picture-perfect. It didn't look like two men were living there.

Phoebe excused herself to visit the bathroom while Heath walked through the French doors to the patio.

'There you are,' he said to his father, who was sitting in the light of the moon.

'Yes, just sitting alone with my thoughts. And here's one of them. Don't look at me as a role model—look at me as a warning... It's not a real life without a woman to share it. Don't leave it too long to look for love again.'

CHAPTER EIGHT

THE NEXT DAY Phoebe was sitting in the cool of her house. It was the weekend, and the previous days had gone by quickly. She had been busy consulting at the practice, but she was a little disappointed that the opportunity to operate with Heath had not arisen again. The way they had preempted each other's needs during surgery still remained in her mind and she looked forward to the opportunity to do it again.

Heath had been at the hospital, presenting some tutorials for the third-year medical students, but they'd caught up at the practice briefly, and talked over any questions that Phoebe had had about her patients. She had reminded herself that with his *rules* they would never be more than friends, but despite her still simmering feelings that she needed to ignore, he was still a fascinating friend to have.

Phoebe was enjoying her work, but the jet-lag had finally caught up with her and she'd wanted to have plenty of rest to ensure she didn't compromise her patients, so she had enjoyed a couple of early nights.

Wondering what to do on a Saturday, she put on a load of washing, did some yoga and although she considered calling her father, it was still Friday in the US. No doubt he would be busy, dealing with some political emergency, so she decided to leave it until the end of his day—which would be just after lunch for her. She didn't dare call her mother, to hear yet another sales pitch about her repentant ex-fiancé, so she decided not to make any calls.

It was much too hot to head to the park or the Botanic Gardens so, while the washing was on its spin cycle, she picked up a magazine that she had purchased at the airport and left on the coffee table and thought perhaps later she would visit the museum or an art gallery.

Suddenly the doorbell rang. With a puzzled expression she looked through the window to see a delivery truck parked outside her home. She tentatively opened the door. Surely there wouldn't be another delivery? It would be the second since she'd arrived in town.

'Phoebe Johnson?'

'Yes.'

'Great,' the man replied, lifting his baseball cap slightly and handing her an electronic device with a signature pad. 'I have a delivery for you. Sign here, love, and I'll bring it in.'

Phoebe signed, then watched as the man disappeared back to his truck. He opened the large double doors and stepped up inside. There were some loud banging and dragging sounds coming from the back of the truck and Phoebe's brows knitted in confusion. She had no clue who would be sending her something. And how big *was* this delivery?

Suddenly the delivery man emerged and jumped down from the truck. He pulled a huge box out onto the road. Then another two smaller packages. He also pulled down a trolley, and piled everything on top and headed back in Phoebe's direction.

'Are you sure all of that is for me?'

'Dead sure, love,' he said, as he waited for her to step aside so he could wheel it inside.

Phoebe followed him and told him to leave it to the side of the living room, near the kitchen doorway. He offloaded all the items and then left, closing the front door behind him.

Phoebe scratched her head as she searched for the delivery note and discovered it was from a local department store. She headed into the kitchen, found some scissors and began to cut open the largest of the three packages.

A moment later she squealed in delight. It was a Christmas tree. But as she pulled it gently from the oversized box she could see it was a very special type of tree.

The branches were the deepest forest-green, and looked so real. She moved closer and smiled as she could smell pinecones. It was just like the tree she'd had back home when she was very young. It was still her favourite Christmas tree of all time, and she had looked forward every year to her mother and father bringing it down from the attic and spending the night decorating it, with tinsel and lights, and baubles with their names handwritten on them in gold. Even the dog had had a personalised bauble...

But the branches had broken one by one over the years, and eventually the tree had had to be replaced. They hadn't been able to find the same one. And the new one had been nice but it was a slightly different green and it didn't smell like pinecones. It just hadn't been the same...

She heard her phone ringing in the other room and raced to pick it up.

'Do you like it?' the very recognisable voice asked. 'I asked them to text me when they'd delivered it. In the catalogue it looked like the one we had when you were a little girl.'

'It is—it's just the same! Thank you so much, Dad. I love it, and it was so sweet of you.'

'Well, I couldn't have my little girl the other side of the

world and all alone for her favourite time of the year without a tree,' he told her.

'But there are two more boxes.'

'You can't have a tree without decorations.'

Phoebe felt a tear trickle down her cheek. 'I miss you.'

'Miss you more—but I have to head back in to deal with another crisis. Middle East is on the agenda again today,' he said, then added, 'I want to hear all about work and your new home. I'll call you again soon.'

'Thank you again, Dad. Love you!'

'Ditto, sweetie.'

Phoebe had planned on putting up her Christmas tree that night, but she got a call from Tilly, inviting her to dinner. It was Ken's birthday.

They were such a social family, and it was stopping her from feeling lonely, so she accepted. It meant spending time with Heath but she hoped that with the family around and by catching yet another cab, she would keep that professional distance between them. But as it was Ken's birthday she realised she would need to race into the city for a gift.

She closed the giant box and dragged it across the polished floorboards into the second bedroom, and then put the boxes of decorations in with it. She looked forward to putting it up another day.

As she closed the door she felt a little ache inside. This should have been her first Christmas with Giles, in their own home as husband and wife. She didn't miss him, but she still felt sad that she was spending it so far from home.

The birthday dinner was lovely. It was the whole family again, and Ken loved the astronomy book Phoebe gave him. Heath was pleasant, but he seemed a little preoccupied as he sat at the end of the table with Oscar by his side.

Knowing what she did about his past, she didn't press him to be anything more than he could be, but she enjoyed his company and found that during the evening that he seemed to grow less guarded, and even smiled once or twice at her stories of growing up in the US. And she managed, with a concerted effort, to keep her butterflies at bay.

The next few days sped by. The weather had thankfully cooled slightly—enough that Phoebe felt the need for a light sweater one night. She had planned on putting up the tree over the weekend, but on Sunday she had slept in and read some patient notes to prepare for Monday's surgical schedule, so it was still packed away.

Ken invited her over on Wednesday for 'hump day takeout'. This time it was just the four of them. And that night Heath took the seat next to her.

Oscar smiled at his grandpa.

And his grandpa hoped Heath was taking his advice on board.

They chatted about work, and then about their lives outside of work. The conversation between Heath and Phoebe continued on the patio as a light breeze picked up and Oscar was tucked up in bed.

'Does it feel like second nature, being in Adelaide now?' he asked.

'It does. In fact this whole experience is strange in that it feels almost like déjà-vu in familiarity. Your family are wonderful—so down-to-earth and welcoming.'

Phoebe looked out across the garden from the wicker chair where she sat. The landscaping wasn't modern and manicured, like Tilly's, it was more like a scene from *The Secret Garden*. The flowerbeds were overflowing with floral ground cover, large old trees with low-hanging branches lined the perimeter of the generous-sized property, and there was an uneven clay brick pathway leading to an archway covered in jasmine.

It was beautiful and timeless and she felt so very much at home in Ken's house. All that was missing, she thought, was a Christmas tree and a hearth in the living room. The hearth would never happen in temperatures over one hundred degrees, but perhaps she could work on bringing a little bit of Christmas to the three men who lived there.

'My family have their moments,' Heath told her.

'Don't they all? But yours don't appear to interfere in your life, which is great.'

Heath shook his head. 'Believe me, they try—but I put a stop to it quickly.' Then he paused. 'The way you said that sounded a little Freudian. Am I to gather that your family *does*?'

Phoebe ran her hand along the balustrade next to her. 'Sometimes.'

Heath sat down in the armchair next to hers. 'Did they try to interfere in your decision to come to Australia?'

Phoebe rolled her eyes and sipped her soda and lime as she recalled the last conversation she'd had with her mother, by the waiting cab.

'I'm taking your expression to be a yes,' Heath commented.

'Well, a yes to my mother—but my father was supportive from the get-go,' she said, putting the glass down on the table.

'Why was that?'

'He knew I needed a break from Washington and he wanted to help.'

'But your mother didn't think you needed a break?'

'Hardly...' she lamented. 'She wanted me to stay and work it out.' Phoebe instantly realised that she had said too much, but the words were already out.

'Work what out?' he asked, leaning forward in the chair with a perplexed look on his face.

'Oh, just things... You know—things that she thought needed to be worked through and I thought needed to be walked away from.'

'No, I can't say I do know what you mean, Phoebe.'

She sighed. She knew she had to elaborate, but she had no intention of going into all of the detail. 'Relationship issues. Some of those just can't be sorted out.'

'With another family member?'

'No, thank God—he never made it into the family.'

'Ah...so an issue with a man, then?'

'Yes, with a man.'

'So you ran away to the colonies of Australia to get away from a man?"

'Uh-huh...' she mumbled, and then, looking at the question dressing his very handsome face, she continued, 'Now you know everything there is to know about me, it's your turn. What is Heath Rollins's story? Have *you* ever run away from anything?'

As she said it she wanted to kick herself. She knew his story, and it was a sad one that begged not to be retold. He had lost both his mother and his wife. And Phoebe suddenly felt like the most insensitive woman in the world to be asking that question.

'I'm sorry, I shouldn't have asked. Please ignore me.'

Heath considered her expression for a moment. There was sadness in her face, almost pity. 'You know about my wife?'

'Yes.'

'Well, you know I did run away from something, then. From overwhelming grief and a gaping hole so big that I never thought it would heal.'

She closed her eyes for a moment. 'I can't begin to know what that feels like.'

He sat back in his chair again in silence, with memories rushing to the fore. 'Did my father let you know or was it Tilly?' His voice was calm—not accusing, but sombre.

'Neither,' she answered honestly. 'It was Oscar. He told me the other day, when we were in the garden at Tilly's. He said that he was very little when his mother died and doesn't remember anything. I assume he must have been a toddler.'

Heath was surprised that Oscar had opened up about it to Phoebe. He rarely spoke of his mother, and particularly not to anyone he didn't really know.

'He was five months old, actually—when Natasha died. He never had the chance to know his mother. To walk beside her or even to hold her hand.'

'Oh…I don't know what to say except that I'm so sorry, Heath.' As she sat on the chair next to him she felt her heart breaking for him. 'After a loss as devastating as that it must have been so hard for you to even begin to find your way through the grief and cope for the sake of your son.'

'It was hard for all of us, watching her die. Knowing there was nothing we could do. It was the hardest time of my life and I was powerless to stop it. I felt guilty for allowing it to happen, for not making her have treatment earlier.'

Phoebe didn't ask what had taken his wife's life. It wasn't for her to know. But she could see he was still wearing the guilt. 'You can't make a person do what you want if it's not their wish. They have to do what is right for them, even if it's not what we see as right. I'm sure she had her reasons for not starting treatment.'

'Yes—Oscar was the reason. She was twenty weeks pregnant when Stage Three breast cancer was diagnosed, and although she could have safely undergone modified chemotherapy during the pregnancy she refused. She wanted to wait until she had given birth, then start the treatment but with the hormones surging through her body she understood there was a chance it would spread. But it was a risk she wanted to take. In my mind, with the oncologist's advice, it was one she never needed to even consider. They took Oscar four weeks early, but the cancer had already metastasised. She underwent surgery and chemo but she knew it was useless. She had done her research and was aware that there was little chance of her surviving.'

'What an amazingly selfless woman.'

'More than you can know. But at the time I was angry with her, for leaving me with a baby to raise and no wife to love.'

Phoebe watched Heath wringing his hands in frustration.

'I can understand your feelings, but I guess I can also understand your wife had a right to do what she thought was best. Sometimes what two people in love want is not the same, and it's not that either is wrong, or not respecting the other, it's just that they see things differently. Their life experience and values alter their perspective. And she was a mother. I can't say it from any experience, since I have never had a child, but I am sure carrying a baby would change everything about how you see the world.'

'But she was so young, and she had so much to live for—no matter how I try I will never understand. I love Oscar so much, and I'm grateful every day for him being in my life, but it was a huge and difficult choice she had to make. And I feel guilty for what happened because it means Oscar is growing up without a mother.'

Phoebe was puzzled at his feelings of remorse. She understood the sadness, but not the guilt. 'I don't know why you would say that. Your wife made the decision—not you.'

'But I should have made her have the chemo. I should have never let her delay it. And perhaps I shouldn't have married her so young. If she hadn't married me then she wouldn't have rushed into having a child, and when she was diagnosed she would have gone ahead with treatment.'

'Heath, you can't know that for sure. Natasha might not have been diagnosed until it was too late anyway. A young woman in her twenties wouldn't have been having mammograms, so it might have gone undetected for a long time—by which time she might have faced the same fate. It's something you will never know. But you have a very special little boy. And you can't harbour any blame—it's not good for Oscar.'

Heath nodded, but Phoebe could see his thoughts were somewhere else, struggling with his memories.

He was thinking back to the day Natasha had died.

It had been Christmas Day.

The next day Phoebe woke early, still thinking about everything that Heath had told her. While the heartbreak Giles had inflicted on her had been soul-destroying at the time, she knew now that it had been for the best. But nothing about Heath's heartbreak was for the best. His wife had died and left behind a little boy who would never know her. And a man who couldn't fully understand or accept her reasons.

She felt a little homesick for the first time, and called her father.

'I assisted in surgery last week, and I'm heading in today to the practice, and then tomorrow I'm in Theatre again,' she told him as she ate her muesli and fruit breakfast with her mobile phone on speaker. 'And I finally met Ken Rollins.'

'That's great. I bet you quizzed him about his papers.'

'I did and he was so generous with his knowledge.'

'How long will his son be filling in before he leaves and heads back to his old position?'

Phoebe's mood suddenly and unexpectedly fell as she listened to her father and was reminded that Heath and Oscar were only transient in her life. She had enjoyed spending time with Heath out of work hours. No matter how much she was looking forward to working with Ken, she knew she would miss Heath. He was charming company when he lifted his guard, and he had managed to make her feel important with the way he listened to her and engaged in their conversations.

He was a far cry from the distracted man who had once held the title of her fiancé. And she suddenly felt a little sad that Heath would be gone in a few short weeks. She knew she wanted more. What that was, she wasn't sure—but she knew even after such a short time there would be a void in her life when he left.

'Um…I'm not sure, exactly,' she muttered, trying not to think about exactly how much she would miss him as she washed her bowl and spoon and put them in the dish drainer. 'I think another four weeks, unless Ken's recovery takes longer.'

Phoebe realised she wouldn't be disappointed in any way if the older Dr Rollins chose to recuperate at home for a little longer than originally planned. She would be

more than agreeable to holding down the fort with his son.
In fact she knew it was something she wanted very much.

But that was in the hands of the universe and Ken's
doctor.

'Well, I miss you, honey, and so does your mother.'

'Miss you too, Dad. How is Mom?'

'Rushing about, keeping herself busy with her charity
work as always.'

'Maybe you could both head over for a short vacation
in sunny Australia in a few months? By then I will know
my way around and I can be your tour guide.'

'That sounds like a wonderful idea—but don't book any
accommodation for us yet. With the presidential election
only eleven months away I can't see sleep on my agenda,
let alone a vacation any time soon.'

'Of course—how silly of me. I guess I was caught up
with my life here and I forgot about everything happening back in Washington.'

'And that's a *good* thing. I'm proud of you, honey, and
you deserve this time away. Just don't come home with
an Australian drawl or I'll need to hire an interpreter!'

He laughed, then said goodbye, promising to call again
that week, and left Phoebe free to get ready for work.

The morning was filled with a few post-operative checks
and one new patient.

Phoebe loved working with Tilly. She was funny and
sweet and made the workplace even more enjoyable. And
she made her feel almost like part of the family.

She just wished that there was a way she could make
Heath feel whole again. But she doubted it. And she had
limited time. His guilt was not allowing him to move on.
Perhaps it also framed his *rules*. For those rules would protect him from getting too close to a woman again.

'Evan Jones?' she called, to the man she assumed was her next patient.

'That'd be me.'

The man in his early thirties stood, and with a strained expression on his suntanned face, using crutches, he crossed the room to Phoebe.

'We can take it slowly,' she said as they walked the short distance to her consulting room.

As she passed Heath's room she felt compelled to look, even though she knew he wasn't there. He hadn't been in all day. He had ward rounds at the hospital, then a short surgical roster to keep him occupied at the Eastern Memorial. She missed seeing his face, and wanted to believe that their current working arrangement could remain in place for a longer time.

Heath was everything she wanted in a colleague, a mentor and a friend. And perhaps even a lover, her body told her, before she quickly brought herself back to the task at hand. She should not be thinking about anything other than work. And definitely not thinking about Heath Rollins.

'Is that an American accent?' the man asked.

'Yes, East Coast,' she told him. 'Washington DC to be precise.'

He hobbled to the chair and rested his crutches against the nearby wall as Phoebe closed the door behind him. His patient notes told her that he was thirty-three years of age, a smoker and had suffered a heel fracture as a result of a fall from a balcony at a party. Without wanting to pass judgement, she couldn't help but wonder if alcohol had been a catalyst for the injury.

'So, Evan, your referring doctor has noted that the fall took place one week ago and that the CT scan she requested has confirmed you have a fractured calcaneus— or, more simply put, a broken heel bone.'

'Yes, my doc said that I smashed it when I fell from Bazza's ledge at 'is bucks' night.'

'It must have been quite the party. When's the wedding?'

'In two weeks. We've been like best mates for ever, and I'm meant to be 'is best man, but I'm gonna give it a miss 'cos I can't get across the sand for the wedding. It's on the beach at Noarlunga. That's what 'is missus wants. So I gotta just watch from the road.'

Phoebe nodded. She had no idea where Noarlunga was, and she was struggling a little with his heavy accent and wasn't too sure she had understood everything, but she knew she would be able to clarify the details during her examination. What she *did* know for a fact was that a best man on crutches, sinking into the sand, would not auger well for a romantic beach wedding, so she silently agreed with the bride's decision.

'Well, let me look at your injury and see if I can at least get you mobile enough to be in the audience—even if it is standing on the side of the road.'

Phoebe slipped the X-rays and the CT scan on the illuminated viewer, switched it on and then donned a pair of disposable gloves while she studied the films. The specific nature of the injury was leading her to concur with the referring doctor that surgery would be Evan's best option.

Kneeling down, she removed his moon boot and began to assess the damage done to his foot during the fall. 'I will chat to you in a moment, Evan, about our options to restore function and minimise pain.'

'Yeah, I'm throwing back painkillers like I got shares in the company.'

'We don't want you to be doing that for any extended period, so let's find a solution,' she replied as she gently elevated his foot. 'Does that hurt?'

'Nah—but I just tossed back a couple of strong ones about ten minutes ago, so ya could probably remove me kidney and I wouldn't feel a thing.'

Phoebe smiled. She still hadn't caught everything, but understood enough to see the humour in his remark. Evan's was the thickest Australian accent she had ever heard, and she guessed he was a not a city dweller. Well, at least had not always been a city dweller.

'Did you grow up in Adelaide, Evan?'

'Nah, I'm from up north. Grew up just outta Woomera, on a sheep station.'

'I'm guessing that would have been pretty dry and hot. Does it get hotter up there than here?'

Evan laughed. 'This isn't *hot*, Doc. Hot's when it's fifty in the shade—or, as you folks would say, about a hundred and twenty degrees.'

'Oh, my goodness. I can't imagine being that hot. I think I would die.'

'Plenty do, if they're not bush-savvy,' he replied with a grin. Then, as she lowered his foot to the ground, he grunted with the pain. 'That did hurt a bit.'

'I apologise, but I just had to check if the skin on your heel is wrinkled—this tells me the swelling has subsided sufficiently to proceed with surgery.'

'No worries. So I'm good to go out there and make a time for the surgery, then?'

'Not so quickly, Evan...' Phoebe removed her gloves and disposed of them in the bin before she took a seat and began reading the referral notes, along with the patient details he had completed for Tilly. 'At your age, and with the extent of the damage that is indicated on the X-rays, I think you're a good candidate for surgery, but I can see here that you wrote down that you're a smoker.'

'Yep, but I can hold off before the surgery, and even a

few hours afterwards. I've cut back heaps on 'em lately. What with the cost and all, it's sendin' me broke.'

'Actually, Evan,' Phoebe continued, looking directly at him with a serious expression on her face, 'you have to quit. Cold turkey, with no soft lead-in time, if we're to complete this in time for you to even be up and around to view the wedding from the side of the road.'

'Why?'

'Because smoking is harmful for wound and fracture-healing. I won't, in good conscience as a surgeon, consider you for surgery unless you stop smoking today.'

'That's a bit harsh, isn't it?'

'Unfortunately, Evan, I can't be gentle if you want me to operate and not compromise your health further. I need your vascular system at its peak to ensure the best results.'

'So say I give up—and I'm just puttin' it out there...not sayin' yet that I *will* give up—but say I do, when will you be operatin' and whatcha gonna do to me foot?'

'I could schedule the operation for approximately ten days from today. The procedure involves cutting through the skin to put the bone back together and using plates and screws to hold the alignment. It's called an open procedure and it involves an incision over the heel. The incision can be likened to a hockey stick, or a large L, where the overlying nerve and tendons are moved out of the way. The fracture fragments are restored to the best possible position. Then I will place a plate and screws to hold the fracture in place.'

Evan shifted uncomfortably in his seat. 'Makes me shiver all ovah. So I'll be right under while ya doin' it?'

'If you mean under general anaesthesia—yes. You will be in hospital and asleep during surgery. We will also use a regional nerve block, which involves a local injection to help with pain control. This block will provide between twelve and twenty-four hours of pain control after surgery. Surgery can be a same-day procedure, or planned with a hospital stay.'

'So will I have a moon boot again afterwards?'

'Post-surgical dressings and a splint or cast will be applied, and you won't be able to put weight on your foot for at least six to eight weeks, until there is sufficient healing of the fracture. The foot will remain very stiff, and some permanent loss of motion should be expected. Most patients have at least some residual pain, despite complete healing. And, Evan, almost everyone who sustains a break of the calcaneus, or heel, particularly involving the joint, should expect to develop some arthritis. If arthritis pain and dysfunction of the foot become severe, then further surgery may be required. These fractures can be life-changing.'

'Hell, can anything *else* go wrong? I mean, I didn't know that I'd be in pain for ever and then get arthritis. Damn—if I'd known all this I'd nevah have taken Bazza's twenty-buck bet to walk on his ledge with me eyes closed.'

Phoebe used all her composure to refrain from rolling her eyes at the idea of risking life and limb for twenty dollars. 'There are always risks, but I would say that in your case, if you give up smoking immediately, the risks are outweighed by the benefits. What line of work are you in, Evan?'

'I'm a sparkie.'

'So you work with fire crackers?'

'Nah!' He laughed. 'Not a sparkler—a *sparkie*…an electrician.'

'Oh, I see.' She smiled at her confusion. 'Well, you will need extended sick leave to heal, and then you should be back to work without this affecting your capacity to earn a living in your profession.'

'So there's, like, no complications other than pain for the rest of me life and arthritis? Like that's not bad enough.'

'I can't say none, as there are always potential complications associated with anaesthesia, and of course there's infection, damage to nerves and blood vessels, and bleeding or blood clots. But I *can* say that in all of my time as a surgeon there has been none of these when patients follow my pre and post-operative instructions.'

'Like quittin' the smokes?'

'Yes, definitely like giving up cigarettes,' she replied as she completed the notes on her computer so that she could send a report to the referring doctor in an email. 'The most common complications are problems with the skin healing and nerve-stretch. Most wound-healing complications can be treated with wound care. Sometimes—and only sometimes—further surgical treatment may be required if a deep wound infection develops. But most times it is cleared up with antibiotics, and nearly all nerve-stretch complications will resolve over time.'

'So do the plates and screws need to be removed later on?'

'No, they don't need to be removed. They stay there—unless they are causing pain or irritation. Then we can talk about removing them. But we'd make sure there was enough fracture-healing before even considering that, and I've not needed to do it up to now.'

'Let's book it in, Doc.' Evan sat back in his chair and looked down at his injured foot. 'Thanks, Bazza. Your harebrained idea's gonna cost me a hell of a lot more than twenty bucks.'

Phoebe nodded and then completed the paperwork, so that Evan could have the result of his bucks' night antics repaired.

* * *

Tilly had left and Phoebe was just finishing up some replies to emails and wondering where Heath might be when he appeared and answered her question.

'So, how was your day, Dr Johnson?'

Phoebe turned to see him leaning in her doorway. He looked as ridiculously handsome as always, but he seemed to have a sparkle in his eyes that she hadn't seen before. There was still a slight reservation to his manner, but now she understood the reason behind it and it didn't annoy her—in fact it was the opposite.

'Very nice, Dr Rollins. And I have tomorrow off, because apparently your father liked to play golf every second Friday and he has no patients booked in. So I'm looking forward to staying up late and having a sleep-in.'

Heath had been looking forward to seeing Phoebe again. All day he had had her in his thoughts. There were so many things about her that made him want to spend time with her. And she made him see life a little differently. He wasn't sure how long the feeling would last, but at least for a little while he thought he felt whole again.

'Then, since you have no curfew, would you like to join me for dinner? Not at my dad's or at Tilly's. Just you and me.'

'I'd need to pop home and change. Will it be like when we went to Hahndorf last week?'

Heath didn't want it to be anything like Hahndorf. He wanted this night to be so much more.

CHAPTER NINE

AFTER A QUICK SHOWER, Phoebe put on a pretty mint-green cotton dress and high strappy sandals.

'Finally ready,' she said, passing Heath the car keys he had left on the kitchen bench while he grabbed a cool drink and made himself comfortable on the sofa. 'Sorry I took so long.'

Heath looked at the woman standing before him and knew he would have waited for much longer. He loved being with her. And even being in her home brought a sense of serenity and belonging to him.

'I'm not in a hurry.'

And he meant it. He didn't want their time to end. He knew it had to. He would be heading back to Sydney in a few weeks but tonight he didn't want to think about it. He wanted to forget the past and not contemplate the future. He wanted for the first time in many years to feel alive in the moment. And he felt more than willing to break another rule.

Heath opened his hand to collect the keys and her skin brushed softly against his. He felt the warmth of her touch and his weakening willpower disappeared completely. He wanted more. He didn't want to wait any longer. He wanted Phoebe. Right there and right then. Gently but purposefully he pulled her down towards him.

'Why don't we stay here for a while? The restaurant isn't going anywhere.'

Phoebe swallowed, and her heart and her head began to race when she sat down beside him and the bare skin of her arm touched his. Their faces, their lips, were only inches apart.

Phoebe felt powerless to spell out the consequences and risks to her heart at that moment. Giving in to the feelings she had tried to ignore was imminent and she felt a pulse surge through her body.

She wanted Heath and from the look in his eyes focused so intently on her, she knew he did too.

'We don't have to go anywhere at all if you don't want to,' she said a little breathlessly.

He answered her with a kiss. And without hesitation she responded, and with equal desire her lips met his and her arms instinctively reached for him. It felt so right.

He pulled her closer and his hands caressed the curve of her spine, before climbing slowly to the nape of her neck. His lean fingers confidently and purposefully unzipped her dress, letting it fall from her shoulders to reveal her lacy underwear. He lowered his head and gently trailed kisses across her bare skin. She arched her back in anticipation and he stopped.

'Are you sure about this, Phoebe?'

Searching her eyes for permission to forgo dinner and seduce her for the rest of the night, he found his answer as she smiled back at him between kisses. He wasn't waiting a moment longer, and he led her to the bedroom.

He was not leaving before the sun rose. He didn't care that he was breaking another rule. He wanted to wake with Phoebe in his arms.

* * *

Phoebe woke from a beautiful dream. Then, feeling her naked body being held tightly in Heath's strong arms, she realised it wasn't a dream.

She couldn't remember feeling so happy. She felt as if she had just come to life. Like a flower in full bloom on a perfect spring day. She had shed her fears and found something wonderful. It was as if before Heath had made love to her she had been merely existing—not living. Her body was still tingling as she felt the warmth of his gentle breathing on her neck, and she remembered the feeling of his moist kisses discovering her naked body.

She didn't want to stir and wake the man sleeping soundly beside her—the man who had made her feel more wanted than she'd thought possible. The security of being wrapped in his strong embrace was like floating in heaven. And she wanted to stay in heaven for a little while longer.

She closed her eyes and listened to the steady rhythm of his breathing. She drifted off to sleep again, knowing that she had made love with a wonderful man. A man who just needed help to heal. A man who had broken one of his rules when she'd met his son. And if he was there in her bed when she woke, then he would have broken another rule. Perhaps all that she had overheard in the changing room would now be in the past.

Phoebe heard the shower stop and moments later heard footsteps coming purposefully towards the kitchen, where she was preparing breakfast. She felt happier than she'd thought possible. And her breath was taken away when Heath appeared in the doorway in a low-slung towel.

His smile was borderline wicked.

And they both knew why.

'So tell me, Dr Johnson, how did I get to be so fortunate? What crazy man would make you leave Washington and head to Adelaide?' Heath asked as he moved towards her, kissed her neck gently, then picked a grape from the bunch on the table and slipped it into his mouth.

'Let's forget the man and call it serendipity.'

'For me it is—but for you I sense there was something a little more serious.'

'Let's leave it at serendipity—it has a nice ring to it.'

Heath was looking at Phoebe intently, a little concerned. 'Are you sure you don't want to tell me? He didn't hurt you physically, did he? Because if he did and I ever meet him I'll kill him.'

Phoebe saw how upset Heath had become. They had shared a wonderful, blissful night together, and she wasn't sure that Giles's name and his abominable behaviour should be raised, but she didn't want Heath to think it was more than it was—and after what he had shared she suddenly didn't want to hide anything from Heath. She didn't want to lie to the man who had shared her bed.

With a knotted stomach, she flipped the spinach-and-mushroom-filled omelette and mumbled quickly, 'It was a broken engagement that made me leave Washington.'

Heath's earlier admiring glance at Phoebe, in a short satin wrap with nothing underneath, suddenly became serious again.

'Seriously? You were engaged and you left him to come here?'

'We weren't suited.' Her response was matter-of-fact and somewhat awkward as she struggled with knowing how much to say and how to discreetly gloss over the embarrassing parts.

'How long were you engaged before you realised you weren't right for each other?'

'A few months. But we were two different people with

completely different views on life and on the meaning of commitment,' she said, hoping that that would sum it up and they could move on to something more pleasant—like spending more time together.

'So just how close were you to getting married?'

Phoebe bit her top lip. He wasn't going to just walk away from this conversation. She knew it would sound bad, no matter how it came out. If she didn't tell Heath the entire story he might think her views on marriage were flippant—as she'd dumped her fiancé the night before the wedding—when he had lost his wife so tragically. But retelling the story of the bridesmaids sleeping with the groom would be humiliating.

She weighed up which was the lesser of the two morning-after-the-first-night-together information evils. Only telling him half of the story might scare him, but the full story might make him feel pity for her.

Her stomach was still churning and her heart had picked up a nervous speed. Neither was a great option, so she decided to omit the most debasing details.

'It was close to the day—but honestly it was for the best. Do you prefer your tomato grilled or fresh? I'm more grilled in winter and fresh in summer...'

'How close?'

Phoebe paused. Heath wasn't making it easy. He had been widowed, which was a tragedy, but she had been cheated on—which was pitiful. And the circumstances made it even more embarrassing. She had no option. She had to tell him the whole shameful story.

The pathetic bride-to-be who couldn't keep her man happy so he found love in the arms of another woman... or in her case women.

'Your omelette cook broke off her engagement the night before the wedding but I had good reason. Very good reason. But I did do it less than twenty-four hours before we were due to walk down the aisle.'

'I'm certain you had a very good reason. I wouldn't take you for the type to change your mind or your heart on a whim. Whatever happened, it must have seemed that you had no choice.'

Phoebe swallowed, and then fidgeted nervously. 'I *didn't* have a choice. It's an incredibly humiliating story… but, in short, I found out that my fiancé had cheated on me the weekend before the wedding. The best man told me and my fiancé didn't deny it. And to make matters worse—not that I thought it *could* be worse—it wasn't just the once. He cheated twice over the same weekend. But please don't feel sorry for me. It's pathetic and embarrassing and I really didn't want to tell you… But I didn't want to lie to you either…'

Heath crossed to her in silence, turned off the gas under the frying pan and spun Phoebe around towards him. He kissed her passionately and without another word scooped her up in his arms and carried her back into the bedroom. Gently he stood her beside the bed, undid the tie on her robe, slid it from her bare shoulders and let the silky fabric fall to the ground.

'The man was a fool…but *I'm* not.'

Heath stayed until just after eight, when he left Phoebe with a kiss at the door and the promise that with her permission they would do this again—very soon. He had a full day's surgery, but hoped to be home by six, when they would go out for the dinner he had promised her the night before.

Phoebe was so happy she could burst. She wasn't sure what the future held, but she had a very good feeling about it. Heath was so much more than she ever dreamt possible—as a man and as a lover. And she realised that if she had stayed with Giles she would have been cheated out of knowing true happiness.

Her body tingled when she walked past her bedroom and saw the bed with its sheets tangled from their early-morning lovemaking. And then she saw her dress on the living room floor and thought back to how he had carried her into the bedroom the night before.

As she soaked in a bubble bath she closed her eyes and thought back over everything that had happened. She thought there was nowhere in the world she would rather be this Christmas. Then she remembered the beautiful tree that was still waiting to be decorated, so she stepped out of her soapy resting place and wrapped herself in a fluffy white towel to dry off, before slipping on some shorts and a T-shirt and beginning the glorious job of putting up her very first Australian Christmas tree.

But first she needed to drag the boxes back out into the living room and then find just the right place for it...

It was almost an hour later that she'd finally finished. It was a huge tree, and filled a whole corner of the room, and the decorations were stunning. Red and gold baubles, tinsel, twinkling lights and hand-painted figurines. And there was also a miniature tree in the box. Perhaps her father had wanted her to have one beside her bed, but immediately she knew a better place for it. The practice—to brighten the faces of the patients.

She had keys, so she would drop it in later and surprise Heath and Tilly.

She stood back and admired the beautiful tree in her living room for a moment longer, and thought to herself how everything was finally right again in her world.

Actually, more right than it had *ever* been. And she hoped in time that she could make things right in Heath and Oscar's world too.

The telephone rang as she was folding the cardboard boxes and putting them by the recycling bin, and when she picked it up she discovered it was Ken.

'I've looked over the paper we were discussing the other night, Phoebe, and I think I can shed some light on those questions you asked me. If you'd like to come over I can elaborate on those areas of research that you raised.'

'That would be wonderful. I can be there in half an hour.'

'Perfect.'

Phoebe changed into a blue and white striped summer dress and flat sandals. Her hair was back in a headband, away from her face, and she slipped on her sunglasses and climbed into a cab, stopping briefly on the way to drop the baby Christmas tree in to the practice. She put it on the reception counter and then locked the door again. She liked the idea of sprinkling the festive spirit around—particularly with her own newfound happiness.

She spent an hour talking with Ken, while Oscar watched his favourite cartoons. Ken explained the benefits of the new process that had confused Phoebe with its invasive and somewhat controversial approach.

'You're a natural teacher, Ken. You should think about doing more of that while you're out of action—and definitely when you're considering retiring in a few years,' Phoebe told him. 'You have a gift for explaining things in an engaging manner, and the medical profession can't afford to lose your knowledge.'

'That's very kind of you, and food for thought, but to

be honest I'm not having much luck engaging with Oscar this morning.'

'Is everything all right with him? He is a little quiet today. Has he been watching television all morning?'

Ken looked over at his grandson. 'Yes, he hasn't wanted to do anything else. He's been a bit down in the dumps. It may have something to do with Heath's talking about returning to Sydney the other day. Oscar wants to stay here,' he replied as he lifted his leg to the ground. 'If only I could find a way to make that happen...'

Phoebe wanted them to stay too.

She looked over at Oscar and lowered her voice. 'Do you think perhaps it would be okay for me to take him into town for the rest of the day? We could have lunch, go to the museum—just get out of the house for a while.'

Ken considered her proposal for only a moment before he willingly agreed to the outing. 'I think that's a terrific idea—if you're okay giving up your day.'

'I'd love to—but only if you're sure that Heath will think it's okay? You know him so much better than I do. Should I call him and check?'

'He's in surgery all day. Who knows when he'll take a break and look at his phone? By the time you get his approval the day will be over. You have my permission as his grandfather and that's all you need.' He turned to Oscar. 'Hey, little matey—fancy the afternoon in town with Phoebe? She wants to take you to the museum, and I'm pretty certain there will be ice cream afterwards, knowing Phoebe.'

They both couldn't help but notice the little boy's face light up as he jumped to his feet. 'Sure would.'

'Then it's settled,' Phoebe announced, reaching for Oscar's hand. 'We're going dinosaur-hunting at the museum, and then we can head to the Botanic Gardens to have a late lunch—and that definitely includes ice cream. But we'll have to stop at my place on the way. I need to pick up a jacket as it might get a little cool out later, by the looks of those clouds.'

Phoebe called a cab while Oscar brushed his teeth. Then, as she was waiting by the front door, there was a knock. She opened it to find an elegantly dressed woman, her soft grey hair cut in a smart bob, with a lovely smile and what looked like a trifle in her hands.

'Is Ken at home? I just wanted to drop this off for dessert for the boys,' the woman said. Her voice was refined. 'I'm Dorothy. I live a few doors down.'

'I'm Phoebe—please come in.'

Phoebe held open the door while the woman entered with the large glass bowl filled with port-wine-coloured trifle. She could see the rich layers of peaches, custard, raspberries and cream.

'I'm sure that Ken would like to thank you himself.'

The moment Dorothy entered the house Phoebe could see that she knew exactly where to go. She moved down the hallway then turned left into the kitchen without any instructions. The woman wasn't a stranger. She looked as if she belonged there. But this was the first time Phoebe had seen her.

She followed Dorothy and saw her open the refrigerator and place the delicious dessert inside. Phoebe smiled. Perhaps Ken had a lady friend after all. He just wasn't sharing that information with Heath or the rest of the family.

While Phoebe waited for Oscar in the hallway, she overheard Ken mentioning to Dorothy that he'd had an epiphany that morning, after chatting with Phoebe, and how he might soon have more spare time, and then he said something about travelling to the Highlands of Scotland.

Oscar suddenly appeared, and with Ken's blessing they headed for the front door, with Oscar's tiny hand in Phoebe's.

'I love dinosaurs!' he told her loudly. 'The triceratops is the best!'

Ken smiled and waved from his chair. 'Stay safe—and have some ice cream for me!'

Dorothy just smiled. But Phoebe couldn't help but notice that it was a knowing smile, and she felt certain after the conversation she had overheard that Ken's visitor was a little more than just a concerned neighbour...

Phoebe asked the cab driver if he would wait outside her home while she ran inside with Oscar to get a jacket. She opened the front door and Oscar raced straight for the Christmas tree. His mouth was open wide and so were his beautiful brown eyes.

'That's an awesome tree.'

'Thank you. I think it's pretty special.'

'I've never had a Christmas tree. Aunty Tilly has one, but I've never had my own tree.'

Phoebe tried not to let Oscar see her surprise at his announcement. 'Well, I'm sure Daddy's busy—and it's a lot of work to put them up and decorate them.'

'I think it's 'cos they kind of make him sad. He gets really quiet when he sees one. So I don't ask for one 'cos I don't want him to be sad at home. But I helped Aunty Tilly with her tree the other day. Hers is really neat too, but not so big as yours. Yours is like the most *giant* Christmas tree maybe in the whole world!'

Phoebe smiled at his wide-eyed innocence. She remembered being only five and how wonderful it had been at Christmas time. Looking up at the sparkling lights and the baubles and the tinsel and thinking that their family tree was the biggest in the entire world.

'Maybe not the most giant, but I think it's one of the prettiest,' Phoebe said as they both stood admiring it.

'Sure is. Does it have lights too?'

'Yes, I'll put them on—but just for a minute while I get my jacket, because the taxi driver is waiting.'

A few minutes later, with the tree lights turned off, they were on their way to the museum. The short trip was filled with Oscar telling Phoebe he knew everything about dinosaurs, and she was happy to see him so excited.

An hour later, as they walked around the displays of giant skeletons, Phoebe discovered that Oscar *did*, in fact, know everything about dinosaurs—she was quickly learning so much about prehistoric times from her tiny tour guide.

Time passed quickly as they moved on to the Egyptian mummy collection, and Phoebe was quickly aware of how much Oscar knew about that ancient culture too.

'Daddy and I watch a lot of TV about this stuff, and he's bought me lots of books too. He's been reading me some ancient books too, from when he was a kid.'

Phoebe laughed. She wondered if Heath thought of his childhood books as 'ancient'. She felt a little tug at her heart as she remembered how Heath had not wanted her to read to Oscar. She'd put it down to him being very possessive. Perhaps being father *and* mother to Oscar had given him that right.

She just hoped that there was nothing more to it. She knew what a dedicated father Heath was, and how he doted on his son. She had nothing but admiration for how Heath had raised him, with equal amounts of love and guidance. Perhaps he didn't want their connection to change. He had every right to want to hold on to those special moments and treasure them.

'Shall we head to the park for lunch?' she asked, bending down to make eye contact with Oscar.

'Sure,' he said, and reached for Phoebe's hand.

She felt an unexpected surge of love run through her for the little boy. She had never thought much about children. It wasn't that she didn't want to have a family—it just hadn't been a priority. But now, feeling the warmth of the little hand slipping so naturally into hers, she knew it was something she wanted very much.

But it wasn't her biological clock ticking. She didn't just want a child. She wanted *Oscar*. He had crept inside her heart.

Just like his father had. Heath had restored her faith in men. In the Australian heat, the ice around her heart had melted too. She had not expected to find anything more than a career change in her temporary home but she had found so much more and it was all because of Heath. It had not been without a struggle, but it had been worth it and more to finally see him break his rules.

They wandered outside and discovered the weather had turned from a lovely sunny day to quite overcast. It was still warm, almost humid, with ominous summer storm clouds looming.

'I think we'd better stay indoors,' she said, with disappointment colouring her voice. She looked up at the dark sky and then back at Oscar protectively. 'I don't think Daddy would like you to go home wet from the rain.'

'No, I don't think he would like that very much.'

Phoebe wondered what they could do. She didn't want to end their day early, but she didn't think the nearby art gallery would hold much interest for her little companion.

Then it dawned on her.

'What if we go to Santa's Magic Cave?'

'What's that?' Oscar asked with a puzzled expression.

Phoebe was taken aback by the question. She may be on the other side of the world, but she'd assumed *every* child would know about Santa's Magic Cave. 'It's where Santa Claus comes every day in December, to meet boys and girls and find out what they want for Christmas.'

'I've never met Santa.'

Phoebe was surprised further at Oscar's response. 'You *do* know about Santa, though, don't you?'

'Yes,' Oscar said with a huge smile. 'I've seen him in pictures and stuff—but not in his own cave. Where is it? In the hills? Is it hard to find?'

Phoebe saw his curiosity was piqued, and couldn't help but smile at his barrage of questions.

'No, it's not in the hills. It's right here in the city—in the department store.'

'Then it's not a real cave,' Oscar said in a five-year-old's matter-of-fact tone, a little disappointed.

'No, it's not a real cave—but it's Santa's workplace when he's not in the North Pole. And being in the city it means all of the children have a chance to meet him.'

'Not *all* children. *I* haven't met him.'

'Well, today you will.'

Phoebe didn't really understand why Heath hadn't tried to make Christmas a happy time for his son's sake, but she wasn't about to say that to Oscar. Heath had been through great sadness, but she hated to think that he would wallow for ever and never let Oscar experience this special family holiday. But it wasn't her place to question Heath. He was a wonderful man, and she assumed he must find the Christmas traditions time-consuming or awkward, without a wife to help with arranging dinner, presents and decorations.

She smiled to herself. *Could she be the one to bring*

Christmas into their lives? And keep it there? Perhaps even take the pressure off Heath being both a father and a mother to his son?

'Today can be your first visit with Santa and you can tell Daddy all about it tonight,' she said as they headed for the pedestrian crossing, hand in hand. 'But first we have to have lunch—'

'And ice cream,' he cut in.

'Yes, Oscar, and ice cream.'

Lunch consisted of mixed sandwiches at a lovely café. Oscar loved the egg and lettuce, but sweetly screwed his nose up at the pastrami and avocado. Then, without any crusts left on the plate, they both had a double-scoop chocolate ice cream cone before they headed off to see Father Christmas.

Standing in line with all the other parents, Phoebe felt a bond growing with each passing moment she spent with Oscar. He was an adorable and caring little boy. Heath had raised him with impeccable manners. Without prompting he said 'thank you' and 'please', and was genuine in his gratitude.

He would one day grow into a wonderful young man— not unlike his father. And Oscar would be a young man Phoebe knew she would be proud to call her son. But she also knew that, no matter what her heart wanted, they were not destined to be together for much longer unless Heath changed his plans and stayed in Adelaide with his family.

Heath and Oscar would head back to Sydney in just over two weeks and her life would feel empty without them. It was a sad fact but the time she had spent with all of the Rollins men had gone a long way towards healing her heart.

And her faith in men.

* * *

'And what would *you* like for Christmas, young man?' Santa asked as Oscar sat on his lap on the large gold padded throne.

Mrs Claus was standing beside him, in a long red velvet dress with white fur trim on the collar and cuffs. She was giving each of the children a Christmas stocking filled with candy as they left.

'I would like to stay here, with Grandpa and Aunty Tilly and Uncle Paul, 'cos we don't have Christmas in Sydney. Daddy has to work, and we don't even have a tree 'cos they make him sad.'

'Daddy's very busy, so Christmas is difficult for him,' Phoebe said in a low voice.

'Well, you're lucky that Mummy brought you to see me today, then.'

'I'm not Oscar's mother—I work with his father...' she began. 'Long story, but today is Oscar's first ever visit to see you, Santa.'

'Isn't that wonderful, Mrs Claus?' Santa said with a hearty laugh. 'So apart from staying in Adelaide, which I'm not sure I can arrange, what else would you like for Christmas this year? You *do* get presents for Christmas, don't you?'

'Yes, Daddy always gets me something. It's usually pyjamas or something. But if I can ask for anything...'

Phoebe could see that he was thinking long and hard about his answer. He was taking the question very seriously. Phoebe, Santa and Mrs Claus were all poised and waiting for the long list of toys they expected he would rattle off. As it was his first visit to Santa, Oscar would no doubt have a backlog to fill.

'I would like a bike helmet with dinosaurs,' he finally

told the jolly man with his gold-rimmed glasses and a mane of long white hair.

'That's a very sensible present, to keep you safe while you're riding your bike. Is there anything else?' Santa asked curiously.

'No. You've got a whole lotta kids in line, and they'll want presents. I don't want to take too many and you run out. Then they'd be sad. The helmet's all I need.'

Phoebe signalled to Santa with a nod that the present would be bought.

'Well, then, Oscar, I think we can manage a bike helmet with dinosaurs for Christmas. And Mrs Claus has a lovely stocking filled with candy for you. I don't think I need to tell you to be a good boy—I think that you're a very good boy.'

Santa lifted Oscar from his lap on to the ground, and his wife held out a Christmas stocking for him to collect on his way past.

Oscar suddenly stopped and turned back to Santa. 'Santa—there's another thing I want.'

'Yes, Oscar.' Santa leant down. 'What is it?'

'I want Phoebe to be my mummy...'

CHAPTER TEN

HEATH CALLED IN to the surgery on the way home. He needed to check his list for the next day as he had an urgent request for a consultation on a colleague's mother, and had no clue as to his availability. As he unlocked the door, his heart felt lighter than it had in many years. He hadn't wanted to fall for Phoebe but he had and he had broken two of his rules in the process. He intended on breaking the third rule, of not sleeping with a woman twice, as soon as possible. Just knowing she would be near him at work made him smile as he walked through the empty waiting room. He knew he should be feeling on shaky ground as his rules had kept him safe, but with Phoebe he was beginning to feel he didn't need to protect himself.

But there had been a strange phone call from his father. One he would deal with when he got home. Apparently there was trifle in the refrigerator, his father wanted to retire and he wanted Heath to take over the practice. It had certainly been a day of major changes. Some he welcomed, but others Heath still wasn't sure about.

Heath thought his father had perhaps gone a little mad from being at home too long.

The cleaner was at the practice when he arrived, and he had piled all the wastepaper baskets in the centre of the reception area to be emptied. Heath didn't see them in the dim lighting and managed to kick them over. He could see the young man, busy in the surgery, with his headphones on, moving to the music as he polished the tiled floor.

He decided to pick up all the paper himself and then remind the young man on his way out to perhaps leave the bins in a safer place. There was nothing confidential—just general waste. Tilly was always careful that referrals with patient details were filed and that anything else of a confidential nature was put through the shredding machine.

For that reason he was very surprised to see the letterhead of another podiatric practice on a piece of paper thrown in with the general waste. It was unlike Tilly. She was more careful than that. He collected all the other waste and tidied the area before unfolding the letter properly to read its contents.

It wasn't Tilly who had thrown the letter so carelessly into the bin. It was Phoebe. The letter was addressed to her. And the letter wasn't about a patient—it was about her. It was the offer of a dream job. As an associate with the largest sports specialising podiatric practice in Melbourne. It couldn't have been more perfect with her qualifications and background.

And she had thrown it away.

His heart sunk as reality hit him.

This time she had thrown it away. But what if she didn't next time she received such an offer? And with her credential those offers would keep coming.

She had no roots in Adelaide, or even in Australia. She could leave at any time. And despite their night together there was no guarantee that she would remain in his life. Or in Oscar's. He spent nights with women and never felt compelled to remain in their lives. Why should she be any different?

She had come into their lives and within a few short

weeks tipped them upside down. He could see Oscar growing closer to her with every day, and now his father had
announced over the telephone that after speaking with
Phoebe that morning he had decided to retire and consult
part-time with the university. He had offered the practice
to his son. And then he had told him about that trifle again.
What was so damned important about a trifle?

Heath suddenly felt overwhelmed. His carefully organised life was going to pot.

As he tried to reconcile his life and find more reasons to
return everything to the way it had once been he thought
about Phoebe's ridiculous love of the Christmas season. It
was completely at odds with his own feelings. In fact now
he thought about it, everything was at odds with the way he
saw the world. Phoebe was taking his life and without his
approval making sweeping changes. Even Tilly had suggested a Christmas tree in their waiting room after hearing
all about the glorious tree back at the Washington hospital.

It had to stop. All of it. Christmas was not something
to be—

His thoughts came to a screaming halt when he saw the
miniature Christmas tree on the reception counter.

Heath was struggling with the control he felt he was
losing. Control of his life…and his heart. Looking at the
crumpled letter in his hand, he knew he shouldn't feel safe
any more. He never should have felt safe with Phoebe.

Phoebe felt as if she knew what true happiness was for the
first time in her life. She was falling in love with the man
who'd left her bed that morning, and she was already in
love with his tiny son. He was the sweetest boy, and a tiny
version of his father. Although not so battle-worn.

'What do you say to us buying a Christmas wreath for
the front door of your grandpa's house?'

'Is that one of those green circle things with gold bits that you stick to a door?'

'Exactly. What if we buy one for Grandpa as a present?'

'Daddy doesn't like those things. He doesn't like Christmas much. So maybe no…' he said, in a little boy's voice but with the sensitivity of someone so much older.

She suddenly realised that behind his sunny disposition perhaps Oscar was battle-worn too. He just didn't wear it on his sleeve.

Phoebe thought about Oscar's wish all the way home. A wonderful maternal feeling she had never experienced before was surging through her and making her smile so wide and heartfelt. She wanted so much to be a part of the little boy's life, but she had never considered for a moment that he would picture *her* in such an important role.

His mother.

It was more than she could wish for, but she felt concerned for the little boy. He had never been able to enjoy a special time at Christmas, and she wasn't sure why, but she would chat to Heath and she felt certain they could work through it. Heath was a wonderful father—perhaps he just didn't see that what he saw as a silly holiday tradition was so much more.

To Phoebe, Christmas meant family.

And now she was beginning to feel as if Heath and Oscar were family too. It had all happened very quickly, but she couldn't help the way she felt.

She had never imagined when she'd left the sadness and indignity of her life in Washington that she would find anything close to happiness. She had just hoped for a respite. For time to find herself and put the pain and humiliation behind her. Love had only ever been in in her wildest dreams. Phoebe would have settled for a pleasant six months and never felt cheated for her efforts.

The joy that had become her life in such a short time was so unexpected. Heath was the most amazing man, and while she didn't know what lay ahead for them she felt certain it was something wonderful.

And he had the most adorable son.

Oscar was so sweet, and Phoebe had grown so fond of him. She thought that being his mother perhaps wasn't such a crazy idea. If it was what Oscar truly wanted, and Heath felt the same way, then one day in the future perhaps it would happen. Life had turned around, and Phoebe felt blessed as they arrived back at Ken's home.

Phoebe paid the fare just as she watched Heath's car pull into the driveway.

'Keep the change,' she said over the sound of the engine, and she handed the driver more than enough for the short trip home. The driver smiled and took off down the street as Phoebe caught up with Oscar.

She wanted so much to throw her arms around Heath and kiss him, but she thought better of it. She didn't want Oscar to feel that she was rushing to greet his father. She wanted any relationship they had to unfold slowly, and in a way that would make Oscar feel comfortable.

Her heart was light with the knowledge that he wished she could be his mother, but in her mind it was important that the little boy knew he would always come first with his father.

'Daddy, Daddy—guess where Phoebe took me today?' Oscar asked excitedly, and then without waiting for a response he continued. 'To the *museum*.'

'That sounds wonderful, Oscar. You *are* lucky that Phoebe spoilt you like that.'

Phoebe couldn't help but notice that Oscar hadn't yet told his father about Santa's Magic Cave.

'We saw dinosaurs and mummies and we had egg sandwiches.'

Phoebe was taken aback that still there was no mention of Santa.

Heath smiled a half-smile at Phoebe. 'Thank you for taking him out. That was very kind of you.'

Phoebe had thought that after the night they'd shared she would not be on the receiving end of a half-smile any more. Something had changed. She didn't know what, but she could tell that in the hours since he'd left her apartment the closeness he'd felt had cooled.

She hoped they could talk about it later. And she wanted to talk to Heath about Oscar too...

'I've put a roast in the oven,' Ken said as they all piled in to greet him. 'And afterwards there's trifle for dessert.'

'What's with the trifle, Dad?' Heath asked in an irritated tone.

Phoebe couldn't help but notice and assumed perhaps there were problems at the hospital.

'Nothing much,' Ken replied in a subdued voice. 'A neighbour dropped it in. They're a friendly lot around here. Someone's always coming by to say hello and check up on me. And I *love* trifle.'

Phoebe was confused that Ken didn't admit where the lovely treat had come from. For some reason he too was not telling Heath the whole story.

Suddenly she started to see that no one was really telling Heath how they felt, or what he needed to hear, they were all hiding parts of the story and telling him what they apparently thought he wanted to hear. Was Tilly hiding her feelings from Heath too?

'Can Phoebe read to me tonight?' Oscar asked his father as they were clearing the dinner table.

The roast had been lovely and the trifle divine, and Ken had had a big smile on his face as he'd eaten it.

Phoebe was clearly thrilled to be asked to read a story, and her smile didn't mask her happiness. But Heath wasn't thrilled. While Phoebe was a wonderful woman, and an amazing lover, he was more than concerned that she was bringing changes into their lives that he didn't think were for the best.

And he also realised that she might not be staying. Well not forever.

Everything was suddenly moving too fast for Heath to consider properly.

His son had never wanted his nanny to read to him. That was Heath's job every night. It was their special time together. It suddenly hit him that perhaps Oscar was becoming too fond of Phoebe, and he didn't want to see the little boy leaning on her when she could soon be gone.

He felt mixed emotions as he looked down at his son. Phoebe's life was in Washington, or wherever her work demanded. And his was in Australia. Oscar might be hurt if he saw more in Phoebe than she was able to give him. Or more than Heath felt ready to ask of her.

Adelaide was a dream. A wonderful dream. But it was one they could all potentially wake up from very soon. The way he'd woken up from the dream of a happy and long life with Natasha. It could all be over soon.

He needed to protect his son.

And himself.

'Phoebe's tired. She's been on her feet with you all day. Brush your teeth and I'll be there in five minutes.'

Heath continued loading the last of the cutlery and glasses.

'Please, Daddy, I want Phoebe to read to me—'

'Honestly,' Phoebe cut in with a smile in her voice. 'I'm more than happy to read to Oscar.'

'No, Phoebe. I will be reading to Oscar tonight.'

As Heath drove Phoebe home she decided to question him over his behaviour. The top was down on the car as they travelled into the city, but the fresh air was lost on Phoebe. She had something else on her mind.

'Is everything good between us?' she asked.

Heath took his eyes from the road for a moment. He saw the look on Phoebe's face and knew exactly why she was asking the question. 'I've had a long day and we can talk about it another time.'

'I think we need to talk about it sooner rather than later.'

Heath pulled up at the front of Phoebe's house. He wasn't sure how he felt, except that he was losing control by the minute. And although he wasn't blaming Phoebe completely, he knew she could never understand the way his life had to be.

'Come inside. We can talk about it for a few minutes. It won't take long.'

'Maybe we should,' he said as he climbed from the car and walked to the front door, before he added, 'But I'm not staying.'

He had been fooling himself to think they could see each other without complications or expectations. He had been swept up in the moment and had forgotten his rules and obligations. Rules that he had created when he'd lost his wife. Rules that he had been ignoring from the moment he'd met Phoebe. He needed to reinstate them.

Phoebe was surprised at the bluntness of his statement. But she put it down to his being tired and thought he might change his mind when he got inside. She turned on the light and Heath's expression grew even more strained at the sight of the huge Christmas tree.

'Didn't they have a bigger one?' he muttered sarcastically, then refused to look at it again.

'My father sent it to me. He thought it might brighten my day. Oscar loved it today, when we called in. I think he wants to embrace Christmas but he knows it makes you sad. He doesn't know why any more than I do.'

It seemed so unfair to Phoebe that other little boys could share Christmas with their families but Oscar, at five years of age, was protecting his father. And she was worried what that would do to the little boy as he grew older. Would he think that his father missed his mother so much that he couldn't find joy even at Christmas? Would he think *he* was the cause of that? There were many widows and widowers out there who still managed to look for some joy in the world, she thought as she closed the front door.

'Oscar's fine.'

'He's wonderful—but do you ever think that you're stopping him from doing what most other little boys his age take for granted? Having Christmas—with a tree, and turkey, and presents, and laughter and the love of family.'

'That's a bit of a sweeping statement without basis, don't you think? He has presents, and we call home to say hello to my father around that time. Don't tell me he doesn't have Christmas. He does.'

'You call home "around that time"?' Phoebe asked, but they both knew it was a statement more than a question. 'You *acknowledge* Christmas, Heath. You don't celebrate it.'

'I don't want to celebrate Christmas. It's just a commercial holiday wrought by multinational companies to get families to spend up, and I won't be controlled as if I have no independent thoughts.'

Phoebe was not sure what was fuelling Heath's antagonism, but she needed to know. He had been so loving the previous night, and even in the morning, but now he seemed so bitter.

She was falling in love with a man who hated Christmas. And she had to know why.

'Christmas is about families, and love, and being together. You can throw away all the advertising and the hype, but you have to see it for its true meaning and what a wonderful day it is,' she continued.

'It's not and never will be a wonderful day. It's a day I dread every year—a day I can't wait to see the back of. It's a day I need to get through, not celebrate. My wife died on Christmas Day, Phoebe. So don't tell me how I should feel about the day. It isn't and never will be a happy day for me.'

He didn't look at her. He looked at his hands and then at the floor. His jaw was clenched and his eyes stared blankly as he stood and began to pace.

'I'm sorry, Heath. I didn't know.'

Phoebe sat in silence for a moment, gathering her thoughts. She understood that losing his wife on Christmas Day had been incredibly sad, but she knew that he needed to move on and be the father to Oscar his wife would have wanted. If he saw the day with dread then everyone around him would see it the same way. As Oscar grew up he too would learn to dread the day he'd lost his mother and, knowing the facts as she now did, he might to some degree even blame himself. Instead of celebrating the woman who had given her life for him.

'You will never, ever understand. I see the way you make Christmas a big event. But for me, for everyone who knew Natasha, the day is filled with sadness.'

'Perhaps.' She hesitated for a moment. 'Perhaps because you're choosing for it to be a sad occasion. It doesn't have to be that way if you can look at it differently.'

'"Look at it differently"? What? Just pretend my wife didn't die and enjoy a perfect *Little House on the Prairie* Christmas? Life isn't like that. You can't make everything right in the world with tinsel and baubles.'

'No, but you can make Christmas a happy time for your son, and for your family and yourself.'

'It's not that simple.'

'It can be, Heath. But you have to *want* to make it happy—and you should try for Oscar's sake.'

'What do you mean? I'm a good father. I take care of him. I doubt that my attitude to Christmas is affecting him.'

'It *does* affect him. He's hiding things from you.'

'What do you mean?'

'Today we went to see Santa. Clearly I didn't know about Natasha's passing on Christmas Day so I took him to the Magic Cave but he couldn't tell you. Obviously he knew it would make you sad. He doesn't know why, but soon he will ask. I wanted to put a Christmas wreath on the door of your father's home as a gift, but he said no, that it would make you sad. He is taking on a role much too onerous for his age. What if one day, in some small way, he blames himself for your sadness and inability to enjoy life? That's a huge burden for a little boy.'

'It won't come to that. He knows I love him.'

'Of course he knows that—but he also knows that you're sad a lot.'

'And why do you care so much? It's not as if you will even *be* here next Christmas. You'll be gone. Back to Washington or somewhere else. I'm sure that Adelaide won't be able to compete with the offers of work that will arrive...or that you will seek out.'

'What are you talking about? I thought after last night and everything I told you that you'd know I'm staying here. If you want me to, I want to be with you—'

'I saw the letter from that sports practice in Melbourne,' Heath cut in as he leant against the doorframe in the kitchen.

'The one I threw in the bin?'

'The one you never told me about...'

'Because I wasn't interested in it.'

'Maybe the terms didn't suit you and you declined the offer, but you applied. They reached out to you. Forgetting what happened last night, didn't you think that as a common courtesy you should have told me you were looking around at other options?'

'But I applied a while back... Before I left the States. Before we even met. Before last night happened.'

'Before we had sex?'

'Before we made love.'

'However you want to say it...' He sniffed. 'There's some double standards here. You sit here and tell me how to raise my child, but you've never had a child. You tell me that Christmas is about family, but your family are on the other side of the world this Christmas. And you want to get close to my son and read him a bedtime story, and all the while you're looking for work in another city? I need to protect my son...from you.'

Phoebe felt a pain rip into her heart. There was nothing

to protect Oscar from when it came to her. She loved the little boy. 'I'm not about to disappear. I would *never* run away and leave you or Oscar.'

'Stop it. I've heard enough. It seems to me that you want to change everything about the way Oscar and I live our lives. Well, we like it just the way it is—so I think *you* are what needs to change. You need to leave, Phoebe. It's for the best. For all of us, and especially for Oscar. I don't want him to get attached and then find overnight that you've taken off, despite what you say. I saw that letter. It was dated a few days ago and you had every opportunity to raise it with me.'

'I told you—it wasn't something I saw as important.'

'And nor is celebrating Christmas for me, so let's agree to disagree.' Heath had no emotion colouring his voice. It was suddenly cold and distant. Like a judge delivering a verdict. 'I won't have a temporary employee telling me everything that's wrong with my life. Take up that offer in Melbourne—it fits better with your qualifications anyway.'

'You sleep with me last night, then end our relationship *and* fire me the next day?'

'I think it's best if you step down. And one night is not a relationship, Phoebe. There is nothing to end.'

To Phoebe it felt like a death sentence to her heart.

She could see his lips moving but she didn't believe the words coming from them. He was telling her to go. Leave the practice and his life and take a job in another state.

She felt pain rip through her. They had shared the most wonderful night and he was trying to find anything as a reason to end what had barely begun.

'This isn't about anything you said. This is about your cardinal rules since your wife died. I know about all of them, and apparently you've broken two of them with me, but clearly you won't break the third. You never want to sleep with a woman twice.'

Heath swallowed and felt his jaw tick. It couldn't have been further from the truth. But if this would push her away and protect his son and himself, then he was happy for her to believe it.

'Fine—whatever. My one-night rule has been working fine for a long time, so there's no need for me to change it.'

Phoebe felt physically sick. Heath had just proved to her that all men were the same. She felt so many emotions building inside her. Anger, disappointment, betrayal and loss. But she would not take it lying down. She would not be told by a man what she should do with her life.

'Has your father agreed to this? He is, after all, my employer—not you!'

'Actually he's not. I am. You see, your talk with him this morning about how great he was as a mentor made him decide to retire and consult part-time at the university. He's asked me if I want to take over the practice. You have put me in the difficult position of uprooting my life in Sydney to relocate permanently to Adelaide, or watching him sell up. That is a lot of pressure that prior to your little chat wasn't even on his radar.'

'Stop being so angry! I'm sure it must have been on his mind, and it's wonderful news. It means you'll be near to your family and Oscar can see them…'

'Oscar is *not* your concern. You seem to be intent on changing everything about us. You want us to be one big happy family. Your way. That is *not* my way—and, again, if family is so important why is yours on the other side of the world? A little hypocritical, don't you think?'

The fairytale had just ended. He knew that a broken heart and humiliation had sent her away from her hometown and he was making her suffer both again.

He had played her for a fool.

'There's no need to come into work again. I'll cover your patients and pay you out for the rest of your contract.'

Phoebe didn't answer him. She didn't want his money. She had wanted his love and she'd thought she'd almost had it.

Refusing to respond to the words he had delivered in such a callous tone, she opened the front door, signalling him to leave. Her heart was breaking as she watched the man who had just shattered her belief in happily-ever-after walk past her. He suddenly looked different to her. Handsome, still—but so cold. She was looking through a filter of disappointment and pain. The rose-coloured glasses lay shattered in a million invisible pieces. Heath would never look the same as he had that morning, when she'd woken in his arms.

'Please say goodbye to your father and Oscar.'

CHAPTER ELEVEN

'WHY ARE WE replacing Phoebe?'

'She's gone to Melbourne. She's taken up an offer with another practice. It's larger and it has a sports focus. You knew with her qualifications that it was always a risk she would move on.'

Ken searched Heath's face for a more substantial answer. 'Just like that? No notice? Phoebe's just upped and left us? That doesn't sound like Phoebe.'

'Well, I guess you never really knew her, then, did you,' Heath returned.

His anger wasn't towards his father—it was at himself and at Phoebe. He was battling his own feelings about what he had done. And about what she had told him about himself.

'How can you think you know someone in not much more than a few weeks?'

'I knew I was going to marry your mother after one week,' Ken said in a calming tone as he patted Heath gently on the shoulder. 'Some people you just know. And I thought Phoebe was one of those people....'

'She wasn't, was she?'

'There you go—getting all uppity again. I mean, what on earth makes a woman leave without any warning when only a few days ago she was happily accompanying Oscar to the museum without showing any hint of a woman about to defect. Not to mention I know you two were getting close. Perhaps think through what has happened, Heath. See if there isn't something you want to do or say to make her rethink her decision.'

Heath's jaw tensed as he recalled the visit that had triggered his need to send Phoebe packing. He couldn't allow a woman to get that close again. He might learn to depend on her and so might Oscar. It would turn them into a family. And then if something happened—if she left, how would he be able to pick up the pieces? He had been fooling himself to think she would stay forever. Her family, her life, they were in America. The letter was just a wake-up call and he felt grateful to have found it.

And even if she wanted to remain in Australia permanently, there was Christmas to consider. She loved everything about it with a passion equal to how much he hated it. Christmas was too painful and it always would be. Christmas belonged to Natasha and it had died with her. He couldn't bring it back to life. A piece of him had died that day, and he had tried but he just couldn't feel any joy about it. He couldn't be happy about a day that had ripped his world in two. He couldn't join the rest of the world in their merriment and trivialise Natasha's passing.

Phoebe would never understand. Just as his family never would. There was no one in the world who could understand.

Christmas was just too hard. He owed it to the woman who had given her life for Oscar to have more respect than to move on.

Before he'd met Phoebe his loyalty to Natasha had not been tested. But the moment Phoebe had fainted and he'd looked into her beautiful eyes as they'd opened Heath had been painfully aware that she would test him more than any woman ever had. Or ever would. But he wouldn't let himself fall in love with Phoebe. He had enjoyed her company, and against his better judgement he had slept with her. But falling in love was not on the table for him.

He had to be the father to Oscar that Natasha would have wanted. And he had to keep his heart locked away. And he couldn't do that if she stayed any longer. She was too easy to fall in love with. That was painfully obvious.

There was nothing he could do or say to Phoebe. He had to push her away. It was best for all of them this way.

Heath had patients on the two days since he and Phoebe had parted and each day he woke with less enthusiasm than the last. Tilly said nothing, but he could tell by the look on her face that she was just as disappointed as Ken—and a little more suspicious.

'Your three o'clock cancelled, but your four p.m. wanted an earlier time, so I've moved Mrs Giannakis forward. She'll be here in fifteen minutes. And I've rescheduled Phoebe's patients. You'll be working late tonight to get through them all, but they've been great and very understanding about the changes. You've obviously got a double patient load now, but I've been in contact with Admissions at the Eastern and we've worked out the surgical roster to make sure that no one is inconvenienced too much by Phoebe's sudden departure.'

'Good,' he responded, without making eye contact.

'You might have to put in a Saturday next week to do the interviews for her replacement. Dad did the shortlisting last night—there's three of them. I'll email them today, if you'll agree to do it on the Saturday. I don't think there's any other way. I can mind Oscar, so you and Dad can both be here.'

Heath shrugged. His mind was elsewhere. He hadn't even considered the interviews that needed to be set up. He had informed his father, who had obviously passed on the news to Tilly, but he hadn't put any more thought into it. His father must have moved on things very quickly. Which was best, since Heath's mind was on Phoebe. And on Natasha. And the mess he had made of everything.

Getting too close to Phoebe had been a huge mistake for both of them.

'I must say I didn't see it coming.'

'What?'

'Phoebe doing a runner. She didn't seem the opportunistic type. I know working for a huge podiatric practice with elite sportsmen and women is a great break, but the Phoebe I know would have given more notice and definitely not run off without saying goodbye. She seemed...' Tilly paused for a moment and put down her pen. 'I don't know—a better person, and more grounded than that. She actually seemed to *like* us, odd as we are, and I know Oscar liked her a lot. It's sad, in a way, and I'm surprised.'

'She doesn't owe us anything. She's from the other side of the world and she needs to make the most of these offers. We're just a small show in a small town. Why wouldn't she want to take up an offer like that?'

Heath knew as the words fell from his lips that Phoebe would never have run off for a better opportunity. He had forced her to take it.

'Perhaps there's more to it. Dad thinks there is.'

'You both need to get over it,' he said tersely as he looked over his day sheet, ticking off those patients he had already seen. He had to end the conversation. It made him uncomfortable and brought up feelings he needed to put to bed. 'There's nothing more.'

* * *

'So, Mrs Giannakis, how are you feeling today? I can see here that it's been two weeks since your surgery.'

As he slowly led the woman down to his consulting room and closed the door behind them Heath noted the relative ease with which she was walking for only two weeks post-surgery. Phoebe's surgical intervention had obviously gone well.

'It's still sore, Dr Rollins, but I can tell that it's improving a little every day,' she told him as she took a seat. 'Dr Johnson did a wonderful job.'

'Yes, Dr Johnson is a great surgeon,' Heath replied as he loosened the woman's padded space boot then slipped on some surgical gloves before he began to gently unwrap the bandage to reveal the site of the surgery. He admired the minimal surgical entry point and the exactness of the stitches.

'And she's so lovely. What a sweet disposition and bed-side manner she has,' Mrs Giannakis said as she leant over to look down and watch Heath's examination.

'Yes,' he responded as he moved her foot slightly to check the return of flexibility.

'I recommended her to my niece last week. Stephanie's a professional netballer and she's always complaining about pain in her feet. She's seen a few specialists, but doesn't seem to be getting it sorted, so I wanted her to see Dr Johnson—but now Tilly's told me she's gone.'

'I'd be happy to see your niece,' Heath told her matter-of-factly.

'Of course,' Mrs Giannakis replied, still looking down at her foot and the slight mauve bruising. 'I'll still be recommending the practice, Dr Rollins, but I thought that being another young professional woman they would hit it off. And I know you would very quickly have found a large sporting clientele with Dr Johnson here.'

The rest of the day went similarly, with Heath seeing a number of Phoebe's patients and all of them speaking highly of her and their physical response to surgery testimony to her skill.

Heath wished his life was different, so that his reaction to Phoebe could be different. He felt powerless to change the way everything had turned out. He wished the manner in which he had ended things had been better, but that could only have happened if they had never become involved.

But they had.

She was irresistible and he'd overstepped the mark. He was angry with himself for leading her on. For letting her believe that there could be more, if that was what she was wanting. In hindsight, he hadn't set the boundaries early on, the way he did with other women. He had let his desire cloud his reasoning and rushed into something that would never last.

Could never last.

He wanted to turn back the hands of time to their meeting and not look into her beautiful eyes when he held her. He should have treated her as a patient who had fainted, checked her vital signs and not looked further. But he had, and he'd seen the most gorgeous woman. And then he'd got to know her more over iced coffee and realised that there was so much more to this slurping princess. She was warm, and sweet, and intelligent, and skilled. And then, when he'd taken her to bed...he'd lost his mind and his heart.

He would regret everything that had followed for ever.

* * *

Heath headed home, trying not to look in the direction of Phoebe's house. He took a longer, more roundabout route to avoid driving past the place where she had lived for those few weeks. He couldn't risk his reaction. What if her suitcases were being loaded into a cab? Would he screech to a halt and pull them from the trunk? Then pull her to his body, claim her lips with his and never let her go?

He couldn't. They had too many unresolved differences. Differences that they could never move past.

He turned left down another side street to take him around the square where she'd lived. Had she left? Would he be faced with a darkened house? Would he slow his car, look at windows with no soft glow from the lamps, and know that the love and warmth was gone?

With a deep breath he left the city and headed along the main road to his father's house. Back to his son.

Heath needed to travel to Sydney to give notice formally to the hospital there. He owed them that. He knew they would understand his need to take over his father's practice, but he wanted to let the Associate Professor and the hospital board know personally.

His flight left early in the morning and he planned on staying overnight. Tilly was happy to look after Oscar for the night.

He travelled light and the meeting went smoothly. While disappointed to lose his expertise, the Associate Professor and the board wished him well. There was little to do but return to Adelaide.

He didn't feel like socialising into the early hours with his peers over drinks, so he enjoyed dinner with three close friends and then caught an eight-thirty flight back to Adelaide. By nine he was at his father's front door.

As he opened the door he noticed that there were no lights on in the living room or out on the patio. He assumed his father had gone to bed early. As he walked past his room he could see a faint glow from under the door. It flickered like a candle. Why on earth, he wondered, was his father in bed with a candle burning?

He opened the door quietly, in case he had fallen asleep. He intended on putting out the candle for safety's sake.

What he didn't expect to see was a woman with grey hair cuddled up beside his sleeping father. Then he recognised her. It was Dorothy Jamieson from down the street. She had been a friend of the family for many years. Her husband had died almost ten years ago.

'Don't worry, Heath, I'll put the candle out before I fall asleep,' she said quietly.

Heath was having breakfast the next morning when his father walked out very sheepishly. There was no sign of Mrs Jamieson.

'And you were planning on telling me about this little fling *when*, exactly?'

'It's not a little fling, Heath. Dorothy and I have been together for three years now.'

'Three years? Why didn't you tell me?'

'Because I was scared you wouldn't approve. You hadn't moved on from Natasha—in fact I know you still haven't. I didn't want to make you feel that I had forgotten your mother. I haven't, and I never will, but being alone won't bring her back to me. I have fallen in love with Dorothy and she loves me. We still have so much of our lives to enjoy. And we want to do it together.'

'So the trifle was made by Dorothy?'

'Yes. She knows I love her trifle, and she wanted to have an excuse to see me while you were staying here. I didn't expect you back until tomorrow, so I asked her to stay the night.'

'So you told me what I wanted to hear?'

'Perhaps. Don't be cross.'

Heath looked at his father and wondered if what Phoebe had said was the truth. 'Does Oscar want a Christmas tree?' he asked.

'Yes, he'd love one but he knows that Christmas makes you sad. So he won't ask for one.'

Heath collapsed back into his chair. Phoebe was right. Everyone was telling him what they thought would make him happy. He had made them into something they weren't and forced them to keep secrets from him.

He hated himself for what he had done. To his family and to Phoebe. She had been the bravest of all. She had stood up to him and told him what he needed to hear.

And he'd punished her for it.

'Anyone home?' Tilly asked as she stepped inside the front door with Oscar in tow.

Heath walked out to greet them. He was still in shock, and feeling more and more by the minute that he had lost the strongest, most wonderful woman he would ever meet.

'Hi, Daddy.' Oscar clapped his hands excitedly and ran to greet his father.

Heath picked him up and hugged him, then kissed his forehead. 'Did you have a nice night with Aunty Tilly and Uncle Paul?'

'Yes—but when is Phoebe coming over again? I miss her. I want to play Snap with her—and maybe we could go to the museum again or the pool. She's fun. I really like her. Don't you like her too?'

Heath's heart fell instantly as he listened to his son and studied the expression on his face. He lowered the little boy to the floor and took his hands in his. He wished he could give him the answer he wanted. But he couldn't. It was complicated in an adult way that Oscar would never understand.

He had broken the heart of a special woman. Phoebe was gone and she wasn't coming back. She would never be back to play Snap with Oscar again. Nor would they go to the pool or the museum. Heath had sent her away. Selfishly and blindly. For reasons that Oscar wouldn't understand.

'Phoebe's gone away to work.'

'When's she coming back?' Oscar asked, with his big brown eyes searching his father's face for the answer. 'I can do some drawings for her. Can you post them to her? Then she'll miss us and come back.'

Heath sat down and put his son on his lap. He knew the answer would not make him happy, but it was for the best. For everyone.

'Phoebe's not coming back, Oscar.'

'She's *never* coming back?'

'No, she needed to go away quickly.'

Heath saw his little boy's eyes grow wider, a little watery, and his lips tilt downwards.

'Too quickly to say goodbye to me?'

'Yes.'

'But I thought she *liked* me,' Oscar said with a furrow forming between his little brows. 'I thought she liked *you*.'

'She does like you, Oscar. She likes you very much.'

His actions had apparently made everyone sad, but Heath doubted it was a call that he could reverse now. Not even if he told her the truth. That he loved her.

'I guess… But it makes me sad for you, Daddy, 'cos you

smiled so much with Phoebe. She made you happy and now you'll be sad again. I don't like it when you're sad.'

Heath felt his heart breaking. He had been so blind to what he'd had.

'Oscar, if you want we can go and buy a Christmas tree. Maybe it would be nice to put one up with Grandpa and—'

'No, I don't want one any more, Daddy. Santa isn't real and Christmas is stupid,' Oscar cut in, his voice cracking a little as he swallowed his tears.

'Why do you say that?'

''Cos I asked him to make Phoebe my mummy. And she left. A mummy would never leave me.'

Heath knew he had been a fool not to let Phoebe make changes to his life. They were much needed changes that everyone else had been too scared to tell him he needed to make.

He had no idea if she would ever forgive him, but he knew he had to try.

CHAPTER TWELVE

PHOEBE SAT STARING at her suitcases and at Oscar's cheerily wrapped Christmas present, standing by the door. Her landlord had kindly agreed to arrange a courier to deliver the dinosaur-patterned bike helmet to the little boy on Christmas Eve. She adored Oscar, and did not want him to stop believing in Santa Claus. His father could dress it up any way he wanted, but Phoebe still believed in Christmas.

Her tears had dried slowly as she'd packed her belongings over the three days since Heath had told her to leave. Regret filled her heart that she had so stupidly seen more in Heath and their relationship than there obviously had been from his standpoint. His one-night rule clearly still applied. She had broken the others, but that one still stood.

There was no regret that she had come to Adelaide. She had fallen in love with Heath and his son, and she believed in her heart that Oscar's innocent feelings for her were as real as her feelings for him. And then there was Ken. He was equally as lovable as his grandson, and she would never regret the time she'd spent with them both.

But allowing herself to fall for Heath would be a lifelong regret. And one she felt sure would haunt her waking moments for ever. She had completely fallen for the man who'd crushed her heart so easily.

Her airline ticket was booked. The destination wasn't

Melbourne, to take up the offer from the sports practice, although professionally it would have been advantageous to take on the role. Phoebe knew it wasn't what she wanted. She never had.

Nor was she heading home to Washington.

Instead Phoebe was heading to London.

'I don't know what to do!' Phoebe had cried into the telephone to Susy two days earlier. 'I thought Heath was the *one*. I feel so stupid for falling so hard, so quickly, but I've never felt that way about any man before in my life. How could I get it so wrong?'

'Because, like I said before, men are from another planet. They don't communicate in the same language. It may sound the same, it may even look the same on paper, but the emphasis is very different. It's like a completely different way of thinking.'

'You're right. He's just another playboy and he definitely played *me*. I should never have doubted my belief that all men are the same.'

'Why don't you come to London and spend some time with me? We can cry into a warm beer at the local pub and then, after a while, you can start planning the rest of your life.'

Phoebe had sat in silence for the longest moment. She had stupidly thought the rest of her life would involve Heath.

'Phoebs, don't go silent on me,' Susy had continued. 'It's a brilliant idea. I'm wrapping up a case now, and I'm due to have at least a week off, so the timing is perfect for you to get your sweet self over here. I miss you, and I'd love to spend time with you. I feel terrible that I couldn't get to Washington...'

Susy had paused as she'd realised that the last time

they'd supposed to catch up had been at the wedding that Phoebe cancelled.

'To witness my vows that never happened?' Phoebe finished drily.

'Sorry, Phoebs…I'm so insensitive.'

'Hardly,' Phoebe returned. 'It's just that your best friend's life is a series of unfortunate love stories. Only this one will be the last. I gave my heart completely to Heath—now there's nothing left for me to give another man even if I wanted to. I'm done.'

'London would be good for you, then. There are a million pubs and a nice fluffy bed in my spare room that can serve as shelter till you've healed.'

Phoebe was hurting more than she had thought possible and doubted she would ever heal, but she knew she had to listen to her father's advice and smile through the heartbreak until it didn't hurt any more.

'Okay, Susy—looks like you have a house guest. A miserable one, but you know that upfront. I'll book my ticket today.'

Phoebe was sitting on the sofa waiting for her cab and looking wistfully around the apartment that had held so many wonderful memories.

The night that Heath had stayed over was still only days before, and she could still feel his presence there. It was as if he might walk back into the kitchen with his towel hung low and tell her that the man who had cheated on her was a fool.

Now she knew the only fool was her, for believing him. For waking in his arms, making breakfast together, opening her heart and having him make love to her as if they were the only lovers in the world. For planning in her head the life and the love they would share together, wherever in the world that might be.

She had not dreamed for a moment that it was just a fling for him. A night like all the others he'd shared with different women.

She had never thought for a moment, as he'd held her naked body against his, that he knew it would end as quickly as it had started.

Her stay in Adelaide had been short and heartbreaking.

Her stomach was churning with nerves and hunger. She hadn't been able to eat for the two days since Heath had ended their relationship—forced her to leave and broken any chance of a future for them. There was plenty of food in the refrigerator, but as she stared at it her mind raced back to that morning when he'd walked out in his towel and she'd been cooking omelettes. Breakfast had been delayed as they'd been hungry only for each other.

Now she had no appetite. She had been too upset to think about food. There was no point cooking because she knew she wouldn't be able to eat. She hoped that on the plane she might feel differently. Or at least when she landed and had Susy's shoulder to cry on for a little while.

She felt more alone now, as she sat waiting for her cab, than she had when she'd arrived at the empty house all those weeks ago. Then it had been almost an adventure—an escape and a fresh start. Now she saw nothing that would ever fill the void in her heart...the hole he had made in her soul that she'd mistakenly thought he would fill with love.

Suddenly she heard a car pull up at the front of her home. Looking at the kitchen clock, she noticed that the cab was a little early. It didn't matter. There was nothing else for her to do in the house anyway so she might as well be at the airport.

She stood and crossed to the door. Her steps were shaky and her emotions like a tiny boat riding huge waves. An unexpected tear slid down her cheek and she wiped it away with the back of her hand as she opened the door without even looking up.

'My bags are there by the door,' she told the cab driver as she turned away. 'I'll get my handbag and coat and we can be gone.'

The driver didn't answer her, and suddenly his scent seemed familiar. She spun around. It wasn't a cab driver at all…Heath was standing in the doorway.

She froze for a second. Then the anger and pain that had been her only companions for two long days and nights found a voice.

'What do you want? Haven't you said everything there is to say? You couldn't make the message clearer or hurt me any more if you tried.'

'I'm so sorry, Phoebe. I've been the biggest idiot.'

'Don't do this, Heath,' she said, shaking her head. 'I don't want to play games. You made it clear how you felt. And I'm not about to waste a minute longer with you and your stupid rules.'

'I never paid attention to those rules once I met you. I just agreed with you so that you would walk away.'

Phoebe met his gaze. She wanted to look at the man who had shattered her dreams one more time. She wanted the image to burn into her heart so she could walk away and never be hurt again.

Her eyes were empty. She had cried the last tear on her way to the door.

'But why? What did I really ever do except try to make you and Oscar happy?'

'That's exactly what you did—and you did even more than that. You challenged me and stood up to me and told me what I needed to hear. When even my father was too scared to tell me what I was doing was wrong, you did.'

Heath moved closer, but he did not attempt to touch her. He knew she was hurting and he knew he had caused the pain.

'I refuse to let it be too late. I'm here because I don't want you to leave. Not now—not ever.'

Suddenly there was the harsh blaring of a cab's horn on the street outside. The cab had arrived on time. Phoebe jolted back to reality. She was about to leave for the other side of the world.

'That's my transport to the airport.'

Heath swallowed hard as he looked over to see Phoebe's suitcases by the door. 'I'm so sorry I asked you to leave Adelaide.'

'*Told* me to, actually.'

'I was a fool.'

'I was too—to think that you actually cared about me.'

Her voice was flat. The bottom had fallen out of her world and she had no intention of letting him back in to hurt her again. He could not just arrive on her doorstep and expect to waltz back into her life.

'I can undo it if you'll let me. I'll fly to Melbourne and sort it through with your new employer. I'll find them a podiatric graduate. Please don't leave, Phoebe. Don't go to Melbourne. I want you here with me. I don't deserve you, but I will do whatever it takes to make it up to you.'

Phoebe drew a deep breath, suddenly feeling light-headed as her heart started racing. 'I'm not leaving for Melbourne, Heath... I'm leaving for London.'

She crossed the room in silence and, feeling a little unsteady, she picked up her handbag from the sofa.

Heath paused, momentarily stunned by the news. 'London? Why London? I thought you wanted to take up the position in Melbourne.'

'You assumed incorrectly. I threw that letter away because I didn't want the job. I told you—I applied for it before I left Washington, but the moment I met you and your family I wanted to stay in Adelaide.'

Heath shook his head in disbelief at his own actions. 'I wish I could take back everything I said that night.'

Phoebe stepped towards the door. 'Well, you can't.'

Her heart was still racing, her head was spinning, and she needed to get away from him. Just seeing him again, being so close to him made it hard for her to breathe. It was hard to think clearly. She didn't want to hear the concern in his voice. She didn't want to question her resolve to leave and never look back. To walk away from the man who had owned her heart but thrown it away. She felt overwhelmed. Heath was pleading his case but she felt so confused.

She was confused by him, by his sudden appearance and by the feelings that she felt welling inside.

She needed air. Her chest was at risk of exploding, and she felt dizzy. The heat was stifling, her head was spinning and she realised the lack of food had taken its toll. It was a recipe for disaster.

Without warning the floor lurched towards her.

And she fainted into Heath's arms.

Phoebe's eyes flickered as they opened. She looked up to see Heath looking down at her, and felt the warmth and strength of his arms wrapped tightly around her as he held her against his chest. They were both on the sofa.

'What happened?' she asked as she tried to pull away from the man she still unfortunately loved with all of her heart but who she knew didn't love her. He had told her to leave and she was still clueless as to why he was in her house.

And why she was in his arms.

'You fainted…and I caught you,' he told her as he put a glass of water near her lips.

She pushed it away. 'I don't need anything from you.'

'You need water—or you'll take two steps and faint again.'

Begrudgingly she sipped the water.

'Phoebe, I was a fool to treat you the way I did,' he said as he put the glass on the table beside them and gently brushed the stray wisps of hair from her forehead. 'I pushed you away because I was scared. You were like a change agent in my life, and I needed it and so did Oscar but I couldn't accept it. I didn't want to accept it. But I should have. I should have welcomed it, and thanked you for what you were trying to do. And I want to now.'

Phoebe inched away from Heath. She didn't know whether to believe him. She didn't want or need another ride on the same emotional rollercoaster.

'I just wanted to bring happiness into your lives—and Christmas. But you hate Christmas, and I understand why, but I wanted you to understand that you *have* to let go and let your son enjoy the day. One day you can explain what happened. But not now. He's too young to understand. He just needs to be a child.'

Heath nodded his agreement. 'I thought no one felt pain the same way and that I had to carry the burden alone.'

'I think that you are not giving anyone credit. Your father lost his daughter-in-law that day, and Tilly lost her sister-in-law. They would have felt it too. Not the same level of pain, but they would still have been hurting.'

Phoebe's words hit a chord with Heath. Simple words that made sense. He had been so tied up in his own grief that he had not considered theirs. In five years he had not looked through any filter other than his own despair. And now he knew that Phoebe knew him better than he knew himself.

'I just saw them all rallying around to help out with Oscar and they seemed to be fine. Their emotions were in check and...'

Phoebe shook her head. 'Of *course* they seemed to be in control. There was a baby to consider. If your family had fallen into a heap they couldn't have supported you through losing your wife or helped tend to your son. They were being strong for *you*, when they knew you couldn't be.'

'I never thought about it that way. I thought they were fine. *I* fell in a heap, and I had to get back up for Oscar.' His hands were raking through his hair as he relived the darkest moments of his life. 'That meant pushing away memories, but I didn't want to forget. I felt so torn about that day.'

'It's normal not to be thinking rationally.'

'The last thing I remember when I left the hospital the night Natasha died was the Christmas tree in the foyer. I wanted to pull it down—throw it to the ground and break it. It was so cheery, and my dreams had just died in my arms, and I couldn't understand what there was left to celebrate. It seemed so pointless and I resented everything about it.'

Heath drew a deep breath and stared straight ahead.

'My father drove me to Tilly's house and she had a Christmas tree up as well. It made me feel ill to see it, so I left and went home—and the first thing I saw was the one that Natasha had insisted on putting up a few days before she was admitted to hospital. Oscar was only five months old but she wanted us all to celebrate his first Christmas. She knew it would be her last. I swore that night, when I went home alone, that I never wanted to see another Christmas tree or celebrate the day again. There was nothing in my mind to celebrate about the day. But now I know that Christmas is about so much more than tinsel and trees— it's about family. It's about appreciation of those you have in your life.'

'Yes, and Oscar needs to know in his heart, as he grows up and discovers the day his mother passed, that you don't believe *he* was the cause of his mother's death and that Christmas was a day of joy for Natasha. A day she wanted to celebrate with him.'

Heath nodded.

'As he grows older he may feel that he robbed you of celebrating that day by being born. He may decide to take on your grief and resentment over the day. That's a heavy burden for a little boy to carry and a tragedy if he takes it on into his life as a man.'

Heath looked at Phoebe and understood why he had fallen in love with her. She was undeniably beautiful, but she was so much more. She had an enormous heart and a level of empathy and understanding that he had never witnessed before. And she saw life for what a blessing it was and made him want to be grateful for it.

'I thought if I ran away and pretended the day wasn't happening I could block out the pain.'

'I think you magnified your distress by trying so hard to ignore Christmas. It's everywhere. And every time you saw a sign it must have ripped your heart in two and made you hate it even more.'

'I do hate it,' he admitted. 'I can't understand how everyone can go on smiling and singing carols as if nothing has happened. It's the anniversary of Natasha's death, and every year I feel like I am drowning in memories.'

'Then stop fighting it, Heath. Embrace what the day

meant to Natasha and how she would want you and Oscar to think of her—and the love that she wrapped around you both.'

Heath was silent for a moment as he looked at the woman he now knew for certain had claimed his heart. 'How did you become so wise?'

Phoebe looked away. She didn't think she was wise. But she knew that Heath was not the selfish playboy who had pushed her away. He was a man who hadn't known how to deal with the pain from his past. But she was hopeful now that he had clarity, and that he and Oscar would be okay. They could move forward and maybe even one day have their own Christmas tree.

The cab blasted its horn again and brought her back to reality.

'That's me,' she said, and she softly placed his hand back on his lap and stood up to walk away.

She understood his pain, but it didn't change anything. She had to leave. Heath would always hold a place in her heart but she needed more than she thought he could offer.

'I have a plane to catch. But I do forgive you and I hope we can always be friends.'

'I don't want to be friends, Phoebe,' he said, shaking his head. 'That is not why I came here tonight. I mean, of course I wanted your forgiveness—but I want so much more.'

'Heath. I'm leaving for London. This was a crazy dream, and we've both grown, but I think it's too late for anything more—'

'I won't let it be too late,' he cut in hastily as he gently pulled her back to him. 'You've never been anything other than loving and understanding, and I've been so consumed with fighting my feelings for you, and with the denial and grief and fear built up over the last five years, that I was blind to how much I love you. I was scared of loving you. *Really* loving you and then losing you. But love is a risk worth taking, and I know that now. I will never be whole without you.'

Phoebe stilled. *'How much I love you.'* Tears started falling from her eyes again. But these were tears of joy, and she let his hand gently wipe them away.

'I love you, Phoebe. I think I have from the first time you fainted in my arms. I don't want to spend another minute without you in my life.' Heath pulled her close to his hard body and kissed her mouth as if she was his life-line. Then, dropping to one knee, he continued. 'If you love me—*and* my dinosaur-crazy son—I want more than anything for you to be my wife. Phoebe Johnson—will you marry me and allow me to spend my life making love to you?'

Heath kissed her passionately, and when he finally opened his eyes they were on her. They didn't look anywhere else. Everything he needed was in his arms.

And Phoebe could see it and she had everything she had ever wanted too. She nodded. 'Yes, I will—because I do love you, and I love your wonderful son.'

EPILOGUE

'Please be careful, darling,' Phoebe said.

'Yes, Daddy, be careful. You're up pretty high.'

Balancing precariously on a ladder, Heath smiled down at his wife and son standing below. In one hand he held a large gold five-pointed star with the letter 'N' decorated in red crystals, while the other hand held on to the top railing.

'As soon as I secure Natasha's star on top of the tree I'll be finished.'

Heath's long arm reached over the top of the ladder and placed the Christmas star atop the ten-foot lush green tree that took pride of place in the living room. It was the same tree that Phoebe's father had sent for her very first Christmas in Adelaide. It was the tree that Oscar thought was the most gigantic tree in the world.

They had added baubles with their names on, handwritten in gold, which they had bought at the Christmas market their first Christmas as a family. And each year they had added more—including one for their beagle, Reginald, who had been rescued from the pound and now sat chewing his favourite toy while eyeing the new kitten, Topsy, who lay on the armchair. She was the most recent addition.

It was their third Christmas together, and Oscar was now eight. Each year Heath took pride in putting their hand-crafted remembrance of Natasha in place.

'Tilly, Paul and the girls are on their way over,' Ken announced as he walked into the room with sparkling fruit punch for everyone.

He placed the tray on the coffee table and took a few steps back to admire the festive decorations before he picked up the individual glasses and gave one to everyone in the room. Then he sat down next to Dorothy and she softly kissed his cheek.

'You know, at this rate, Phoebs, I'll be making an annual Christmas pilgrimage to your home Down Under,' Susy said as she sipped her chilled drink. 'This is my third, and it won't be too difficult to convince me to leave the snow behind to sunbathe and swim to the sounds of Christmas carols again next year—and the one after that. A white Christmas in England is quite spectacular, but I would never refuse the opportunity to exchange my Wellingtons for flip-flops.'

She looked down at her feet and with a huge smile wriggled her bare toes.

'Now all I need is an Aussie lifeguard to make my Christmas complete.'

'We're just glad you could make it again this year,' Phoebe said with an equally happy expression. 'We hope you can always share Christmas with us—and I'll keep a look-out for that lifeguard...then you might move here permanently.'

'You've outdone yourselves—all of you. Your home looks beautiful,' Phoebe's father said as he came down the stairs from the guest bedroom, carrying colourfully wrapped gifts he had pulled from the suitcases and handed them to Phoebe's mother, who was arranging them on the floor with the others already there. 'And I haven't seen a prettier tree ever,' he added with pride.

'It's the best, Grandpa John,' Oscar said as he dropped

down cross-legged on the patterned rug, patted Reginald's head and then looked up with a toothy grin at the huge expanse of green foliage, sparkling lights and glittering decorations.

Heath climbed down from the ladder and folded it up against the wall. His smile grew wider as he reached around and gently pulled his pregnant wife against his chest. With a heart filled with love, he said, 'And it's all because of you.'

'No, not me,' she told him gently, with a smile in her voice. 'It's because you were ready to believe in Christmas again.'

'And love,' he reminded her with a kiss.

* * * * *

HIS CHRISTMAS
BRIDE-TO-BE

ABIGAIL GORDON

For Glenn, Emma, and healthcare in all its many forms

CHAPTER ONE

THE TAXI THAT had brought her from the airport had gone, and surrounded by the baggage that contained her belongings Emma took a deep breath and looked around her.

When she'd been driven through the town centre it had been as if nothing had changed while she'd been gone for what seemed like a lifetime. The green hills of Gloucestershire still surrounded the place where she'd been born and had never imagined leaving. Everywhere the elegant Regency properties that Glenminster was renowned for still stood in gracious splendour to delight the eye, while, busy as always, the promenades and restaurants had shown that they still attracted the shoppers and the gourmets to the extent that they always had.

All that she had to do now was turn the key in the lock, open the door and step inside the property that had been her home for as long as she could remember, and of which she was now the sole owner. The act of doing so was not going to be easy. It felt like only yesterday that she had fled in the night, heartbroken and bewildered from what she'd been told, as if the years she'd spent in a land far away had never happened.

During all that time there had been no communication between herself and the man she'd always thought was her father, and now he was gone. Since receiving the news that he had died, all the hurts of long ago had come back. What he had done to her had been cruel. He'd taken away her identity; made her feel like a nobody. Turned the life she'd been living happily enough for twenty-plus years into nothingness.

He had been a moderate parent, never very affectionate, and she'd sometimes wondered why. He'd provided the answer to that by telling her on the night she'd left Glenminster in a state of total hurt and disbelief that he wasn't her father, that he'd married her mother to give her the respectability of having a husband and a father for her child when it was born as the result of an affair that was over.

Emma had directed the taxi driver to take her to lawyers in the town centre where the keys for the house had been held in waiting for when she made an appearance. Once she had received them she had been asked to call the following day to discuss the details of Jeremy Chalmers's will.

She'd been informed previously that he'd left her the house, or she wouldn't have intended going straight there on her return. She was uncertain if she would be able to live in it for any length of time after her father had disowned her that night long ago in such a cruel manner, but it would be somewhere to stay in the beginning while she slotted herself back into life in Glenminster.

Back in the taxi once more, having been given the house keys, she'd given the driver the directions for the last lap of her journey back to her roots and had thought grimly that it was some homecoming.

Gazing down at the keys, the memory was starkly clear of how she'd packed her cases and left the place that was dear to her heart that same night, intending to start a new life to replace the one that Jeremy Chalmers had shattered and made to sound unclean.

Her only thought as she'd driven out of the town that lay at the foot of the Gloucestershire hills had been to go where she could use her medical skills to benefit the sick and suffering of somewhere like Africa and start a new life as far away as she could get.

Until then they had been contained in the role of a junior doctor in a large practice in the place where she had been happy and content, but that night the urge to leave Glenminster had been overwhelming.

The last thing Emma had done before departing had been to drop a note off at the home of Lydia Forrester, the practice manager, to explain that she was about to do something she'd always wanted to do, work in Africa for one of the medical agencies, and that had been it without further explanation.

* * *

Time spent out there had been a lot of things, fulfilling, enlightening, exhausting and *lonely*. If she stayed and went back to work in the practice that she'd known so well in the busy town centre, would the memory of that night come crowding back, she asked herself, or would it be like balm to her soul to be back where she belonged and lonely no more?

Yet was *that* likely to be the case in the house where it had happened and which was just a short distance from the surgery where her stepfather had been senior doctor?

Emma had joined the staff there as soon as she'd got her degree in medicine and had been carefree and happy until that awful day. The job had absorbed her working hours and mixing happily with her own age group in her free time had made up for the atmosphere at home, where there had just been Jeremy Chalmers and herself, living in separate vacuums most of the time.

She'd lost her gentle, caring mother too soon and had been left with only him as family—a bridge-playing golf fanatic in his free time, and at the surgery a popular GP with an eye for the opposite sex. He had proved how much on the night when he'd told her that she was going to have to move out, find herself somewhere to stay, as he was getting married again and his new wife wouldn't want her around.

'Fine,' she'd told him, quite happy to find a place of her own to settle in, but the way he'd said so uncaringly that he was going to replace her mother and that *she* was in the way had rankled and she'd said, 'I *am* your daughter, you know!'

He'd been to the golf club and had told her thickly, 'That is where you're wrong. I married your mother to give her respectability and you a father figure. You're not mine.'

'What?' she'd cried in disbelief. 'I don't believe you?'

'You have to. You've no choice,' he'd said, and added, turning the knife even more as he'd begun to climb the stairs, 'She never told me who your father was, so you can't go running to him.'

As the door swung back on its hinges at last, reality took over from the pain-filled past. Nothing had changed, Emma thought as she went from room to room. There had been no modernisation of any kind.

The new bride must have been easy to please. So where was she now that her father had died from a heart attack on the golf course? It was all very strange. Had the widow moved out at the thought of a new owner appearing?

It would be time to be concerned about that when she'd spoken to the person who had taken over the running of the practice after her father's death. The absence of the new woman who had been in his life could be shelved until she, Emma, had been brought up to date with the present situation there.

But first, before anything else, there was the matter of arranging a suitable farewell for the man she'd thought, for most of her life, was her father. Jeremy had been well known in the town and there would be many wanting to show their respects.

The first she had heard about his death had been a month after the event, when the organisation she was working for had contacted her in a remote region of Africa to inform her of it and had explained that back in the UK her presence was required to organise the funeral as she was his only heir and would need to be the executor of his will.

It was a chilly afternoon, winter was about to take over from a mellow autumn, and having become accustomed to tropical heat Emma was grateful to discover that it was warm inside the house with the old-fashioned radiators giving out welcome heat.

Once her unpacking was finished hunger began to gnaw at her and when she looked in the refrigerator she found it was stocked with the kind of food that had become just a memory while working in the heat and dust of Africa.

It was a comforting moment. Someone had been incredibly thoughtful and had pre-empted her needs on arriving back home in such sad and gloomy circumstances, yet who had it been? There had been no evidence of anyone living there as she'd unpacked her clothes.

It was a Friday, and once she'd been to the law firm the following morning the weekend was going to be a long and empty affair until she'd got her bearings. With that thought in mind she wrapped up warmly, which wasn't the easiest of things to do as all her clothes were for a hotter climate, and decided to walk the short distance to the practice in the town centre before it closed to see if there was anyone left on the staff that she knew.

The darkness of a winter night was all around Emma by the time she got there and the surgery was closed with just an illuminated notice board by the doorway to inform the public what the opening hours were and what numbers to ring in an emergency.

As she turned away, about to retrace her steps, a car door slammed shut nearby and in the light of a streetlamp and the glare coming from the windows of a couple of shops that were still open she saw a man in a dark overcoat with keys in his hand walking towards the practice door with long strides.

On seeing her, he stopped and said briskly, 'The surgery is closed, as you can see. It will be open again at eight-thirty tomorrow morning and will close at twelve, it being Saturday. So can *I* help you at all?'

'Er, no, thank you, I'm fine,' she told him, taken aback by his manner and sudden appearance.

'Good. I haven't a lot of time to spare,' he explained. 'I just came back to pick up some paperwork, and after that have to be ready at any time to welcome back the prodigal daughter of our late head of the practice, which is a bind as I have a meal to organise when I get in.'

Emma was observing him wide-eyed. He was no one she recognised from the time when she'd been on the staff there and she thought he was in for a surprise.

'I have no idea who *you* are,' she told him, 'but obviously you're connected with the practice, so maybe I can save you one of the chores that you've just described. My name is Emma Chalmers. Does it ring a bell? I've returned to Glenminster to take possession of the property that my...er...father has left me *and* to find occupation as a doctor should I decide to stay.'

As he observed her, slack-jawed with surprise, she turned and began to walk back the way she'd come.

It was nine o'clock when the doorbell rang and Emma went to open the door cautiously because her knowledge of neighbours or local people was scant after her absence, so she slipped the safety chain into position before fully opening the door to her caller.

It was him again, the bossy man in the overcoat, on the doorstep and as she surveyed him blankly he said, 'You will guess why I'm here, I suppose.' She shook her head.

'I've come to say sorry for being such a pain when we met earlier. My only excuse is that I have my father living with me and he likes his meals on the dot as eating is one of his great pleasures in life.'

'Er, yes, I see,' she said, 'but why were you, as a stranger, going to be the one who welcomed me back? Surely there is someone still there who remembers me?'

'Possibly, but I am filling the slot that your father left and so was chosen to do the honours. Everyone will be pleased to see you again, I'm sure.'

'Hmm, maybe,' she commented doubtfully, with the thought in mind that there was still the matter of the missing wife to be sorted.

'We had a message from Jeremy's lawyers a couple of days ago,' he explained, 'to say that you would be arriving tomorrow, so back there when we met it didn't occur to me that you might be already here and installed in this place...which isn't very palatial, is it?'

Emma ignored the comment and said, 'I was fortunate when I arrived to find that the kind person with amazing foresight who had switched on the heating had also filled the refrigerator, as I was both cold and hungry after the journey and the change of climate.'

He was smiling. 'Lucky you, then.' Seeing her amazing tan, he asked, 'How was Africa? I'm told that is where you've been. I'm behind on practice gossip as I've only taken over as head of the place since your father died.'

'It was hot, hard work, and amazing,' she said, and couldn't believe she would be sleeping in the house that she had never wanted to see again after the night when Jeremy had removed the scales from her eyes in such a brutal manner.

Her unexpected visitor was turning to go and said, 'I must make tracks.' Reaching out, he shook her hand briefly and said, 'The name is Glenn Bartlett.'

Taken aback by the gesture, Emma said, 'Where do *you* live?'

'In a converted barn on the edge of the town.'

'Sounds nice.'

'Yes, I suppose you could say that,' he replied without much enthusiasm, and wishing her goodbye he went.

Driving home in the dark winter night, Glenn Bartlett thought that Emma Chalmers was nothing like her father if the big photograph on the practice wall was anything to go by. Maybe she'd inherited her dark hair and hazel eyes from her mother, although did it really matter?

He was cringing at the way he'd called her the 'prodigal daughter' as he knew absolutely nothing about her except that she was Jeremy Chalmers's only relative, from the sound of things, and his moaning about how busy he was must have sounded pathetic. Would Emma Chalmers have wanted to hear the gripes of a complete stranger?

Yet they were true. Unbelievably, he'd made time that morning to switch the heating on for her, do a dash to the supermarket to fill the empty fridge in the house that she was coming to live in, and put a slow casserole in his oven for his and his father's evening meal.

Back where he had left her, Emma had found some clean bedding in one of the drawers and was making up the bed that had been hers for as long as she could remember, while at the same time remembering word for word what the stranger who had knocked on her door had said.

It would seem that, apart from the father that he'd mentioned, there was no other immediate family in his life, and where had he come from to take over in Jeremy's place? Whoever he was, he'd had style.

The next morning she awoke to a wintry sun outside her window and the feeling that she didn't want the day to get under way because she had little to look forward to except the visit to the law firm in the late morning. Her instinct was telling her not to expect any good news from that, except maybe some enlightenment regarding the missing wife.

When she arrived there she was told that Jeremy's car was hers for the taking in the scheme of things. She felt that explanations were due. It seemed that the man sitting opposite her in the office of the law firm was not aware that she wasn't a blood relation to the deceased until she explained, and when she did so Emma was told that under those circumstances she wasn't entitled to any of his estate, except the house, which he had willed to her when her mother had been alive.

'The car was all that he had left,' the partner of the law firm went on to say. 'There were no financial assets. It would seem that our man Dr Chalmers was something of a high-flyer.'

It was at that point Emma asked if he had married again, as that was what he had been contemplating, and if so his new wife would be his next of kin.

Observing her with raised brows, he said, 'Dr Chalmers didn't remarry, as far as we are aware. Maybe his sudden death prevented him from accomplishing such a thing. So if no one else comes forward to claim the car, it will be yours if you want it.'

Emma left the office feeling weary and confused about life in general.

A time check revealed that the practice building only minutes away would still be open and she decided to stop by and say hello to whoever was on duty, admitting to herself that if Dr Glenn Bartlett was one of them it would be an ideal moment to see him in a different light after being taken aback by his unexpected visit the night before.

He wasn't there, but there were those who knew her from previously and in the middle of carrying out their functions either waved or flashed a smile across until such time as they were free to talk.

As she looked around her Emma was aware that the place had been redecorated since she'd last seen it. The seating and fabrics were new and there was an atmosphere of busy contentment amongst staff that hadn't always been there when Jeremy Chalmers had reigned.

'Emma!' a voice cried from behind her, and when she turned she saw Lydia Forrester, the practice manager, who ran the business side of the place from an office downstairs, was beaming across at her.

'I hope you're back to stay,' she went on to say. 'I've missed you and wasn't happy about the way you disappeared into the night all that time ago. It was a relief to hear from your father's solicitors that you'd been located and were coming home to arrange Jeremy's funeral. He was very subdued for a long time after you left.'

'Did he marry again?' Emma questioned. 'I've wondered who was going to be the bride.'

'Marry!' Lydia exclaimed. 'Whatever makes you ask that?' She looked around her. 'How about us going down to my office for a coffee? They are too busy here to have time to talk. It will quieten down towards lunchtime, and then we can come back up.'

'Yes, that would be great,' Emma replied, and followed her downstairs.

Lydia was silent as she made the drink and produced biscuits to go with it, but once they were seated she said awkwardly, 'I would have been the bride, Emma. Your father was going to marry me. We had been seeing each other away from the practice for a few months and when he asked me to marry him I said yes, never expecting for a moment that he would want to throw you out of the house. When he confessed that he'd told you to find somewhere else to live and that you'd gone that same night I was appalled and called the wedding off. So, my dear, you have the missing bride here before you.'

'You!' Emma exclaimed incredulously, with the memory of Jeremy's hurtful revelations about him not being her father just as painful now as they'd been then. 'You gave up your chance of happiness because of me? I wouldn't have minded moving out, especially as it was you that he was intending to marry.'

She couldn't tell Lydia the rest of it. Why she'd gone in the night, feeling hurt and humiliated, desperate to get away from what she'd been told, but holding no blame against her mother. She'd dealt with women and teenage girls in the practice in the same position that her mother had been in and had sympathised with their problems.

The practice manager was smiling. 'Your disappearance saved me from what would have been a big mistake, marrying Jeremy. I'd never been married before. Had never wanted to, but as middle age was creeping up on me it was getting a bit lonely and… well you know the rest. But happiness doesn't come at the expense of the hurt of others…and ever since I've looked upon it as a lucky escape.'

'I'm so glad you've explained,' Emma told her. 'From the first moment of my return I've wondered why the house felt so empty and cheerless. I've felt that I couldn't possibly live in it under those conditions, but now I might change my mind and make it fit to stay here.'

Feet on the stairs and voices were coming down towards them. It was twelve o'clock Saturday lunchtime, the practice had closed, and as friends of yesterday and newcomers she had to get to know crowded round her, for the first time it felt like coming home.

'Where is Glenn this morning?' she heard someone ask, and before a reply was forthcoming he spoke from up above.

'Did I hear my name mentioned?' he asked from the top of the stairs, and as he came down towards them he smiled across at her and asked the assembled staff, 'So have you done anything about arranging a welcome night out for Dr Chalmers?'

'We were just about to,' someone said. 'It's why we're all gathered below decks, but first we need to know if Emma would like that sort of thing.'

'I would love it,' she told them with a glance at Lydia, who had brought some clarity into her life and was smiling across at her.

'So how about tonight, at one of the restaurants on the Promenade that has a dance floor?' Mark Davies, a young GP trainee and a stranger to her, suggested. 'Any excuse for food and fun.'

As the idea seemed to appeal to the rest of them it was arranged that they meet at the Barrington Bar at eight o'clock. As they all went home to make the best of what was left of Saturday, Emma felt that it was beginning to feel more like a homecoming, although she had no idea what to wear.

There had been no time or inclination to dress up where she'd been. It had been cotton cropped trousers and a loose shirt with a wide-brimmed hat to protect her face from the heat of the sun, and any clothes that she'd left in the wardrobe here would be reminders of the hurt that being told she had been living there on sufferance had caused. They would also smell stale.

So after a quick bite in a nearby snack bar she went clothes shopping for the evening ahead and found the experience exhilarating after the long gap of wearing attractive outfits. Her euphoria didn't last long.

There was the arranging of Jeremy's funeral that had to be her first priority after the weekend, and if she'd needed a reminder the amount of black outfits in the boutiques and big stores would have given her memory the necessary prod.

As she made her way homewards with a dark winter suit and matching accessories for the funeral, and, totally opposite, a turquoise mini-dress for the night ahead with silver shoes and a white fake-fur jacket, Emma was remembering that it was the new head of the practice who had prompted the staff to arrange the welcome-back occasion of the coming evening. Would he be there?

Glenn Bartlett knew her less than anyone and, having seen him in the smart black overcoat, she imagined that he would turn up well dressed.

He did come, looking more like an attractive member of the opposite sex than a sombre well-wisher, and suddenly the evening felt happy and carefree after her time of hurt and toiling in hot places.

For one thing, Lydia had solved the missing wife mystery that had been concerning Emma, and for another the surgery crowd, apart from a couple of newcomers, had been delighted to see her back in Glenminster. *And to feel wanted was a wonderful thing.*

The Barrington Bar, where they were gathered, was one of the town's high spots as it boasted good food in a smart restaurant area beside a dance floor with musicians who were a delight to the ear, and as she looked around her the new head of the practice said from behind her, 'So is it good to be back, Emma?'

'Yes,' she said, sparkling back at him, and he thought that the weary-looking occupant of what had been a drab, deserted house had come out of her shell with gusto. The dress, jacket and shoes were magical.

Some of the practice staff had brought partners with them but not so Glenn Bartlett. There was a look of solitariness about him, even though he was being friendly enough after their uncomfortable first meeting.

Did he live alone in the converted barn that he'd mentioned when he'd rung her bell last night? she wondered. Someone had said when they'd all been gathered at the practice earlier that he'd been taking his father with the big appetite home.

At that moment James Prentice, a young GP who had recently joined the practice, appeared at her side and asked if she would like to dance. As Emma smiled at him and took hold of his outstretched hand, the man by her side strolled towards the bar and once he'd been served seated himself at an empty table and gazed into space unsmilingly.

He'd been a fool to come, Glenn was thinking. The fact that he'd suggested a welcome homecoming for Jeremy Chalmers's daughter would have been enough to add to switching on the heating and filling the refrigerator in that ghastly place, without turning out for a night at the Barrington Bar. It would have been a tempting idea at one time but not now, never again.

If it hadn't been for the fact that Emma Chalmers had returned to the Cotswolds for a very sad occasion he would have left her to it, but common decency had required that he make sure she had food and warmth and the pleasure of tonight's gathering to make her feel welcome because she'd looked tired and joyless on her arrival, which was not surprising after a long flight and a funeral to arrange as soon as possible.

Glenn finished his drink and, rising from his seat, told those of his companions who were nearest that he was leaving, going home to enjoy the peace that his father's departure had restored.

Emma was still on the dance floor in her partner's arms and as she glanced across he waved a brief goodbye and was gone.

Back home he sat in silence, gazing out into the dark night with the memory of Jeremy Chalmers's last moments on the golf course starkly clear. He'd known him before stepping into the vacancy that his passing had left.

The then head of the practice and his father had met at university. Jeremy, who had been on the point of retiring, had invited his friend's son, also a doctor, to stay for the weekend to familiarise himself with the running of the practice with a view to taking over as his replacement in the very near future after the necessary procedures had been dealt with.

They'd gone for a round of golf after lunch at the club and while on the course Jeremy had suffered the heart attack that had proved fatal. In intense pain he had managed to gasp out his last request and he, Glenn, working on him desperately as he'd tried to save him, had been stunned when he'd heard what it was.

'I have a daughter,' he'd croaked between pain spasms, 'and I upset her gravely some years ago, so much so that she left to go where I don't know, except it wasn't in this country. Emma is a doctor and most likely has gone to one of the hot spots where they need as many medics as they can get.'

'Bring her home for me, Glenn, back to where she was happy until I told her some unmentionable things about me.'

His lips had been blue, his eyes glazing even as the sound of an approaching ambulance could be heard screeching towards them, and his last words had been, 'Promise you will?'

'Yes, I promise,' he'd told him gravely, and then his father's friend had died.

Now, sitting sombrely in the attractive sitting room of the property he'd bought on the occasion of taking over the practice, Glenn was remembering the time and effort he'd put in to discover the whereabouts of the missing daughter. He was upset to think that he hadn't tuned in to who she was outside the surgery the night before.

Fortunately he'd made sure that the house that had been her home previously was warm and habitable a day early and had had food in the refrigerator. Then had gone the extra mile by suggesting that the folk from the practice make her welcome with an evening in one of Glenminster's high spots.

Now just one thing remained regarding his promise to her father, and when that was done maybe he would be able to have a life of his own once again. The task of locating Emma Chalmers had been mammoth.

He would be there for her at her father's funeral and once that ordeal was over he was going to step aside and let her get on with her life. The same way he intended to carry on with his own, which was empty of womankind and was going to stay that way.

Drawing the curtains across to shut out the night, he went slowly up the spiral staircase that graced the hallway of his home and lay on top of the bedcovers, his last concern before sleep claimed him being the stranger that he had reluctantly taken under his wing.

What was her story? he wondered. Had she been close to Jeremy and they'd rowed about something that had made her go off in a huff? From what he'd said in his dying moments, it had seemed that Jeremy had been the reason for Emma's departure and whatever it had been he'd had cause to regret it.

Since coming back to her roots she had never mentioned him, which was not a good omen, and what about the mother that she'd lost not so long before her hasty departure? What sort of a marriage had she and Jeremy had?

CHAPTER TWO

THERE WERE A few offers to see Emma home safely when the Barrington Bar closed at the stroke of midnight heralding the Sabbath, but Lydia forestalled them by saying, 'I'm in my car, Emma, and haven't been on the wine. Would you like a lift as I have to pass your place?' And added to the rest, 'That leaves two more empty places if anyone wants to join us.'

The offer was immediately taken up by older members of staff, one of the practice nurses and a receptionist, both of whom lived just a short distance away, and when they were eventually alone in the car Lydia said, 'So how has your first full day back in Glenminster felt?'

'Very strange,' Emma told her, 'and unexpectedly pleasant. But that feeling isn't going to last long when I start making the funeral arrangements for Jeremy. He wasn't my father. Did you know that, Lydia?'

'No, I didn't!' she gasped 'How long have you been aware of it?'

'Just as long as it took him to let me see how little I meant to him—which was immediately after he'd said he wanted me gone, out of the way.'

The house was in sight and when Lydia stopped the car she said dejectedly, 'And all of that was because he wanted to marry me? Surely he didn't think I would allow him to hurt *you* so that he could have *me*. None of it brought him any joy, did it? Without even knowing about what he had said regarding him not being your father, I refused to go ahead with the wedding when he told me that he'd made it clear that you wouldn't be welcome around the place once we were married. Sadly, by that time Emma, you'd gone and not a single person knew where you were.

'Jeremy was with Glenn when he had the heart attack and made him promise to find you and bring you back to Glenminster to make up for all the hurt he'd caused you. So he did have a conscience of sorts, I suppose. Glenn, being the kind of guy who keeps his word, spent hours searching for you in every possible way until he finally located you. No doubt once the funeral is over he will be ready to get back to his own life, hoping that yours is sorted.'

Shaken to the core by what she'd been told about the man she'd been going to marry, Lydia was about to drive off into the night when Emma asked, 'Was it Dr Bartlett who saw to it that there was heating and food in the house?'

'Yes,' she was told. 'Glenn mentioned that he was going to deal with those things and you almost arrived before he'd done so by appearing a day early. Now, one last thing before I go—have you enjoyed tonight, Emma?'

'It was wonderful,' she said, 'and would have been even more so if I could have thanked Dr Bartlett for all he has done for me, but as I didn't know about it I shall make up for my lack of appreciation in the morning.'

Glenn was having a late breakfast when he saw Emma appear on Sunday morning, and as he watched her walk purposefully along the drive he sighed. What now? he wondered. He didn't have to wait long for an answer as once he had invited her inside she told him, 'I'm here to say thank you for all that you've done for me, Dr Bartlett. I had no idea until Lydia explained on the way home last night that my father had put upon you the burden of finding me, and that it was you who had made my home-coming as comfortable as possible with food and warmth. It must have all been very time-consuming.'

He was smiling, partly with relief because she wanted no more from him and because she was so easily pleased with what he'd done for her. At the beginning Emma Chalmers had just been a lost soul that Jeremy had asked him to find so that he could die in the hope that he, Glenn, would bring her back to where she belonged. Difficult as the process had sometimes been, he'd had no regrets in having to keep the promise he'd made.

Pointing to a comfortable chair by the fireside, he said, 'It was in a good cause, Emma, and having now met you I realise just how worthy it was. Whatever it was that Jeremy had done to you it was clear that he regretted it. I could tell that it lay heavily on his conscience, and as my last involvement in your affairs, if you need any assistance with the funeral arrangements, you have only to ask.'

She was smiling but there were tears on her lashes as she said, 'I will try not to involve you if I can, but thanks for the offer.'

As she rose from the chair, ready to depart, he said, 'My parents will be at the funeral. They are a crazy pair but their hearts are in the right place and I love them dearly. It was my dad who told Jeremy that I was a doctor and had come to live in the village after leaving a practice up north. So that was how I came to be with him on the day he died.

'Jeremy had been to see me and, having been told that I'd been doing a similar job to his in the place that I'd left, asked if I would be interested in replacing him at the practice in Glenminster as he was ready to retire. Once I'd seen it and been introduced to staff I was keen to take over, and that is how I come to be here.'

'Going through the usual formalities with the health services and the rest took a while but I had no regrets, and now we have his daughter back with us, so hopefully he will rest in peace. You don't resemble him at all, do you?' he commented.

He saw her flinch but her only comment gave nothing away.

'No,' she said in a low voice. 'I'm more like my mother.' Having no wish to start going down those sort of channels in the conversation, she said, 'Thanks again, Dr Bartlett, for all that you've done for both me *and* him.' On the point of leaving, she commented, 'Your home is lovely.'

He nodded. 'Yes, I suppose it is, and with the hills above and the delightful town below them, I am happy to be settled here.'

'So do you live alone, then?' she couldn't resist asking.

There was a glint in the deep blue eyes observing her and Emma wished she hadn't asked as his reply was short and purposeful, and to make it even more so he had opened the door and was waiting for her to depart as he delivered it. 'Yes. I prefer the solitary life. It is so much easier to deal with.'

She smiled a twisted smile and told him, 'I've had a lot of that sort of thing where I've been based over the last few years and to me it was not easy to cope with at all. Solitariness is something that takes all the colour out of life, so I'm afraid I can't agree with you on that.' And stepping out into the crisp Sunday morning, she walked briskly towards the town centre and the house on the edge of it that the man who hadn't been her father had left to her for reasons she didn't know.

There had been no generosity in Jeremy on that

awful night and ever since she had needed a name that wasn't his: the name of the man who had made her mother pregnant. Did he even know that he had a daughter?

Common sense was butting in, taking over her thought processes. So what? You had a fantastic mother who loved and cherished you. Let that be balm to your soul, and as for that guy back there, doesn't every doctor long for peace after spending long hours of each day caring for the health of others? If you've never had the same yearning, you are unique.

Back at the property that Emma had admired, Glenn was facing up to the fact that his description of his home life must have sounded extremely boring. With a glance at the photograph on his bedside table he wondered what Jeremy's daughter would think of him if she knew why he needed to be alone.

Serena was gone, along with many others, taken from him by one of nature's cruel tricks, a huge tsunami, unexpected, unbelievable. Since then he had lived for two things only, caring for his parents and his job, and there were times when the job was the least exhausting of the two.

They'd been holidaying in one of the world's delightful faraway places when it had struck. The only reason he had survived was because he'd taken a book with him to one of the resort's golden beaches and had been engrossed in its contents, while Serena had been doing her favourite thing, swimming to a rock that was quite a way out and sunbathing there.

When the huge wall of water had come thundering towards them, sweeping everything out of the way with its force, they'd both been caught up in it. Glenn had been closer to land and had surfaced and managed to hold onto driftwood before staggering towards what had been left of the hotel where they'd been staying. But of Serena, his wife, sunbathing on the rock far out, she and others like her had disappeared and had never been found.

Weeks later, with all hope gone, Glenn had arrived back but had been unable to bear to stay where they'd lived together so happily. So he had moved to a new job and a new house in the town where his parents lived, telling the older folk that he didn't want his affairs discussed amongst the residents of Glenminster, or anywhere else for that matter.

The only way he had coped after leaving the practice up north to join the one in the town centre had been by giving his total commitment to his patients, and when away from the practice shutting himself into the converted barn that he'd bought and in the silence grieving for what he had lost.

That day on the golf course had been a one-off. Jeremy had persuaded Glenn to join him there for a round or two much against his inclination because it would be interrupting the quiet time that he allowed himself whenever possible.

When the other man had collapsed with a massive heart attack in the middle of the game and hadn't responded to Glenn's frantic efforts as they'd waited for an ambulance, Jeremy had begged him with his dying breath to find his daughter and bring her home to Glenminster. Though aghast at the request, as it had seemed that no one had known where she was, he had carried out Jeremy's wishes faithfully. Once the funeral was over Glenn was fully intent on returning to his reclusive evenings and weekends.

The fact that Emma, having only been back in her home town three days, had visited him on the third one had not been what he had expected. Neither was it what he was going to want once he began to live his own life again.

He'd seen to it that she was back home where she belonged and on a grey winter's day had made sure she would be warm and fed when she arrived. He had even gone so far as to make sure that she received a warm welcome home from the practice staff at the Barrington Bar, of all places, which had not been the kind of thing on his personal agenda. Once his duty had been done he had been off home to the peace that his bruised heart cried out for.

Only to find that Emma had good manners. On the quiet Sunday morning she hadn't picked up the phone to thank him for all that he'd done on her behalf, which until her chat with Lydia she'd had no knowledge of, but had come in person. So why was he feeling so edgy about it?

Was she going to want to come back into the practice? They needed another doctor. But was the daughter of chancer and man about town Jeremy Chalmers someone he would want around the place?

He spent the rest of the day clearing up fallen leaves in the garden and at last, satisfied that all was tidy, went inside when daylight began to fade and began to make himself a meal.

As he was on the point of putting a piece of steak under the grill the phone rang and when Glenn heard Emma's voice at the other end of the line he sighed. She didn't hear it, but his tone of voice when he replied was enough for her to know it would have been better to have waited until the following morning to report the conversation she'd just had with a funeral director.

'I'm sorry to disturb you again, Dr Bartlett,' she said. 'It is just that I've been speaking to the funeral firm, who have been waiting for me to appear with regard to a date for the funeral that has been unfortunately delayed because of my absence, and they pointed out that as my—er—father was so well known in the practice and around the town, maybe a Sunday would be the most suitable day. Then all the staff would be free and more of the townspeople would be able to attend, it not being a regular working day for most people.'

'Yes, good thinking,' he agreed, relieved that the

final chapter of the sad episode on the golf course was to be soon for her sake as well as his. 'Why not call in at the practice tomorrow so that I can help you with the rest of the arrangements?'

There was silence at the other end of the line for a moment and then Emma said haltingly, 'Are you sure you don't mind me butting into your time there? I'm afraid that I've been in your face a lot since I returned.'

Glenn thought that she'd picked up on his moroseness and his desire to be free of his commitment to a man he'd hardly known, so he told her, 'No, not so. Once the funeral is organised and has taken place we can both get on with our lives.' But as the steak began to sizzle and the vegetables he intended having with it came to the boil Emma had one last thing to say and he almost groaned out loud.

'Just one thing and then I really will leave you to enjoy your Sunday evening. It is with regard to the food that you provided me with. How much am I in your debt?'

'You're not. You owe me nothing,' he said abruptly. 'It was part of the promise that I made to a dying man.'

Her response came fast. 'So let me make you a meal after the practice has closed tomorrow evening. It would save me butting into your lunch hour to discuss the arrangements for next Sunday.'

His reply was given at a similar speed. 'No! I've told you, Emma. You owe me nothing. I'll see you tomorrow at midday.' And as she rang off without further comment it was clear to her that he was more than eager for the role he had played during recent weeks to be at an end.

Glenn had been looking forward to the meal he'd cooked, but every time he thought about how uncivil he'd been when she'd wanted to thank him for what he'd done for her the food felt as if it would choke him.

Emma would have understood if you'd explained that you still mourn the loss of your wife under horrendous circumstances, he told himself, and that after a week at the surgery you want to be left in peace.

Pushing the plate away from him, he poured a glass of wine and went to sit in front of the log fire that was burning brightly in the sitting room. Gazing morosely at the dancing flames, Glenn admitted to himself that it was most unfair to transfer the pain of his shattered life to a stranger such as her.

He was behaving like a complete moron. Why in heaven's name didn't he explain the reason for his behaviour and try to get it in perspective? Otherwise people would start asking questions that he didn't want to answer.

For one thing, Emma wouldn't want to feel that his attitude was another dark chapter of her life to add to the fact that she had to attend the funeral of a man who had confessed to causing her great hurt.

With determination to atone for the rebuff he'd

handed out when she'd wanted to make him a meal, Glenn decided that he would call at her house on his way home the following evening if she didn't appear in the lunch hour, and do all he could to show Emma that he felt no ill will towards her. That his behaviour came from pain that never went away, so he needed to focus on work.

As his first appointment of the day arrived on the following morning he settled down to what he did best: looking after his patients.

The staff of the practice consisted of Lydia, the practice manager, six GPs with himself as senior, two trainee GPs, who were there to earn their accreditation after qualifying as doctors, and four incredible receptionists who held it all together.

Once the man who had been his predecessor had been laid to rest, the gloom that had hung over the practice might lighten. As a new era began, was Jeremy's prodigal daughter going to want to join the practice, or had he put her off completely? he wondered.

Back at the house the night before Emma had been deep in thought as she'd cleared away after a solitary meal, and they had not been happy thoughts. Did she want to be in the first funeral car on her own? There was no one who should rightly be with her. Her mother had left no relations, neither had Jeremy—and she had no knowledge of who her birth father might be.

Maybe Lydia would join her. If she did it would help to take away some of the dreadful lost and lonely feeling that she'd had ever since she'd been told with brutal clarity that the man she had always thought to be her father, in fact, was not.

The other concern on her mind was the fact that she was having a bad start in getting to know the man who had replaced Jeremy in the practice. She was experiencing a kind and thoughtful side to his character that was contradicted by his brusque attitude on occasion.

It was clear that Glenn was not a good mixer. It would be interesting to find out what sort of a man he was if she joined the practice staff. She did want to feel happy and fulfilled back in Glenminster, if that was possible.

She didn't want to return to the heat and endless toil of Africa until she had recharged her batteries in the place where she had grown up and where she'd had a job she'd loved until the bubble of her contentment had burst.

With those thoughts in mind she presented herself at the practice in the lunch hour. When Glenn's last morning patient had gone, and before the afternoon's sick and suffering began to arrive, he left his consulting room and went to see if Emma had come, as he'd asked her to. He was relieved to find her outside in the corridor deep in conversation with Lydia.

On seeing him the older woman suggested that Emma come down to her office for a coffee before she went, and left them together. So Glenn opened the door that he'd just come through and when Emma was seated on the opposite side of his desk at his invitation he asked, 'So how are you this morning?' He followed it with another question. 'Are you any nearer to knowing how you want the funeral to be arranged?'

Emma was looking around her. The last time she'd been in the room Jeremy had been seated where Glenn was now. The memory of her last day in Glenminster came back so clearly it was making her feel weak and disoriented, although Jeremy hadn't delivered the actual body blow until late that evening, when he'd been drinking and had been about to climb the stairs to sleep it off.

Glenn watched the colour drain from her face and came round the desk to stand beside her, concerned. But Emma was rallying, taking control of the black moment from the past. Managing a wan smile as he gazed down at her anxiously, she said, 'I'm all right, it was just a memory of the last time I was in this room and what happened afterwards that knocked me sideways.'

Straightening up in the chair, she said, 'In answer to your question, I'm fine. I've just asked Lydia if she will join me in the one and only funeral car that will be needed instead of my being alone. I have no relatives that I could ask to keep me company on such a depressing occasion. Obviously there will be other people following in their cars, but that is how it will be for me.'

'And what did she say?' he asked uncomfortably, knowing that he should have given some thought to Emma's solitariness on the day instead of being so wrapped up in his own feelings.

'She said yes, that she will be with me.'

'Good. I hadn't realised just how alone you are, Emma,' he commented. 'If Lydia hadn't been able to do as you asked I would have volunteered. Though whether you would have wanted someone you hardly know with you on such an occasion seems unlikely.'

He glanced at a clock on the wall and commented, 'I can only give you half an hour before my afternoon patients start arriving so what exactly do you want to discuss?'

'I'm going to have an announcement in the local press, announcing that the funeral will be on Sunday at the crematorium at three o'clock, for the benefit of anyone wanting to take part in the service or just to watch,' she told him, 'and I'm arranging a meal for afterwards for the practice staff and any of his close friends.'

'That sounds fine,' he agreed. 'What about flowers?'

'No. Instead, I'd like donations to be made to the Heart Foundation, or locally to Horizon's Eye Hospital, which is an amazing place. Do you think those kind of arrangements will be suitable?' she enquired. She was ready to go and leave him to his busy afternoon, aware all the while that the time she had taken out of his lunch hour might leave no opportunity for him to have a snack or whatever he did for refreshment at that time of day.

But remembering Glenn Bartlett's rebuffs of the previous evening, there was no way she was going to concern herself about that. He was the one who'd suggested a chat in the lunch hour, and in the days when she'd been employed there she'd often missed her lunch due to pressure of work.

'Yes,' he told her, unaware of the thoughts going through her mind. 'Just one question. Am I right in presuming that it will all start from what is now your house?'

'Yes, of course,' she replied, the cold hand of dread clamping on her heart. Until the man she'd thought had been her father had been laid to rest she couldn't even contemplate what she was going to do in the future if Glenn didn't want her back at the surgery.

It was possible, taking note of his manner towards her, that he could be feeling that enough was enough. That having found her and brought her back to where Jeremy Chalmers had wanted her to be... and the rest of it, he'd had enough without her being forever in his sights.

Maybe after Sunday, in the relief that the slate had been wiped clean, she would be able to see everything more clearly. As far as she was concerned, it couldn't come quickly enough. So, getting up to go down to Lydia's office in the basement for the coffee that she'd suggested, Emma wished Glenn goodbye and left him deep in thought.

In the days that followed Emma felt as if she were in some sort of limbo. She wandered around the shops for suitable clothes to fill her wardrobe against winter's chill, while trying to ignore signs of the coming of Christmas already on view in some of them.

It was the last thing she wanted to contemplate, spending Christmas in the house that had been left to her in its present state. It had always been basic and she'd often wondered why her mother had never complained, but now she understood. Maybe Jeremy had expected gratitude instead of requests for a brighter home from the woman he had married to save her name.

She supposed she could give the place a makeover or alternatively put it up for sale and move to somewhere smaller and more modern and not so near the bustle of the town, but until Sunday's ordeal was over she couldn't contemplate the future.

It was done. The event that Emma had been dreading had taken place and, with Lydia beside her and Glenn Bartlett hovering nearby, she had coped. There had been a good turnout, as she'd expected, and now the staff of the practice and a few of Jeremy's golfing friends were gathered in a restaurant in the town centre for the meal she'd organised.

Emma was feeling that now the future was going to open out in front of her, though not as an exciting challenge. More as if it was hidden in a mist of uncertainty. As she caught the glance of the man who had brought her home from a foreign country to an uncertain future, she felt her colour rise at the thought of asking for a return to her previous position in the practice. He was so obviously wanting an end to their unwanted connection.

Did he ever smile? she wondered. If his expression was less closed and sombre he would be the most attractive man she'd ever met. His hair was dark russet, his eyes as blue as a summer sky—but always with no joy in them.

It seemed that he was unmarried, not in a relationship of any kind, and lived alone in his delightful property, with the occasional visit from his elderly parents.

Her smile was wry. It seemed as if neither of them was fulfilling their full potential. His life sounded almost hermit-like. Or was it that he had enough to think about with the job and being there for his folks? Although they sounded anything but fragile.

She was being observed in return. What was it that Jeremy Chalmers had done to cause his daughter the degree of hurt that he'd confessed to when he'd lain dying? Glenn asked himself. It had been enough to make her leave Glenminster and only be prepared to return in the event of his death.

Emma didn't come over as the weak and whingeing type. Whatever it was, she didn't carry her sorrows around with her, as he did. Maybe they weren't as dreadful as the burden he was carrying, having Serena there one moment and the next gone for ever. If they'd had a child to remember her by he might be coping better.

The funeral party were getting ready to leave. He got to his feet and joined them and as Emma shook hands and thanked them for their time and their support, he waited until they'd gone and asked, 'Do you want a lift home, Emma?'

She smiled. 'No, I'm fine. Lydia is going to take me, but thanks for the offer. And also thanks once again for the way you have been there for me, a stranger, at this awful time.' Her smile deepened. 'I promise I will not cause any more hassle in your life.'

Before he could explain that his moroseness came from coping with terrible grief every moment of every day, she had gone to where the practice manager was waiting for her, leaving him to return to the empty house that he had turned into his stronghold against life without Serena. For the first time since he had gone to live there Glenn was reluctant to turn the key in the lock and go inside, and when he did so, instead of its comforting peace, a heavy silence hung over every room.

CHAPTER THREE

WHEN EMMA AWOKE the next morning the first flickers of daylight were appearing on the wintry horizon and she thought that it would have been so much easier to have returned to Glenminster in summer, with long mellow days to provide some brightness to the occasion.

The feeling of closure of the day before was not so strong in the moment of awakening to the rest of her life, because in the background was, and always would be, the shadowy figure of the man who was her birth father.

But there were two things to look forward to that hopefully would not have any painful attachments to them. First, the opportunity, if Glenn Bartlett was agreeable, for her to apply for the GP vacancy at the practice where she'd been so happy and fulfilled before, and, second, house hunting for a modern apartment bought from the proceeds of the sale of the house that she had returned to so unwillingly.

With regard to the practice, Glenn couldn't stop

her from applying for the post, but his obvious eagerness to be left in peace after spending so much time on her and her affairs indicated that he might not be bubbling over at the thought of her being still in his life to some extent. The only way to pursue that matter was to get in touch and sound him out about joining the practice.

Before she did either of those things there was something she wanted to do first and that was to put flowers on her mother's grave in a nearby churchyard, knowing that it would have been sadly neglected during her absence as Jeremy hadn't been into that sort of thing.

It had been on her mind ever since she'd come back to Glenminster but she had needed to be clear of her responsibilities regarding *him* before bringing her life back to some degree of normality.

As she approached the grave with an array of winter flowers, Emma stopped in her tracks. It was clean and tidy but already had a display of roses gracing the centrepiece that looked as if they had been put there recently.

The only person she could think of who might have done that was Lydia from the practice. The two women had been great friends and she had called off the wedding when she'd discovered how Jeremy had been planning to treat her dead friend's daughter.

The church was open and rather than not place the flowers she'd brought on the grave Emma went inside and asked the verger if she could borrow a vase for a short while, and was told to help herself to any that were standing idle on the window sills.

When she'd arranged the flowers to her satisfaction and had placed them next to the others, she stood back and observed them gravely. For the first time since Jeremy had left her feeling lost and joyless there was peace in her heart and it was all due to an attractive stranger who had searched for her high and low to keep a promise he had made.

After leaving the cemetery Emma went to the garage where Jeremy's car had been kept awaiting her return to claim it. A large, black, showy model, it had no appeal whatsoever, and with the manager's agreement she changed it for something smaller and brighter. She came away with cash to spare and the feeling that for once everything was going right, or at least it would be once she'd thanked Lydia for looking after the grave in her absence.

She had to pass the practice on her way home and intended to stop to do that, and at the same time ask Glenn about the vacancy for another doctor.

She found them both having just come up from the monthly practice meeting in the basement. For once there was a smile on his face when he saw her and no sign of the weary tolerance of previous meetings. She decided that it must be the pleasure of being off the hook that was making him look happy to see her. But how was Glenn going to feel if she wanted to be back in the practice, always around in some form or other?

'I came to see you both for different reasons,' she told them, 'and won't keep either of you for more than a few moments.'

'Fine,' he said. 'I'll be in my consulting room when you've had your chat with Lydia,' and strolled off in that direction.

'Is anything wrong?' the practice manager asked anxiously.

'No. Not at all,' Emma told her. 'I've just been to put flowers on my mother's grave and there were already some there, beautiful cream roses, when I was expecting it to look totally neglected. I thought that only you would think to do that in my absence. So thank you, Lydia.'

'You're mistaken,' the practice manager told her gently. 'You are right in thinking I had a mind to keep it clean and with fresh flowers, but I haven't done so recently.'

'And you don't know who else might have done?' Emma asked incredulously.

'No. How very strange.'

'Isn't it? I shall have to keep a lookout for the mystery grave-visitor,' she said slowly, 'and will let you know when I discover who it is.'

When she knocked on the door of Glenn's consulting room and was told to enter she was still in a state of amazement. He said, 'What gives? You look as if you've seen a ghost.'

'Not exactly,' she told him, 'but something along those lines.'

'Nothing to do with me, I hope?'

'No. I came to ask if I could talk to you some time about the vacancy for another doctor here at the practice.'

'I see,' he replied thoughtfully. 'So what is wrong with now? The place is empty. We don't make appointments for the afternoon when we have the monthly practice meeting in the morning, so I am free and would like to hear what you have to say.'

'I would like to join the practice again if you would be happy about that,' she told him. 'I would never have left it in the first place if Jeremy hadn't told me something one night that hurt so much I just had to get away to face up to what it meant. I left the next morning.

'It is something I don't want to discuss, but as everyone else in the practice who was present at that time is aware of how I left without saying any goodbyes, I felt that I should explain the reason for my absence to you.'

'You don't have to explain anything to me about your private life, Emma,' he said levelly. 'Mine is buried deep in a black pit that I never seem to be able to climb out of. As to the rest of what you've said, I am concerned that you seem to think I wouldn't be happy to have you as part of the practice. If I have given you that impression, I'm sorry.

'The vacancy has arisen because one of our GPs has gone to live abroad unexpectedly with very little notice. Having once been employed here, you will be aware that in the town centre the pressure is always on. So shall we fix a starting date? And I will deal with any necessary paperwork regarding you coming back to us.'

He was observing her thoughtfully. 'Maybe you should give yourself time to unwind before you come. Your own health is just as important as the health of others, and stress is something that can wind one down into a dangerous state of exhaustion. I know because I've been there.'

Emma could feel tears threatening. The very person she had thought would be dubious about the idea of her rejoining the practice was being kind and thoughtful, so much so that if she didn't make a quick departure she would be weeping out her pain and loneliness in front of him.

'I'll be fine,' she told him hoarsely. 'I need to be with people of my own kind, Glenn, and after the sort of life I've been leading for the last few years nothing I have to deal with at the practice is going to stress me out. Thanks for being so considerate. It is a long time since anyone took the trouble to notice that I was there.' And before he had the chance to make any further comment she went, hurrying through the empty surgery with head bent.

He'd touched a nerve there, Glenn thought when Emma had gone. Had he been so wrapped up in his own sorrows that he hadn't noticed that Emma was not the calm unflappable person that she appeared to be on the outside? The few words of concern that he'd felt obliged to express had opened a floodgate of pain from somewhere. At least he had his parents to give his life some purpose, but there had been no mention of anyone close to her, or surely they would have been at yesterday's funeral.

Lydia knew Emma better than anyone else, it would seem. Maybe she could throw some light on the distress of a few moments ago. He found her on the point of leaving, ready to take advantage of the empty surgery, and asked, 'Can you spare a moment?'

'Yes,' was the reply. She liked the reserved but totally dependable head of the practice. After Jeremy's comings and goings and afternoons on the golf course when he should have been holding the place together Glenn Bartlett was a pleasure to work with.

'Just a quick question,' he said. 'I've had a chat with Emma about her joining the practice in the near future. It seems that she is keen to be back where she belonged before going to Africa and will be with us soon.'

'I am so glad about that,' Lydia said. 'She has had a hard time over the last few years. Emma lost the mother that she adored when she was very young and ended up with just Jeremy in that dreadful house until he upset her so much that she left in the middle of the night. Until you found her no one knew where she was. I am sure she is going to be all right now, Glenn.'

'I hope so,' he said doubtfully, 'but when I suggested that she take some time to recover from the last couple of weeks and have a rest before stepping back into the practice she became so upset I wished I hadn't spoken. Why do you think that was?'

'It could have been because it is so long since anyone showed her any consideration,' was the reply, which was almost word for word what Emma had said.

Lydia could have told him how Emma had been informed that she was a nobody in the unkindest possible way, cast aside by the man she'd thought was her father, and it was his concern for her well-being that had broken through her reserve. But there was no way she was going to tell a virtual stranger about the tricks that life had played on someone that she was so fond of.

One of the reasons Lydia had agreed to marry Jeremy had been the desire to be a good stepmother to his motherless daughter, and also she'd been weary of returning to an empty house at the end of each day at the practice.

But he had been his own worst enemy when he'd been too quick to tell Emma that she was going to be in the way when he married for a second time, without divulging the name of his bride-to-be. When Emma had voiced a mild protest, in his drunkenness Jeremy had wiped out her identity, so much so that when he'd woken up the next morning she'd gone.

'I see,' Glenn said, breaking into her thoughts. 'I knew nothing about Emma as she was long gone when I joined the practice. Until Jeremy begged me to bring her back to where she belonged that day on the golf course. Having done as he asked, I have wanted to get back to my own life, such as it is. I will bear in mind what you have said, Lydia. I'm sorry to have kept you.'

'It has been good to talk,' she told him, and clutching her car keys disappeared into the winter night.

He was the last to leave, the rest of the staff having taken advantage of the absence of patients because of the meeting in the basement. When Glenn turned to go to where his car was parked, after securing the outer door of the building in the light of streetlamps, he was reminded of the night he'd first seen Emma hovering hesitantly outside the locked building and had mistaken her for a patient. He had never expected in that moment of meeting that her connection with the practice was going to be the same as his own to a lesser degree.

The thought of it was fine, just as long as his life away from the place was not going to be a furtherance of the responsibilities he had undertaken on her behalf that day on the golf course.

It occurred to him that maybe some shuffling around was required with regard to who was allocated what consulting room. There a vacant one next to his so maybe a transfer for one of the longer-serving members of the practice staff would work, with Emma installed in a room further down the corridor.

As he left the practice Glenn was tempted to call on her to make sure that she was all right after her emotional outburst earlier. He pointed his car in the direction of her house, but drove straight past on observing the flashy vehicle that belonged to James Prentice parked on the driveway.

Trust that one to be first in line when a new woman appeared on the scene, he thought grimly, with the memory of the trainee GP monopolising Emma at the Barrington Bar on the night when the members of the practice had gathered to welcome her back home.

Yet why not? Just because his life was grey and empty there was no reason why those who had a zest for living should be denied the pleasure of it. At least seeing Prentice's car outside Emma's house had brought with it the relief of knowing that she wasn't alone and sad back there after her emotional exit from the practice earlier.

That line of reasoning lasted until he was pulling up on his own drive and knew that he had to make sure that she was all right whether Prentice was there or not. He thought grimly that he really was carrying his promise to Jeremy Chalmers to the extreme. But he was already reversing and when he approached Emma's house once again he groaned at the sight of the same car still on the drive.

But the thought was there that maybe she hadn't invited him, that the pushy Prentice had invaded her privacy for some reason. After seeing him perform at the Barrington Bar the other night there were a few reasons why he had an uneasy feeling about him.

After parking across the road from the house, Glenn rang the doorbell and adopted a casual approach when the door was opened to him, but there was nothing casual about Emma's expression when she saw him standing there.

'Glenn!' she breathed, stepping back to let him in. 'Is everything all right?'

'Er…yes,' he told her. 'I just wanted to make sure that you'd arrived home safely and realise that I needn't have concerned myself as I see that you have Prentice here.'

'What gives you that idea?' she exclaimed. 'I'm on my own. I haven't seen James since that night at the Barrington Bar.'

'But the car on the drive,' he persisted. 'Surely it belongs to him?'

'Not to my knowledge. The only one out there is mine. I did an exchange with the garage on the car that my…er…father left me, for something more trendy. I must have chosen a model similar to that of James without being aware of it as I've never seen his car.'

'Ah, I see,' he said uncomfortably, and followed it with, 'I'm sorry to have bothered you.' He was ready to get off, with the feeling that Emma must be totally weary of him fussing over her like some bore with nothing better to do when his day at the practice was over. Wasn't he supposed to be eager to get back to the days before Jeremy had gasped out his last wishes and placed the burden on him that he'd so wanted to relinquish?

'Have you eaten?' she asked softly.

'Er...no, but I intend to shortly.'

'I could make you a meal if you would let me,' she volunteered. 'I owe you such a lot, Glenn.'

'You owe me nothing,' he said with a wintry smile. 'Except maybe to cherish the life that I've brought you back to with every ounce of your being. Because it can all slip away when we least expect it to.'

With that comment he went striding off into the night to where he'd parked his car. As Emma closed the door slowly behind him his description of what his life was like came to mind. She wished she knew what it was that was hurting him so much, that was responsible for the black pit that he'd described.

But the chances of finding out were slim as Glenn was the most private person she'd ever met. The least she could do was to respect that privacy and get on with adjusting to life back at the practice.

Back home for the second time Glenn was squirming at the thought of the mistake he'd made regarding Emma's car. She must think him an interfering fusspot, he thought grimly. If they were going to be working together at the practice he needed to be around less in her private life.

Having been looking forward to the time when he

could let her get on with it, he'd just made a complete fool of himself and it was not going to happen again.

Not in the mood for cooking, he made a sandwich and a mug of coffee and settled down by the fire, waiting for the silence of the room to wrap itself comfortingly around him as it always did. But not tonight, it seemed. The events of the day kept butting into his consciousness and he couldn't relax. The thought uppermost in his mind was that Emma Chalmers was beginning to be a disturbing influence in his life, which was something he could do without. Maybe agreeing to her coming back to the practice was *not* such a good idea.

There were other practices equally as busy as theirs that would welcome her with open arms on hearing the details of where she'd spent the last few years. But would she want to work for them? Had he brought Emma home to places she loved only to want her elsewhere?

The irony of the situation was that he who knew her the least out of the folks at the practice was the one she was having the most to do with. He hadn't intended it to be like that.

But recalling Lydia's veiled comments about Emma's past hurts and the practice manager's obvious desire to have her back amongst them, he was going to have to stick to the arrangement he'd made with Jeremy's daughter while keeping his distance at the same time.

If Glenn had spent a restless evening, so had

Emma. It hurt that he hadn't let her offer him any hospitality. Not being aware of the chat he'd had with Lydia after she had left him in an emotional state the other day, Emma was unaware that his concerns on her behalf had been brought to the fore again when, on arriving at her house, he had thought that she had been socialising with the practice womaniser.

Walking slowly up the stairs to bed with the restlessness still upon him, Glenn stood in front of his and Serena's wedding picture on the dressing table and asked gently of his smiling bride 'Why couldn't you have stayed on the beach, you crazy woman?'

The next morning, with Emma's time her own until a date had been fixed for her to start at the practice, she went to check if the strange flowers were still on the grave beside the ones she'd put there. On discovering that they were, she decided that they were a one-off of some kind, and once faded would not be replaced.

With that reassurance in mind she went on her way to her next important errand, which was regarding house prices in the area. She came away having surprisingly developed a yearning to stay where she was and create something beautiful out of her house during the long winter months.

Glenminster was busy with early Christmas shoppers and Emma didn't want to linger too long anywhere near the practice with the memory of her visit the previous day. So she parked the car and went for a coffee in a bistro on the other side of town, where she sat hunched at one of the tables, drinking the steaming brew and digesting mentally the idea of giving a makeover to the drab place that was still her home and so convenient for the practice.

Just thinking about the two places made her impatient to be involved with them both. As if Glenn had read her mind, there was a brisk message waiting for her when she got back to ask how about her returning to the practice the following Monday. For the first time in what seemed like an eternity bells of joy rang in her heart.

She rang back immediately with a reply of just two words, 'Yes! Please!' And for the first time since meeting him she heard him laugh.

'That's good, then,' he told her. 'We look forward to seeing you on Monday next, if not before.' And was gone.

She spent the rest of the day with literature she'd picked up from a local builder while out and about earlier. The ideas suggested for modernising old properties were fascinating, so much so that it was evening before she knew it and Lydia was knocking on her door on her way home from the practice with the news that there were fresh flowers on the grave that hadn't been there the day before.

'After what you told me yesterday I took a stroll through the churchyard in the lunch hour and there they were,' she said.

'But I was there myself first thing!' Emma exclaimed.

'So it must have been after that. When you'd been and gone,' Lydia reasoned. 'But why now, when there was nothing like that all the time you were away? I used to put flowers on occasionally but there were never any others already in place.'

'Glenn goes through the churchyard as a short cut, instead of driving there, when he goes to visit old Mrs Benson. He might have seen someone bring the flowers. Shall I ask him?'

'No,' Emma said uncomfortably. 'I'll keep a lookout myself, he has been involved enough with my affairs and I think is weary of the hassle.' Then she took a leap in the dark. 'Why does he refer to his life so miserably, Lydia? What do you know about him?'

'Nothing,' was the reply. 'Nothing at all regarding his private life, but what I see on the job is a different thing. Glenn Bartlett is the best head of the practice ever. I've seen a few mediocre ones come and go in my time, including Jeremy.

'Which reminds me, Emma, do you have the urge to change your name from the one you thought was yours, considering the heartbreak he caused you, or stay with it to avoid questions?'

'What would be the point of changing it now?' she asked flatly, 'I could always change it to my mother's maiden name, I suppose, but everyone knows me as Chalmers. And as I haven't a clue what my birth father's name is or was, I can scarcely change it to that. If I ever found out, that would be the time to decide.'

'Yes, I guess so,' Lydia agreed, and on the point of departing suggested quizzically, 'With regard to what I came about, we will have to take turns watching out for the phantom flower-bringer, I'm afraid.'

'It will be someone who is putting flowers on the wrong grave and will realise their mistake sooner or later,' Emma said firmly, having no wish to discuss the matter further, and when Lydia had gone she picked up the brochures on home conversions once more.

But her concentration had diminished with the memory of Lydia's comments about Glenn now uppermost in her mind, and her eagerness to be back working in the practice overwhelmed her. Just seven days to go and she would be back where she'd been happiest amongst those of a like kind, and with her boss, the man who had brought her back to Glenminster. What more could she ask?

Over the next week Emma didn't hear from Glenn. And as the days passed, with no glimpses of him driving past on his home visits, or signs of him anywhere in the vicinity of the house where he lived the quiet life away from the surgery, Emma found she missed him. So by the time Monday morning came she was surprised how much she wanted to see him again.

She was to be disappointed. There was no sign

of him in the practice building and Lydia met her with the news that Glenn was taking a break and would be back in a week's time. With a doctor short, her presence would be welcomed by the rest of the staff. As Lydia pointed out the consulting room that would be hers, Emma thought they wouldn't exactly be tripping over each other when he did put in an appearance, as it was just about as far away from his as it could be.

But there was no time for wishing and wondering. No sooner had she settled herself and her belongings in the room that was to be hers than patients allotted to her by the receptionists were beginning to appear. She had a warm welcome for those she knew and a cautious approach for those she didn't, and the time flew with her disappointment regarding Glenn's absence forgotten.

But it returned at six o'clock with the switching off the lights and the locking of the doors. As Emma drove home in winter darkness there was the question of why, when Glenn had rung to tell her that she could start back at the practice today and that he would see her then, he hadn't kept his word.

Where was he and who was he with? she pondered. None of the rest of the staff had shown surprise at his absence so it must have been general knowledge to everyone except her that he would not be there on her first day back to welcome her as promised. But after all why should she know? She was just an additional staff member, a new member of the team, no one of particular importance.

The sea was calm, unbelievably so, but all his memories of it were of a gigantic wall of water sweeping everyone and everything before it into total destruction.

The rock where Serena had gone to sunbathe still rose majestically out of clear blue water, just as it had done on that day when his life had changed for ever.

The rebuilding of the hotel where he and Serena had been staying was finished. It had taken three years to make it fit to live in again and the same applied to the rest of the resort that had been their favourite holiday venue.

At long last he was coming to terms with what he had always felt to be the unfairness of being left to live the empty life that had been thrust upon him. He'd been back a few times since it had happened, looking for solace, for answers that might make his life worth living again, but none had ever been forthcoming. Even the strange friendship with Emma Chalmers, which had come out of nowhere and was pleasing enough in its own up-and-down sort of way, wasn't enough to take away the pain of loss.

She had been forced to cope with a loss of her own in the short time since he'd brought her back from Africa, but hadn't felt much grief as far as he could see.

He would be flying back home in the next few

hours, feeling guilty at having not kept his promise to be there on her first day back at the practice. An early morning news item a week ago had alerted him to the fact that the rebuilding of the devastated holiday resort was complete. And that those who had lived there and lost everything in the disaster were returning in the hope that soon the tourist trade would be back and flourishing.

On hearing it, Glenn's first thought had been that he never wanted to go there again. But there had been others that followed it, the most overwhelming one being that he needed to say goodbye to the place, and with it his farewell to the wife he had lost so tragically.

His father had once given him good advice, unwanted at the time. 'Let her go, Glenn. Serena wouldn't want you to live a life of loneliness and grief,' Jonas had urged, but Glenn had ignored him. It was only today, seeing the sea calm and still, the buildings rebuilt and the gardens back to their previous glory, where there had been carnage, that had finally given him the will to let go.

They were waiting for him at the airport, the parents that he loved, elderly and temperamental but mostly on his wavelength. Typically his father's first comment was, 'You left that young daughter of Jeremy's high and dry on her first day back at the practice. Did you forget?'

'No. I didn't,' he told him. 'It was just that when

I heard about the rebuilding on the six o'clock news that morning I knew I had to go. Everything else seemed blurred and vague, and I got the first flight of the day out there. I will speak to Emma in the morning and I'm sure she will understand.'

'And?' his mother interrupted gently. 'How did it feel to see it all made good again? Was the rock still there?'

'Yes, it was,' he told her, 'and it was strange because seeing it comforted me. I felt that at last I could say my goodbyes to Serena.'

'And you'll have a word with that girl of Jeremy's tomorrow?' his father insisted, tactless to the last.

'Yes, of course. I've said I will, haven't I?' he told him as the three of them boarded a waiting taxi. Emma wasn't going to lose any sleep over his absence, he thought. It was the job she coveted, not a washed-out widower like him.

But the time he'd just spent in a place that would be in the background of his life for ever had been well worth the effort. He was ready to accept what he had been given, make the best of it, and it was a major step forward. It was a pity that his father couldn't see it that way, instead of fussing about what he saw as letting down a comparative stranger.

It seemed that he had gone to the practice to pick up a prescription and seen Emma's expression when she'd discovered that his son was not around on her first morning at the practice, and like an elderly knight of old had taken up her cause. For heaven's sake, Lydia would have been there to make Emma welcome and young Prentice wouldn't have been far away, that was for sure.

When the taxi stopped outside the neat semi-detached where his parents lived Glenn paid the driver and then saw them safely inside before walking the short distance to his own home. On the way he had to pass the drab property that was Emma's residence and when he glanced across saw that in spite of the fact that it was well gone midnight there was a light on in an upstairs room, and he thought wryly that maybe she had found it easier to find solace than he had.

She was very noticeable with her long dark hair and big hazel eyes, he thought, and now that she was back in civilisation who could blame her if she found some of the men she was getting to know exciting to spend time with.

Yet from what little he knew of Emma it was strange that she should already be so close to someone of his gender after so short a time, if that was the case. And he might have thought it stranger still if he had known that Emma was propped up against the pillows all alone, studying builders' estimates as if there was no tomorrow.

As for himself, for the first time in ages he slept the moment his head touched the pillow, unaware that Emma's last thought before sleep had claimed her had been of him and his disappointing absence

on her first day at the practice. It had taken some
of the pleasure out of her return to work, but not
all of it. She had slotted back in again as if she'd
never been away and hoped Glenn would approve
whenever he came back from where he had disappeared to.

CHAPTER FOUR

DESPITE THE LATENESS of his return the previous night Glenn was at his desk when Emma arrived at the practice the next morning. Having left the door of his consulting room open, he was watching for her arrival and called her in the moment she appeared.

Beckoning for her to take a seat, he asked levelly, 'So how did your first day go, Emma? Was it up to expectations? I had expected to be here, but something completely unexpected took me to foreign parts and I didn't get back until very late last night.'

'Yes, it was fine,' she told him, 'just like old times, only better since having worked abroad.'

'I passed your house on the last lap of my way home,' he said, 'and saw that one of your bedroom lights was on at that late hour, so it would seem that you are settling in amongst us satisfactorily.'

'Yes, I suppose you could say that,' she agreed coolly, 'if you would class leafing through a pile of builders' estimates as "settling in".'

Ignoring the implied rebuke, he said, 'You mean

you're considering giving your house a face-lift? All I can say to that is good thinking.'

'It will be my Christmas present to myself.'

He didn't like the sound of that. Surely Emma had someone to spend Christmas with? It was clear from the funeral that she had no close relatives.

But it was still some weeks away. There would be time for both their lives to change before then: his because of what had just happened in a faraway place, and Emma's because by then she would have found new friends and made her house beautiful.

Any other surmising had to wait as there were voices to be heard nearby, the waiting room was filling up, and as Emma turned to go to her own part of the busy practice he said, 'I'm here if you have any problems, so don't hesitate to ask.'

Glenn watched her colour rise at the reassurance he was offering and wondered if he had hit a sore spot of some kind. Had she thought that he was forgetting her past position in the practice and hinting that her absence over the last few years might have made her less than capable with her own kind?

If that was the case Emma would be so wrong. There was an air of efficiency about her that showed she knew what she was about, and he wasn't going to interfere regarding that.

She didn't reply to the offer he'd made, just smiled, and as she turned to go to her consulting room he pressed the buzzer on his desk and the day was under way.

In the early afternoon Glenn had a house call to make at a farm high on a hillside. During the lunch break he went to find Emma with the intention of suggesting that she accompany him to renew her acquaintance with the more rural parts that the practice covered, now bare and leafless in winter's grip.

He discovered that she was nowhere around and concluded that she'd gone to do a quick shop somewhere in her lunch hour, until Lydia, observing him finding Emma missing, explained that she was most likely to be found in the churchyard.

When he asked why, the answer was that her mother's grave was there, and Glenn was immediately aware of the strange arrangement of her parents being buried in different places, as Jeremy had been laid to rest in the local cemetery.

Not wanting to question Lydia further, he strolled towards the church and, sure enough, Emma was there, arranging fresh flowers on one of the graves, and he wondered why, as there was an abundance of them there already.

When his shadow fell across them she looked up, startled, and asked, 'Have you come to tell me that lunchtime is over?'

'No, not at all,' he said, feeling a little awkward that he was interrupting something special. 'I'm driving up into the hills to do a home visit for my next patient and thought you might like to renew your acquaintance with the green hills of Gloucestershire. They're as beautiful as ever above the Regency finery of Glenminster.

'My mother was born in this place, but when I came along they were living in Yorkshire because of my father's job. She was so homesick they christened me Glenn after the place she loved so much. At the first opportunity he brought her back to Glenminster and they've been here ever since.

'Not me, though. I met my wife when we were both studying medicine up north and when we married we stayed up there content with our lot until it all fell apart and I came back here to pick up the pieces.'

Emma was listening to what he had to say with wide eyes. Was this the same man who valued his privacy, wouldn't let her make him a meal, and now was putting the blame for his peculiarities on to a failed marriage?

'It would be a pleasure to be up amongst the hills again,' she told him, and with a last look at an abundance of cream roses on the grave she turned away and they walked back to the practice building in silence.

Once they were there Glenn said, 'Can you be ready in twenty minutes? Have you had some lunch?'

'Yes,' she told him, and feeling that she ought to explain said, 'The reason you found me beside my mother's grave is because since I've come back I've discovered that someone is mistakenly putting flowers on it and I need to know who they are.

'I thought it might be Lydia because the two of them were good friends. But it isn't and she is just as curious as I am, as I have no relatives that I know of.'

Glenn was observing her sombrely. What was it about Emma that brought out the need in him to look after her? It wasn't because his return to the place where his life had been resurrected a few days ago had made him want to find a replacement for Serena.

That had just brought some peace to the empty shell that he lived in. That being so, as they drove towards the farmhouse high up on the hillside where his patient lived, he felt free to offer his services with regard to the mystery mourner. He said, 'If there *is* someone bringing flowers in remembrance of your mother, we need to find out why, don't you think?'

'Yes, I suppose so,' she agreed. 'Yet it is a long time since she was taken from me, though not to someone else, it might seem, unless they're putting flowers on the wrong grave. The hurt is always there. I loved her so much, but today I don't want to think about the past. I just want to look and look and look at my favourite places.'

'And so you shall,' he promised, 'when we've seen the farmer and sorted out his health problems. You may remember him from before you went away. Does the name Jack Walsh ring a bell?'

Emma swivelled to face him in the confines of the car. 'Yes, his son was in my class at school. What's wrong with his father?'

'An injury while harvesting that occurred during

your absence. Every so often his spine seizes up and he has to go for hospital treatment. He won't make the effort until I insist on it, and with Christmas coming up he will be reluctant to miss the festivities. Luckily his wife, who knows him better than he knows himself, rang to say that he could hardly walk.'

'So who runs the place?' Emma asked.

'The rest of the family,' was the reply as he brought the car to a halt outside a farmhouse built from the local golden stone that was so popular amongst the builders and house owners of the area.

They found Jack Walsh reclining on a couch, watching television. When he spotted Emma he groaned.

'You're Jeremy's daughter, aren't you?' he asked. 'Come back, have you, now that he's gone?'

Glenn watched the colour drain from her face and anger spiralled inside him. 'Dr Chalmers is here to assist, not to be insulted!' he told him. 'So how about a demonstration of your mobility as that's what we're here to observe? Your wife thinks that it's worse.'

As Jack eased himself off the couch and, leaning on a stick, moved slowly across the room Emma was wishing herself miles away. There had been something in his comment regarding herself that had made her cringe because it had brought back the memory of that awful night when she'd fled from her home.

At that moment Mrs Walsh appeared and greeted

them with a relieved smile and the conversation became medical again. Glenn sternly insisted that the regular physiotherapy sessions that Jack had been giving a miss should be started again immediately unless he wanted to be totally unable to enjoy the pleasures of Christmas.

'Your muscle control is very poor, more from lack of effort than anything else,' Emma told him when both doctors had examined the patient.

'Dr Chalmers is right,' Glenn told him, 'so back to the physiotherapy and we will see you again before Christmas is upon us.'

'Aye, if you say so,' Jack agreed irritably. 'It's all right for some.'

When they left the farm it was three o'clock and Glenn thought there wasn't going to be much time for Emma to renew her acquaintance with past memories. 'It will be dark soon,' he said. 'What would you like to do most in the time we have left before we need to return to the practice?'

Her answer was prompt. 'Watch a winter sunset on the horizon.'

'Right, we will do that, but from inside. How about afternoon tea, somewhere with a good view?'

She hesitated. 'Won't we be needed back at the practice?'

'Not for a couple of hours. My father is insisting that I make it up to you for not being around on your first day there.' Glenn smiled as he drove into the parking area of a cosy-looking café. 'So here goes, afternoon tea up amongst the hills.'

They had a table near the window, the food was delicious, and as the winter sun sank below the sky-line Emma thought it was the first time she'd felt really happy in years.

As he watched Emma, Glenn thought that this stranger that he had bought back to Glenminster was very easily pleased. She made no demands, just quietly got on with the life she had come back to, but he sensed that deep down she was hurting and it almost certainly had something to do with Jeremy.

A smile tugged at the corner of his mouth as he compared Emma's father to his own. His was a 'do-gooder', which was the main reason why his mother sometimes threw him out because he overdid it and his concern for others got her down. While she just wanted a pleasant retirement he was busy looking after all the waifs and strays of the neighbourhood. Glenn understood both their points of view.

He sometimes thought that if he could have given his parents a grandchild to love in their old age it would have been different, but a terrifying act of nature had put an end to that dream for always.

As they watched the sun go down he said, 'I am very impressed to hear that you're going to give the house a face-lift, Emma, but it will be a huge undertaking for you on your own, Why did Chalmers let it get so run-down? He was always smartly dressed, had a big car, and was never away from the golf club, so I'm told, yet the house is a mess.'

'It was just a place to sleep—that was how he saw it,' she told him, 'and if my mother ever asked for anything new, he wasn't interested.'

'Yes. I see,' he commented, and thought that all of that went with Chalmers's type. On the heels of that thought came another that he was already putting into words and thinking he was insane.

'If you decide to go ahead with the renovations, I will be only too pleased to help in any way I can,' he said gently. 'You have only to ask, Emma.'

He watched her colour rise as she turned to him in confusion and said, 'I wouldn't dream of involving you in doing anything like that, Glenn. You did enough in finding me and bringing me back home.'

'Yes, well, we'll see about that if and when the time comes,' he said. 'In the meantime, take everything one step at a time.'

What did he mean by that? she wondered. Was it a reference to her impulsive decision to give the house a makeover, or was Glenn aware that she was attracted to him—a lot?

It was time to change the subject, she thought as they drove back to the practice. 'I've loved being back amongst the hills, Glenn,' she said. 'Thank you for taking me with you. I thought it would be just a matter of a house call to a difficult patient, but it was much more than that.'

He smiled in response, and the thought came to him again that Emma didn't take a lot of pleasing.

But how long was she going to be pleased with him safe behind his touch-me-not barricades? He found himself worryingly close to thinking about her in a way he hadn't envisaged before, so bringing a lighter note into the moment he said, 'So can I tell my father that I have redeemed myself for being missing on your first day at the practice?'

'You can indeed,' Emma assured him. 'Today has been my first happy day in ages. I would be totally content if it weren't for the flowers that keep appearing on my mother's grave.'

'Yes, that I can understand,' he said gently. 'We need to do something about it. I sometimes use the churchyard as a short cut so will be on the lookout. And I'm sure Lydia will be keeping a close watch too, and of course you will be. So between us we should be able to come up with an answer sooner or later.'

When they arrived back at the practice Glenn had a patient waiting and Emma was involved with assisting the practice nurses with a cluster of school children brought in by their parents for the nasal flu spray vaccination, and for the rest of the afternoon the happy moments up on the hillside seemed far away. But in the quiet of the evening the memory of the time spent with Glenn was there again and with it the same amount of pleasure.

* * *

During the following fortnight the mystery of the flowers seemed to have gone away and Emma began to think that maybe it had been someone's mistake as no more strange blooms appeared. The only flowers on view were the ones that she took herself and she was relieved to discover that it was so.

But just when she had started to forget about them the flowers reappeared. Engrossed in her plans for renovating the house, Emma decided to ignore them. Not so Glenn and Lydia, who kept watch for a while, but without any success. Eventually Emma placed them on a grave that was always bare, only to find the unknown mourner not fazed by that as fresh flowers continued to arrive alongside her own.

With Christmas approaching and nothing to look forward to socially, Emma was pleased to hear that there was to be a staff party on the Saturday evening a week before the festive occasion. She felt that it called for something special to wear, especially if Glenn was going to be there. Although she had her doubts that he would be.

Ever since the afternoon spent with him up on the hillside Glenn had been distant when in her company and she wondered if he still spent every moment of his spare time closeted in his house. He had referred to the ending of his marriage with cold clarity and she wondered where his ex-wife was now.

Nevertheless, it didn't stop her from buying a

dress that brought out the attractions of the dark sheen of her hair and pale smooth skin, and as the occasion drew near she resigned herself to being an odd one out in the hotel that had been chosen by those who knew the night life of the town, as it was now, far better than she did.

Lydia would be there and had suggested that they share a taxi to get there but had explained that she would be staying the night at the hotel after the party and so wouldn't be around for the home journey.

'But I'm sure that Glenn will give you a lift home if you ask him,' she'd said. 'He never stays over on those occasions. Just puts in a courtesy appearance and once the meal is over expresses his best wishes to the staff and goes back to the peace of that lovely house of his. That is if you don't want to stay long, of course. Otherwise it will need to be a taxi again,' she told her.

'Right, I'll remember that.' She wondered if deep down she really wanted to go. There were decisions to make about the house, alterations that she wanted done as soon as possible. A quiet night in would help to move the project along more quickly, but there was the beautiful new dress. She did want to wear it when Glenn would be there to see her in it...

In the meantime, as the days spent at the practice went too fast and were so busy, Glenn wasn't looking forward to Christmas any more than he had over the last few years. He may have made his peace regarding losing Serena, but the loneliness was still there.

Restless now in the quiet of his home, unable to relax, he knew he had to do something about it, but what? As head of the practice he was committed to going to the staff Christmas party, which was looming up in the near future. He realised with a combination of pleasure and pain that Emma would be there.

Glenn had shopped already for his Christmas gifts to his parents. As was the routine since losing Serena, he would be spending the two festive days with them at their house, with his mother doing all she could to brighten the occasion and his father restless and on edge because he longed for grandchildren and his son never did anything towards granting him his wish.

He had wondered a few times what Emma's Christmas would be like in that ghastly house on her own. If his two days of festivities were heavy going, hers would probably be worse, unless she had something planned that he knew nothing about.

As far as she was concerned, it still upset her that Glenn hadn't let her thank him for his kindness on the occasion of her return to Glenminster and she intended using the approaching festivities to make up for the lapse in some way.

As the days went by she was beginning to feel a loneliness that had never been there before at Christmastime, even while she'd worked abroad. Although it hadn't exactly been joyful in past years, with just Jeremy and herself to share the event with their opposing lifestyles and little in common, it hadn't felt as empty as this, she thought as she wandered around Glenminster's delightful shopping promenades for a gift for Lydia and a magical something to present to Glenn if he would accept it.

On one of her shopping trips she met Glenn's parents, and his father, Jonas, introduced her to Glenn's mother Olivia as 'Jeremy's daughter come back to the fold' and asked how she intended spending Christmas.

It was an awkward moment. Emma knew that he was always on the lookout for waifs and strays and didn't want to be classified as such, but was lost how to reply to the question. Luckily, Glenn's mum provided an escape route by saying that her husband was always looking for helpers with his good works and on Christmas Day was masterminding a free Yuletide lunch for the needy in the town centre.

'I would love to help with that,' Emma told him with complete honesty, 'either by cooking, serving, or helping generally.'

'I'll accept the offer,' he told her promptly with gruff gratitude, 'but only on one condition—that you dine with us in the evening.'

Emma felt her colour rise at the thought of Glenn's expression when he discovered that she was going to be part of his Christmas celebrations—if that was the correct word to describe the foursome that his father had suggested. Uneasy at the thought, Emma made a weak acceptance of the invitation and braced herself for explaining how it had come about to Glenn the next time they came face to face, which turned out to be the following morning at the practice.

Glenn had been engrossed in a report he'd received from the endocrine clinic in Glenminster's main hospital concerning a patient whose calcium levels had been rising dangerously over past months, according to his recent tests. When he looked up to see Emma standing in front of him she looked very serious, so he asked her what was wrong.

'It's about Christmas Day,' she said awkwardly. 'Your father has invited me to dine with the three of you in the evening and I really don't want to intrude, but hesitate to offend him.'

'I didn't know that you were on visiting terms with my folks,' he commented dryly. 'How did that come about?'

'I offered to assist with the Christmas lunch he's organising for the lonely and needy folks around the place, and the invitation to dine with your parents and yourself in the evening became part of the arrangement.'

'So why the fuss? If you don't want to do that, tell him so. My dad is a great guy for organising other people's lives, whether they want him to or not. But he means well and when it comes to the lonely or isolated he excels himself.'

'And is that how you see me?' she said quietly. As a pathetic loner? You don't know the half of it.' And on that comment she went to her consulting room and prepared to face the day.

When Emma had gone Glenn squirmed at the way he'd been so offhand with her. What was he thinking? The thought of her beside him on such a special day of the year was magical. It would help to take away some of the emptiness that he lived with, but instead of telling her how much he needed her he had sent her away after showing little interest in her plea for his advice. And as the morning progressed there was no opportunity to tell her how much he would like her to be there on the evening of Christmas Day.

The flowers were still appearing on the grave and Emma had decided that if in some way her mother was conscious of them and content to receive them, she was going to let the mystery of them lie like a blessing. So that lunchtime she went into the churchyard as she sometimes did and spent a few quiet moments there to calm the confusion of her conversation with Glenn earlier.

As she turned to go he was there, seemingly having read her mind. Observing her quizzically, he said, 'Do you ever regret coming back to Glenminster, Emma?'

'No, of course not,' she said immediately. 'I belong here and nowhere else, but there are unsolved questions I have to live with.'

'Such as the mystery flowers?'

'Yes, that in part; but bigger issues than that haunt me. I envy you your parents, Glenn. You are so fortunate to have them here in your life every moment of every day. Although I am so sorry that your marriage didn't work.'

'Is that what you think?' he exclaimed. 'That I'm divorced or something of the sort?'

'Well—yes, I assumed.'

'I'm not divorced, Emma,' said Glenn. 'My wife is dead. Swept away in a tsunami when we were on holiday some years ago.'

'Oh, how awful for you!' she breathed. 'I had no idea. Do, please, forgive me for jumping to the wrong conclusion.'

'It's an understandable mistake to make,' he said. 'Only my parents know what happened and at my express request they don't discuss my affairs with anyone. It's something I don't like to talk about, and I would be obliged if you would do the same.'

'Yes, of course,' she told him, still stunned by what he had told her. 'I really am so very sorry, Glenn. If ever there is anything I can do to help, do please say so.'

He was smiling a tight smile. 'There *is* one thing. In spite of my having put the dampener on it earlier, how about you sitting beside me on Christmas Day night to please my parents? I'll pick you up at seven o'clock if that's all right.'

'Er...yes,' she replied, wondering what he would say next to amaze her, and asked hesitantly, 'What shall I bring?'

'Just yourself will do fine,' she was told, and with a glance at the clock in the church tower high above them added, 'We had better get back to our patients or we'll have a queue.'

Emma smiled across at him, happier than she'd felt for ages. The invitation to join Glenn and his family for a Christmas meal made her feel more wanted than she had done in a long time. But poor Glenn! What he'd had to say about the loss of his wife was heartbreaking and explained so many of the things about him that had previously puzzled her.

It was the day of the staff party and with that and Christmas the following week, with all the excitement and nostalgia that entailed, there was a lovely heart-warming atmosphere in the surgery. Everyone was looking forward to the festive season and a well-earned rest. It was midday and most of the staff had already gone to enjoy their weekend when a phone call came through to say that Jack Walsh needed to see a doctor urgently. Glenn sighed. Jack had a high temperature and it sounded as if he might have some sort of infection. After checking that the building was empty, he locked up and went to his car, ready to drive up to the remote farm.

At that moment Emma drove onto the practice forecourt and he observed her in surprise. Having noted that her consulting room was empty, Glenn had taken it for granted that, like the rest of the staff, she had gone to enjoy the weekend ahead.

As she got out of her car he wound his window down and asked in surprise, 'Where have you been? Everywhere is locked up. I'm off to see Jack Walsh at the hill farm. He has a high temperature and from what his wife says seems to be heading for something serious.'

'Can I go along with you?' she asked. 'I missed the hills so much while I was away and loved it the other time you took me up there.'

'I would have thought that you'd have lots of nice things planned for the rest of the day,' he said. 'Come, by all means, if you wish, but it won't be much fun up there on a day like this. There is a definite nip in the air and the sky is dark and lowering.'

Emma was already easing herself into the passenger seat beside him and flashed him a smile. 'It's a case of anything to get out of my stately home,' she teased, and he could understand that.

'Where have you been?' Glenn asked as he drove off the forecourt of the practice.

'To see a child with 'flu,' she replied. 'I hope I don't get it for Christmas.'

So do I, he thought. The party later that night and having Emma with him at his parents' house on Christmas Day were beginning to stand out in his mind like stars in a dark sky.

By the time he pulled up at the Walsh farm it was snowing. Large flakes were falling all around them, silently forming a white carpet that was getting thicker by the moment. Glenn said, 'Are you wishing you hadn't come? We could be snowed in up here and it's the staff party tonight.'

The question had an answer that was making her heart beat faster. Emma wanted to be wherever Glenn was, be it the smart hotel where the staff party was to be held or on the Walshs' ramshackle farm, so as Mrs Walsh opened the door, Emma's smile was serene.

'Doctor, he's bad this time,' she said worriedly, as she led the way to a drab bedroom on the ground floor of the building. 'He's hot as fire, his breathing is difficult, and he isn't talking sense.'

'How long has he been like this?' Glenn asked, as he bent over the feverish figure on the bed.

'He's gradually been getting worse since yesterday,' was the reply.

Glenn frowned.

'It could be pneumonia or something worse,' he said when the two doctors had finished examining him. 'I'm going to phone for an ambulance and hope that it will be able to get here before this place becomes inaccessible.' He sent a wry smile in Emma's direction. 'So much for life in the fast lane.'

'I don't mind,' she told him, and she really didn't

as long as she was with him. Although Glenn was still an unknown quantity as far as she was concerned. Since they'd met he'd wanted nothing of her or from her, and as far as she knew nothing had changed.

It was still early afternoon. They might get to the party yet if the snow eased off and an ambulance managed to get through. She would still be able to wear the dress that she'd been hoping would make Glenn see her how she wanted him to.

CHAPTER FIVE

AN HOUR LATER an ambulance did come trundling through the snow with its siren screeching. After a quick word from Glenn the sick man was taken on board and was on his way to the nearest hospital, leaving the two doctors to get back to civilisation the best they could.

After a mile of careful driving with visibility almost nil the car became stuck in a snowdrift. Glenn had been worried when they'd set off, but now anxiety on Emma's behalf spiralled as there was no signal when he tried to phone for help. He got out to assess the situation and was hit straight away by the severe cold.

'I should never have let you come with me!' he said when he opened the door to ease himself back in. 'I suggest that you climb over onto the back seat and if I leave the engine running you may be able to keep warm while I dig us out of this mess. I keep a couple of shovels in the boot for situations such as this.'

'Give me one and I'll help,' she said immediately.

He shook his head. 'No! You stay put and keep trying to get a signal on the phone while I'm out there, digging.'

As she was about to protest at his refusal to let her assist he said tightly, 'Do as I say, will you?' And she obeyed meekly.

A short time later he got back behind the wheel but had no luck—the car was still stuck. He groaned as he climbed into the back seat beside her and asked grimly if she'd been able to get a signal.

When she shook her head Glenn held out his arms and when Emma made no move towards him he said dryly, 'I don't bite. I am merely offering body warmth because the car heater doesn't seem to be working.'

With a wry smile she went into his hold and as he held her close against his chest, in spite of the snow drifting silently and thickly around the car, she had never felt so safe in her life before. Beside her, Glenn was thinking that it was the first time he had held a woman in his arms since he'd lost Serena and it was arousing all the passions he had kept so tightly under control ever since.

Because it wasn't just any member of the opposite sex he was holding close. It was the daughter that Jeremy Chalmers had confessed to having done some great hurt to as he'd been dying, and he, Glenn, would very much like to know what it was.

'So tell me what it was that Jeremy did to you

that hurt so much,' he said gently, when they'd sat in silence for a while.

Her face clouded and Glenn thought she was going to refuse, but after a pause she sighed. 'He had been out drinking and came home late. Then he told me that I would have to move out of the only home I'd ever known. That he was getting married for a second time and that I was not welcome to stay where I had lived all my life,' Emma said. 'And when I protested that I was his daughter and didn't deserve such treatment, he informed me that he was not my father. He had married my lovely mother to give her respectability, and her child—me—a name. And as a final hurtful truth he told me that he had no idea who my father was, that my mother had never told him, so I was a nobody.

'Unable to bear the thought of staying in Glen-minster after listening to his nastiness, I left during the night and had no intention of ever returning until you got in touch and brought me back to the place I loved.'

She turned, looked up at him from the circle of his arms and said softly, 'I will always bless you for that, Glenn.'

Emma's mouth was only an inch or two away. It would be so easy to kiss her, he thought achingly, kiss away the hurts that Jeremy had caused in his spiteful drunkenness, and make love to her in the privacy of the snowbound car.

Tilting her chin with gentle fingers, he looked

down at her upturned face and it was there, the feeling of togetherness that she aroused in him, and letting desire take hold of his senses he kissed her just once long and tenderly, then it was gone, swept away by the happenings of the past that still had him in their grip.

The mighty wall of water surging towards him that, when it had taken its toll of the holiday resort, had also taken Serena, along with many others, and ever since he'd carried with him the guilt of being spared when she had been lost.

The torment of the thoughts that wouldn't allow him to hold Emma any closer was broken by the sound of some sort of vehicle approaching through the swirling white flakes and she cried, 'It sounds like a truck of some sort, Glenn!'

Relief washed over him, mixed with regret that he hadn't taken advantage of the magical moments when he'd held her in his arms, but her safety had to come first and he said, 'It's a snow plough, Emma. We might get to the staff party after all if they can pull us out of this drift.'

At that moment a voice could be heard across the divide between the two vehicles.

'Are you folks OK?' a voice called. 'The ambulance crew phoned to say you might have problems getting back to civilisation, so we're here to clear the way for you to drive back to Glenminster.'

'Yes, we're fine,' Glenn told them. 'But the drifts around the car were getting a bit worrying, so the sooner you can get us moving again the more grateful we will be. We're so thankful for your help. Where have you come from?'

'We're from a farm not far away,' was the reply. 'The police and local council know I have one of these things and we have an arrangement that I come out to tow folks like you out of the drifts.' The young guy seated beside him jumped down onto the snow with ropes in his hands and attached them to the front of Glenn's car. 'This is my son. He knows what he's doing. We'll soon have you free and on your way.' When the car suddenly lurched forward onto level ground they knew that it wasn't a vain promise.

As he thanked them before moving slowly onto the main road that would take them back to the town Glenn said, 'If ever I can do you a favour you have only to ask.'

The farmer laughed from high up on the driving seat of the snow plough and said, 'I could do with something for my indigestion.'

'So shall we see you at the surgery on Monday morning, then?' Glenn grinned.

'You might,' was the reply as the man went trundling off into the distance.

On the way back Glenn was silent. Emma wondered if he was already regretting those moments when they'd been so close, surrounded by drifting snow with the moment to themselves. As if he sensed her thoughts he said, 'That wasn't the best drive back, was it?'

Stung, she replied, 'I thought that some of it was very pleasant.'

'Yes, maybe,' he said, 'but circumstances can sometimes create illusions that are not meant to be.'

Her house had come into sight and when Glenn stopped the car outside he said, 'So are you going to the party? There is still time. I'm going as I have no choice. As head of the practice I have to keep putting in an appearance at these sorts of things, but I don't intend to stay long.'

'Yes, I'm going,' she told him. 'I was looking forward to it, but suddenly it has become a chore.' She felt like telling him that she'd bought a special dress for the occasion, but wouldn't be wearing it after the way he'd put the dampener on those magical moments in the car.

'That's good, then,' he said, ignoring her downbeat comment.

Without her there the event would mean nothing to him in spite the downturn in his mood.

As Emma watched him drive off into the night the memory of being in his arms on the back seat of the car was warming her blood, bringing desire again into the moment.

Yet how crazy had that been, acknowledging their attraction to each other at such a time. The memory came to mind of the Sunday morning when she'd gone to his house to thank him for all that he had done in preparation for her arrival and had asked if he lived alone.

'Yes, I do,' he'd told her, and had sent her on her way with the feeling that he was a loner and preferred it that way. Since then she had got to know him better and, knowing that he had lost his wife in the most awful circumstances, she decided if she let herself fall in love with a man who still lived in the past she must be crazy.

By the time Lydia arrived to pick her up, Emma had changed her mind about the dress. She would wear it after all. Whatever Glenn thought of their relationship, there was no call for her to dress down because he wasn't interested in her. She owed it to herself, if no one else, and was determined to enjoy the evening no matter what.

Glenn's spirits rose as he caught his first glimpse of her coming out of the cloakroom, having dispensed with her warm winter coat. How could he not want her? Emma was special, dark-haired with smooth creamy skin, curves in all the right places, and tonight she looked bewitching in a black dress with silver trimmings. So why couldn't he tell her he was sorry about what he'd said on the way home from the farm? Why couldn't he give them both a chance to get to know one another better?

Yet Glenn found he couldn't. As their glances held he turned away and went to chat to other staff members who didn't have the same effect on him as Emma did. As the evening progressed his only communication with her was to ask briefly if she was all right after the snow hazard they'd encountered. Emma's brief response that she was fine gave him no further encouragement, so he left her chatting to James and wished him miles away.

Glenn got up to leave after the meal and to say goodbye to Lydia and Emma, who were seated nearby. 'Why are you going so soon?' Lydia asked.

'It's been a long day,' he said, his smooth tone covering up his turbulent feelings. 'Has Emma told you we had to be rescued from a snowdrift by a local farmer and his son in their snow plough?'

'Er…no,' Lydia replied, and he smiled tightly.

'Maybe you didn't think it worth mentioning,' he said, turning to where Emma was sitting.

'Some parts of it were and some weren't,' she told him quietly, intent on not revealing the hurt of his comments on the way home.

'Ah, yes,' he said, and looked deep into her eyes. 'I'm sorry if I offended you, Emma.'

'It's forgotten,' she said, and wished it was true. But she *had* felt hurt and there was no way she wanted that to become common knowledge.

Glenn left then, striding purposefully towards the door. Heads turned at the sight of his looks and stature and Emma swallowed hard. His leaving felt like another rebuke in her empty life and she wished she had stayed at home and planned the alterations to her house instead.

'What have you done to upset Glenn?' Lydia asked curiously, breaking into her thoughts.

'Nothing at all,' she said tightly, and added, in a moment of sheer misery, 'Why does no one ever want me, Lydia? First there was my unknown father, who can't have wanted either my mother or me, then Jeremy told me to leave, and now Glenn, who I admire and respect, wants me to keep my distance.'

'I don't know about the rest of it,' Lydia said comfortingly, 'but for some reason Glenn has no wish to settle down, which is a shame because I've never seen him look at any other member of our sex like he looks at you. Try not to be too sad, Emma.'

As she listened to what Lydia had to say she remembered Glenn confiding in her about how he had lost his wife and requesting her not to discuss it with anyone. She couldn't tell Lydia what she knew so without further comment, when James appeared at her side once more she excused herself and let him take her onto the dance floor just once more. Then she rang for a taxi.

On the way home she did a foolish thing. Instead of letting the taxi driver take her straight home, Emma asked him to drop her off beside the church and beneath the light of a full moon made her way towards the grave, curious to see if any more flowers had been left there.

As she drew nearer she saw someone standing motionless beside it and increased her pace. But by the time she got there whoever it was had gone and as the quiet night surrounded her once again she looked down at the grave and they were there again, flowers from someone who must have known her mother.

As Emma walked the short distance to her dismal home she wished that Glenn was by her side and for once her wish was granted. He pulled up beside her from nowhere and without speaking opened the car door for her to get in.

Once she was seated he asked, 'Emma, what happened to the taxi that you set off for home in? Lydia rang me to say that you had left the party early too and she was worried about you. So I went round to your place to make sure you were safe and found it in darkness.'

'Yes, I know,' she admitted meekly. 'It was a crazy thing to do but as the taxi was about to go past the church I had a sudden urge to check if any more flowers had been put on the grave. So I paid the driver and went to see.'

'And?' he questioned.

'There was someone standing beside it in the moonlight, Glenn, but by the time I was near enough to see them clearly they'd gone. When I looked down fresh flowers had been put in the vases.'

'And did you have time to see what gender this person was?' he asked. 'It's unlikely a woman would be found in a churchyard after dark.'

'No,' she told him. 'It is as I said. They'd gone

by the time I got to the grave. Maybe they heard my footsteps on the flagged path.'

'Has it made you nervous?'

'A bit, I suppose, but it was my own fault.'

The car was already pointing in the direction of Glenn's house. Emma sat bolt upright in shock when he suddenly said, 'I'm going to take you to my place for the night. I never feel easy about you being in that house on your own after dark, and just in case the person in the graveyard saw you, or already knows where you live, we aren't going to take any chances.'

'Do you have a spare room?' she enquired faintly.

'Yes, of course I have! I've got two, as a matter fact, and you'll be quite safe in whichever one you prefer.'

'You know that I'll be green with envy while I'm inside your house, don't you?' she teased.

'There's no need to be,' he parried back. 'Like they say, a home is where the heart is and mine is in a place far away.'

Glenn watched the light go out of her eyes and the colour drain from her face and wished he hadn't been so clumsy.

You are crazy to have brought her here, he told himself as he put his key in the lock when they arrived at the converted barn that appealed to her so much. Especially after the way the two of you were up there in the snowdrift. She's beautiful and kind. For pity's sake, don't hurt her because you've been hurt. Emma has had enough sadness in her life already. Don't get involved in promising her something that you aren't able to give.

When he turned to face her, though, he was smiling, and as she observed him questioningly he said, totally out of context, 'The dress is lovely, Emma. Just so right for your colouring. I intended telling you that at the party but the opportunity didn't present itself.' Unaware of what had been in his mind just a few moments ago, she asked a question that he would rather not have had to answer.

'What was your wife like, Glenn?' she asked, and his smile disappeared.

'I have her photograph in my bedroom. If you would like to see it I'll bring it down,' he volunteered.

'Only if you want to,' she told him. He went upstairs and brought the picture back, and as Emma observed the smiling golden-haired woman in the photograph she could understand his abiding affection for her. But if Glenn's wife had loved him as much as he loved her, surely she would have wanted him to find happiness again with the right person?

Her own track record of not being wanted meant that she certainly wasn't at the top of anyone's yearning-for list. She could only imagine that happening in her dreams.

Emma was unaware that Glenn was watching her, taking in her every expression. He felt full of tenderness for her, but someone like Emma deserved better than him. Despite that, as he listened to her

telling him gently that his wife had been very beautiful, for once he was more enraptured by a woman
other than Serena.

As Emma handed the photograph back to him
Glenn said, 'If you'd like to come upstairs I'll show
you the guest room. Feel free to get up whenever
you like in the morning. It's Sunday, so there's no
rush. Would you like a hot drink before you settle
for the night?'

'Er...no, thanks,' she replied. 'I had plenty to
eat and drink at the party. Glenn, I'm sorry that
I've caused you concern by my actions. It was stupid of me to go into the churchyard at that hour. I
don't know what possessed me,' she added guiltily.
'I won't stay for breakfast. I'll leave early so as not
to cause further disruption of your organised life,
and see you back at the practice on Monday.'

'I don't think so,' he said. 'Breakfast is part of
the arrangement of you sleeping safe and sound beneath my roof for once.'

It had been a long day and Emma was tired, but sleep
was evading her because the events of the day had
been so strange. It seemed unbelievable to her that
Glenn could be sleeping only feet away in the master
bedroom of his converted barn. His last comment
before he'd closed the door had been to tell her she
would find a selection of nightwear in the dressing-
table drawers.

And now wearing a long chaste-looking nightdress of white cotton that seemed more like something that belonged to his mother than Glenn's cherished wife, Emma was sleepless still because the very idea of being so near yet so far from him in every other way during the night hours was incredible. And in the morning there would be joy in her heart when she went downstairs and he was there.

Glenn's bedroom door was wide open when Emma sallied forth fully dressed the next morning and she smiled at the thought of seeing him. It would be just two people getting to know each other, sharing their different joys and sorrows, she thought, and what could be wrong with that?

What *was* wrong with it was that Glenn was nowhere to be seen anywhere in the house. She went from room to room with the minutes ticking by, but there was no sign of him. There was no kettle boiling or bacon sizzling to create a breakfast atmosphere.

Outside, the drive and gardens were also deserted, and Glenn's car was nowhere to be seen. The only thing that *was* of interest were brochures about holidaying in Italy on the hall table, and she wondered if Glenn was planning a trip abroad.

Surely he hadn't already gone and in a rush to be off had forgotten she was there from the night before? It would fit in with how she saw herself as someone of little importance.

Though why should she be so quick to expect that he had left her like that? Glenn was thoughtful and caring. But annoyance was building up inside her and in her confusion she was hurting because he had insisted on her staying the night and now he was gone and she didn't know where.

Reaching for her topcoat hanging up in the hall, Emma gathered the few belongings that she'd had with her from the staff party. Two could play at that game, she thought tearfully and stepped out onto the drive, intending to make her way home on foot. Only to be brought to a halt when Glenn's car appeared. Within a matter of seconds he was out of it and observing her with a questioning smile that was the final irritation of the morning.

'I'm sorry, Emma,' he said. 'You must think me very rude to have been missing when you came down for breakfast.' She observed him in chilly silence. 'I got my timing wrong, I'm afraid. My mother phoned me before daybreak to say that Dad wasn't well. He's got some sort of throat infection and has a temperature, so she asked me to go and examine him.

'As there is rarely anything serious when they ring me on these occasions I went straight away, without disturbing you or leaving a message. I expected to be back within a very short time, only to get there and find him unwell with what seems like tonsillitis.

'So I had to write out a prescription and go and pick it up at an all-night chemist. I have promised to call again later. Could I persuade you to come back inside for some breakfast?'

She didn't say yes or no, just asked tightly, 'So why didn't you wake me up or leave a note? I would have been only too willing to have gone with you and done anything to help that I could.'

'What, after the day that you'd had?' he protested. 'Being insulted by that insolent Walsh fellow at the farm, and then caught in a snowdrift, followed by enduring my miserable comments on the way home?

'I scare myself sometimes when reality hits me. It takes me out of my safe cocoon and reminds me that life has to go on, that I'm not the only one who lost someone they loved on that dreadful occasion.'

He took her hand and drew her gently towards the door, wide open behind her, and once they were inside he unbuttoned her coat, slipped it off her shoulders and, holding her close, asked, 'So what would madam like for breakfast?'

'I'm not hungry,' she told him, stiffening in his arms. She wasn't hungry, for food anyway, reassurance maybe, and Glenn was offering a plateful of that.

'I can't believe it,' he said gently, and planted a butterfly kiss on her cheek. 'How about that for starters, followed by food, glorious food?'

She was smiling now, the feeling of being left out in the cold disappearing, and when they'd eaten and she'd helped him tidy the kitchen Emma went with Glenn to visit his parents. She envied him the closeness of his small family.

If there was just one person *she* could call family and give her love and affection to now that her mother was gone, she would be content. But there was no one.

'You are so lucky to have your parents still with you,' she told Glenn as he drove her home in the quiet Sunday morning. 'I lost my mother some years ago and Jeremy wanted me gone as soon as he found someone to replace her.'

Glenn didn't comment but rage swept over him in a hot tide at the thought of what Jeremy had done to Emma. It wasn't surprising he'd been desperate to go to his maker with a clean slate. As far as Glenn was concerned, the man had done him a favour by asking him to find her, wherever she might be.

But his attraction to Emma was something new in his life and he was going to have to decide where he was going from this moment in time. Glenn would have liked to have spent the rest of the day with her, but once he had satisfied himself regarding his father's condition Emma had explained that she was expecting the builder to call with regard to the alterations she was planning and wanted to be there when he arrived.

'So, until tomorrow at the practice,' Glenn said, as he braked the car in front of her house, and with colour rising Emma thanked him for his hospitality, kissed him lightly on the cheek and was gone, leaving him to go back to make sure that his father really was improving with the touch of her lips against his skin feeling like a combination of a promise and a goodbye.

The patient *was* feeling better, his temperature was down, the inflammation in his throat reducing. Typically Jonas was now in a more upward mood with his thoughts turning to the event he was planning for the old and lonely on Christmas Day and wanting to know if Emma was still available to keep her promise of assisting.

'Yes, as far as I know,' Glenn told him. 'The surgery will be closed so she should be free, unless she has changed her mind.'

'And is she still going to dine with us in the evening?' his mother questioned.

'I suppose the same applies,' he said dryly, and left it at that, knowing that if Emma kept her promise and came to eat with them as arranged, whatever else there was between them it would be the best Christmas he'd had since he'd lost Serena. Which led him to wonder how was he going to make her aware of his feelings. He wanted to, needed to, because if nothing ever came of their attraction to each other, at least she had brought some joy into his empty life.

It was Monday morning and Emma was feeling miserable because the builder's quote for her requirements had been far above what she could afford, but she was excited about something else.

She'd noticed during her stay at Glenn's house that the one next to his was for sale and she'd gone home with an idea. It was of a similar design, though smaller, but just as attractive, and when the builder had left without an order Emma had rung the estate agents who were handling the sale and had discovered that it would cost less to buy it than do the extensive amount of work that her own property would need.

With excitement mounting, she'd asked the estate agents if they would be interested in selling hers as well. If things worked out, she hoped she would be able to buy the house next to Glenn's, which was empty at present.

It would be heavenly to live in a place like that. She'd been unable to stop thinking about it for what was left of the weekend. But would she be able to sell her own monstrosity? And, more importantly, would Glenn want her as a neighbour?

'How did you find your father when you checked on him again yesterday?' was Emma's first comment when they met up on Monday morning in the passage outside their respective consulting rooms.

'Much better,' Glenn replied. 'And to prove it he was asking if you are still available to help with his Christmas Day event. My mother also wanted to know if you will be joining us as planned later in the evening.'

'The answer to both those questions is yes,' said Emma. 'I'm looking forward to both very much.'

'How did you fare with the builder?' he wanted to know, concealing the pleasure that her reply had given him. 'Did he go away with a big order?' When she shook her head Glenn asked in surprise, 'Why ever not? I thought you were all set for a big face-lift for your house?'

'His quote was too high,' Emma explained, 'and I've had a change of plan over the weekend.'

'Meaning what?'

'I've put my house up for sale and I'm going to buy the one next to yours if it is still on the market when I've sold mine.'

'I see,' he said in a monotone. 'And where has that idea originated from?'

'I've liked where you live from the word go, and something small but similar would be just right for my requirements.'

'And what if yours is still unsold when a buyer turns up for the one next to mine?' he asked in the same flat tone. 'What do you do then?'

'I'll worry about that when and if it happens,' Emma said, and called in her first patient of the day without further discussion.

CHAPTER SIX

EMMA'S FIRST PATIENT the next day was Anna Marsden, who had been in recently for her yearly checkup and was now back to have a chat about the results.

Newly retired from the position of manageress of Glenminster's largest womenswear boutique, Anna and her husband had been looking forward to a stress-free retirement. So Emma was not relishing having to let her know that the tests had shown that Anna had a type of blood clotting that showed signs of leukaemia and was going to need further investigation and treatment.

Anna's reaction to the news was typical of her. She listened to what Emma had to say and then responded calmly, 'Where do I go from here?'

'You have an appointment next Monday at the hospital,' Emma told her. 'Once you've chatted to the doctors there, you will have a clearer idea of what is involved.'

The woman seated across from her in the small consulting room smiled a twisted smile. 'Yes, of course, and at least I'll be able to have a lie-in when I feel like it now that I'm retired.'

When Anna left, the morning took its usual course of a steady flow of the sick and suffering coming and going. It gave Emma no time to question Glenn's reaction to the possibility that she might one day be living in the house next to his.

But in the lunch hour when Emma had a moment to spare and think about it properly, it became clear to her that although they'd spent some quality time together over the weekend he was still living in the past. There was no way she wanted to be in the background, chipping away at his love for the wife he had lost.

Yet it wasn't going to stop her from buying the house next to his if the opportunity presented itself. If Glenn was going to resent having her so near in his free time as well as being around constantly at the practice she would just have to accept the fact and get on with her life.

Glenn had just returned from visiting a patient who lived at the other end of the church graveyard from where the practice was. He popped in to inform her briefly that while there had been no sign of anyone hanging around the grave in the light of day, there had been fresh roses in one of the vases. Emma's niggling feeling of unease came flooding back.

With Christmas just a week away and her rash promise to spend some of the time with Glenn and his family hanging over her, Emma went to shop for the event on her way home that evening with little enthusiasm. She would be dining on one of the special nights of the year with people she hardly knew and could see it being an ordeal.

The daytime activity she'd volunteered for was different because she would be doing something useful in helping Glenn's father to bring some light into the darkness of other folks' lives. She wondered what his son would be doing while they were so employed. Putting up a fence between his house and the one next door?

Jonas had asked her if she could be at the community hall in the town centre for eight o'clock on the morning of Christmas Day as there were turkeys to be cooked in its spacious kitchens, along with all the other trappings. Within minutes of arriving Emma was at work along with a group of other volunteers who were mostly known to her from the practice, plus a couple of strangers. Glenn's father introduced her to one of them. His name was Alex Mowbray and he had lived in Glenminster many years ago before going to live abroad with his sick wife.

'I never wanted to leave this place,' Alex said, 'but my wife had a long-term serious illness. She wanted to move where it was warmer so I had no choice but to take her to live abroad.

'She died recently and my yearning to come back to Glenminster clocked in. So here I am, getting to know old friends who are still around and remembering with sadness those who are not.'

He seemed a decent sort, Emma thought as Alex Mowbray went back to his allotted task of preparing the vegetables that would be served with the turkey. Tall, with silver hair and kind blue eyes, he was easy to talk to, which was more than she could say for the man she was falling in love with. When she looked up, Glenn was there, having just arrived with a carload of provisions for the meal and an overwhelming urge to be near her.

So he wasn't going to be shut away in his castle for the day, like she'd expected, Emma thought joyfully. For at least part of the time he would be where she could see him.

Having unloaded the produce he'd brought, Glenn was beside Emma in a flash, smiling at the chef's hat she was wearing and asking if she was all set for the evening.

'Yes, if you still want me there,' she said. 'You didn't seem enthralled when I told you that I might be coming to live in the house next to yours.'

'That was merely the surprise,' he protested, 'and also because I don't take well to my secluded life being invaded.' It didn't seem like the moment to tell Emma that he wanted her living with him in his house, not in the small dwelling next to it.

Glenn looked around him. 'Dad is beckoning. He's going to tell me not to interfere with the workers. I'd better be off as I'm in charge of making sure that anyone unable to walk has transport to get here, which is going to involve half the practice staff making their cars available.'

'And I thought that you wouldn't be getting drawn into today's event,' she teased.

'What! With a father like mine?' He laughed and was gone again, leaving Emma to observe his father and Alex, who had appeared in their midst, chatting amicably as they performed their chosen tasks. Meanwhile Glenn and whoever was available from the practice staff were organising the transport that was going to be needed.

It was almost time for lunch and the kitchen staff were taking a short break before the diners arrived when Glenn's father informed Emma that he had invited their new acquaintance to dine with them that evening.

'Alex Mowbray lives alone,' he said, 'and that shouldn't happen to anyone at this time of year, so I've invited him to join us tonight.'

'Have you told your wife?' Emma teased, and he smiled.

'Yes, but she knows what I'm like. Olivia would be surprised if I *hadn't* invited someone else as well as you.'

'Is Glenn going to be happy, having me there?' she asked haltingly. 'I'm tuned in to how much he cherishes his privacy.'

'It has been difficult for him since he lost

Serena,' his father said, 'especially in such a dreadful way. May I be allowed to say that since he brought you back to Glenminster out of nowhere, his mother and I have begun to hope.'

'I don't think you should if you don't mind me saying so,' Emma told him. 'We get on well most of the time, but the barriers that Glenn lives behind are not going to come down with me, I'm afraid.'

Glenn appeared at that moment with an elderly couple that he'd driven to the community hall and cast a quick glance at his father and Emma in a deep discussion that tailed off while he was finding seats for his passengers.

When Glenn had done that, he turned to go for his next lot of guests and found Emma beside him, smiling her pleasure at being near him again.

'So how many more journeys do you have to make?' she asked, and there was no smile in return.

'Just a couple,' Glenn replied, and then said, 'I hope that there's a table set for all the kind folk who have been doing the chauffeuring at my request.'

'Yes, of course,' she assured him, 'and tonight your parents will have another stranger at their table. Your father has also invited Alex Mowbray, who has recently returned from abroad after many years away.'

'Fine,' he said, and was off to pick up the last of the guests without giving her time to reply.

After the Christmas dinner was over, the guests had departed and the volunteers had tidied the place up, Emma began the short walk home. She hadn't wanted to take up a parking space, which would be in big demand, at the community hall so she'd walked there earlier. She could have waited for a lift from Glenn but along with the other car drivers he was busy taking guests home, while his father had gone to take the hall keys back.

Emma had only been on the way a matter of minutes when Alex's car pulled up beside her. Winding the window down, he asked, 'Can I give you a lift?'

'Er…yes, if it won't be out of your way, Mr Mowbray,' she said, deciding she'd like to get to know this amiable stranger better. 'I live just a short distance down the road.'

As she settled herself in the passenger seat next to him he said, 'So you'll know Waverly House, then?'

'Yes, I do,' she told him. 'It is a beautiful old property.'

'Yes, indeed,' Alex agreed. 'It was where my wife and I lived before we moved abroad and I have gained much comfort in finding it for sale and bringing it back to its former glory. Although sadly there will be no one for me to leave it to as we were never able to have children because of her health problems.'

What a charming man, Emma thought as she thanked him for the lift and went to prepare for the day's next big event. This time it would be Glenn who would be driving her to her destination and as she showered and dressed for the occasion the promise of the evening ahead was like a precious Christmas gift, probably the only one she was likely to receive.

But that didn't matter as long as Glenn liked what she had bought for him. She would never forget as long as she lived how he had painstakingly found her and persuaded her to come home. She could scarcely believe he was now the centre of her universe.

Glenn had said he would call for her at seven o'clock and as the clock climbed slowly towards that time every moment felt magical. Until it went past seven, then eight, and was teetering on nine. He must have had better things to do and had changed his mind about picking her up she thought dejectedly.

The phone rang at last and her heart skipped a beat when she heard Glenn's voice. 'I am so sorry, Emma,' he said contritely. 'I was involved in a pile-up as I was leaving the town centre.'

Her heart missed a beat. 'Are you hurt?' she gasped.

'No. I just had to help treat the casualties, who are now safely in A and E. I should be with you in minutes so don't run away.'

'Does your mother know?' Emma asked.

'Yes. She's been holding the meal back but is now ready to serve when we put in an appearance. I couldn't get in touch with you earlier as the accident occurred on the bottom road and I couldn't get a signal. We had to drive the casualties ourselves until we were higher up and then ambulances came speeding out to them. All the time I kept thinking that you would be judging me as yet another person letting you down. Tell me truthfully, did you?'

'Er...yes,' Emma said with painful honesty, 'because I know that in spite of our friendship you prefer to be alone, and I do understand that, Glenn.'

There was silence for a moment and then he said, 'I'll be with you in a matter of minutes—and be prepared. Dad is going to be wearing his Father Christmas outfit.'

As she watched for his car Emma felt ashamed for being so quick to judge him. She knew Glenn was decent and honourable and she loved him, she thought glumly. But the chances of her love being returned were not evenly balanced.

Glenn was as good as his word and his car pulled up outside within a matter of minutes. Emma saw immediately that what must have been a smart suit was ripped and bloodstained, but he was unharmed. In her relief at seeing that he wasn't hurt she leaned across the passenger seat and kissed his grimy cheek. 'Please, forgive me for doubting you,' she said softly.

'Of course,' Glenn said, reflecting that if he wasn't so scruffy and if his parents weren't patiently waiting for them to arrive, he might stop the car and show Emma how much she affected him. Within minutes they were pulling up outside his parents' house.

'Helping in an emergency such as tonight's is the

penalty of being a doctor,' Glenn said, as his mother held him close for a moment.

Alex nodded his agreement.

Glenn's father was helping Emma to take off her coat and when it was done he kissed her cheek lightly beneath the mistletoe and she felt tears prick her eyes.

They were a lovely family, she thought wistfully. What a shame that their daughter-in-law hadn't lived to give them grandchildren.

Glenn had disappeared in the direction of the bathroom and minutes later he appeared scrubbed and clean in casual clothes. They sat down to eat with a small gift from their hostess beside each plate, leaving Emma to wonder when she would get the chance to give Glenn what she had bought for him.

It came when the meal was over and the two of them were clearing away while the older folks relaxed after their exertions of the day in front of the sitting-room fire.

'I have something for you, Glenn,' she said awkwardly. He looked at her questioningly, and she said, 'Christmas seems an appropriate occasion to show my gratitude for all that you have done for me.' Taking a small gift-wrapped box out of her handbag, she offered it to him.

Glenn didn't accept it at first, leaving her standing with it in her hand. After a moment's silence he took it from her and said in a low voice, 'Whatever it is that you want to give me there is no need, Emma. What I did for you I would have done for anyone.'

'Yes. I know,' she said, feeling hurt that he had put her in her place. 'If you don't want to accept it, fine. The gift doesn't carry with it any commitments, just my grateful thanks.' She left him with the small package unopened in his hand and went to join the others, the question uppermost in her mind being how soon she could go home without causing offence.

When she'd gone back into the lounge Glenn groaned at his tactlessness. Why couldn't he have explained to Emma that he couldn't bear the thought of hurting her at some time or other by letting his dedication to Serena's memory come between them?

He had something for her that he was going to present in privacy tomorrow. He had already asked Emma out to lunch and he wanted to put his present where it belonged on her finger. But he knew that their relationship was not the usual kind and had no idea how she would react when she saw his gift.

When Glenn removed the wrappings and Emma's gift was revealed he swallowed hard. It was a gold pocket watch. He had admired a similar one belonging to a patient and Emma had remembered.

He opened the sitting-room door and when she looked up he beckoned to her. Unobserved by the others, who were engrossed in a carol service on television, she went to join him in the hall.

Taking her hand in his, he said softly, 'Your gift

is lovely, Emma. I am a tactless clod.' Pointing to the mistletoe sprig above their heads, he bent and kissed her long and lingeringly. He would have continued to do so if he hadn't heard movement coming from the sitting room because the programme they had been watching had come to an end.

Opening the door, Glenn smiled at them and said, 'Anyone for coffee?'

'Not for me, thanks,' Alex said. 'I came on foot and don't want to be too late getting back.'

'I'll be taking Emma home shortly,' Glenn said, 'and could drop you off after I've seen her safely home.'

Alex smiled. 'In that case, a coffee would be most acceptable.' And Emma thought, So much for the kiss. Apart from the time spent in the kitchen clearing up after the meal and the magical moments in the hall when Glenn had kissed her, they hadn't been alone for a moment all day. And now he was making sure they weren't by taking her home first.

There was the dry taste of anguish in her mouth, but pride stiffened her resolve and when Alex asked if that would be all right with her Emma flashed him a smile and said, 'Yes, of course.' And the matter was settled.

The fact that Glenn had spent no thought with regard to a Christmas gift for her was immaterial. Emma hadn't given him the watch expecting something in return. But it couldn't help bringing back that feeling of being of no importance, which had never gone away since the night Jeremy had told her she wasn't his and he wanted her gone.

They were outside her house and as she opened the car door and stepped onto the drive Glenn went round to her side and said in a low voice, 'It's late. I want to see you safely inside before I go. Emma, the reason I'm dropping you off first is because I want to know more about this stranger who has appeared out of nowhere. You have lived here a lot longer than I have, yet he isn't familiar to you, is he?'

'No, but Glenminster is a town, not a village where folks are much more likely to know each other,' she said. 'And from what Alex says, he has been long gone from here.' She glanced across to where he was waiting patiently for Glenn to get behind the steering-wheel again. 'All I know is that he seems a really nice man, and that he's rebought the house he used to live in and has refurbished it. It's a dream of a place.'

Emma instantly mellowed and, smiling at Glenn, said, 'I will be ready at twelve, as requested.' As the door closed behind her he got back into the car and drove off with his mind full of questions that had no answers.

When Glenn came for her the next day Emma was wearing the white fake-fur jacket and turquoise dress that she'd appeared in on that first night when everyone from the practice had welcomed her back to

Glenminster. His heartbeat quickened at the thought of what he was going to say to her over lunch.

'So what did you find out about Alex Mowbray?' she asked, when they were seated at the table that had been reserved for them in the Barrington Bar.

'Not a lot,' Glenn said. 'Except that he is a really nice guy who kept the faith with a sick wife but always wanted to come back here if the opportunity arose.'

'Do you know what was wrong with her?' asked Emma.

'Yes, advanced Parkinson's disease, which, as we both know, is an illness that doesn't carry with it an early death. The years must have crept by before he was able to come back to the place he loved best. But I didn't bring you here to talk about Alex,' he said with a change of subject. Now it was Glenn's turn to produce a small gift-wrapped box, which he put on the table in front of her.

'I know you must have thought me mean for not having a gift for you yesterday,' he explained, 'but I couldn't give you this then as what I have to ask you is private and very personal.' She sat watching him, transfixed by the moment, and he said, 'Maybe you would like to unwrap it to understand me better.'

'Yes, of course,' croaked Emma. She went weak at the knees when she saw that resting in a small velvet box was a solitaire diamond ring. It has happened at last, she thought joyfully. He wants me, he loves me. I can't believe it!

His next comment brought her back down to earth. 'I may never be able to be to you what you want me to be,' Glenn said gravely. 'To be totally committed I would have to give myself to you whole-heartedly, and I can't guarantee that I can do that by shutting Serena out of my life. So would you accept second best? I care for you a lot, Emma, I really do. And maybe one day I can be the way you want me to be.'

'No,' she breathed, and watched him flinch. 'I've had enough of being second best. I want to be with a man who will cherish me and who I can love in return, without making do with what is on offer. I only want your ring on my finger because you can't live without me and if that isn't so I will do without.'

Emma was getting to her feet and picking up her belongings, desperate to escape from the awful moment of humiliation. When she'd collected her coat from the cloakroom she went into the foyer and flagged down a passing taxi to take her home, leaving Glenn to stare stonily at the ring she had cast aside.

Lying on top of the bed covers, gazing blankly up at the ceiling, Emma heard Glenn's car pull up in the drive below and turned her face into the pillows to deaden the sound of the doorbell when it rang. It continued for some minutes and then stopped, and she heard him drive off into the afternoon. When she went onto the landing and looked down into the hallway the box with the ring inside was lying on the doormat. It was then that the tears came as she went down slowly, picked it up, and without opening it again placed it in a nearby drawer.

When Glenn's father was driving past Glenn's house in the late afternoon he saw his son's car parked outside so stopped to have a chat. 'Where's Emma?' he asked in surprise. 'We thought that you weren't coming to us today because you had plans to spend it with her.'

'Yes, I did,' said Glenn, 'but it would seem that I presumed too much and she doesn't want my company.'

'I see,' Jonas replied, and asked disappointedly, 'What makes you think that?'

'I was a tactless fool, expecting too much of her,' Glenn replied bleakly, 'wanting what was best for me instead of her, and she refused.'

'Serena loved you,' his father said. 'Do you honestly think she would want you to cut yourself off from finding love again because she was taken?'

'Probably not,' Glenn agreed, 'but I still feel guilty because she wanted us to holiday somewhere else for a change, and I preferred to go to our usual place. She only went along with it to please me.'

'Yes, but you weren't to know that a tsunami was on its way that day,' Jonas protested.

'There is no answer to any of it,' Glenn replied.

'We've been through this discussion too often. I'll be fine here, getting some paperwork done, and will pop round for a bit later on if that's all right.'

'You know it is,' his father said. 'You've fed me often enough when your mother has had her fill of me. So we'll see you later, unless you've made friends with Emma again in the meantime.'

As if! Glenn thought bleakly. Emma brought out all his protective instincts one moment and the next stirred the heat of desire in him, and he wasn't getting any of it right.

When his father had gone Glenn left what he'd been doing and went for a brisk walk in the winter afternoon. He met Alex, doing the same thing. When he saw him Alex hailed him in his usual friendly manner and Glenn said, 'Are you looking forward to spending New Year in Glenminster?'

'You bet I am,' Alex said. 'I've wanted that for years. I was never able to come back to my roots until my wife passed away. I always had many precious memories of this place but it isn't the same as actually being here.'

'And I'm just the opposite,' Glenn told him. 'My memories are all in a faraway place and the last of them is not good.'

Having turned the screw on his heartstrings once again, Glenn went on his way with the thought that, like Alex, Emma was delighted to be back in their homeland, despite the gloomy nature of her return.

* * *

Unlike the two men, Emma was huddled beside the fire in her dismal sitting room with no inclination to move. The phone rang and Lydia's bright and cheerful voice came over the line.

'How are you fixed for coming to join me and mine for supper this evening?' she asked, and into the silence that followed she continued, 'I have visitors with me, relatives on holiday from Canada who have called unexpectedly, and I could do with some support.'

'Er...yes, I'm free tonight,' Emma told her reluctantly. 'What time do you want me there?'

'Seven o'clock, if that's all right,' Lydia replied.

'Yes, no problem,' she agreed, trying to sound enthusiastic.

When Lydia went on to say that she'd been trying to get in touch with Glenn to invite him round to give the occasion some support it was a relief for Emma to hear that she hadn't been able to contact him. The events of earlier in the day were still like a knife thrust in her heart.

Asked if she'd seen anything of Glenn, it hurt to admit that they'd met briefly at midday, but she had no idea what his plans were for the rest of it. With a sinking feeling inside she said goodbye to her friend and wondered where she was going to find the zest to socialise with Lydia's relatives.

CHAPTER SEVEN

WHEN GLENN RETURNED from his cheerless walk he found a message from Lydia awaiting him, and his reaction to it was the same as Emma's. The last thing he wanted to do was chat to strangers but Lydia was a tower of strength at the practice and a good friend so he didn't want to let her down.

The least he could do was help her to entertain her visitors and if Emma was there it would be a bonus. Even if she didn't want to have anything to do with him, just to be able to see her would help to lessen the nightmare he had managed to create for himself in the season of goodwill.

Emma was the first person Glenn saw when he arrived at Lydia's home. She was looking pale but composed with a wintry smile for him when he greeted her, which was in keeping with the weather outside and the misery he was experiencing inside being near her again.

What had she done with the ring? he wondered.

She'd put it with the rubbish in the waste bin most likely. Someone at the waste-disposal place might get a pleasant surprise, and if they did, good for them, as Glenn didn't want to see a reminder of his big mistake ever again.

He hoped and prayed that Emma wouldn't do a disappearing act again, as she'd done after Jeremy's hurtful treatment of her. He needed to be able to see her at the practice and around the place like he needed to breathe.

The Canadians were a pleasant lot, easy to get on with, and as the night progressed with a buffet that Lydia had arranged and lots of chatter Emma began to relax. At least the evening was proving to be a good opportunity for her to meet up with Glenn before seeing him at the practice when Christmas was over.

They had both walked the short distance to Lydia's house, thinking that driving wasn't a good idea if the wine was going to be flowing. At the first opportunity Glenn said to her in a low voice, 'No walking home alone, Emma. If you don't want me around, ring for a taxi.'

Emma nodded mutely as tiredness lay upon her like a heavy shawl after the day's events. There was no chance that she was going to opt for walking anywhere, she decided, and hoped that Lydia's guests might be feeling the same, having travelled quite some distance to see their hostess.

Yet it was midnight before the party was over and, doing as Glenn had suggested, Emma rang for a taxi. As it was the festive season there were long queues and it was going to be some time before her request was dealt with.

Glenn was observing her expression and guessed what the problem was. As they said goodbye to Lydia and her guests and went out into the night beneath a star-filled sky he said, 'You're going to have to let me walk you home, Emma.'

'I'll be fine on my own,' she told him flatly, and almost tripped over a tree root outside the house, but he caught her as she fell. As Glenn looked down at her in the circle of his arms he said, 'If you don't want me at your side on the way home I will be just a few paces behind you until you put the key in the door of your house. I will only leave you when you are safe inside. We still don't know the identity of the person who seems to have an endless supply of cream roses.'

As they set off, with Glenn walking a few paces behind, as promised, he said, 'There must have been other men in your mother's life, like the man who fathered you, for instance, and then disappeared.'

'If there were I never knew about them because I always thought that Jeremy was my father,' Emma said bleakly. 'And I had no reason to question it until that awful night when he put me straight and made me feel so unwanted.'

Glenn ached to hold her close, wanted to cradle

her to him instead of bringing up the rear, but after the dreadful mistake he'd made in showing Emma the ring and telling her she could only expect to be second best, hoping she could cope with that, he'd known that he had blown it with her. And rightly so, as far as she was concerned.

Glenn had said what he had because of the dread of not making Emma as happy, as she deserved, because in the dark corners of his mind there was always the memory of what had happened to Serena making him slow to make another commitment that he might fall down on. And yet it was Emma who was always the centre of his imaginings.

When they stopped at Emma's door she put the key in the lock and said meaningfully, 'You've seen me home safely, Glenn, and now my key is in the door.' She added, as it swung back on its hinges, 'So the only thing left to say is…goodnight!'

'Yes, all right, I get the message,' he said levelly. 'I just wanted to be honest with you, Emma, that's all.' He was striding off into the dark night when she called him back. When he turned round, Emma was standing holding the box, which she'd taken out of the drawer in the hall. 'You will need this when you find someone willing to accept second best,' she said tautly, giving it back to him. And as Glenn looked down at it bleakly, lying on the palm of his hand, the door was closed against him and Emma was walking slowly up the stairs to her lonely bed.

* * *

It was New Year's Eve and Emma was greeting the occasion with little enthusiasm. She had nothing planned and was intending to spend it alone in any case when the phone rang. It was Glenn's mother, to ask whether, if she wasn't booked to go anywhere, she would like to join them for supper as they welcomed in another year on the calendar.

When Olivia said that there would be just the three of them there—Jonas, Glenn and herself—the vision of Glenn insisting on her not going home alone came once again and she excused herself by pleading a headache and having an early night.

It didn't get her far. Olivia must have reported their conversation because minutes later Glenn was on the line, wanting to know if she had any medication for the headache, and if she didn't could he bring something round?

'I'll be fine,' she told him. 'I'm hugging a hot-water bottle and expect to be asleep in moments.' She knew that if he came round, and doctor that he was guessed that there was nothing wrong with her, it would be very hurtful for his parents. She liked them both a lot and didn't want to upset them.

'All right,' Glenn said. 'I don't expect you would have wanted to come in any case, but my parents aren't aware that we are not communicating so you will have to make allowances for them. They both set great store with the coming of a new year and are disappointed that you won't be there to share the moment with us. As far as the headache goes, if it starts to give you any problems I'll come round— *as a doctor, of course,*' was his parting comment, which left her feeling even more miserable.

Once the New Year was firmly established Emma didn't see much of anyone socially, except for Alex, who seemed to be the most agile out-and-about person amongst those who lived nearby. Emma had the feeling that the wanderer who had returned to Glenminster couldn't settle in his gracious house so she invited him round for coffee a couple of times.

Alex was an interesting person to talk to and she could imagine him being a loving father if ever he'd been blessed with children. Glenn would too, she mused ruefully. He had all the time in the world for the little ones who were brought to the practice by their parents with childish ailments.

Emma's closeness with Glenn had died after the business of the ill-fated proposal and although the days went by in a flash, the nights were long and lonely.

There had been a few viewers interested in her house. She had to show them round at weekends as her weekdays were swallowed up by the demands of her job. But she had received no offers for it so far. With the idea of living next door to Glenn no longer in her mind, she wasn't pushing for anything in particular yet she was still leaving her property on the market as daylight hours were becoming longer and

Easter was on the calendar. Soon those who sought a change of residence would be out and about.

Glenn observed her from a distance. At the practice Emma was still a dedicated doctor, putting her patients before anything else, but on the rare occasions when he saw her out of hours she had little to say and looked pale and remote. So much so that he wondered how long he could stand having to live with the evidence of how much he had hurt her.

Glenn cringed every time he thought back to his blundering proposal. It now seemed arrogant and hurtful, like a request for the best of both worlds. It also registered that she was seeing more of Alex Mowbray than him when she was away from the practice.

Yet Glenn was aware that sometimes young, insecure women often turned to older men for comfort and reassurance. Although the way that Emma had sent him packing didn't exactly indicate insecurity, more like outrage if anything.

The house next door to Glenn had been sold, but the board outside hers indicated no buyers as yet. Right now he would give anything for Emma to live near if he couldn't have her with him.

Flowers were still being placed on her mother's grave by an unknown hand and it seemed as if Emma was accepting the fact without further questioning. It was as if she was past caring. But Glenn wasn't prepared to let it rest at that. It was spooky and required an answer for Emma's sake, but short of him camping out in the churchyard it was almost as if the unknown visitor knew when to visit the grave and when not to.

And for Emma, who was all alone in the world—or at least didn't appear to have any other family—Glenn felt that if only he could bring a feeling of belonging into her life he would have done something to make up for his own lack of commitment.

Glenn was beginning to think of Serena less and Emma more but maybe that was because of the situation he found himself in: wanting Emma but afraid to give his heart to her completely and betray his love for his wife that he carried like a sacred torch.

There was one occasion when the flame of their attraction was ignited to fever pitch when Emma had driven to a hotel in the Gloucestershire hills to relieve the boredom of an empty weekend and Glenn was out walking with rucksack and walking boots for the same reason.

Easter would soon be upon them and with the awakening of plants and flowers and a pale sun above, the day had brought out those, like themselves, who loved the countryside.

Emma was about to order afternoon tea when his shadow fell across the table where she was seated out in the open, and he said gravely, 'Do you mind if I join you?'

'Er...no,' she said weakly, as the sight of him so near and unexpected made her blood warm and made her cheeks go pink.

A waitress was hovering to take their order and when that was done Glenn took the pack off his back and, facing her across the table, asked, 'So how are you, Emma? What brings you up here?'

She shrugged slender shoulders and told him, 'For the lack of anything else to do, I suppose. When the practice closed for the weekend at lunchtime I felt that I just had to get some fresh clean air after the long winter.'

'Me too,' Glenn agreed. 'Although I'm surprised not to find Alex with you. He told me once that he comes up here a lot to revive old memories, whatever they might be.'

'He's a lovely man,' she commented. 'But lonely, I feel. Alex once said that he came back because all his most precious memories are here. Whatever they might be, he was obviously happy in Glenminster, which is more than either of us can say, isn't it?'

As soon as she'd thrown that comment into the conversation Emma couldn't believe she'd said it. She'd given Glenn an opening for more aggravation and he was quick to respond.

'Which, I suppose, is my fault for being too faithful to the wife I lost?' he said, and got to his feet just as the waitress was bringing the food.

Emma felt the wetness of tears on her cheeks as he slung the bag he'd been carrying onto his back again and, leaving ample money on the table to pay for what they had ordered, set off back down the track on which he had come up.

She was on her feet, running after him. She caught up with him at the side of a deserted hayloft belonging to one of the farms. When Glenn turned to face her, Emma said breathlessly, 'Forgive me for my lack of understanding, Glenn, and for forgetting how you brought me back out of limbo. I will never forget that, no matter what.'

Her glance went to the hayloft, a close and sheltered place where they could be alone for a while. As if reading her mind, Glenn said, 'If ever I made love to you it would be on our wedding night, not in somewhere like that. Do you understand?'

'Yes, I do,' she said in a low voice. 'I understand perfectly and you have no idea how much it hurts to know how little chance there is of that.'

Glenn nodded and without speaking pointed himself homewards on the hillside, while she walked back to her car with dragging feet.

Following a miserable weekend that had seemed never-ending to Emma, they met again on Monday morning when she knocked on the door of his consulting room. After he opened it Emma said, before she choked on the words, 'I am sorry about what I said on Saturday, Glenn, and do hope you will forgive me.'

He reached out, took her hand in his, and pulled her into the room, closing the door behind her. 'There is nothing to forgive,' he said gently. 'I was too quick off the mark, Emma. But I have to tell

you that you would be better off with someone unlike me, whose heart and mind are free from pain
and sorrow.

'You are young and beautiful and deserve someone who isn't living in the past. It worries me that
you are so alone, without family, with just a few
friends. If we continue as we are doing one day you
will wish that you'd never met me, because all your
chances of happiness will be gone, lost in a relationship without roots, like your mother's was, from
what I can gather. Do you really have no idea at all
who your father was, or is? Have you ever seen your
birth certificate?'

'No,' she said. 'I've never had any need to look
for it, before now, and assumed Jeremy's name was
on it. But I can't find it anywhere, so maybe my real
father's name is included. I should get a copy and
see what comes to light.'

'Yes,' Glenn agreed. 'It can't do any harm. You
need to go to the register office where you were
born to apply for a copy. You will have to pay for it,
together with postage, on the spot. I'm told that it
doesn't take long to arrive.

'I'll come along to give you moral support if you
like and will be there for you when it arrives.' Then,
as the surgery doors were opened at that moment at
the start of another busy day, they separated, each
with a mind full of questions that needed answers.
And in the middle of it all Glenn prayed that the information Emma received from her birth certificate

would bring some degree of contentment into her life and help to take away the loneliness.

They went the next day in their lunch hour to the local register office to fill in the necessary paperwork for a copy of her birth certificate, and when they came out of the building Emma was smiling because, thanks to Glenn, hope had been born inside her. He pointed to a café across the road and said, 'How about a quick bite before we go back to the practice?'

'Yes, please,' she told him, and as they settled themselves at a table by the window Alex passed by on the other side of the street. He observed them and thought what a happy couple they made. He would have liked to go across and join them but didn't want to butt in and went on his way.

It was true. Emma had been happy on that day, just being with Glenn and knowing that soon one of the blank chapters of her life might be opened up to her. Her happiness lasted until the certificate she was waiting for arrived, with the information regarding her father described as 'unknown'.

It had been amongst her mail one morning and she had badly needed Glenn to hold onto for support. But he was missing from the practice that day, having to be present at the monthly meeting of senior medical staff in the town that was held in the board room of its biggest hospital. Without him the day seemed never-ending.

Glenn rang just as she was about to leave for home to see if she'd heard anything about her birth certificate. When she told him tearfully that she had, he told her to stay where she was at the practice, which was now empty as all the other staff had gone home. His meeting was over so he could be with her in minutes. Emma obeyed with the feeling that her life was keeping to its familiar pattern of emptiness.

When Glenn came striding in he held out his arms and Emma wept out her disappointment as he stroked her hair gently and asked, 'So what did it actually say?' As if he didn't know.

'It said "unknown",' she told him wearily, and as she looked up at him he bent and kissed her, gently at first and then with kisses that made her forget everything except that she was where she wanted to be.

When he released her from his hold and they locked up and went out into the dark street, it was as if the winter moon above was shining more brightly amongst a sky full of stars. Turning to her, Glenn asked softly, 'Shall we find somewhere to eat, Emma?'

'Yes,' she said, but when she looked up into his eyes she saw regret there and knew he was wishing they could be back to the way they had been before, which was not on kissing terms. Although there had been no lack of tenderness and desire while she'd been in his arms.

There was a restaurant not far away and Glenn steered her towards it, devastated that the thing that Emma so much needed to know hadn't been forthcoming. He was also cross with himself for allowing her to hope for something again.

'Would you like to stay at my place tonight?' he asked when they left the restaurant. 'I don't like to think of you all alone with such a disappointment to cope with.'

The offer was tempting, but there was no way that she wanted to be so close to him yet out of bounds, so reluctantly she said with a catch in her voice, 'Thanks for the offer, Glenn, but I'll be fine. I might do some searching around the house to see if there is anything that might guide me to who my father was. I doubt it, though, because the last thing that Jeremy said after taking the ground from under my feet was that my mother had never told him the name of the man who had made her pregnant. So I don't see her leaving any names or addresses around, do you?'

Glenn sighed. 'No, not really, I suppose, and are we really saying that she married Jeremy and put up with him for twenty-plus years so you would have a father?'

'Yes, it seems to have been that way,' said Emma sadly, 'and I never knew anything different until Jeremy enlightened me.'

'What did your mother die from, Emma?'

'She was frail, probably from unhappiness that she never let me see, and had a heart problem that culminated in a sudden serious heart attack one day. She was rushed to hospital but it was too late to save her, which left Jeremy and me to jog along as best we could with nothing at all in common.'

They had parked their cars not far from the place where they'd gone to order the birth certificate, and Glenn was only sorry that it had proved fruitless. There was nothing more to say, it was time to say goodbye, but he wasn't willing to give up on it. He said, 'If you don't want to stay at my place, shall I stay with you at yours?'

She flashed him a tired smile. 'No, I'll be fine. Don't worry about me.'

'All right,' he agreed. He couldn't blame her if she wanted to hold him at bay, but he still couldn't help feeling concerned. 'I'll go, but only if you promise that you will ring me if you need me at any time during the night, and that you will come to me for breakfast before we start at the practice. Otherwise I will come to your place to fetch you. Right? Understood?'

'Yes,' she replied. Despite her anxieties about their relationship, his concern on her behalf felt like healing balm. Feeling better, she drove off into the night.

Glenn stopped off at his parents' house on the way home and asked if either of them knew of anyone who might have had an affair with Emma's mother before she'd married Jeremy Chalmers.

They both looked at him blankly, and Jonas said, 'No, we don't. Emma's mum was local, while Jeremy came from somewhere near where she'd worked before Emma was born. Emma was just a toddler when he came as head of the practice.'

And his mother chipped in with, 'Why do you want to know something like that?'

'It was just that I was curious,' he told her, 'because Emma tells me that she and Jeremy weren't at all close.'

Olivia laughed. 'So aren't you the lucky one to have people like us as your parents?'

'I certainly am,' he replied, holding her close, while his father's comment was to the effect of when was he going to give them some grandchildren? At other times the question had irritated him because of his devotion to Serena's memory, but this time it had its appeal as suddenly the thought of having a little girl or boy who looked like Emma was firing his imagination.

When Emma appeared at his door the next morning, geared up for the coming day amongst the sick folk of Glenminster, Glenn breathed a sigh of relief.

He hadn't slept well at all because he'd kept imagining her being sad and lonely in the night hours and now, observing Emma, she looked the more rested of the two of them.

Glenn had gone to the trouble of making a cooked breakfast with all the trimmings, which was the last thing he would ever normally contemplate on a working day. When she saw what was on offer Emma said, 'Glenn, this is delightful. I will enjoy every mouthful.' How great it would be if they could have breakfast together every day after sleeping in the same bed, she thought. Her colour rose at the idea, and then their glances held. He smiled across at her and said, 'We must do this again some time.'

'Yes,' she said, glowing at the thought, 'that would be lovely.' And suddenly the misery of the previous day seemed far away. That was until they got to work and Lydia told them that on arriving at the practice she had seen an abundance of fresh flowers on the grave. And the same question about who the mysterious person who had known her mother could possibly be haunted Emma once more.

Glenn was close behind her and as he watched the colour fade from her face the determination within him to solve the mystery once and for all hardened. Anything to take away the hurt Emma felt every time it happened, even if he had to stay up all night.

There had to be a reason why the flowers were always cream roses, especially when golden daffodils and hyacinths were in bloom and there was cherry blossom on the trees. These roses were hothouse-grown, and if they were chosen for a special reason Emma had no knowledge of it.

Observing the number of blooms that had been put there only minutes ago it seemed logical to expect that it would be some time before the phantom mourner came again. When he or she did Glenn was determined he was going to be ready.

'Who can it possibly be, Glenn?' Emma said as they went inside the practice together. 'I know all my mother's friends and none of them frequent the graveyard or relieve the florists of most of their stock in one go.'

'I don't know,' Glenn said grimly, 'but I'm going to find out, and when I do they will have some explaining to do.' His voice softened. 'You don't deserve this, Emma. I want you to be happy and carefree.' She stared at him doubtfully, and he added, 'Yes, I know I haven't been helping that along much, but I have the matter in hand.'

It was only as they separated, each to their own consulting room, that Emma wondered what that meant.

It was half-term and quite a few parents were there with their young ones for various reasons. As ever on days like this the sound of young voices and small feet came from the play area of the practice, put there to keep the young patients happy until their names were called.

There was also the sound of fretful crying from one little one who had just arrived with worried parents. Glenn must have heard it as he came out of his consulting room as the patient he'd just seen was leaving and told them to take their little girl inside immediately.

Not long after he came out and told Reception in a low voice, 'We need an ambulance fast.' He turned to Emma, who was nearby and had heard the little one's crying. 'I suspect meningitis. The dreaded red rash is there and the other symptoms also make it look likely.'

His comments brought a sudden hush amongst those who were near enough to have heard what he'd said. After the ambulance had been and gone, with siren blaring as it sped on its way, a sombre silence hung over those who were still waiting to be seen.

After the dreadful beginning the day settled into a more normal routine and as the ills of winter became the main topic of conversation in the waiting room someone who had been absent for a while turned up in the form of James Prentice. He had been on a two-month course up north in a hospital there and was back with a new girlfriend in tow and expecting everyone to be as bowled over by her as he was.

With just a momentary lull following his arrival and a few quick handshakes for the new woman in his life because everyone was so busy, James left after announcing that they were getting engaged and would be in the Barrington Bar that evening if anyone would like to join them for a drink.

'That would seem to be a whirlwind romance,' Glenn said whimsically, as he and Emma were about to leave the practice at the end of what had been a very busy day. 'Are you intending to go to this evening's get-together? I shall go for a while to represent the practice but won't be staying long as I've got paperwork to deal with. I never seem to have the time to get to it during the day. So I can give you a lift there but can't promise to be able to bring you back.'

'Thanks for the offer,' she told him. 'I would appreciate it as my car is due for servicing. I can get a taxi to take me home if you've gone when I'm ready to leave. So what time will you pick me up?'

'Is seven o'clock all right?'

'Er...yes,' she replied absently with her mind elsewhere. 'Have we any report yet on the little girl with suspected meningitis?'

'It came through just a few moments ago,' Glenn said. 'She does have it, but they are hopeful that it was caught in time, so she should avoid any serious complications and she'll recover.'

'Poor little one,' Emma said sadly. 'I hate to hear of a child suffering.'

'I'm afraid that goes with the job,' Glenn said, 'but there is the other side to what we do for sick children—we make them well again in most cases because of our treatment and care.' Suddenly feeling that he was walking on eggshells, he said, 'Do you ever want children, Emma?'

She swivelled to face him. 'Yes, of course,' she said immediately. 'To have someone that I belong to and who belongs to me would be a dream come true. But I can't produce them without some assistance, I'm afraid.'

'Were you and Serena planning on having a family?' she asked with a casual sort of interest that was meant to preclude any kind of offence.

He took her breath away with his response.

'Yes, we wanted children,' Glenn told her, 'and we'd already done something towards that end. Serena was four months pregnant when that tsunami came out of nowhere. Mine was a double loss, so can you blame me for doing nothing about it when my parents bemoan their lack of grandchildren? I never told them about the pregnancy. I felt they had enough to cope with with the loss of their daughter-in-law.'

Emma's eyes were big and tears hung on her lashes as she turned to face him, stunned to hear that Glenn had been carrying around an even bigger burden than she'd known. Reaching out, she stroked the hard line of his jaw tenderly and with a groan he pulled her into his arms and held her close. And in that moment Emma knew that if he should never want her to be permanently in his life she would abide by it. That there would never be any other man that she would love as she loved him.

CHAPTER EIGHT

WHEN GLENN CALLED for her, as promised, at seven o'clock Emma was ready but showing little enthusiasm for the unexpected get-together that James had arranged. Observing her expression, he said wryly, 'Something tells me that we're not going to be the life and soul of the party tonight.

'I'm sorry, Emma, I would never have told you about the baby if the subject hadn't come up, and I don't want it to put a blight on your life too. I've learned to live with it. In these kinds of situations one has no choice. At least there's one bright side to tonight's event.'

'And what's that?' she questioned.

'Now he's engaged, Prentice will stop hanging around you. One day the right man will come along and you will find the happiness that you deserve.'

'Don't preach to me, Glenn,' Emma said tightly. 'You've made it clear that I'm not part of your agenda. And as I've already had the unpleasant experience of being told I wasn't wanted by my stepfather, the two together are enough to make me shy away from any future relationships on a permanent basis.'

'Wow! What did I do to deserve that?' he asked, swivelling to face her. 'I was merely referring to the many surprises that life always has in store and thinking how much Jeremy hurt you. I don't want to follow it with something similar.'

When there was no reply forthcoming, he asked, 'So, are you coming or not? Like I said, I'm going but not for long, and the night will be gone if we don't make a move.'

'Yes, I'm coming,' Emma told him, not willing to miss spending some time with Glenn regardless of what she'd said before. So soon they were amongst the rest of the staff, drinking champagne and toasting the newly betrothed couple with smiles that gave no hint of any inward turmoil.

An hour later, when Glenn said reluctantly that he was ready for the off and reminded her to travel home by taxi, with no detours near the church, he added, 'I am determined to find this mysterious person who puts the flowers on your mother's grave so frequently. In the meantime, Emma, don't let it upset you.

'You'll be the first to know when I solve the mystery and I think you will feel better if you keep away from it for a while.'

Emma nodded, ashamed of her earlier outburst, and with that, Glenn was gone.

As he drove the short distance home Glenn was remembering what he'd said to Emma about the grave. It was true that so far he was clueless, and a graveyard wasn't the best place to hang out, but he had to sort it out for her sake.

He felt sure he was missing something that was staring him in the face. And somehow it had to be connected with Emma—but what? Was it from her past, or her mother's? And if it was, how did he unravel the mystery? There must still be people around in Glenminster who had known Emma's mother and who she was seeing before she fell pregnant.

What about his parents, for instance? He'd already tried to sound them out, to no avail. But they'd lived in Glenminster as long as he could remember and his father had always socialised a lot. Maybe he should have another go at sounding him out and seeing if he came up with anything of interest? Mind you, knowing his dad, Jonas would have said if there was anything that he, Glenn, ought to know in connection with his friendship with Emma. Besides, his parents didn't know about the cream roses that graced the grave so regularly.

When he arrived home Glenn put the problem to the back of his mind while he attended to the demands of the practice. But once that was done it was there again, the niggling worry that there might be something that was going to cause Emma pain one day if he didn't pin it down for her.

From the size of the floral display it could be

two to three weeks before the next visit from the mystery mourner. Whoever it was must have had a great deal of regard for the woman buried there, and would surely come back. Hopefully, by then he might have a plan ready that would bring the person into the open.

In the meantime, there was a severe cough doing the rounds that had some of the patients barking in the waiting room, and amongst the elderly, who were only just warming up after winter's chill, there were cases of bronchitis, while for the rest there was a virus here and there, and always a full list.

But during each busy day Glenn could rely on Emma and the practice team with their skills and dedication to their professions. He was more content than he had been for a long time, until the cream roses began to droop and he knew the time was approaching when he might come face to face with the person who might somehow be connected with Emma. He really hoped he could come up with a solution to the problem.

But would Emma want to meet the person who must have known her mother so well that they brought flowers so often and in such a secretive manner? Would he if it were him? Whoever it was, they had given Emma no means of discovering his or her identity.

Having no wish to spend twenty-four hours of every day in the churchyard, Glenn had changed his consulting room with that of one of the other doctors because it overlooked the grave in question. He'd also asked the vicar to keep an eye open for anyone bringing flowers to it around the time he thought they were due.

But as the days went by no one went anywhere near the grave for any reason whatsoever. The only folks around seemed to be just local people taking the same short cut that he did when he went to visit his elderly patient on the road that led past the church. In the end Glenn had to accept that maybe the strange behaviour of the person he sought had just been a joke or a fad, and that there was no cause for concern on his part.

As the time continued to pass uneventfully Glenn had to tell Emma when she asked that so far it seemed that either the person knew they were being watched and had given up the practice of leaving flowers on the grave, had gone to live elsewhere, or it had been some kind of a long-term mistake. Emma had accepted his comments at face value but deep down wanted an answer, a name to set her mind at rest.

The first thing Glenn did on arriving at the practice the morning after that conversation was to go into the churchyard to inspect the grave. He was relieved to find it still empty of fresh blooms, but by lunchtime they were there again. He thought that, short of keeping watch out in the cold all the time, the mystery could go on for ever and he had patients already arriving who needed his time much more than a display of cream roses.

Emma had seen Glenn go across and when he came back could tell from his expression that the flower person had returned from wherever they had been. Observing how much it upset her, Glenn knew that he couldn't proceed with his plans for the Easter weekend if it meant leaving her behind in that sort of a situation.

With Easter approaching had come light and brightness after winter's dark days. Before the mystery flowers had reappeared Emma's spirits had been lifted for quite some time, while Glenn had been considering doing what he always did at Easter.

The practice would be closed for the long weekend and he had intended following his usual routine and spending the time in Italy, where he was in the habit of renting a house on the Amalfi coast that belonged to a friend from his college days.

He always found the change of scene therapeutic and restful, but this time he felt that he couldn't relax knowing that he would be leaving Emma behind to cope with her dark moments and that he was responsible for some of them.

As the time drew nearer he wondered what sort of a reception he would get if he invited her to join him for the Easter break purely as a friend, putting aside all other thoughts and just enjoying themselves in the magic of Italy.

Knowing that he wouldn't rest until he'd asked

her, Glenn waited until they were the first arrivals at the practice one morning and asked if she had a moment to spare.

'Well, yes,' Emma said laughingly, as her glance went around the empty waiting room and on the forecourt outside, and he wondered how long her light-heartedness would last when she heard what he had to say.

It seemed as if he had reason to worry as Emma's smile had disappeared within seconds and she was shaking her head. 'I don't think so,' she said in a low voice. 'That part of Italy is incredibly romantic and beautiful and I would love to go there, Glenn, but feel that it would be more sensible to stay at home. Thank you for inviting me and I hope you have a lovely time.'

He gave a twisted smile and, not wanting to give up easily, said, 'Do you think either of us will have a "lovely time" in one of the world's most beautiful places if we are on our own?'

'No, I suppose not,' she agreed weakly, and decided that it was only four days in Italy they were discussing, not a lifetime. And it *would* be a relief to be away from the mystery of the never-ending flowers on the grave.

'When would we fly out if I came?' Emma asked doubtfully.

'Thursday night, so as to be already there for Good Friday,' Glenn replied, and hoped that she was weakening.

The house had four bedrooms so Emma could have her choice, and there was no likelihood of him being missing when she woke up as when he was there he was always on the patio, soaking up the sun, at an early hour.

'So do I book you a flight for Thursday night or not?' Glenn asked patiently, as the practice began to come alive with the sound of voices inside and out.

'Er...yes...I suppose so,' Emma said. 'It would be a brief change of scene and I need something like that.' And before he could comment further she went to where her first patient of the day was waiting.

So much for enthusiasm, he thought, but at least she'd said yes.

Enthusiasm was more in evidence when Glenn called to pick her up on the Thursday night to go to the airport. There was a smile for him and as he observed Emma's outfit of leggings with a smart silk shirt above them and her weekend case, waiting to go into the boot of his car, his spirits lifted.

They chatted easily enough during the flight and he hid a smile at Emma's expression when she saw the house. It was a very attractive residence, overlooking the sea, and moonlight was shining on the water. It was already quite late after their evening flight.

'There are four bedrooms,' Glenn told her. 'Choose whichever one you want. There's a chef who lives nearby who comes in to do the food, so for a short time we shall be living in style. I've got a hire car due to arrive tomorrow, so shall we drive along the beautiful Amalfi coast? Or do you want to just laze about as we've got here so late?'

'It all sounds fantastic,' Emma said. 'I was crazy not to want to come, but nothing seems right in my life any more except my job at the practice. I am totally content with that. But the mystery of the flowers gets me down and...'

'Go on, say it,' Glenn told her. 'You don't get much joy out of me either. I know what you thought about my proposal. I must have been out of my mind to be so patronising. I hope that one day you can forgive me, Emma.'

'I think I already have,' Emma replied. 'It was wrong of me on that occasion not to take into account the memory of how Serena died and how difficult that must be to live with all the time.'

Glenn was smiling. 'So shall we put all our sad thoughts to one side and enjoy our time together for the next few days?'

'Yes, why not?' Emma agreed, and kissing him lightly on the cheek went slowly up the stairs to the bedroom she had chosen, content to know that Glenn would be near while she slept. Anything further than that would happen only if they both wanted it to, and finally it seemed as if that might be the case.

The following morning they swam in the pool and lay in the sun and the day dawdled along contentedly with every glance, every touch a promise. When it was time to go up to change for the evening meal Glenn bypassed his room and followed Emma into hers. He slipped the towelling robe that she'd been wearing by the pool off her shoulders and kissed every part of her that wasn't covered by her swim-suit until she was melting at his touch. It was like coming in out of the wilderness to happiness and joy.

But the telephone on the bedside table had other ideas and when Glenn released her to answer its strident ring Emma saw his expression change. Her heart missed a beat as he said, 'We'll get the first flight out and go straight to the hospital.' As he re-placed the receiver he said grimly, 'That was my mother. Dad climbed a tall tree in the garden this afternoon to rescue their cat, which had gone up it to escape next door's dog. When it wouldn't come down he stretched an inch too far to reach it, over-balanced and fell down onto the stone path below.'

'And?' Emma questioned anxiously.

'He's in hospital with a fractured arm and leg and my mother needs me, I'm afraid.'

'Yes, of course,' Emma agreed immediately, with a vision of his energetic father hurt and fretful. 'I'll tell the chef that we have to leave while you book a flight.'

'So much for our special time together,' Glenn said flatly. 'I was going to suggest that we go along the Amalfi coast tomorrow. Do you think it wasn't meant to be?'

'No, of course not,' Emma told him gently. 'At present your parents have to come first.'

'Yes, of course,' he agreed, 'but it is typical of Dad that he thinks he can shin up a tree at his age without getting stuck. He sees himself as Superman, thinks that he's invincible. Apparently while he was lying at the bottom of it the cat came down of its own accord without any trouble and ran off.'

They found Jonas sitting up in bed, looking bruised and crestfallen to have been the cause of them having to fly home so soon. Emma told him gently that there was no blame attached to what he had done, and said to Glenn that he was lucky to have a father to love and cherish him. In the silence that followed there was no one amongst them who wanted to contradict that.

A nurse was hovering with the comment that the patient needed some rest and would be in a better condition for chatting the following day, and as they prepared to leave, Jonas said to Glenn, 'Be sure to come tomorrow. We need to talk, and it will give your mother a chance to rest.'

'Yes, sure,' he agreed, 'and in the meantime don't go climbing any more trees.'

'You might be thanking me for climbing that tree soon,' was the reply, and they left the patient in the care of the nurse and took Glenn's mother home to rest.

'I didn't want to bring you back from your break,' Olivia said, 'but Jonas insisted and made such a fuss he was causing alarm amongst the nursing staff.' She turned to Emma. 'You must think us a strange family, my dear.'

'As someone who hasn't got one, I envy you more than words can say,' she replied, and felt like weeping.

'I want you to stay at my place tonight,' Glenn told Emma as they drove the short distance to his house after seeing his mother safely settled. 'Not for any other reason than I want you to be where I know you are near. It has been a strange day. Only hours ago we were in Italy and then we got that phone call. Did you think Dad was OK when we got there? He seemed strange, don't you think?'

'Yes,' Emma agreed. 'It was as if he knew something that we weren't aware of, unless he was suffering from concussion.'

'We'll have to see what tomorrow brings,' Glenn said. 'Are you hungry? We haven't eaten in ages.'

'Just coffee and a biscuit will suit me fine,' Emma said softly. 'Thank goodness that it's Saturday tomorrow.'

'I couldn't agree more,' Glenn said, and added, 'The guest room is ready, just help yourself to anything you find there. I'll bring your case up so that you have your own nightwear available if you would prefer it. Emma, there won't be any locked doors between us.'

'Good,' she said. 'So if I'm up first am I allowed to bring you a cup of tea?'

'Yes, of course, but I haven't brought you here to wait on me. I just want you where you are safe and free from care, and I never feel that you are either of those things in that house of yours.'

'I can't do anything about that until I find a buyer,' Emma said, 'and I'm sure you will agree that it isn't the usual "desirable residence" that the average house hunter is seeking.'

She was asleep within moments of settling into Glenn's guest room this time and when she awoke the next morning, with a bright sun shining up above, the memories of the day before came back— the delights of Amalfi and Capri that hadn't materialised, the moment when Glenn had caressed her and held her close, only to have it taken from them by the news of his father's fall from the tree that had caused their hasty return to Glenminster.

What would today bring? Emma wondered. Some degree of recovery for Glenn's father hopefully, but he was elderly and a fall of that severity could have serious after-effects.

When she went down to breakfast, having showered and changed into fresh casual clothes, Glenn was on to the hospital, asking when it would be convenient to visit his father who, it seemed, had been restless in the night and impatient to see his son.

'Shall I drop you off at your place on my way to

the hospital when we've had breakfast?' Glenn suggested, after assuring the hospital that he would be there as soon as possible.

'Yes, that would suit me fine,' Emma told him. 'It would give you some private time with your family and I can check the post and get in touch with the estate agent to see if there have been any viewings of the house while I've been away. Before we separate, would you like to come there for a meal this evening? It's time that I offered you some hospitality for a change.'

Glenn hesitated for a second and then said, 'That would be great, Emma, but I'm not sure what the day is going to bring with regard to my father. Can we put that on hold for the time being?'

'Yes, of course,' she agreed, with the feeling that maybe Glenn was relieved that their closeness of the last couple of days was being slowed down by unexpected circumstances. And she was back to her feeling of aloneness, knowing that he was the only person who could change that.

There was no mail when Emma arrived back at the house, which was not surprising considering the short time she'd been away, but a phone message from the estate agent was waiting to the effect that there had been a viewer in her absence who might be interested in her property, but instead of feeling uplifted at the thought, Emma's feeling of being surplus to requirements gained momentum.

* * *

When Glenn arrived at the hospital two things were obvious. The first was that his father was in full control of all his faculties, and the second was his eagerness to pass on to his son the reason why he had actually fallen from the tree, which in the first instance sounded less believable than Glenn could have imagined.

'I fell because Pusscat had taken herself high up onto one of the branches to get away from next door's dog,' Jonas explained, 'and as I was reaching for her and in full control of the situation I glimpsed someone going past on the pavement across the way, carrying a large bunch of cream roses. And as I stretched myself further along the branch to get a better look, it gave way.'

'So you didn't see who it was, which gender?' Glenn asked.

'No. All I saw after that was stars as I hit the ground.'

'Did you manage to see what this person was wearing?'

'Only a glimpse before I lost my balance. It seemed like a long grey belted raincoat with a pull-down hat as it was raining at the time, and then I was falling.' Jonas was nearly back to his usual self. 'But I shall expect to be referred to as Sherlock in any future confrontations.'

'You're amazing,' Glenn told him gently, 'to risk life and limb like that for Emma's sake.'

'Aye, maybe,' he replied, 'but I didn't find out who the cream roses were from, did I?'

'Not yet, but it's a lead that we can follow.'

The nurse that Glenn had spoken to on the phone was near and she said gently, 'It is time to rest now that you have seen your son, Mr Bartlett. The doctor is on his way to see how you are this morning and we don't want you tired or overexcited, do we?'

'You're not going to raise any false hopes for Emma, are you?' was his father's last comment as Glenn prepared to leave.

'No, not until I have the right answer,' Glenn replied, and added as he left, 'And now do as the nurse says, Dad, and get some rest.'

On the way home, Glenn stopped off at the church to check if flowers had been recently placed on the grave, and sure enough they were there. But who had brought them and why was something he had yet to discover.

The wording on the gravestone referred to Emma's mother's maiden name, rather than her married one, which was strange. It had a sound of Jeremy about it, and meant that anyone knowing Helena from the distant past would have no knowledge that Emma was her daughter.

It was not surprising that Emma hadn't known about her real father until Jeremy had told her the truth so brutally and she had fled Glenminster until he had tracked her down and brought her home.

On his way home Glenn called to see Emma to

make sure she was all right after he had left her so abruptly to visit his father, but there was no answer when he rang the doorbell. As midday was approaching he stopped off at one of the places where they had lunched a couple of times in the hope that she might be there.

But it was not to be, and despite his efforts he couldn't find her. So once he had eaten he went to report the patient's progress to his mother, who had been having a quiet morning knowing that he would have seen his father. She was preparing to go in later for the afternoon visiting.

'Where's Emma?' she wanted to know. 'I was so sorry to have dragged you both away from the delights of Italy after such a short stay.'

'I would have been sorry if you hadn't,' he told her, 'and so would Emma. She is somewhere around but I'm not sure where. I've just called at her place but she wasn't there. She stayed at my house last night as I didn't want her going back to that dismal place of hers after Italy.'

Emma was in the town centre at the offices of the estate agent, following up the message that she'd received about an interested viewer of her house. When she got there she discovered that they had seen the house a second time that morning and had made an offer.

'Really?' she exclaimed. 'I can hardly believe it.'

The estate agent explained that the house was big

and well built even if it wasn't exactly the last word in design, which had helped it to sell. He asked if she was going to accept the offer.

'Yes, please,' she said. The thought uppermost in her mind was that with money in the bank she would be free to go where she wanted. And if Glenn continued to keep her at a distance, she could start again somewhere new, where there was no pain or longing.

CHAPTER NINE

EMMA RANG GLENN that evening and the lift in her voice said she had good news of some sort to impart.

'I've got a buyer for the house,' she told him, and there was silence for a moment.

'Wow!' he exclaimed. 'Fast work! Well done! And where are you planning to move to?'

Your house, with you, Emma would have liked to say, but it would seem that thought hadn't occurred to him, or surely he would have suggested it?

'I have no idea at the moment,' she replied. 'I only learned this afternoon that I had a buyer.'

'Yes, of course,' Glenn said. 'Why don't I come round and take you to dine somewhere nice to celebrate the occasion? Would you like that, Emma?'

Would she like it? Of course she would! 'Yes, that would be nice,' Emma said. 'I'll need some time to get ready, though.'

'How long?'

'An hour or so. But what about your father, Glenn? Oughtn't we to go to evening visiting instead?'

'We'll go to the hospital first and dine afterwards, if that is all right with you.'

'Yes, I'd love to do that. Your family are amazing,' Emma said. 'I do so envy you, Glenn.'

He wanted to tell Emma about the person in the grey raincoat carrying the flowers, but he was worried that it might spoil their evening. There would be time enough to tell her when he'd eventually found the identity of the mystery donator.

Emma had dressed with care in a wraparound cream silk dress that enhanced the dark attraction of her hair and eyes, and with complementary jewellery to match and shoes that brought her almost level with Glenn's height. She surveyed herself before answering his ring on the doorbell. She thought she must be crazy to think there was anything other than mild interest from Glenn. Ever since they'd had to leave Italy he had seemed withdrawn. And yet she still felt compelled to dress with care. Yes, she really must be crazy.

Her efforts, it seemed, did not go unnoticed. When Glenn saw her, there was longing in his glance, tenderness around his mouth and hope was born in her again, briefly. But it faded when he commented that, it being a mild evening, she might not need the jacket she'd brought with her. And in the car as they drove to the hospital there was no closeness, just the same small talk.

* * *

Jonas shot Glenn a questioning look when they appeared and when his son shook his head, the patient tutted his impatience. He reached for a fruit drink that was standing on the locker next to his bed, and as Emma chatted with Olivia, who had come back for evening visiting, Glenn whispered, 'I'm working on it, Dad. Woe betide anyone wearing a grey raincoat who comes into my line of vision! But it might have to wait until we have another shower. It could be a garment that only comes out in wet weather. And there's also the fact that it might just be a coincidence. You could have seen someone with the same kind of flowers.'

'Yes, I know,' Jonas said, 'and I'm fidgety. I want to be out of this place to help you find this person, but the doctor says not yet.'

'A rest for once will do you no harm,' Glenn told him, 'and I'll be in touch the moment I have any news, all right?'

'Yes. Now, go and enjoy your evening and perhaps you could drop your mother off on the way to wherever you are going.'

'Of course,' Glenn said, and thought how fortunate he was to have both of his parents still fit and well, apart from his father's injuries. Thankfully the fall from the tree hadn't done too much damage and he was responding satisfactorily to treatment. If only there was a family like his for Emma, where she could feel loved and wanted.

He could give Emma one that was theirs alone if she would only let him, but she needed to know where she came from before that and just who it was who was so interested in her mother's grave.

Glenn had booked a table at a restaurant on one of the tasteful shopping promenades that Glenminster was famed for and as they waited to be served, he said, 'So tell me what your mother was like, Emma. Do you resemble her at all?'

'No, not in any way,' she said. 'Mum was blonde with blue eyes, while my hair is dark and my eyes are hazel. We were of a similar build but that's the only resemblance. Why do you ask?'

'Just curiosity, that's all,' Glenn said easily. 'What sort of a job did she have before she had you?'

'She was secretary to the manager of one of the big banks in Glenminster, but had to give it up when I was born. Jeremy told me on the night I left that she had only married him to gain respectability and to give me a father.'

'And did you believe him?'

'It might have been true in one way, but she certainly paid the price for it. He ruled the roost and was prone to remind her frequently how much she was indebted to him, which I didn't understand at the time because I had no reason to think that he wasn't my father.'

'So you really have no idea who your birth father could be? No special friends of your mother's?'

'No, I'm afraid not,' Emma said regretfully. 'I
remember when I was small my mother cried a lot.
As I grew older we were very close, like sisters almost, but she never breathed a word. And after she
died I jogged along with Jeremy's fads and fancies,
having no idea that he wasn't my father. Until, as I
told you, he wanted to remarry, told me to go, and
when I protested, put me well and truly in the picture with such devastating results.'

'The low-life!' he gritted. 'But why didn't he remarry?'

'It was Lydia that he wanted to marry, but as soon
as she realised how he had treated me she called it
off.'

The food they had ordered was being placed in
front of them and when Glenn smiled across at her,
Emma said, 'Glenn, why all the questions? Are they
why you suggested that we dine out tonight?'

'Not especially. I was just interested, that's all,
and felt that you know a lot more about me than I
do about you.'

'And does that matter?' Emma asked.

'It might do at some time in the future.'

'Such as…?'

'There are lots of times when the foundations of
our lives are of interest to others.'

Emma gave up on that pronouncement and turned
her attention to the food, while Glenn reflected that
once he had found out the identity of the visitor to
her mother's grave and presented them to her, he

was going to say something to her that was getting to be long overdue. In the meantime just to have her near was absolutely magical.

When they left the restaurant they walked slowly to the car, holding hands beneath an Easter moon, and Emma's doubts and uncertainties melted away until Glenn pulled up outside her house, kissed her gently on the cheek and said, 'If I'm not around tomorrow, I'll see you at the practice on Tuesday.'

'So you don't want to come in for a coffee?' Emma asked.

Glenn shook his head. 'No, because if I do it will be much more than that I want.' He drove off into the night without further comment, leaving her to wonder what he could possibly mean.

It was busy at the practice on the Tuesday morning after the Easter weekend and Glenn had been hoping that he might have had some good news regarding the long grey raincoat to impart to his father. But ever since Jonas had fallen out of the tree the sun hadn't stopped shining, and there had been no call to ask Emma if she could identify its owner. Besides, Glenn hadn't wanted to mention it to her yet in the vain hope that he might be able to present a complete answer to the question that was eating at him so much.

Quite a few of the regular patients were missing, having been away for the holiday weekend, and as Glenn drove past the mainline railway station on his way back to the practice after a house call in the late morning he saw a few of them homeward bound, unloading themselves and their luggage from a London train. It was then that he spotted the likeable Alex Mowbray amongst them, *and he was wearing a grey belted raincoat.*

As Alex went to join the taxi queue outside the station Glenn pulled up beside him and asked if he wanted a lift, and the offer was gratefully accepted.

'I've been to London a few times over the last couple of months,' Alex explained, as Glenn pulled away from the pavement, 'seeing the shows and generally getting to know the place again after a long absence, but it isn't much fun when one is alone and I'm soon back here in the place I love the most.'

'There is a lot to be said for family life,' Glenn said conversationally. 'I'm fortunate that I still have my parents close by, unlike poor Emma Chalmers—she has no one. Her mother died a few years ago and she has never known who her father is.'

'I hadn't realised that," said Alex. 'Poor Emma, that's very sad.'

'Jeremy Chalmers was Emma's stepfather, he filled the gap left in Emma and Helena's lives when Emma's real father left Helena pregnant, and she never knew the difference. Until in a moment of spite Jeremy enlightened Emma about her true father and she flew the nest to get away from him.'

The colour had drained from the face of the man beside him. 'You are telling me that I have a daugh-

ter, is that it?' Alex croaked. 'That I made Helena
pregnant on the one and only occasion we made
love? It was the night that I was due to leave the
UK. I left the next morning to take my sick wife to
a gentler climate.

'Helena and I loved each other deeply but my duty
was to the woman that I was married to and it was
only when she passed away recently that it felt right
for me to come back to Glenminster.

'But how did you find out about us? I had prayed
that I might find Helena still here and was devastated when it was not to be. I have found solace in
putting her favourite flowers on her grave. And then
I got to know Emma through your father, with no
idea she was my daughter. Glenn, take me to her,
please, I beg you!'

Glenn smiled. 'Emma will be busy at the practice
at this moment, but if you could wait until tonight I
could arrange for the two of you to meet in privacy
at my house. It's thanks to my father I've discovered the truth and you have found the daughter you
never knew you had.'

'He saw you walking down the road, carrying
cream roses, while he was at the top of a tree, trying to get his cat down. He fell off in his excitement
and ended up in hospital. But before he fell he noted
the raincoat that you're wearing.'

'I can't believe this is happening to me,' Alex said
brokenly. 'I have been lonely for so long.'

'Not any more when Emma knows who you are,' Glenn promised. 'Seven o'clock at my place?'

'Yes, absolutely,' Alex agreed, and as his house came into sight he smiled. 'This will be Emma's one day.'

When Glenn arrived back at the practice he told Emma that he would be entertaining a visitor that evening and hoped that she would join them as they would very much like to meet her. Emma's spirits plunged downwards as her first thought was that Glenn had found someone to replace Serena and wanted to break it to her gently.

But she dredged up a smile and asked, 'What time do you want me there?'

'Is seven o'clock all right?'

'Yes, that will be fine,' Emma agreed, and went back to her patients with the thought uppermost in her mind that whatever he had in store for her she would not let him see tears.

When she arrived at the stated time she saw a car on the drive next to his that looked familiar, though she wasn't sure why. Although why it really mattered when she had to get through the evening she didn't know. The sooner this ordeal was over the better.

When Glenn opened the door to her he was smiling, and as she stepped inside he said, 'Someone is waiting to be introduced to you, Emma.' But as she followed him into the sitting room the only person present was Alex Mowbray, who was beaming across at her, and after greeting him she turned to Glenn and said, 'I don't understand. I already know Alex. We are good friends.'

'Er...yes, you do know him,' he agreed. 'You know him as a friend, but Alex is something else as well that you have no idea of. So I'm going to leave him to tell you what that is.' As Emma gazed at him in bewilderment he left them alone with each other and closed the door behind him.

When Glenn had gone, Alex pointed to the sofa and said gently, 'Come and sit by me, Emma, while I tell you something that is wonderful and amazing.' She did as Alex asked, observing him in puzzlement, and he continued, 'I have discovered today from Glenn that we are not just good friends, you and I, but we are also blood relations.'

'How can that be?' Emma asked in amazement. 'I have no family, Alex, none at all.'

'Yes, you have,' Alex said gently. 'Your mother and I loved each other very much, but I had a sick wife I was committed to and Helena and I knew that nothing could come of our love for each other. But on the night before I left this country with my wife, your mother and I slept together.

'I must have made her pregnant, and in keeping with the vows we'd made never to see each other again she didn't get in touch to tell me what had happened. Never betrayed the vow we'd made to keep our love for each other secret for my wife's sake, and it was only today, when Glenn gave me a lift from the station, that my life became worth living again.

'When my wife died only a few months ago I came straight here, but saw the grave and knew I was too late to be with Helena. So I resorted to putting cream roses, her favourite flowers, on it, and would have continued to do so if Glenn's father hadn't seen me on my way there on Good Friday with more flowers. So can you accept me as your father, Emma, someone who will love and cherish you always?'

'Yes, of course,' she said tearfully. 'I have been so lonely, and I liked you from the moment that we met, but never dreamt that we might be related. We have Glenn to thank for this.'

'And my dad, don't forget,' Glenn said, as he came in with flutes of champagne. 'There will be no holding him down after this. So shall we drink to Alex being one of the family and there to give you away, as fathers do, on our wedding day?'

'Yes, please,' she said softly, as all her doubts and fears disappeared, and as they raised their glasses the father that Emma had never known wiped a tear from his eye.

After Alex had gone, quietly radiant, and they were settled in front of the fire, holding hands, Emma said, 'I've thought since we came back from Italy that you were relieved to have an escape route in the form of your father's accident presenting itself to avoid spending time with me, and I am so ashamed.'

'Don't be,' Glenn said gently. 'It was perfectly understandable. The words have been on my lips constantly but I made myself wait until I'd solved the puzzle of the flowers. I can't believe what a wonderful solution it turned out to be.'

'I will never forget that you gave me a family,' Emma said softly, 'and one day hopefully there will be another one, yours and mine, to gladden the hearts of their grandparents. Serena if we have a girl child and Jonas for a boy?'

'Yes, please,' Glenn said, with his arms around her, holding her close in what felt like the safest place on earth. 'And I have some more news concerning Dad. Mum rang earlier to say that he has been discharged from the hospital. They let her take him home with her after this evening's visiting.

'Shall we go round there and tell them the good news that Alex is going to be part of the family for evermore, and that one day they may be granted their greatest wish of the patter of tiny feet all around them?'

'Yes,' Emma said joyfully. 'Your father deserves to hear something good after what happened to him, and your mother will be delighted to know that you and I love each other, and that we are going to spend the rest of our lives together.'

'You came out of nowhere and captured my heart, brought me joy out of sadness at Christmastime,' Glenn told her. 'Would you be prepared to wait until it comes round again for a Christmas wedding?'

'Yes, that would be lovely,' Emma said without hesitation, smiling up at him with the promise of all the happiness to come in her bright hazel gaze, 'just as long as I can live here with you from this day on, which is something I've always wanted.'

'That goes without saying,' he said tenderly. 'Where else would I want you to be but in my home, in my heart?'

When his parents had heard all their news, they rejoiced to hear that not only was Alex Emma's father but he would be at the engagement party that the two doctors were planning on having with family, friends and the practice staff in the near future. It seemed that Jonas's glimpse of him before the branch had given way had provided the answer to the mystery of the cream roses, and in spite of his injuries he was a very happy man.

Emma and Glenn had decided to hold their engagement party at Glenn's house with outside caterers in charge of refreshments. When they went into work the next day they amazed everyone except Lydia by announcing their engagement and inviting them to celebrate it with them some time in the near future. For the rest of the day it was the main topic of conversation.

That evening, wanting to have all ends tied up of what was going to be one of the happiest times of his life, Glenn said, 'What kind of a ring would you like, Emma? Something other than that ill-fated solitaire diamond that I made such a hash of when I produced it?'

Emma smiled across at him. 'I would like the diamond if you still have it,' she said softly. When Glenn looked at her in surprise she added, 'I have realised since that the way you explained it when you offered it to me was because you cared about me, and needed to make me see how much you would never want to let your painful past hurt me as it hurts you. I misjudged you, Glenn. So if you still have it, that is the ring I would like to wear.'

'You are incredible,' he said gently, 'and, yes, I have still got it in a drawer in my bedroom, so shall I go and get it?'

'Yes, please,' Emma told him, happy that the dark moment from the past was turning into a joyful one, and when Glenn took her hand and placed the sparkling ring on her finger, there was brightness all around them.

The engagement party was like a dream coming true for them as they greeted their guests on an evening in early June, and when Alex arrived and held her close for a fatherly moment, Emma's contentment was complete.

She had been round to his place on a few occasions to get to know him and it was always a time of fulfilment and thankfulness when she thought of

how Glenn had brought him to her out of nowhere
and into her life.

It seemed that Alex had been the bank manager
of one of the biggest banks in Glenminster and
Helena had been his secretary. They had fallen
deeply in love with the knowledge that there had
been no future for them to be together because Alex
had been unable to leave his sick wife, and she,
Emma, had been the result of wishing each other a
passionate goodbye.

But a warm June night with love in the air and lots
of nice food and wine to partake of in the company
of friends was not the occasion for sad memories,
and when Glenn asked Emma if she was happy, the
answer was there in her eyes and the tender curve
of her mouth, and as Lydia watched them she felt
a rush of thankfulness in knowing that there was a
happy ending for Emma's hurts of long ago.

EPILOGUE

CHRISTMAS HAD COME again and in the ancient church next to the practice the wedding march was being played as Emma walked slowly along the aisle in a dress of heavy cream brocade designed to keep out the cold, carrying a bouquet of roses of the same colour. She was holding onto the arm of her father, who was observing her with loving pride and joy as the solitaire diamond on her finger sparkled in the light of many candles.

All around them was the Yuletide smell of fresh green spruces and as Glenn stood waiting for her at the altar he sent up a silent prayer of thankfulness for the joy she had brought into his life and the lives of others, including that of his elderly best man, who had risked life and limb on their account.

Tonight he would keep the promise he had made to Emma at the side of the empty hayloft that day. There had been times over recent months when it had been a hard promise to keep, but tonight when they were alone Glenn would show her how much he loved her and always would.

And as Emma came to stand beside him, looking beautiful beyond telling, he felt Serena's presence, as he sometimes did, close by and peaceful in the ether, and contentment filled his heart as he and Emma made the vows that would last a lifetime.

They were going to honeymoon in Italy in the beautiful house where they had stayed so briefly before the phone call from Glenn's mother had brought them swiftly back home. But on this occasion they fully intended to enjoy the beauties of the coastline, now that they had all the time in the world to adore each other. And on their return to Glenminster there would be all the things that were precious in their lives waiting for them.

Such as their parents, Glenn's house, which Emma had adored ever since she'd first seen it, and their all-consuming work at the practice amongst the sick and suffering, with their love for each other their strength in all things.

* * * * *

A FATHER THIS CHRISTMAS?

LOUISA HEATON

To Mum and Dad,
who bought me a beautiful manual typewriter
one Christmas and released the story-writing bunny.

Lots of love, your loving daughter. xx

CHAPTER ONE

'QUICK, EVA, TAKE my pulse!'

Eva turned to her friend. What was wrong?

'What? Are you ill?'

She placed her fingers on Sarah's pulse point on her wrist and looked with concern at her friend as she counted beats. But Sarah wasn't looking at *her*—she was focussed on something or *someone* behind Eva, across the minors department, towards the entrance. She was seemingly fascinated, with a sparkle in her eyes and a slow smile creeping across her face as she looked someone up and down.

'Sex on a stick at one o'clock.'

'What?'

Why was she being ridiculous? Eva swivelled in her seat to see who was making Sarah act like that and her eyes fell upon the one man she'd thought she'd never, ever see again.

Jacob.

Dressed all in black, in what had to be tailored clothes, considering how well they fit, with his tousled dark hair and a five-o'clock shadow, a red-tubed stethoscope draped casually around his neck, he looked stunning.

Well dressed, powerful.

Virile.

More so than four years ago, if that were possible. Time had been overly generous to Jacob, bestowing upon him masculine maturity in a well-defined body that simply oozed sex appeal.

She'd begun to believe that she'd imagined this perfect man. That her one hot night with him that Christmas Eve four years ago had been a figment of her imagination. Despite the obvious, startling reminder that it *hadn't* been imaginary.

Their son.

Eva wanted the earth to swallow her up. Because then she wouldn't have to face him. Wouldn't have to explain to him that he was a father.

She could hardly believe that she had slept with a man she had only known for such a short time. Just because of something she'd felt when she'd looked at him. Taking him at face value—because, really, what else had she had to go on? He'd been in her arms, and they'd danced together in a slow, sultry melting of bodies... The way his hips had swayed, his groin had pressed against hers, the *feel* of him...

But now she was different. Stronger. She was no longer the young woman who had given her heart to a man who had only been a fantasy for just one night—a man she'd dreamed of after the fact.

Now she was more mature. A strong woman. A confident doctor. And there was no way she was going to let Jacob know how she was really feeling.

Terrified.

Still attracted...

I'm not! Just because it feels as if my heart is trying to leap from my chest...

She let go of Sarah's wrist and deliberately turned her back on him.

There was so much he needed to know! So much she needed to tell him. She'd searched for him. Tried to let him know about Seb. But it had been impossible! Would he understand?

Her mouth felt dry, as if it was full of sawdust, and she knew if she were to talk to him her tongue would just stumble over the words. She groaned as her stomach flipped and swirled like snowflakes in a snow globe.

'It's probably that new doctor Clarkson mentioned earlier.' She tried to sound as casual as she could. When Dr Clarkson, clinical lead of their A&E department, had mentioned they were getting a new doctor she'd initially been thrilled. Who *didn't* need an extra pair of hands in A&E after all? Even if it *was* just temporary cover for Christmas.

But he hadn't told her who was coming. Who the new doctor actually was.

Jacob Dolan.

The doctor who'd slept with her and then run off to Africa. The doctor who'd got her pregnant and then disappeared without leaving a trace!

Why did he have to look so good?

Sarah leaned forward to whisper to her, 'Oh, my goodness, I'd really love to find *him* in my Christmas stocking...' She licked her lips. 'How on earth are we going to get any work done with him hanging around? I'm going to be spending all my time wiping drool off my chin and hoping the cleaners have enough wet-floor signs to dot around me.'

Eva grimaced a smile, but went back to her paperwork. All she had to do was write these notes. Write these notes and then maybe get the earth to open up and swallow her or something. Once he realised she was here—once he realised that she was the woman who had slept with him four years ago...

She could grab her coat and go. She could say she was sick or something.

No...that wouldn't work. You only get a day off if you're dying—nothing less...

Their son.

She could tell Dr Clarkson it was something to do with Seb.

This was her dream come true and her worst nightmare all rolled into one! Whilst once she had dreamed about what life might have been like for the pair of them if Jacob hadn't disappeared, she was now faced with the fact that he was back. Here. In her department. And he would eventually need to be told about Seb.

She'd tried to tell him before.

I tried. I tried to track him down. But there was no trace! This isn't my fault! He can't hold me responsible for this!

She didn't have to think about him being here. About him actually being in her A&E department. Standing mere metres away, looking even more alluring than he had before, if that were possible.

She'd hoped her imagination had got it wrong. That her memories of him were impaired. That perhaps he'd *not* been that stunning. That perhaps he'd have more in common with Quasimodo, or a troll, or something hopeful like that.

'*Look* at him, Eva.' Sarah glanced at her friend and frowned. 'Eva? Why won't you look at him? Oh, he's coming over...' Sarah scraped back her chair and stood up.

Eva sucked in a deep, steadying breath and felt her heart pound against her rib cage. This couldn't be true! This couldn't be happening! Not now. She wasn't prepared for it. She'd dreamed about finding him and telling him about Seb for years, but now that the opportunity was upon her she was terrified.

'Eva?'

That voice.

Chills trembled down her spine and she felt every single goosebump that prickled her skin.

She could see Sarah glance at her in surprise that somehow Eva *knew* this man. No doubt there would be an interrogation later, and she'd want all the details, but Eva was mindful that not only was this her workplace but she was a professional—and what business was it of anybody but her?

She dredged up what she hoped was a pleasant smile from somewhere—hoping it didn't look like a ghastly rictus—and turned around, praying to any god that existed that she didn't flush like a menopausal woman or look as if she was going to pass out.

Those blue eyes...

'Jacob! Nice to see you again. It's been a long time.'

Was her voice as strangled as it sounded to her? She hoped not. She was determined to be as professional as she could be. Professional and *distanced.* She was at least grateful for the fact that her voice was actually working. She'd felt so trapped and cornered suddenly she was amazed her voice hadn't disappeared altogether, in a case of phobic aphasia.

She held out her hand for him to shake, as one colleague would to another. He raised a quizzical eyebrow and shook it, smiling that kilowatt smile.

Oh, help...

Eva kept the smile plastered on her face, not knowing what else to do. She had momentous, life-changing news for this man. But how could she tell him? Everyone knew she was a mother—it was bound to be mentioned to him at some point. All she needed was for someone to mention how old Seb was and Jacob would do a little maths, and then—

'How have you been?' he asked, smiling, looking her up and down. 'You look great.'

She lifted her chin and smiled. 'I've been fine. You?'

What had she expected? For him to say that his life had been awful without her? That after their one night he'd dreamed about her the way she had about him? *Hah!* Jacob Dolan had most likely coped absolutely fine without her!

'I've been good. I can't believe you actually work here.'

'Well, I do.' She struggled to think of something else to say. Something pleasant. Something…*neutral*. 'This is Sarah Chambers—another A&E colleague.'

She introduced her friend and Sarah practically melted over him, shaking his hand as if she'd never let go, as if his hand was somehow magically feeding her oxygen or something.

Eva rolled her eyes at her friend's blatant fawning, and when she could finally stand the overt flirting no longer she deliberately walked between them, so that their hand-shaking had to be broken off to allow her through.

'Let me introduce you to everyone.'

Jacob dropped into step beside her. 'Thanks. So…you're going to be my new boss?'

She shook her head. *No. Definitely not.* 'Dr Clarkson is clinical lead.'

'How long have you been here?'

'Since before I met you.' She grimaced at how easily she'd referred to when they'd met. Now he would be re-membering it, too.

She almost stopped walking. Couldn't believe she'd referred to it. Her stomach became a solid lump of cold ice. Her feet felt as if they were inside concrete boots and walking was like trying to wade through molasses.

How do I tell him?

'How was Africa?'

There. That was better. Turn the focus back onto him. It gave her time to breathe. Time to think. Time to formulate the answers she knew she'd have to provide.

'Hot. And dry. But amazing. Life-changing.'

There was something odd in his voice then, and she voluntarily turned to look at him, trying not to be pulled by the lure of those sexy blue eyes that had got her into so much trouble in the first place.

'It's been life-changing here, too. But it sounds like you might have a few stories to tell?'

She could tell *him* a few! About what had happened after he'd left. About the decisions she'd had to make. How she'd done everything alone—as always. But she couldn't right now. How could she? He'd only just got here. He'd only just arrived. Let the poor guy take his coat off before—

'I certainly do. We ought to catch up some time.'

He paused briefly, then reached out to catch her arm. Electricity crackled along her skin like a lightning strike.

'I'm glad you're here.'

His touch burned her skin and she stared at him in shock before pulling her arm free. Unable to stand his close contact, and the effect it was having on her breathing and pulse rate, she stepped farther away, putting a trolley between them and distracting herself by fiddling with the pressed bed sheets, pillowcases and yellow blankets piled upon it.

She picked up one or two and took great interest in folding and refolding them, giving herself time to recover from his touch. To cool down. For her heart rate to slow.

Time to think of something to say.

How *did* you tell a man that he was a father? Completely out of the blue?

By the way, you ought to know...you're a father.

No! She couldn't say it like that. It wasn't something

you could come straight out with. There had to be some sort of preamble. An introduction.

Jacob? You remember that night we spent together? Look, I know we used protection, but somehow it didn't work and...

Hmm... That didn't seem all that marvellous, either.

Jacob...there's no easy way to say this, so I'm just going to come straight out with it...you're a father.

'Let me show you around the department' was what she came up with.

That was easier. By being professional, by not actually looking at him, she could almost forget...almost pretend he was someone else. A junior, maybe. A complete stranger.

She led him around the Minors area and then into Majors, Resus, Triage, the waiting room, stockrooms, sluice and cubicles, talking nonstop about all kinds of things—hospital policy, staff rotas, tricks to know when dealing with the computer—anything and everything but the one thing she wished she *could* talk to him about but was afraid to tell him.

She was talking so he didn't have the chance to ask questions. And all the while aware of his proximity, his dark brooding outline, his expensive clothing, the feel of him near her once again.

She knew she was babbling. He was playing havoc with her senses. It was as if her body had been awoken by his presence. The way a flower reacted to the sun.

Her mind devilishly replayed a memory of his kiss. How his lips had felt upon hers. How they'd drifted ever so lightly across her skin, sending shivers of delicious delight through her body, arousing her nerve endings to touch in a way they had never been before, making her ache for more.

Eva could remember it all too well.

Every sizzling second of it.

Jacob had made her feel so *alive*! She'd had a long day at work that day, and when she'd made it to that party she'd felt exhausted—bereft of feeling. Yet in his arms she'd become energised, had tingled and yearned for his every touch, savouring every caress, consuming every desire and gasping her way through her ecstasy.

Feeling alive once again.

That one night had changed her entire life.

She shivered at the thought, those goosebumps rising again and her nipples hardening against her bra in expectancy. He was the only man who had ever made her feel that way. The only man she'd ever slept with since that night. The memory of him, the experience of him, had stopped her being intimate with any other. No one could measure up to his memory.

Not that there'd been anyone to challenge it, really.

Eva mumbled her way through the details of the filing system and how to operate the computer patient files, work through any glitches on the system, then asked him if he'd like to take on his first patient.

He cocked his head as he looked at her, trying to get her to make eye contact. 'You okay? I mean, I hope our having to work together isn't going to be uncomfortable?'

No, I'm not okay. You're back! You're back, and I had no warning. No time to prepare. And I have something momentous to tell you. And it will change your life. And I'm so aware of that and—

'I'm fine. It's…just been a difficult morning.'

He nodded in understanding. 'Anything I can help with?'

'No.'

He raised his eyebrow in such a perfect arch it was all she could do not to race into his arms there and then.

'Are you sure?'

How are you with kids? Do you even like children? Because I have some news for you...

Eva sighed and shook her head.

No, she wasn't sure.

She wasn't sure at all.

How to tell him that he was father to a beautiful, bright, funny, gorgeous three-year-old boy, who obsessed over lions and tigers and looked *exactly like him*?

She swallowed a lump in her throat as fear overturned her stomach. Nausea unsettled her. A close sweat beaded her brow as guilt and shame overflowed from the box where she normally kept all those feelings tightly locked away.

What was she to do?

Eva slammed a patient file down hard on the doctors' desk, the slap of cardboard on table echoing around the department, then sank heavily into a chair. Her fingertips punched into the keyboard as she began to write up some notes. She had no time. They were already running behind. Patients were filling up the waiting area and two were about to breach the four-hour limit.

Patients who had turned up because there were no district nurses to unblock catheters. Patients who were filling the corridors because there were no beds to put them in. Patients who were turning up just because they didn't want to be alone at home and they needed someone to talk to just a couple of weeks before Christmas.

The need to immerse herself in work and forget about the new doctor was overwhelming.

If she absorbed herself in work it wouldn't give her any time to think about *him*.

The guy who'd turned her neat little world around in just one night.

Even now she told herself she still didn't know what had happened that night. How had he managed to put her under his spell? She knew it had been a difficult and long day at work. She'd almost not gone to that stupid party. But it had been Christmas Eve, and she'd put herself down to work on Christmas Day, and the need to celebrate the season, despite not having any family of her own, had made her go. Just to have a drink or two with friends. Chill out for a moment.

And she'd done that. Had actually been enjoying herself for a brief time when she'd noticed him across the room.

Those eyes. Those piercing blue eyes. But she had noticed something in his gaze. A loss—a grief so deep it had called to her.

She'd recognised emotional pain. And, having been in a similar place herself, she'd hoped she could soothe him. No one had ever helped *her*. But maybe she could help him? Just for a moment, if nothing else.

Then, when he'd noticed her, something had happened. Something weird and dreamlike. As if the rest of the world had melted away and it had been just the two of them, standing in front of each other. Close. Almost touching. He'd said his name and then she'd been in his arms. Dancing with him. Swaying with him. Their bodies mirroring the other, blending together, matching the other.

Melting into one.

There'd been something magical that night.

And it seemed he was still magical now!

How involved would he want to be with his child? He might not even care! He might not want anything to do with them! Perhaps he'd be the type of guy who only paid child support. She wouldn't hate him for that. She'd be disappointed, but in fact she quite liked the idea that she wouldn't have to share Seb. She enjoyed it being just the two of them. It had always just been the two of them. She'd never had to share him.

Jacob could be in a relationship already with someone else. A man who looked the way he did? Of course he would be! A man like him wouldn't be single. If she'd ever entertained any grand idea that they would somehow end up together...

Her hand holding the pen trembled. She put it down for a moment and just sat for a second or two to pause and gather herself, to take in a deep breath and steady her jangled nerves. She could feel her heart slowing, could breathe more easily. Could act the professional doctor she believed herself to be.

Picking up her patient notes, she strode off to Minors.

Leo Rosetti had been brought in by his wife, Sonja. His knee hurt, and despite his taking painkillers at home nothing would touch it.

Eva entered the cubicle smiling, and closed the curtain behind her. 'Good morning, Mr Rosetti. I'm Eva, one of the doctors here in A&E. Can you tell me what's happened this morning to bring you in?'

There. That was better, she thought. Focus on the patients. Not on the fact that a certain someone had re-entered her life and turned it upside down and inside out.

'Well, Doctor, I've got this terrible pain here.' He leaned forward on the bed and rubbed at his left knee through his trousers. 'It's awful, I tell you. Really hurts.'

'And how long has it been like this?'

'Since the beginning of December now, and I really don't feel well in myself, either. It's not good for a person to live with pain day after day.'

No. It wasn't. Especially the emotional kind.

'He's diabetic, Doctor,' the wife interjected. 'And he's got osteoarthritis in both his knees. Had it for years. But he says this is different.'

Eva asked if he could roll up his trouser leg and she examined the grossly swollen knee. 'Are you on any meds, Mr Rosetti?'

'Leo, Doctor, please. I'm on metformin for the diabetes.'

She gave him a general check and then carried out a primary survey, asking questions about his general state of health, taking his BP and arranging for a full blood count and an X-ray, even though Leo said he hadn't knocked or damaged the knee as far as he knew.

'Will he be all right, Doctor? We're going away this weekend.'

'Oh, yes? Anywhere nice?'

'Africa—well, Kenya specifically. We're going on safari. Thought we'd do something different for Christmas, now that the kids have flown the nest.'

Africa. What *was* it with Africa?

She coloured as she thought of Jacob and what it had been like to see him again. That intense look in his eyes. Still with the power to make her go all weak at the knees as it once had.

Feeling guilty at having let her mind wander whilst she was with a patient, she smiled quickly. 'I'll be back in a moment to do the bloods.'

She pulled the curtain across and exhaled quietly and slowly, closing her eyes as she tried to gather her thoughts, her hand still clutching the curtain.

Seriously—what was going on here? Why was she allowing herself to get so worked up?

So Jacob was here? Big deal! He was just a guy. Just a...

I need to pull myself together!

This was not like her! She was normally an organised person. Efficient. She didn't get distracted at work! There was too much at stake to let personal feelings get in the way whilst she was there.

A distracted doctor was a dangerous doctor.

She hurried back to her seat to write up her notes, managing a weak smile as Sarah settled next to her.

'You okay?'

'Sure!' She tried to answer cheerily. 'Just…you know… busy.'

'Really? You seem a bit flushed about that new guy. Anything I can do?'

'Short of growing another pair of arms? Seriously, I could really do without having to babysit a new doctor—'

'So how do you know him?'

Her cheeks burned hot. 'I don't—not really. We only met once before.'

'Come on! He knew your name! You *know* him. How come?'

Eva stared hard at her friend, afraid to give the answer. Afraid to voice the thing that mattered the most to her in the whole world.

Because he's Seb's father.

She muttered something unintelligible and hurried away.

Her patient, Leo, had his bloods done and sent off, and also an X-ray that showed osteoarthritic changes and some mild widening in the joint space of his knee. The blood cultures wouldn't be available for three days, but his Hb levels were normal.

As the knee itself was hot and swollen, she felt it was wise to do a fine needle aspiration to draw off some of the fluid for testing. As she did so she noted that the fluid was quite cloudy, and she marked the tests to check for white blood cell count with differential, gram stain and culture.

She suspected a septic arthritis, and knew the joint would probably have to be drained until dry, as often as was necessary.

'It shouldn't affect your holiday as it's important you keep moving, Leo.'

Mr Rosetti and his wife smiled at each other, and she was about to leave them alone and send the aspirated fluid to Pathology, when Jacob pulled open the curtain and asked if he could have a quick word.

Excusing herself from her patient, she stepped outside of the cubicle with him, feeling her heart race once again. What did he want? Had he found out about Seb?

Her brain quickly tried to formulate an answer about that. 'Look, I meant to—'

'There's been a road accident. We've been phoned to let us know that a number of child casualties are coming our way.'

Children? Eva's heart sank. She could only hope that the children about to come into the department would have simple minor injuries.

They began a hurried walk to Resus. Eva's mind was focused firmly on the news. 'Any idea of the number of casualties?'

'Not at this stage. But it was a school minibus carrying a number of children across town. The police suspect they hit some black ice.'

Her heart thumped hard. She knew Seb's school had been attending a Christmas church service today.

'What age range?'

'We don't have any more details yet.'

It *couldn't* be Seb's school, Eva thought. Someone would have phoned her already.

'Has anyone let Paeds know?'

He nodded. 'I did. They're sending a team down as soon as they've got people to spare.'

'There's no one free *now*?'

What was she doing? She shouldn't raise her voice at him. It wasn't his fault, was it?

They burst through into Resus.

'What's the ETA?'

A nurse put down the phone. 'Seven minutes.'

'Let's get organised. Check equipment trolleys, monitors, sterile packs, gauze—everything and anything. We've an unknown number of paediatric casualties coming in and I want this to run smoothly. Let's prepare for crush injuries, possible fractures, whiplash and maybe burns. Have we ordered blood?'

Sarah and another doctor, Brandon, arrived in Resus. 'We're on it.'

She nodded at both of them. 'I'll lead team one—Sarah, you can be team two... Brandon three.'

'Where do you want me?' asked Jacob.

Ideally as far away from me as possible.

'Work with Brandon.'

'Okay.'

He wrapped a plastic apron around himself and grabbed for gloves before glancing at the clock, walking away to join Brandon.

She watched him go, knowing that at some point she was going to have to tell him the truth.

Just not now.

Six minutes to go.

Eva pulled on her own apron and donned gloves, her

heart pounding, her pulse thrumming like a well-oiled racing car.

Five minutes.

All eyes were on the clock.

Watching it tick down.

CHAPTER TWO

AMBULANCE SIRENS GREW louder and closer as the staff waited, tense and raring to go. These were the moments that Eva both loved and hated.

Loved because of the way Resus went quiet as they all waited, pensive, with adrenaline urging their muscles to get moving.

Hated because she never quite knew what horrors she might yet encounter.

Still the paediatric team had not arrived.

Outside, there was the sound of rumbling engines and then the distant beeping sound of a reversing vehicle. Hospital doors slid open as the first patient came in.

Eva spotted a small dark-haired child, wearing a neck brace and on a backboard, and heard the paramedic firing off details about the patient.

'This is Ariana, aged three. Ariana was restrained by a seat belt but endured a side impact of about thirty miles an hour. Head to toe: small abrasion on the forehead, complaining of neck pain, score of eight, bruising across the chest and middle, due to the seat belt, lower back and pelvis pain, which is secured with a splint, GCS of fifteen throughout, BP and pulse normal.'

Ariana? Didn't her son Seb know a girl in his nursery school called Ariana?

Eva tried not to panic. She had to focus on the little girl in her care. Surely the school would have rung her if anything had happened to Seb? Although her phone was turned off, of course, and in her locker. She'd run and check as soon as she got the chance. Ariana was her priority right now.

'Ariana? My name's Eva. I'm one of the doctors here and I'm going to look after you.'

The way you dealt with any patient was important, but when it came to dealing with children—children who didn't yet have their parents there to advocate for them— Eva felt it was doubly important. You *had* to let them know it was okay to be scared, but that they would be looked after very well and that the staff would do their utmost to get the child's parents there as quickly as possible.

Ariana looked terrified. She had a bad graze on her forehead, probably from smashed glass, and her eyes were wide and tearful. Her bottom lip was trembling and it was obvious she was trying not to cry.

Eva's heart went out to her. How terrifying it must be to be that small, alone and hurt, in a strange place that smelled funny and sounded funny, surrounded by strangers who all wanted to poke you and prod at you and stick you with needles, saying they'd make you feel better.

'We need to check you're okay, Ariana. What a pretty name! Now, I'm just going to use this—' she held up her stethoscope '—to listen to your chest. Is that all right?' Eva always made sure her paediatric patients understood what she was doing.

Ariana tried to nod, but her head's movement was restricted by the neck immobiliser. 'Ow! It hurts!'

'Which bit hurts, honey?'

'My neck.'

'Okay, I'll check that out for you in just a moment.'

Ariana's chest sounded clear, which was a good sign. However, neck pain was not. It could simply be whiplash, but with neck pain you never took a chance.

'We'll need to take a couple of special pictures. But don't you worry—they won't hurt. It's just a big camera.'

She looked up at the team she was working with, awaiting their feedback. One was checking the patient's airway, another was checking her breathing, another Ariana's circulation. One would get IV access for the admission of drugs or painkillers or blood, if it was needed. Each doctor or nurse was calling out a result or observation. They all worked as a highly efficient team so that patients were quickly and perfectly assessed as soon as they arrived in Resus.

Ariana was looking good at the moment. With the exception of the neck pain and the pelvic brace she was doing well, and she was responsive, which was very important. Her blood pressure was stable, so hopefully that meant no internal bleeding at all for them to worry about.

Behind her, Eva heard the Resus doors bang open once again as another patient arrived from the accident. She risked a quick glance to see who had come in. She knew Sarah or Brandon would take care of the new patient and she could focus all her attention on Ariana.

'Have the parents been called?'

One of the nurses replied, 'We believe the school are trying to contact parents now.'

'Good. Did you hear that, Ariana? We're going to find your mummy and daddy.'

She couldn't imagine what it must be like to get that call, being a mother herself. Luckily, so far, Seb hadn't been involved in anything serious like that. The only time she'd ever been woken by a phone call was when he'd gone for a sleepover at a friend's house and the mother had rung at about eleven o'clock at night to say that Seb couldn't get to sleep without his cuddly lion.

Nothing like this, thank goodness.

But having Ariana in front of her was making her doubtful. This sweet little girl looked familiar, and she felt *so sure* that Seb had a girl in his nursery class called Ariana...

If it *was* the same preschool as Seb... If he'd been hurt...

Her stomach did a crazy tumble.

She glanced across at the other teams. Sarah was busy assessing a patient and Brandon and Jacob were looking after their own little charge.

She turned back to Ariana, who was now holding her hand, and showed her the Wong-Baker FACES pain-rating scale—a series of cartoon faces that helped really young children scale their pain.

'Which one of these are you, Ariana? Zero? Which means no hurting? Or ten? Which means hurting the worst?'

She watched as Ariana looked at all the little cartoon faces and pointed at four—'Hurts A Little More'.

Good—the painkillers were taking effect. Hopefully that four would drop. Earlier, the paramedic had said her pain score was eight, so it was better, even if it wasn't perfect.

Eva continued to hold Ariana's hand. It was a soothing thing to do whilst they waited for their turn at CT and X-ray. If it had been Seb trapped in a hospital bed she would hope that the doctor caring for him would do the same thing, too, until she arrived.

Ariana's CT scan was clear. The computer tomography scan showed internal slices through the body, so that breaks or bleeds could be seen much more clearly. Her pelvis was fine, as was her neck. Eva decided that she'd wait until they got back to Resus before she took off the immobiliser from Ariana's neck and the brace from her pelvis.

As they wheeled her out of CT one of the nurses let Eva know that Ariana's parents were on their way.

When they arrived back in the department Eva made the decision to take Ariana to the cubicles. Minors was busy, as some of the lesser injured children from the minibus had filled it up, and they still had a waiting room full of patients who hadn't been involved but had come in with various ailments or injuries.

'We'll wait in here for Mummy and Daddy. This is much less scary than where we were before, isn't it?' She smiled at her patient.

Ariana was looking much happier now that the immobiliser and brace were off. She'd been a very lucky girl.

'Ariana...I know you were going on a trip with your nursery. Which nursery do you go to?'

Please don't say Pear Tree Pre-School!

'The one next to the big school.'

Pear Tree Pre-School was next to an infant school...

'What's your teacher's name?'

Seb's teacher was Miss Dale. She was a very pretty young woman, with the sweetest nature, and Eva secretly wondered how she managed to keep her perfect composure all day long when surrounded by thirty-odd preschoolers.

'Miss Dale.'

Oh, my God! Seb!

'Ariana, I just need to check on something. Stay here, honey.'

She yanked open the curtain and fled from the cubicle, flagging down a passing nurse to sit with Ariana before heading straight to the minors board, looking for her son's name.

Her eyes skim-read all the names until she saw it: Corday, Sebastian.

Please let him be all right!

She was about to rush off and find him when she did a double take, noticing the name of the doctor tending to him.

Jacob Dolan.

A sick chill had pervaded her body and her limbs felt numb and lifeless.

Jacob was with his son and he didn't even know it!

Seb was talking to his father and he had no clue!

She forced her limbs to move. Forced her heavy body to start making its way to the cubicle where her life would change drastically.

Cubicle number four.

What were they talking about? Seb couldn't be that injured if he was in Minors, but how bad was he? Was he sitting up in bed, chatting with his father? Was her secret out already?

No, not possible. Surely...?

Eva walked towards the cubicle with its closed curtain, a feeling of dread sitting low and heavy in her stomach. She could hear laughter inside, and Seb's gentle chuckling.

She was just about to pull the curtain back when she felt a hand on her arm.

Sarah and Brandon wanted to give feedback. One child had a small fracture of the wrist and severe bruising where the seat belt had crossed the body. Another had dislocated her shoulder, but it had been reduced and put into a sling. The teacher driving and all the other adults had got away with nothing more than whiplash and bruising.

'Nothing more severe? Thank goodness for that. They've been lucky, all of them.'

As Sarah and Brandon went back to their respective

charges Eva couldn't help but relax her shoulders, but she took a deep breath before she whipped back the curtain.

Seb was sitting up in bed, a broad smile on a face that was peppered with cuts. Jacob was seated on a stool next to him, about to glue a cut on his scalp.

'Mummy!' Seb saw her and lifted his arms for a cuddle.

Eva hurried over to him, waiting for the axe to fall, waiting for Jacob to do the maths and accuse her of being some heartless witch...

'Seb! Are you okay?'

Jacob held off with the glue, giving them a moment. 'Hello, Seb's mum.'

She chose not to look at Jacob, knowing that if she did her eyes would give her away. Instead, she rapidly checked her son over, her hands grasping at his limbs, feeling for hidden injury. Apart from the cut on his scalp, he didn't seem too bad.

She picked up his chart from the end of the bed and read through it. 'Nothing serious, thank goodness.'

Jacob was watching her. 'Just some minor cuts and scratches, thankfully. His head was banged against the side window, which has given him the small laceration that I was going to glue. He should be fine.'

'Does he need a head CT?'

'Dr Ranjit has checked him and said it wasn't necessary.'

Dr Ranjit was a paediatric neurologist, so she had to assume he was right. 'I see...'

'Seb and I were just talking about lions. Apparently they're his favourite animal.'

'He loves lions.'

Jacob tilted his head at her curt tone, looking at her curiously. Then he asked Seb to put his head back against the pillow so that he could administer the glue. 'Be brave, now—this might tingle a bit.'

Eva gripped her son's hand tightly, smiling brightly into his face to encourage him to be brave.

He looked *so* like Jacob! Couldn't Jacob see it? They both had the same almost black hair, slightly wavy. The same bright blue eyes...the same nose and mouth. It seemed that when genetics were being decided upon Mother Nature had decided to give Seb only his mother's skin tone—very pale and creamy, with hints of pink in his cheeks. Apart from that, he was the spitting image of his father.

And this was not how she'd wanted Jacob to find out. She'd wanted to be able to tell him somewhere peaceful and neutral—perhaps the hospital grounds in a secluded corner? To buy him a coffee and ask him if he had time for a chat, and then slowly drip feed the information about what had happened after he left.

Not like this. Not in front of her son!

Seb winced as the glue went onto the edges of his wound and Jacob pinched them together to help them adhere.

'You're doing great, honey.' Eva rubbed his hands in hers and wished she could take away the pain. The discomfort. Do what she could to make her son feel better.

'I didn't know you were a mother.'

She looked at Jacob quickly, and then away, guilt flooding her cheeks with heat. 'No, well...things change.'

'How old are you, Seb?' he asked, frowning.

'Three.' Seb smiled. 'It doesn't hurt now.'

Jacob nodded and let go, and the wound's edges stayed together. He pulled off his gloves and smiled. 'There you go. It doesn't need a plaster or anything. Just don't get it wet. Well done, Seb! You're very brave.'

Seb beamed with pleasure.

'Can I take him home now?' Eva started to gather her son's things. His backpack had been put on the end of his bed, and his jacket.

'He needs to stay here for an hour or two for observation. He *has* had a bump to the head.'

He was staring at her, his eyes full of questions.

He knows!

She had to get out of there! She did not want to have this conversation in front of Seb! She would *not* have this conversation in front of him. No. Not at all.

But he had to stay. For observation. Couldn't she observe him at home? She was an A&E doctor after all…

'May I have a word with you, Dr Corday?'

Oh, this is it. Here it comes…

'Sure. But…um…later, maybe? I need to arrange cover if I'm going home.'

'Could we talk *now*?'

She looked at Seb. Then back at Jacob.

'Let me get him sorted first.'

She rummaged in his backpack and found his reading book. She passed it to him.

'Have a read of your book, Seb. I'm just going to step outside the curtains and have a talk with Dr Dolan.'

Eva followed Jacob from the cubicle and went with him over to the quiet corner by the Christmas tree.

It looked beautiful this year. The team had really done themselves proud. For years they'd had a tired old fake tree that had been packed away each year in an old cardboard box, battered and unloved. But this year they had a real tree, beautifully decorated in gold and silver, with lots of pretend presents underneath.

Eva and Seb had been really looking forward to Christmas. This year it seemed Seb really understood what was going on, and what was happening, and the story of Santa

Claus had got him so excited! They'd already put their own tree up at home.

But Eva wasn't excited right now. She felt dread. And guilt. All those emotions she'd kept hidden away for years, since that first night with Jacob, neatly locked down, were now threatening to overwhelm her with their enormity.

She stood in front of Jacob like a naughty child before the headmaster. But then she thought about how he was guilty, too. About his part in all of this.

She squared her shoulders back and looked him in the eye. 'Yes?'

'You seem a little...distracted.'

She said nothing. Just stared at him. Waiting for the axe to fall.

'Seb's a great kid.'

'He is. The best.'

'You weren't a mother when we met.'

Her cheeks flamed. 'No.'

'But you are now. And he's three?'

'Yes.'

Jacob seemed to be mulling over his next words. Thinking about what he might say next. Whether she would rebut his words or accept them.

'He looks like me.'

Eva stared deeply into his bright blue eyes...eyes so much like Seb's. She couldn't—wouldn't—deny him the truth. He deserved that.

'Yes.'

Jacob's voice lowered. 'Is he mine, Eva?'

Of course he's yours! Surely it's clear to everyone?

She wanted to yell. She wanted to confirm it to him angrily. Rage at him for all he'd put her through after he left. But she didn't. She knew that could come later. Right now he just needed the plain facts.

'Yes. Seb's your son.'

He stood staring at her, his face incredulous.

The Christmas tree twinkled between them.

She couldn't help but notice how his broad shoulders narrowed down into a neat, flat waist. How his expensively tailored trousers moulded his shape, his long, muscular legs. He looked mouth-wateringly good. The years he'd spent in Africa had obviously been good to him. He was vital and in peak condition.

Years before, when they'd met at that party, there'd been only hints of the man he was to become. But even then he'd been delicious… Now the heavier muscle and perfectly toned body looked amazing on him…

She swallowed hard.

All she'd known about him that night was his name and that he was going to work for some charity. That he was a doctor, like her, and was going to Africa. But just because that was what he'd said, she hadn't been sure it was true. People lied. Especially at parties. To make themselves sound better or more interesting than they actually were.

Jacob. In *her* A&E. Standing there. As large as life. As gorgeous and as sexy as he'd ever been. A hundred times more so.

He was just staring back at her, his mouth slightly open, as if he'd had something he was about to say only it had never come out.

She couldn't just stand there! Waiting for the axe to fall. To see his reaction. Waiting for him to reject them.

So Eva turned and headed in the opposite direction— back through the curtains of the cubicle that held her son.

Their son.

If she just accepted right now that Jacob wasn't going to be sticking around—he was just a locum after all, here for the busy Christmas period—then it wouldn't hurt as badly.

She couldn't expect him to stay. She and Seb deserved to be loved 100 percent. Eva refused to accept anything less.

'Seb will be okay to go home soon. I'll have to take the rest of the day off. There's no one else to take him, and I can't get my neighbour Letty in—not after this.'

'The new doc can pick up the slack,' Sarah said.

'Jacob.' Her mouth and lips and tongue flowed over his name like a caress.

Eva turned to go and get Seb, then realised her coat and bag were in her locker on the other side of the department. She hurried to get them, flushing as she went past the double doors to Resus.

She had to be quick. Her fingers fumbled over the combination lock and her hands were shaking by the time she managed to open it.

She'd worried so much about how Jacob would react upon finding out he had a son that she hadn't given a thought as to how *Seb* might react if he found out! He didn't even know he *had* a father. Seb hadn't yet asked, and she'd been too afraid to broach the subject with her very young son, deciding to wait until he was older to tell him what little she knew about Jacob.

Eva hurried from the staff locker room and headed for the cubicles.

She wanted to go home *now*!

CHAPTER THREE

HE HAD A SON? A *son*!

That little boy. Seb. He'd just been *talking* to him, taking care of him, and he'd not once suspected that he was his son.

But why would he? Just because the boy had had the same hair as him and the same eye colour…that didn't mean he should have suspected at all…

Why the hell hadn't Eva told him about Seb? Why had she kept him a secret?

He couldn't bear that. Secrets were dangerous.

He had to talk to her. Find out more. Find out what had happened after he left.

Walking away from the Christmas tree, he headed back to the cubicles—only to find Eva there, putting on her coat and scarf.

'Where are you going?'

'Home. I can observe Seb there. I *am* qualified.'

'He needs to stay here.'

She looked at him. 'This is nothing to do with you. You don't have to pretend to care.'

'Seb is *everything* to do with me—and not just as his doctor. And I do care.'

Eva stared at him, and as he waited for her to say something Seb peeked at him over his book and smiled.

Jacob couldn't help but smile back. Seb was a cute little guy.

Then he looked back at Eva. 'You both need to stay. We need to talk.'

She shook her head. 'I'm not ready for this right now.'

'Tough. It's happening.'

He dared her to defy him. If she chose to walk away right now, then he had no idea what he would say. He'd probably have to chase her until she gave up and headed back to A&E. But thankfully he didn't have to do any of that.

Eva let out a big huff, and then removed her scarf and unbuttoned her coat. 'Fine.'

Jacob let out a breath and his shoulders sagged down. He hadn't realised how tense he'd been. He couldn't help but look at Seb now.

He looked tall for a three-year-old. Like himself, he supposed. He could remember his mum saying that he'd always been tall for his age. Then again, Eva wasn't short, either. But now, the more he looked at his son the more he could see himself in the little boy. Seb's eyes were the same shape and colour as his, he had the same wavy hair, the same shaped mouth...

It was like looking at a mini-me.

And he was *three* years old...

Three years that he had missed out on. Three years of important milestones—his first word, his first steps, his first tooth, his first Christmas!

I've missed everything. Birthdays and Christmases...

How had he not known about his own son? More important, why had Eva kept it from him? For three years! The last woman who had kept a secret from him had almost destroyed him.

Jacob called for one of the healthcare assistants to sit

with Seb. 'Don't let him out of your sight,' he said, then guided Eva into the staff room and slammed the door closed behind them.

Three years! I've had a son for three years and she never told me!

Fury and rage that he'd never thought it possible for one human being to contain filled his body, making it quake, and he had to grit his teeth to try to bring it under some form of control.

'What the *hell* have you done?'

She looked up at him, her eyes wide and defiant as a solitary tear dribbled down her face. Even crying she was beautiful, and he hated her for that. Why couldn't she look wretched? Why couldn't she look awful, as if she were suffering for the pain she'd caused him?

He recalled Michelle standing in front of him, crying, begging for his forgiveness...

'I've done nothing wrong.'

He looked at her, incredulous. 'Nothing *wrong*?'

'I'm raising a boy on my own and I'm doing a damned fine job, thank you very much!'

'Oh, I'm sure that you are—but what about me? Did you not think our son deserved a father?'

'Of course I did!'

A horrible thought occurred to him. 'Are you with someone else? Is another man raising my child?'

She shook her head. 'No.'

'Then, why didn't you find me and tell me?'

'I tried! Believe me, I tried! But I only had your name, and I knew you were going to work for a charity in Africa. I had no way to track you down.'

'Did you even try?'

She wiped the tear from her cheek. 'Do you know how

many charities do work in Africa? Do you know how much research that would have taken?'

'You could have asked my friends from the party! They would have known!'

'I did! They told me you were working with Change for Children, but when I contacted them, they told me you'd already left!'

He stared at her. It was true. He had worked for them, but only for a little while. And then he'd met that doctor working for a different charity and he'd gone with him, hoping to assist with an eye clinic...

Had he told anyone? Had he told anyone the specifics of where he was going next? He couldn't remember. Surely he must have said something? But even if he had, would she have been able to track him down? He'd still been running then. He would not have left a way for himself to be traced by his family...

Was all this *his* fault? If he'd only thought to leave a forwarding address... Only he hadn't, had he? Because he'd been trying to avoid his family tracking him down and sending him letters, bothering him with all their worry and their 'Are you all right?' and 'Are you coming home?'

He'd always assumed that when the time came he would be there for his children. As his father had been for him. He'd imagined what it might be like to hold his baby in his arms... And Eva had had his child, not found him to tell him about it, and his own son had been without him for three years. If he'd known he wouldn't have stayed in Africa for so long...or even gone there in the first place!

Words couldn't adequately describe how angry he felt right now.

And for it to be *Eva* who had done this to him. The woman who had sashayed into his life one night, blown his mind and made him feel more alive than he'd felt in a year! The woman who'd filled his dreams for many a night subsequently. The woman who'd made him regret leaving England. The woman he'd thought about coming back home for.

He'd never have expected that *she* would do this to him!

'So…what does Seb know about me?'

She folded her arms. 'Nothing yet. He's too young to have asked about his dad. I had planned, when the time came, to tell him that you were in Africa, with no means of communication.'

'Africa…'

He'd loved it there. It had been such an education for him—would have been for any doctor—to go from a high-tech medicalised hospital to work in a ramshackle, dusty building that barely had instruments, lights or monitoring equipment. Many a time he'd been so frustrated at the lack of equipment, at the numbers of people they'd lost because they didn't have adequate resources, that he'd decided to come home again and again, after every loss, but he never had.

If only I had…

Then he might have learned about Seb sooner. Learned about Eva. Could he forgive her? This was Eva—the woman he'd…

Jacob cleared his throat. 'I've lost so much time with him already. He needs to know who I am.'

She stood up instantly, her body blocking the door. 'You're not going in there to tell him right now.'

He raised an eyebrow. 'He needs to know.'

Eva nodded. 'Then, I'll tell him. At home. In his own space. Then maybe… I don't know…perhaps you could come round later? Get to know him? Next week, perhaps…'

'Give me your address. I'll be round tonight.'

'Tonight? I don't—'

'Tonight. I've already lost three years.'

She looked down at the ground. 'I need more time.'

Jacob stepped forward so that he faced her, his nose mere inches away from hers. 'You've already had three years. Tell him today. Or we both tell him tonight, when I come round. Your call.'

Eva backed away from the intense, angry stare of Jacob's eyes. She'd had no idea of how angry he'd be. Or, really, what type of man he was. She'd allowed herself to be seduced by a stranger that night. She only knew one side of him.

'I'll tell him. I was the one who kept it from him after all.'

The way she looked at him then, with those beautiful crystal blue eyes of hers—the palest of blue, like snow ice on the polar caps—he had a flashback to how those eyes had looked into his that night they'd spent together, and a smack of desire hit him hard and low in the groin.

How could he still desire her when she'd just driven him mad with anger?

'You know what hurts the most, Eva?'

She shook her head, her full, soft lips slightly apart, so he had to fight the urge to kiss her. It was as if there was a battle going on in his body. Half of him wanted to be furious with her; the other half wanted to take her to bed and make her gasp with delight.

'Not only did you keep Seb from *me*, you also kept Seb from my parents. Grandparents who would love him. Aunts and uncles who would adore him. Cousins who could be his friends. My family would *adore* Seb.'

'They still can...'

'But only because I came here.' He reached up and re-moved a wave of red hair from her cheek, then realised what he was doing and dropped it like a hot coal. 'How much longer would you have kept the secret if I'd gone elsewhere?'

She seemed nervous of his touch, her breath hitching in her lungs and then escaping when he let go of her hair. She was breathing heavily, and he felt empowered to know he had that control over her. That she still responded to his touch.

He'd never forgotten that one night…

'Jacob, I—'

'What's your address?'

Reluctantly, she told him.

He stepped past her and yanked open the locker room door.

'I'll be round at six.'

And then he left, leaving her alone.

Eva stood gasping like a landed fish after he'd left the locker room. As the door slowly closed behind him she sank down onto the bench and let out a long, slow, breath.

Jacob knew. And it had been every bit as horrible as she'd feared.

She felt she should have told him when she'd had that moment in Resus. Perhaps it might have gone better? If she'd been honest with him when she'd had the chance? But, no, she hadn't said anything. Instead, she'd sneaked away like a frightened mouse. And now look what had happened.

She'd *wanted* to tell him. She'd wanted to tell him ever since she'd discovered she was pregnant! But…

She hadn't been able to find him. She'd blamed him for being untraceable.

She'd wanted Seb to have it all! A mother *and* a father. As she'd *never* had. She'd promised herself that when-ever she had kids her children would have the firm foundation of a loving family. Of growing up surrounded by love and security.

When she'd realised she couldn't trace Jacob she'd quickly accustomed herself to the idea of raising Seb alone. Of relying only on herself—the way she'd always done! Seb would be able to rely on her. She'd be the best mother she could be. Her child would have the certainty that she was there to stay and she would love him more than life itself. Do the job of both parents.

Her feelings for Jacob she could control. What had they been but fantasy? He was a man she'd been able to put on a pedestal because she hadn't known him long enough to discover otherwise. Who knew what he was really like?

She could *do* this.

It would be easier now. They would be able to work together and she wouldn't have to worry anymore about him finding out about Seb. The worst was over.

Wasn't it?

She caught her own worried gaze in the mirror. Maybe it wasn't. Maybe Jacob would let Seb get to know him and then he'd disappear again? He had a temporary post here—perhaps he'd be a temporary father?

Eva got up and went over to the sinks to splash cold water on her face. She stared again at her reflection in the mirror, dabbing her skin dry with the paper towel.

'Jeez…you really didn't handle *that* very well at all,' she told herself, trying out a tentative smile.

That was better. She needed to look human again before she went to collect Seb. She didn't want him to notice she'd been crying. After today he needed to see his normal mum—the one in control. The one who soothed his brow when he was sick…the one who read to him at nights until he fell asleep. He'd need everything to be normal after the frightening start to his day in the minibus.

But I'm going to have to tell him about Jacob...

Exactly how *did* you tell a three-year-old about his father? Would he even be able to understand what she was telling him? Or would he accept it easily? In her experience her little boy was very adaptable. Maybe he'd take it in his stride?

She threw the paper towel into the bin and continued to look at herself in the mirror. She blinked quickly. The redness in her eyes was almost gone now. By the time she got out there to Seb she should look fine.

Eva opened the door.

Seb was still in his cubicle, but Jacob was with him, holding on to Seb's little fingers as he spoke to him. Seb looked intrigued. So happy. She wondered what they were talking about. She watched them together. The way Jacob spoke, the way he laughed—he was so like Seb. And Seb looked *so* like his father, with his wavy dark hair and intense blue eyes. They were the spitting image of each other. He was so obviously Jacob's little boy.

And I didn't persevere in trying to find him. I should have! We could have had everything we ever wanted...

Yeah, right. As if *that* would ever have happened...

Seb spotted her and waved. 'Can we go home now?'

Jacob didn't smile at her.

'Soon. We need to stay for a while so the doctors can keep an eye on you.'

'Because I banged my head?'

'That's right.' She glanced at Jacob.

He looked to his son. 'You know what, Seb? I'm going to come round to your house tonight. Is that okay?'

Seb nodded emphatically. 'Yes! You can tell me more about lions.'

He smiled. 'I will. I'll tell you anything you want to know.'

Eva stared at him hard, but he looked away from her and down to his son, ruffling his hair.

He'd kept them there as long as he could, but eventually Jacob had watched as his son and Eva left the department.

Hell of a first day!

He'd expected fireworks. He'd expected ups and downs. But not this. Never this!

Three years. He'd been a father for three years. Years that he'd spent in Africa, tending to the poorest and sickest of people, with almost no modern medical facilities. Watching people die needless deaths, getting depressed, drinking too much...

Thank goodness he'd stopped with the alcohol. That had been a stupid path to go down. But what with Michelle and The Wedding That Never Was, he'd felt entitled to a drink. And the drink had helped numb his thoughts. About Michelle. About Eva.

She'd been the last thing he'd expected at that party.

He'd gone there expecting to say goodbye to a couple of friends—people who had been there for him after Michelle, who had let him crash on their floors despite the stuff going on in their own lives—and there she'd been. Standing on the far side of the room, in a dress that hugged in all the right places. That flaming red hair had made her stand out in a room of mousy browns and she'd had the bluest eyes he'd ever seen, her lips curved in a half-smile.

Something about her had intrigued him.

Who *was* she? What was she doing there?

The very fact that he'd actually been thinking those questions had woken something in him. Something that he thought had died along with Michelle. And when he'd held her in his arms to dance, her soft curves moulded into his body, as if she'd been carved specifically for him, he'd turned to mush.

He'd wanted to kiss her. Had wanted to taste her. Possess her. All other thoughts—all the pain, all the grief, all the torment that he'd spent months trying to get rid of—had suddenly dissipated.

All there had been was Eva.

And she'd kept quiet. Not told him he was a father. Not tracked him down. If she had he could've been… He could've had…

He shook his head to clear his thoughts.

She was doing it again. Muddling his mind. What *was* it with women who did this?

He had to think clearly again. There was a reason he didn't like to revisit his past.

Jacob strode back into the department and picked up a patient file. No matter what, life was now going to be different. He'd get to know Seb. Slowly. Not rush it. He'd get to know his son. Let Seb get to know him. *Do I want to see my family again?*

The last time had been on his wedding day. The day that Michelle had died. Almost five years ago.

Since then, he'd been running. Running from his family…running from those who said they loved him because he couldn't cope with them. Couldn't think about dealing with their pity and their sympathy and their sad looks, their supportive pats on his back. He'd not wanted to face any of that. Nor would they have wanted to give it if they knew the whole truth of what had happened that day…

But he could be different now. Couldn't he? It wasn't just him anymore—he wasn't alone now. He had a son, and his son would need him. He refused to let Seb be without his father for a moment longer.

And it was nearly Christmas. Traditionally a time for

family. Perhaps now was the time for him to start building some bridges? Maybe let his parents know about Seb? Maybe Eva would let him take Seb for a visit? They'd love that. Love Seb. And Seb would love Jacob's old childhood home. The smallholding. The animals there. The old orchard where Jacob had spent so many hours himself.

I can't go. There are too many memories there of Michelle...

It was too much to think of going there.

Michelle had grown up right next door. His English rose, with her gorgeous straw-coloured hair that had floated and billowed in the breeze. He could picture her everywhere there. In the orchard. The barn. The house. He could hear her laughter even now, as she danced away from him, always out of reach.

His parents' grief and Michelle's mother's grief would be too much to deal with! How they all managed to still live there, he had no idea!

I bet they still have that picture of us both on the kitchen mantelpiece...

Their engagement picture. He'd felt so happy when she'd said yes.

If only he'd known of the pain she would eventually cause.

CHAPTER FOUR

TELLING SEB ABOUT Jacob was a lot easier than Eva had been expecting.

He sat there on the couch, looking up into her face with those eyes that were so like Jacob's, and she told him the momentous news.

'Seb, I want to talk to you about your daddy.'

'My daddy?'

She'd never really heard him say the word, and to hear it now felt strange. Odd. But she guessed she ought to get used to it. Jacob was back, and from what she'd seen so far he was going to stick around long enough to meet his son. Whether he *stayed* around... Well, that could be another thing entirely. When had anyone ever stuck around for her?

'Yes. You know the man today at the hospital, who helped glue your head?'

'Yes.'

'Well, that was him. That was your daddy.'

Seb seemed to think about it for a moment, his head tilted to one side and his eyes screwed up with concentration. Eva knew she had to say something else to make things clear for him.

'Daddy has been working away since you were born, Seb. In Africa. Remember he told you all about the lions? Well, he was doing very important work, being a doctor like Mummy, so he didn't get a chance to meet you. But now he's back, and he's excited to get to know you, so tonight he's coming to see you.'

'Okay,' he said, and simply went back to watching his television programme.

Eva sat next to him quietly. Waiting to see if he'd say anything else. Ask anything else. But Seb seemed engrossed.

Assuming he was fine, she got up and went into the kitchen. She was thrilled he'd taken it so well, but children were very accepting, in her experience. Until now she had been all that Seb needed.

Eva knew what it was like not to have parents. Growing up in the foster system had been a lonely experience. Some places she'd stayed longer than others, but as she'd been pushed from pillar to post she'd always felt alone and separate. Dependent only on herself for her own happiness.

She'd got used to not relying on other people. Used to people walking away. And she'd known that those who did stay, stayed only until she was sent elsewhere. She'd been a foster child. The families she'd gone to had known she wouldn't be staying forever, so there had always been that detachment. They'd never got close. Never cared for her too much, or loved her too much.

She never got attached to anyone. There was no point. The only person she'd allowed herself to love was Seb, and he meant the world to her. If Jacob was here for now, then great. But she knew she had to hold a piece of herself back from him. A piece of *Seb* back from him.

Just in case.

Because what had life proved to her so far? People pretended they were going to be there forever. Some would even promise it. They'd promised Eva that she would never have to get used to another home ever again. And what had happened? Real sons and daughters had been born and suddenly she'd been cast out. They'd sit her down, then have *that* talk with her about how things weren't working out.

There was no point in getting attached to people.

They just let you down.

And she'd promised herself—and Seb—that if she ever did meet someone she thought could be the great love of her life, then that person would have to love her and Seb 100 percent. She refused to be anyone's second best. Refused to be the 'reserve' love interest.

Eva spent the afternoon getting the place ready for Jacob's arrival. Due to her working full-time, and being a single mother, the house wasn't as presentable as she would have liked. There were stray plastic bricks and action figures everywhere. There was even a platoon of storm troopers guarding the bottom of the stairs.

She cleared away what she could and vacuumed through, polished and cleaned. The Christmas tree was looking a little sad in the corner, so she rearranged some of the ornaments and switched on the lights to give it some life. She laid the dining table with her best china, in case he stayed long enough to sit and eat with them. She cleared the hallway of coats and shoes.

It had become a veritable graveyard of outdoor stuff, even though there was just the two of them, but there was a mix of wellingtons, work shoes, Seb's shoes, trainers and slippers there, all waiting to be tripped over.

She was quite pleased with how neat it all looked when it was cleared away. She'd never been much of a housekeeper, having never had a real home except for this one, and she did her best.

Now, the big question was whether to get dressed up for Jacob's arrival?

If she tried too hard he'd know it. If she dressed casually would that take away from the enormity of the occasion? But didn't Seb need as much as possible to stay the same?

She certainly didn't want Jacob thinking she was dressing up especially for *him*, so she decided on casual. After a quick shower, she dressed in blue jeans and a fitted white T-shirt. Over that she wore a short taupe cardigan. And even though she'd decided not to make herself up especially for Jacob she painted her toenails, because she liked to go barefoot in the house. After a quick blow-dry of her hair, a swipe of mascara, lip gloss and a squirt of perfume, she felt ready.

Two minutes before six the doorbell rang.

Eva swallowed hard and felt her already jangling nerves turn into a cacophony of chaos.

He was here.

Seb's father.

'It's him! It's him!'

Seb rushed past her to get to the door first and she followed sedately after him, to give herself a few last seconds of trying to calm her nerves. She almost felt as if she was walking up to the gallows. She had no idea of how Jacob would be with *her*, but she hoped he would be pleasant in front of Seb.

The mirror in the hall told her she looked just fine. If a little apprehensive...

Seb pulled open the door and beamed at his father. 'Hi.'

'Hello, Seb.' He stood in the doorway, wearing jeans and a T-shirt with a black leather jacket over the top.

She was glad he'd chosen casual, like her, but *his* casual managed to look oh-so-sexy.

In his hands he held a gift-wrapped present, which he handed to Seb. 'This is for you.'

'What is it?'

Seb gave it a shake and Eva recognised the sound of many somethings with many pieces waiting to be built—or eventually, knowing them, sucked up into her vacuum cleaner.

'You'll need to open it to find out. Hello, Eva.' He was now looking at her, his gaze intense and unreadable.

She had to be welcoming and friendly, especially in front of Seb, so she smiled. 'Jacob. Come in. It's cold out! No need to stand in the doorway.'

She held the door open for him, inhaling the scent of him as he passed, the smell sending her back to that night she'd spent naked in his arms, writhing and tingling and gasping her pleasure...

She blinked rapidly. 'Go straight through. Seb, why don't you show your daddy into the lounge?'

She closed the front door and watched Jacob and his son disappear into the room ahead of her.

Get a grip!

She let out a harsh, short breath, then squared her shoulders and headed into the room with them.

Seb was ripping off the wrapping paper on the parcel to discover a large jigsaw puzzle of his favourite cartoon characters. He dropped to the floor in delight so he could study it better.

'You bought him exactly the right thing. He loves jigsaws,' she said, glad she hadn't already bought it and put it under the tree.

Jacob knelt on the floor and watched his son. 'My sister has a son. I tried to remember the sort of thing he was into at this age.'

At the mention of his sister, of Jacob's nephew, Eva felt chastened. She stood in the doorway, not sure what to say next.

Seb looked up from his present and beamed a smile,

then ran over to Jacob and threw his arms around his father's neck. 'Thanks, Daddy!'

Jacob looked surprised at how easily Seb was being with him, then relaxed and hugged his son back. 'No problem.'

Seb let go, and then took a step back and looked at his father. 'I'm Seb.'

Jacob smiled. 'I'm your dad. Pleased to meet you.'

They shook hands, and then Seb giggled and went back to his puzzle.

Jacob looked up at Eva and smiled hesitantly. 'He took it well, then?'

'Yes. Easier than I expected.' She sat down on the couch near him. 'It's been a big day for him, what with the accident this morning and then you. I'm sure all his questions will come later, when it begins to sink in.'

'I'm sure they will, too. He's still okay? After this morning's accident?'

She nodded. He seemed fine.

'Hey, Seb... Want me to help you do it?'

'Yes, please!'

As they huddled together on the carpet, with Jacob pretending to struggle to find pieces, she watched him—this man who had fathered her child. She'd always wondered what he would be like with his son, and here he was, playing it out live in front of her. Jacob seemed at ease with Seb, which was good, and Seb, in turn, seemed comfortable with Jacob.

Eva headed into the kitchen to make them all a drink.

She made up a tray of tea for the two of them, including a real teapot, and a juice for Seb, before heading back out into the lounge. She put the tray down on the coffee table and asked him whether he'd like sugar and milk.

'Milk without, thanks.'

She poured the drinks and sat back.

It was strange. It was almost as if they weren't strangers at all. Seb was laughing and chatting with Jacob, trying to show him how the pieces fitted together and which pieces matched which, and Jacob was laughing and smiling, and it was like watching friends who had known each other for years.

She almost felt like an outsider. The way she had felt as a foster child. Being apart from the family unit, as if she was a visitor.

Her stomach coiled in on itself at the too-familiar hurt and, feeling uneasy, she decided to interrupt. 'Is there anything you want to ask?'

Jacob looked up at her, as if he'd forgotten she was even in the room. She saw him look her up and down and then away. 'I...er...have a lot of questions, actually.'

'Okay. Fire away.'

'You were on your own? For the pregnancy? How did it go?'

She nodded and took a sip of her tea. 'Yes. Totally on my own. When I found out I was pregnant I was shocked. The doctor said I was about two months gone, and pretty much after that the morning sickness started.'

'Was it bad?'

'Pretty bad. I was okay in the mornings, but late afternoons and evenings were the worst—which weren't great whilst I was working shifts at the hospital and getting tired.'

'But you coped?'

'I always do.'

He looked at her then, his eyes holding hers just for a moment longer than was comfortable. 'Any cravings? My mum craved apple pie and custard with me.'

She shook her head. 'No. Not really. But I couldn't stand

the smell or sight of blood…which isn't ideal for an A&E doctor.'

He smiled as he clipped his jigsaw pieces together. 'What did you do?'

'I made sure there were plenty of those cardboard sick bowls in the room with me and got on with it. I wasn't going to have the hospital make special provisions for me.'

'Why?'

'Because I wasn't special.'

She wasn't going to tell him the real reason. That when she was growing up no one had ever made special provisions for her. That she was the one who made provisions for others. Fitting in around everyone else. She'd never received special efforts from anyone. Why would she have expected her colleagues at work to do that?

'And the birth? How did that go?'

Seb looked up. 'Mummy borned me in the water.'

Eva smiled. 'That's right, Seb. It was a water birth. After an extremely long and tiring labour.'

'How long?'

'Forty-two hours.'

'Ouch.'

'Ouch, indeed.' She smiled at him.

He was smiling, too.

When they realised they were smiling at each other they stopped, Jacob looking back down at the jigsaw pieces and Eva down at her cup.

What was she *doing*? She wasn't meant to be getting friendly with him. She was just meant to be polite. For Seb's sake. Nothing else was going to come of this.

'And…er…he was healthy?'

'Very healthy. Nine pounds in weight. Were you a heavy baby?'

'No. A seven-pounder. You?'

'I don't know what I was.' She could see he looked confused. Most people knew how heavy they were when they were born. Their parents usually told them. But she didn't have that information. Had never thought to ask for it, either. 'I didn't have parents,' she explained. 'I grew up in foster care.'

'Mummy had lots of homes!' Seb said, passing Jacob a piece he needed to complete the corner of the picture.

'I'm sorry to hear that.'

He sounded it, too. Genuinely. Which made her look at him carefully. He really had a kind face. It was easy to see in the wide openness of his eyes, the laughter lines around them and the generous smile of his mouth. His features were soft and rounded. There were no sharp lines, no bony angles, no harshness to his features.

She'd always believed you could see the kindness of a person in their face. If someone was a nice character, kind and gentle, then you could see it. But if someone was cruel or nasty or vicious, then you could see that, too. The meanness would be plain to see.

Jacob had a good face. A beautiful face.

And she felt a small amount of hope. That he would be a good dad to her son and remain that way. Seb deserved it. Not that she'd ever let him want for anything. He wasn't spoiled. But he *was* loved. And he knew that he was loved, and she'd tried to love him enough for two. Her guilt at not being able to give him the father he needed had hurt for a long time. But he did have *her*. He had his mother. Which was more than she had ever had.

Jacob hadn't known about his son for three years, though! He'd missed so much! How could she ever make up for that?

'I'll just check on dinner. Would you like to stay?'

Jacob looked up at her...*so* delectable. Heat flooded her cheeks at the thought.

'That would be nice. Thanks.'

'It's just pasta. Crab linguini. Is that all right with you?'

Jacob smiled. 'That would be great. Anything you're having will be fine.'

At that moment he looked so charming and approachable she had to remind herself that even though she'd once slept with this man, made a child with him, they were still strangers.

It was hard for her to get up and move away from them, from their sudden cosy family unit, to go and cook the pasta. But she figured she needed to leave them—to give them some time together without her there. A bit of father and son bonding.

Just cook the pasta. That's all you have to do.

She was successful at that, then hurried to the fridge to prep the crab. She mixed the crab meat with fresh herbs, salt and pepper and a small amount of chilli. It was good to be doing something with her hands, because before she'd been beginning to feel like a spare part. Now she felt useful. As if she was contributing.

She figured she'd better get used to it, because there were bound to be more meetings like this as Jacob and Seb got used to one another. They had so much to learn about each other. Three years of catching up to do.

How many times were you meant to apologise to a man when you'd kept him from knowing his child?

She felt incredible guilt. She'd apologised, but now she was trying to put everything right. But there was no need for her to feel beholden to him. They were both at fault for Seb not having had his father around.

The fork she was using slipped from her fingers and

clattered to the tiled floor. Sighing, she bent to pick it up—but Jacob got to it first.

She'd had no idea he'd followed her to the kitchen and she was surprised and shocked to find him there.

So close…

They stood up together and he held the fork out for her to take.

'Thank you.' Her fingers brushed his and she tried not to show how much his contact affected her.

Such an innocent, brief connection.

But such an effect.

Her heart pounded—so much so that it sounded as if it was in her ears and not her chest. Her mouth went dry, as if she'd spent months in the desert, and she fought to stop her hands from trembling as she put the fork into the sink and got another one.

Could he see her hands shaking?

Now was probably not the best time to pick up a heavy pan of pasta, but it was done and she needed to drain it. The pan wobbled slightly, but she hoped he couldn't see.

'Why don't you get Seb to wash his hands? This'll be done in a minute or two.'

She heard him go and let out a pent-up breath. At the same time the steam from the water billowed up around her face as she strained the pasta.

How had it come to this? Yesterday she'd not had a care in the world. She and Seb had been good. School was good. Work was good. Home life was good. They'd been looking forward to Christmas, just a couple of weeks away—Seb praying for snow, as always.

It had all been *good*.

And yet today… Today her son had been in an accident and had been brought to her A&E. Jacob had turned up out of the blue. Her body had fired off little shots of adrenaline every time he came near and now he'd discovered he was father to her son!

How could just one day change so much?

Eva mixed in the cooked crab, then took the bowl of linguini and the side salad into the dining room and called them through.

Jacob came in with Seb on his back and set him down by his chair.

'This looks great.'

She nodded her thanks and bade them sit. Seb helped himself first, and Eva served up salad to everyone's plates as Jacob served the pasta.

They all began to eat, at first in silence, enjoying the food, and then Seb asked his first question of the night.

'Were there big lions?'

Jacob finished his mouthful of food before answering, 'In Africa? Yes, there were!'

'Whereabouts in Africa were you?' Eva asked.

Jacob smiled at her. 'Lots of places, but mostly I was in the Manyara region of Northern Tanzania. Do you know where Tanzania is?' He looked to his son.

Seb shook his head.

'It's between two countries called Somalia and Mozambique. I'll show you on a map later, if you'd like?'

'And you were doctoring people?' Seb pushed a huge forkful of linguini into his mouth, sucking up a stray strand of pasta.

Jacob laughed. 'I was. It was a lot of hard work!'

Eva watched the pair of them talking across the table. Seb looked so much like his father. It was hard to think that they had only met today. They even held their forks the same way.

Seb nodded. 'Why didn't you phone me?'

Jacob looked awkward. What would he say? Eva wondered.

'There were *some* phones there, Seb, but they were old, and lots of them were broken, so a lot of the time they were useless. And I couldn't use my mobile because... Well, there just aren't any antennae over there. I'm sorry. I would have phoned you if I could.'

Jacob glanced over at Eva and she looked down and away, thankful that he hadn't blamed her outright, in front of their son, for his not even knowing about his existence.

Jacob *would* have called his son if he'd known about him! That was what he'd been trying to say with that look. With just a single glance from those blue eyes of his.

The pasta suddenly seemed inedible to her, sticking in her throat, and she had to take a large drink of juice to wash it down. Then, feeling very uncomfortable and needing some fresh air, she quickly stood up. 'Excuse me a moment,' she said, and disappeared back into the kitchen.

Leaning back against the kitchen units, she held her hand to her mouth. Would Jacob ever let her forget what she'd done? Would he always try to punish her for not trying harder? She wasn't sure she'd be able to put up with those reproachful eyes of his for evermore...

She opened her fridge to check on dessert. The chocolate mousse was set, so that was fine. All she had to do was go back into the dining room and continue to pretend to Seb that everything was fine...

Back at the table, Jacob was showing Seb something on his phone. 'Do you see? That's my parents' place. Your grandparents. They own over ten acres there, and have it full of all the animals you'd find on a farm. Chickens, goats, alpacas...' He sounded wistful.

'What are *they*?' Seb was flicking through the pictures on Jacob's phone.

'They're like llamas.'

'Don't they spit?' Eva cringed.

Jacob laughed. 'Sometimes. But alpacas are gentler, I think. Or so my parents used to tell me.'

'Can we go?' Seb looked to Jacob, then to Eva.

Eva saw the look of joy and hope on his face. How could she say no?

It would give Seb a chance to get to know his grandparents. Now that he *had* some. All he'd ever had family-wise was her. Now he had grandparents and uncles, aunts and cousins. Seb's world was about to get a whole lot bigger. And though she'd wanted that for him, now that it was a reality she worried about it.

She'd have to get to know them. She'd have to sit in front of them and be judged. Like before. When she was a child. And she wanted no one judging Seb like that. Seb was her son. The one thing in this world that she had to protect. Jacob's family were strangers and she knew nothing about them.

'I suppose… But maybe in a few weeks? If Daddy is happy to take you?'

Jacob looked down at the floor. 'Er…sure.'

Eva could see that something wasn't right. Jacob didn't seem too keen on the idea. Why did Jacob seem apprehensive?

Seb's his son, too. Remember that.

She'd never shared her son. *Ever.* And now Jacob would introduce him to his new family. And she had no idea how far away their place was, or what type of people they were, and there was black ice on the roads. Today had proved how dangerous it was to travel.

What would they make of him? His grandparents?

What was she thinking? They'd *love* him. Of course they would! A new grandson to spoil. They'd love and adore Seb, surely. Welcome him into the Dolan fold without a backward glance.

Hopefully…

She had no idea what it was like to have grandparents. She could only imagine what they would think of *her*.

They'll judge me. Keeping their grandson from them for all these years…

Seb looked disappointed at her response. She could see he was keen to go. Jacob was staring at her.

'They *will* look after him.'

'I'm sure they will. It's just—'

'They're his grandparents.'

'I know they are. So…why don't *you* seem to want to go?'

Jacob looked down at his plate and she could see he was clenching and unclenching his jaw.

'It's a long story.'

'Well, maybe I need to hear that story before I let you take my son somewhere that might not be safe.'

'It's safe!' He almost laughed out loud. 'What…? You think there are monsters there or something?'

Eva glared at him. Talking about monsters in front of Seb! He had no idea how his son might feel, hearing his daddy talk about monsters! Seb could be terrified—Jacob wouldn't know!

'People aren't always the nicest.'

'My family are *very* nice.'

'So why don't you want to go?'

He looked cornered, looking to Seb first, then back to Eva. Eventually, he let out a breath. 'Because they don't know I'm back in the UK yet.'

'Why not?'

'I have…reasons.'

'I'd like to know what they are.'

Seb sucked up another long piece of pasta and grinned at his dad.

'We haven't spoken for a while. There wasn't a falling out—there weren't any arguments—it was just that I needed to get away for a while, and I didn't contact them or speak to them in the time I was away. The longer it got, the more difficult it became and now it's…almost impossible.'

Eva considered his words. 'You haven't spoken to them for *four* years? If there were no fallings-out, then ring them. I'm sure they'll be thrilled to hear from you.'

'I'm sure, too.'

'Yet you still haven't done it?'

'No.'

Jacob pushed some pasta round his plate. She watched him as she absentmindedly used her fork to twist and turn her own pasta. Seb was still eating hungrily. Her son's eyes were gleaming and bright, full of childish enthusiasm.

Jacob watched his son—gazing upon his mirror image, taking in all the details of Seb's face. The chicken pox scar above Seb's left eyebrow. The small mole below his ear. The light smattering of freckles across Seb's nose that were more Eva than him.

Eva thought back to when she was pregnant. Desperately trying to track him down and let him know about his child! Unable to find him. She'd been so upset at not being able to give her son his father! But he'd moved on, as people always did in her life, and the disappointment at that fact had hit her so hard. She didn't know why she'd expected it to be any different with him.

And it was then and only then that she had truly understood just how alone in the world she was…

She'd so wanted him to know! So wanted to have someone else there. To hold her hand. To reassure her that she could do this. To let her know that someone else cared about this baby with her—wanted to nurture it and love it and take care of it. To tell her that no longer would she have to walk through this world alone and on the edges of everyone else. That she would be a part of something. A team. United against the world.

But no. He'd gone. And so she'd faced it alone.

Until now.

Those two were already bonding. Quicker than she'd ever imagined. She knew Seb had been excited to learn his father was back, but she'd expected him to question it further. To hold something of himself back, taking his time to decide whether or not he could trust his father. But, no, Seb hadn't been like that at all! He was happy his father was here and he was carrying on as if they'd been together for always!

Or maybe those were her own thoughts?

While she'd carried Seb in her belly she'd tried over and over again to find Jacob. But eventually she'd had to admit defeat. As far as Eva had known, Jacob might never come back. As far as she had known his note might have been a lie—he might not have even been going to Africa, but slept with her and then disappeared because that was the type of man he was.

Though there had been that look in his eyes that had told her he was different. She'd wanted to find him—she really had—but after she'd hit that dead end…life had got in the way. Looking after herself and then Seb had taken over, and then too much time had passed, and…

She began to understand a little as to why Jacob had not contacted his family. The more time that passed, the more difficult it got. Perhaps they were more alike than she'd realised?

Eva excused herself and scraped back her chair, taking away the pasta still on her plate and then coming back

for theirs. Jacob and Seb had both cleared their plates—
a first for Seb, who usually left something. She raised an
eyebrow at his empty plate and was rewarded with a grin.

'Ready for dessert?'

They both nodded and looked up at her at the same time,
and the looks were so devastatingly identical she felt her
insides contract.

In the kitchen, she scraped the plates and put them in
the dishwasher, then she got the mousse from the fridge.
She served it into three bowls and carried it back out to
the table, serving Seb first, then Jacob. She sat opposite
and mutely spooned up the chocolate.

Normally it would have been delightful...enjoyable.
But right now, she couldn't taste anything and she might
as well have been spooning sawdust into her mouth. It felt
cloying and heavy and she didn't enjoy it at all.

Perhaps this was what second-guessing yourself felt
like? Whatever it was she was doing, it wasn't pleasant.

Somehow she finished the mousse. So did Seb and
Jacob. She took their dishes into the kitchen, only to hear
Jacob follow her in and set down the condiments he'd
brought through from the table.

'Thank you for dinner. I didn't know you were such a
good cook.'

'Well, there's probably a lot we don't know about each
other. But when you're alone you either learn how to cook
well or how to cook quick, and I never was one for micro-
wave meals.' She turned to face him and once again tried
to ignore the effect of his looks. He was effortlessly attractive and she found that annoying. Or was it the fact that
she was still attracted to him that irritated her?

The father of her child stood mere inches away, after
all this time. A man she hadn't seen for years now back,

tanned, matured and still making her nerve endings sing like a performing choral act.

The last time I saw you we were naked.

And that was the problem. She could still picture that night. Still remember the effect of his touch…still recall how he'd made her feel, how he'd made her yearn for more. How they'd made a child that night and how it had been magical.

The way he looked at her now wasn't innocent, either. Could he remember, too? Did he remember how she'd ground herself against him? The way she'd gasped in delight at his touch?

'I'm sorry, Jacob.'

He raised an eyebrow. 'For what, exactly?'

'For not finding you. For letting you work with me this morning and still not telling you until I was backed into a corner.' She bit her lip. 'I should have persevered. I should have kept trying to find you.'

He said nothing. Just stared at her. His eyes bored into her soul so intensely she got lost.

'Okay. Thank you. Seb wants me to stay for a bit longer. So I can be here when he goes to bed and read him a story. Is that all right with you?'

She nodded. 'Of course.'

Seb's bedroom was a little boy's dream, as far as Jacob was concerned. The walls were blue and covered in lion posters. There was a small low bed, and Jacob could see tubs and tubs of toys. There was a giant beanbag in one corner, and a small desk and chair piled high with books. A garage set lay under the window and from the ceiling hung many different plane models and homemade paper chains.

Seb's room was perfect for a boy, and he could imagine what it must be like to enjoy this room as a child.

'Wow! Great room, Seb.'

'Mum painted it. I did this bit.' Seb pointed.

Jacob made a point to study the windowsill. 'You've done a great job. You sure you haven't done this sort of work before?'

'I paint pictures in nursery.'

Jacob nodded. Seb was already in his onesie and had climbed into bed. 'So what book are we reading?'

'That one.' Seb pointed at a book.

Jacob settled down next to his son and felt envious of all that he'd missed. Cinema trips, meals out, watching Seb grow… Being there for illnesses and birthdays. And for all those other times when nothing actually happened but you were just in each other's company, watching television or sitting on the sofa.

Christmases…

All those magical times he'd not been there. It made his heart feel leaden even to think about it. But was it best that it had happened this way? Would he have been ready for this kind of responsibility three years ago?

Jacob picked up the book, found the bookmark and opened up the pages. 'I've not read this one.'

'We've read it lots of times.' Seb fiddled with his quilt. 'Will you go back to Africa?'

Jacob looked hard at his son and saw fear in Seb's eyes. 'I said I would, but… You've grown so big and I've missed so much…I don't want to miss a single second more.'

Seb smiled and snuggled down into his bed. 'Will you read to me *every* night now?'

'I'll try. I'd better ask your mum first—if I can come round every night.'

His son propped himself up on his elbows and frowned. 'But don't you *live* here?'

How could he explain? How could he explain to Seb

that his father and his mother had never even been in a proper relationship? That it had been one night when he'd let himself get carried away by a redhead with a body that wouldn't quit and the kind of lips that ought to have come with a health warning.

It was all too complicated. And he didn't want to blame Eva in front of Seb, either.

'I wasn't sure if your mum would have room, so all my things are at my flat.'

'But now you can bring your clothes here.'

Jacob ruffled his son's hair, marvelling at the softness of it under his fingers. 'Maybe. Settle down, then—let's read you the next chapter of this story.'

But his private thoughts lingered on how to sort out this situation between himself and Eva.

Clearly Eva hadn't told Seb the truth about their relationship. How could she? Seb was so young still. He could understand that. *He* wouldn't want to tell a child about that, either.

He'd been so apprehensive about coming here tonight. Learning about Seb had been such a shock to his system. One minute he'd been a single guy, with his only commitment being a temporary contract with the hospital, and the next, he'd found out that he was a father! And not to a baby about to be born, but to a three-year-old child!

He'd been furious after Eva had left the hospital. Livid. But then, after a bit of fresh air up on the hospital roof, other thoughts had entered his head. What if he wasn't a good dad? What if he had no idea of how to do it? It had been so long since he'd last allowed himself to care for someone. To love someone. He'd spent so long with his heart locked away in a box...

But a child needed love. *Deserved* to have it!

He wished he'd found out about Seb sooner, but there

was no way he could have done—no way he could have predicted the consequences of that night. He'd used protection with Eva. He'd only known her first name, and he hadn't taken her number or found out where she worked. It had been first names only and one hot, unforgettable night. He hadn't asked her any questions, because he hadn't needed to know.

She'd been his gorgeous redhead, his mesmerising siren, and he hadn't wanted to talk, or to think, or to second-guess. He'd wanted simply to go with the flow and enjoy the ride his body was taking him on. To allow her to soothe his soul. And though it had only been one night, it had made him feel alive once more. He'd hardly been able to believe it had made such an impact on him.

She'd filled his dreams for weeks afterwards. Every now and again he would think he'd caught the scent of her perfume, even though he'd known she was on a different continent!

He'd have had no way of tracking *her* down, the same way she hadn't been able to find him. Although he supposed he could have asked his friends. The ones at the party. Though actually they had been more friends of friends. But he could have asked them who the mesmerising redhead was, who Eva was...

Which, technically, he *had* done when he'd got back to the UK.

He shifted slightly and turned a page of the book, not really in the story, but lost in his own thoughts.

Upon his return to England he'd called a friend from the party that night. He'd asked him vaguely, as if it weren't important, if he could remember that night. If he could remember someone called Eva.

Mark had joked and joshed with him about it, and said

that he couldn't, but then later that day Jacob had received an email from him, with Eva's full name.

It had been as simple as that to find out where she was currently practising. Thank goodness she wasn't called Smith or Jones. Thank goodness she wasn't married! Because she might have been—there was no reason why she wouldn't have met someone else in the time they'd been apart. She probably wouldn't even remember him.

But he'd wanted the chance to see her again. Because for some reason—even after all those years—he'd never been able to get the image of her out of his head. She'd done something to him that night—something otherworldly that had brought him back to who he really was—and he'd wanted to feel that way again. Being in Africa had taught him that something was missing in his life—and he'd thought maybe, if he was brave enough to seek out Eva, he'd find it once more.

But he'd come back and discovered that he had a son...
Wow.

He wanted to know his son—although just looking at him it already felt as if he'd known Seb his whole life. It was like looking at a mini-me, only with paler skin and freckles.

The burden of responsibility hit him hard. A *son*! A three-year-old boy who would want to look up to his father and emulate him. Could he be that role model?

There was no question about it.

It was a tough situation, and he'd had enough of those to last him a lifetime: Michelle... The Wedding That Never Was...

Over time it had been easier to lock away his heart for good, to disappear when things got tough—to take a breather and throw himself into work until he could get his head around how he was feeling.

But finally he'd felt ready to come back. Strong enough to find Eva and to continue to be the best doctor he could be. Only now he could add another role to the one of doctor.

Father.

And he wanted to be the best father he could be…

For Seb…and for himself.

Eva had cleared away the dishes downstairs, cleaned the kitchen and sat down on the sofa, fidgeting with her mug of tea as she waited for Jacob to reappear.

This was the first night in a long time that she had not read her son his bedtime story.

Because his *father* was doing it! Jacob. The one man all other men had had to live up to. Not that there'd been many other men. Not seriously anyway. She'd had the odd dinner date, or been invited out to coffee, but she'd always stopped it at that. Though it had been nice to know that men still found her attractive, she'd made it clear to each and every one of them that it would not get serious. Because after a couple of dates they'd always wanted to get more involved in her life than she was prepared for—they'd wanted to meet Seb.

And none of them had been Jacob.

She'd fantasised about what might have been for so long—had stupidly almost fallen in love with her one-night stand and allowed herself to put him on a pedestal.

The night they'd spent together had been the best night she'd ever had. Of course she was bound to be sentimental about him. He'd made her *feel* for the first time in ages! Besides, they'd made a child together. Without Jacob there'd be no Seb. And her son was her world. By having her own child she'd discovered how it felt truly to love for the first time ever. To feel connected to another human being.

Of course Jacob had known nothing of the feelings he'd engendered in her. He'd slipped away into the night, never to be seen again.

Until today.

She'd always been sceptical about people who believed in love at first sight! What a cliché! Things like that didn't happen in real life, did they?

Only it had. She'd gone to her friend's party out of a sense of obligation, really. But once there she'd decided to live a little, to have a few drinks and, for once, to lose herself in the moment.

And suddenly, across the room, her gaze had collided with his. He'd stood there, half a foot taller than everyone else, and those piercing cobalt eyes had pinned her to the spot with their intensity.

The music had been blasting out, people had been talking loudly and laughing all around her, but, caught in his gaze, all she'd been aware of was her mystery man.

Her body had tingled with awareness, each nerve ending lighting up like a beacon. And when she'd realised he was coming across the room to her, without breaking eye contact, her limbs had turned to jelly, her mouth had gone dry and she'd had to physically remind herself to keep breathing.

Up close, he'd been devastatingly handsome. Tall, broad, athletic. A shock of dark hair. He'd lifted up a tress of her own hair, letting it run through his fingers, his gaze focusing on her open lips before he'd said, 'I'm Jacob. Dance with me?'

It was as if time had stopped. As if everyone else had no longer been there and it was just the two of them in that airless room. The heat, the lights, the music and them.

A slow tune had come on and he'd led her into the small dance space, his fingertips deftly pulling her after him, and then he'd spun her around and pulled her into his arms, so that she was pressed up close against his body, her hands against his chest, feeling his heart beat…

It had been magical! His touch… The connection she'd felt with him… As if that moment had always been meant to be. If she'd said that to anyone else they might have laughed at her, but she'd felt it to be true.

He'd held her in his arms and she'd rested her head against his chest and listened to his steady heartbeat, moving with him, against him, moulded into him, fitting into him perfectly.

And then the music had stopped.

She hadn't heard the next tune. She'd just been aware of his eyes, of the heat in his gaze as he'd lowered his lips to hers…

Even now, thinking about it all these years later, she could feel a shiver down her spine as she recalled how he'd slowly lowered his mouth to hers and finally—*finally!*—claimed her lips for his own.

That soft, gentle kiss had turned into a hungry demand for more, and with her silent consent he had led her out into the candlelit garden and found a summer house.

After closing the doors they'd ripped at each other's clothing, tossing it to the floor, and tumbled onto the futon inside, a mass of laughter and limbs. And then he'd taken her, his mouth insatiable as he'd tasted every inch of her, making her writhe and contort and gasp his name. She'd unashamedly clasped his hair as he'd tasted her intimately, and when he'd kissed her again she'd tasted herself on his lips. The taste, the scent of their sex had driven her on, and she'd clambered on top of him, riding him so forcefully and so deeply she'd noticed bruises on her knees days later that had made her smile with the memory of their night.

Afterwards they had lain side by side on the futon,

laughing and giggling into the early hours. Eva had fallen asleep briefly, and when she'd woken Jacob had been gone. His clothes had been missing. Her own naked body had been covered by a crocheted throw.

She'd found a folded note on the pillow next to her.

Had to leave. Africa calls!
You were amazing!
Love, Jacob x

She'd dressed quickly, ashamed at what she'd done, but glad that the party was still in full swing so she could sneak out without anyone noticing.

Eva had been forlorn. How typical of her to fall for someone who had disappeared to another continent…to Africa. Unless his note had been a joke…?

But, no, he'd left without a trace.

She'd tried to forget him. To forget that night. But then she had discovered that she was pregnant.

She hadn't believed the little blue cross at first—they'd used protection; there was no way she could be pregnant, and from one night, too.

Abortion had never been an option. She hadn't been able do it—she'd wanted her baby. No one else was going to make the decision for her. She would make it work—she would *have* to make it work. She would try to find Jacob. Try to track him down. How hard would it be?

Eva had craved to hear Jacob's voice, to feel his touch upon her one more time. She'd cried when he'd not been there to see the first scan, or to help her with nursery decoration ideas, or to help her through her contractions during labour, or to be there to hold his son after he was born. But as time had passed it had become easier. She'd become more able to bear the pain and the longing.

Until now.

And she could still feel that pull. That pull of attraction that hit her low and deep in her gut each time she looked at him. That *need* she had for him—still with her after all this time. How *could* he still have that effect on her? How did one man hold such sway over her emotions? It was like living in an emotional pinball machine, being ricocheted from one feeling to the next—fear, excitement, doubt...arousal.

But what was going on with his family? Why had he been out of contact with them for so long?

When he'd first found out about Seb he'd said to her that one of the worst things she'd done was to keep Seb from the family who would love him. Adore him. Jacob had given her that whole speech about uncles and grandparents and cousins. And yet he showed obvious reluctance to connect with that family.

Why?

She didn't need anyone else's drama. She didn't need anyone else's family issues impeding on the life she lived with Seb. They had a good life—a happy, stable life. She didn't need to take Seb down that road. The road of being judged and found wanting. Of being rejected. She wouldn't allow it.

What were they talking about up there?

She longed to be able to hear. But then she heard Jacob's footsteps on the stairs, and soon he was standing in the doorway, looking as irresistible as when she first saw him.

'How did it go?'

'He's asleep.'

'Good.' She smiled.

Jacob perched on the edge of her sofa. 'He wants to know why I'm not living here.'

Her breath caught in her throat. 'And what did you say?'

'Just that all my things were at my flat.'

'I see…' That was a difficult one.

'He wants me to read to him every night. Would that be okay? To come round in the evenings?'

That could be awkward. 'Erm…'

'I've missed enough nights, don't you think?'

'You'd practically be living here.'

'Just when my shifts allow? If it's really late maybe I could sleep on the couch?'

She'd never get a wink of sleep, knowing he was so close!

'I don't know…'

'I think we should do it. For Seb. I'd do anything for him. Now that I know I have a son I'm not going to let him down. If he wants me here every night, then I'd like to be. I'll keep out of your way.'

She stared back at his beautiful blue eyes. *How?* How would he stay out of her way? The place wasn't that big.

'Okay.'

Had she really just said that?

'Thank you. I'll go home tonight, but I'll bring a few things over tomorrow for when I have to stay.' He attempted a smile. 'I promise my toothbrush won't take up too much room.'

'Right…'

This was all moving so fast! The man she'd wanted for the past four years was practically moving in!

Jacob closed Eva's door behind him and let out a big sigh into the cold night air. The evening had gone better than he'd thought it might. He hadn't been sure how Eva would be with him. Whether she'd be treading on eggshells around him or whether she'd have loads of questions that he just wasn't ready to answer yet.

About that night. The one they'd spent together. About him leaving and never saying goodbye.

She had every right to challenge him about it. He would in her position. There was plenty she could choose to ask about, but she'd not said a thing. She'd given him the time and space he'd needed to be with Seb, and for that he was grateful.

Seb was a great kid, from what he could see. Eva had done a fabulous job in raising him thus far. But now Seb would have his father in his life and things would be different.

Jacob smiled as he walked to his car. Seb was a good-looking boy, with his wavy dark hair and blue eyes, and that alabaster skin. Girls wouldn't stand a chance when he was older! Eva had skin like that... The palest of skin tones, clear, unblemished, to the point where it almost didn't look real. The type of skin you wanted to reach out and touch, just to make sure.

He'd known he was going to find Eva in that A&E department. And, yes, he'd wanted to know more about her. There was something about her that called to him, as if she was some sort of siren singing an enchanted song that only he could hear. He'd never stopped thinking of her in Africa and that had scared him. How could a one-night stand feel like so much more?

What if they became close? What if they had a relationship? Could he keep himself emotionally separate?

Not from Seb. Seb was his son, and already he could see how easy it was going to be to love that boy, and he'd protect him to the ends of the earth if he had to. But Eva? What would happen there?

She'd already got under his skin. She'd ignited something in him that he hadn't felt for a long time. And the last time he'd felt that way... Had *thought* he felt that way...

No...I don't want to think of that anymore.

Could he even trust his own judgement? How could he know that he was making the right decisions? When he'd trusted himself before he'd been blind to what had truly been going on...

He closed his eyes and pictured the way Eva had moved that night. The way she'd felt on top of him, writhing and sweating as he'd felt himself deep inside her, as she ground him into her with a steady, yet deep rhythm. How it had made him feel to hear her gasping, to feel her hot breath blowing into the side of his neck, her fingernails scratching into his back as she'd clutched him to her as if she'd never wanted to let go...

That night had been amazing. But then he'd watched her fall asleep, her back to him, and he'd felt immense guilt, knowing he was going to have to slip away to catch his flight.

He should never have slept with her before he left for Africa. He should never have slept with *anyone*. He'd known he was leaving in a few hours and he'd not been in the right headspace—so what the hell had happened?

He hadn't even considered how she might feel afterwards. That she might feel used or abandoned when she woke up alone.

No. That wasn't true. He *had* thought about it. Worried about it. Had felt guilty about it. He'd treated her badly. Should have told her the truth from the start. He'd never forgive himself for that, even if she did.

But now he needed to be the best father that Seb could ever have. To be there always for his son. Never to let him down. Never to make a promise that he couldn't keep. To make Seb feel cherished and adored by *both* his parents.

He could do that.

Easily.

But he'd treated Eva badly once before—how would he know not to do it again? Perhaps if he stayed away from Eva and focused just on Seb, then that would be safer for them all?

He'd once felt this way about Michelle. A deep-down attraction that had pulled at his very being. And look how wrong *that* had turned out to be.

She'd seemed a safe option. The girl next door...his childhood sweetheart. Michelle had seemed so right. And yet it had all gone wrong! She'd professed to love him, professed to be true to him, and she'd ended up sleeping with somebody else. His friend! The one person he should have been able to trust most.

It had been a huge shock. Yes, Michelle had seemed more and more distracted, but he'd put it down to the wedding and how all the preparations had needed so much organising. Brides were *meant* to worry about their weddings—he'd thought her preoccupation was normal. But it had been something else...the sordid details of which she'd finally disclosed to him on their wedding day.

He hadn't seen Michelle's affair coming... Could he trust his instincts now?

CHAPTER FIVE

EVA HAD BARELY been at work for five minutes before Sarah found her and turned her round in her chair.

'So how's Seb?'

Eva thought about how best to answer her. He'd had a few aches and pains this morning, a bit of a headache, but generally seemed fine. In fact he'd seemed more than fine, and she put that down to the fact that he'd spent a few hours getting to know his father.

But did she want to tell Sarah that Jacob had been round at her house last night?

'He's good, thanks.'

'No after-effects from the accident?'

'Nothing much.' She smiled and tried to get on with her work, but Sarah wasn't going to let it go. Apparently her questions about Seb were only a preamble for her questions about Jacob.

'And Dr Dolan?'

Her fingers froze above the keyboard. 'What about him?'

'Well, you never did get the chance to tell me how you know him.'

Eva looked about them, to make sure no one else was listening, but the only witnesses were the Christmas decorations, already wilting.

'He's…um…Seb's father.' She looked up guiltily at her friend, hoping and praying that she wouldn't over-react whilst they were at work.

'Seb's dad? Really? Wow, you kept that one quiet.'

Eva nodded, her cheeks aflame. 'And there's more to it than that. I, er, only told him about Seb yesterday.'

'What?' Sarah looked totally amazed, her eyes wide, her mouth gaping, until she closed it promptly. 'What did he say when you told him?'

'He was…shocked.'

'I bet. What did he say?'

'He said I had to tell Seb. That he was going to come round.'

'And?'

'And what?'

'How did it go?' Sarah asked, as if she were an imbecile.

'Fine.'

'Fine? What? That's *it*? No furtive, lingering looks between the pair of you? No unfinished business?'

'We finished our business nearly four years ago. All that matters now is Seb.'

'But aren't you going to find out if he's single?'

Eva frowned. 'Why?' There was no point, really. It would be too much to expect that life would actually start working out well for her. That they could be a happy family unit with Jacob. *Hah!* As if *that* was ever going to happen.

Sarah shook her head in disbelief. 'Because *you're* single, Eva! And don't forget…he's hot.'

'He's unreliable. Disappears when you want him and leaves no trace. It was like trying to track down a spy. And he's only here temporarily. Once his contract is over he'll move on and we'll never see him again.'

She felt awful for saying it, but it was what she truly expected. No one ever stuck around for her. No one ever wanted to keep her in their life. Why would Jacob be any different? No matter how much she wanted him to be.

Sarah picked up a treatment card for the next patient. 'If he really was a spy that would make him hotter.'

'You're incorrigible!' Eva laughed. 'Why don't *you* get a boyfriend so you can stop trying to fix me up?'

'I'm married to my job.' She skipped off without a backward glance and left Eva pondering over Jacob.

What did she really know about him? Okay, so he was a doctor—which gave him brownie points from the get-go, didn't it? His interest in medicine meant that he spent his day helping people, and he'd even flown off to a developing continent and offered to help people there, in what must have been difficult conditions. He'd discovered that he was a father and, after his initial shock, had showed up, played with his son, eaten with them and read Seb a story. He'd even promised to come round every night, when he could, so there were signs of commitment there...

But he *had* seduced her and then left without a trace. He'd given her the barest information about himself, so that she'd been unable to track him down. Although she'd *known* it was going to be a one-night stand. She'd *known* it was going to be a one-time thing. But it hadn't mattered. She'd wanted it as much as him—had succumbed to their primal connection and lost herself in the moment.

She'd wondered then, as she had many times since, what had been driving him that night. And what had he been running away from...? She'd seen that he was in pain emotionally. In some torment. And rather than scaring her off it had drawn her to him. Two damaged souls merging together, soothing each other, before they parted ways, never to see each other again.

Although now she knew that he had turned his back on his family—but why?

He had family who cared about him—he'd mentioned that earlier, and that there hadn't been any huge falling-out. But he'd stayed away from them when quite clearly they would have supported him through whatever it was. And if there *was* something he was still running from, was he the sort of person she wanted around her son? Did he flee when the going got tough? Should she be letting Seb get to know him? Because if Jacob was going to bolt then she needed to know.

She brought up the staffing schedule for the day and saw that Jacob was supposed to be at work in Minors again today.

I need to get on with my work. I can talk to him later.

She picked up her next patient file and headed off to call the patient through, but as she walked through Minors a cubicle curtain swished open and there he was.

'Hello.'

'Hi. You okay?' he asked.

His patient smiled and hobbled past them on crutches, one ankle bandaged neatly.

She waited until the man was out of earshot. Then blew out a breath to calm herself, tucking her hair behind one ear and using the moment to try to focus.

'I'm fine. I'm glad I ran into you, though. I wanted to have a quick word about our…situation.'

'Oh…?'

She looked up into his eyes and once again found herself cursing his parents for giving him the most startling blue eyes she'd ever seen on a man. He had sickeningly long lashes, too, all dark and perfectly outlining his almond-shaped eyes. Any woman would kill to have lashes like his.

'Have you got a minute?'

'Sure. Fire away.'

'I need to know your intentions.'

He looked puzzled. 'My what?'

'Your intentions. With Seb. With the future.'

'I'm sorry, I don't under—'

'You're on a temporary contract here. For the Christmas period. I…er…I need to know if you're going to be temporary elsewhere, too.' She babbled her words, rushing to say them, to get them out of her mouth so that they wouldn't be clogging up her brain any more.

Jacob looked at her, his brow furrowed with lines.

'Are you a stable influence for me to have around Seb? Because if you're not, if you're going to disappear again, then I don't want you around him. Getting to know him. Being in his life for five minutes and then disappearing. Leaving me to handle the fall-out again—only this time with a small child in tow, who will ask questions and be hurt that his father couldn't stick around.'

He looked annoyed that she would even suggest it. 'I'm going to be there for my son.'

'Always?'

'Always.'

'Good.'

She'd believe it when she saw it. She wanted to trust him. Desperately so. But life had taught her that it didn't always work that way.

He laid a hand on her arm and looked her deeply in the eyes. 'When I came back I didn't expect to discover that I had a child. But I do, and I'm thrilled, and I'm going to be the best father he could ever have.'

She tried not to think about his hand on her arm. Warm and reassuring.

'Right. Glad to hear it.'

'Don't ever doubt me when it comes to Seb.'

She looked up into his dark blue eyes and nodded.

* * *

Somehow, magically, there was a brief lull in patients. The waiting room had almost emptied and Jacob took a brief moment to sit outside, cradling a hot cup of coffee and wrapped up tight in his jacket and scarf.

He could feel the weight of his phone in his pocket. Could feel it burning into him as he debated making that call back home. Imagining the scenarios, the conversations, the questions he would no doubt receive.

Could he face them and tell the truth finally? He'd decided in Africa that he could. But now that the time was upon him—the time to pick up that phone and make the contact that he knew his parents and family would crave—he felt anxious.

He knew they'd ask. He knew they'd want answers. So would he in their position.

I should never have let so much time pass without contacting them.

He was angry with himself for that. Angry with himself for a lot of things. He'd been responsible for what had eventually happened. He'd worked too hard, he'd taken for granted Michelle's feelings for him, and once he'd got that engagement ring on her finger he'd stopped trying. Stopped showing her how much she meant to him. No wonder she'd ended up with another man. His best friend!

That betrayal had hurt. The woman he'd professed to love and his best friend… It had been obvious afterwards. The amount of time they'd spent together… And to think he'd been so pleased that Michelle and Marcus got on so well together! Working together to plan the wedding!

I pushed them together. It was my fault.

Accepting his part in it had been a major trigger point for his coming home. He'd spent a couple of years blaming *them*. *Their* betrayal, *their* deceit, *their* cheating. It had been uncomfortable to turn that questioning on himself. But when he had… He'd taken some time to admit it, but he had found *himself* wanting. Had accepted what he'd done on their wedding day, yelling at her like that, causing her to rush off in tears, crying at the wheel…

He pulled the phone from his pocket and brought up his list of contacts. He scrolled down to M and found the listing he wanted.

Mum and Dad

Jacob let out a sigh and looked about him. An ambulance had just pulled up and was offloading a new patient, strapped to a backboard. Briefly he thought about going in to help out, but dismissed the idea.

He needed to do this. Make contact. He'd spent too long shutting the door on painful things in his past and he'd vowed to himself that when he came back from Africa he would face everything. He'd call his parents. He'd tell them the truth of what had happened that day. He'd tell them what he had done wrong. He would tell them everything…

He could imagine hearing their voices. How delighted they'd sound. He knew they wouldn't be cross. They weren't that type of people. His parents were easy-going and caring. They'd have *worried*, sure. They'd have fretted. Big time. But they wouldn't greet him with anger.

So just do it already!

He pressed his thumb to the screen and then put the phone up to his ear. He felt odd. Not nervous. Apprehensive…? But he sucked in a breath and knew he could handle this. He was ready now. He never had been before. But now he needed his family as he never had before. Now that he was a father himself. Now was the time to reconnect. Because of Seb.

'Hello?'

'Dad?'

A pause. *'Jacob?'*

He smiled. 'Yeah, Dad. It's me.'

A little boy had been brought into A&E by his terrified father. Separated from the mother of his child, he'd been looking after his son and had woken him from a sleep to find a lump on his forehead that had appeared suddenly.

Eva had called the mother in from work and the two parents had been at loggerheads from the get-go.

'You must have *some* idea, Lee! Did he fall? Have an accident? Go out on the ice?'

Lee looked utterly perplexed. 'No! *Nothing!*'

'Were you drinking again?'

Eva stepped in between them as their voices began to carry across the department. 'That's enough!' She eyed both of them, the look on her face the only warning they'd get, watching them both, making sure she had their attention. 'You can argue later, but right now we have to look after Ben. Okay?'

The father nodded quickly, the mother reluctantly, mumbling under her breath, 'I should never have trusted you in the first place.'

Eva could understand her distress. It was a mother's worst nightmare to find out that something was wrong with her child whilst she was at work. The most obvious explanation for Ben's large bump would be an accident, but Ben's father had denied that—and if things were as bad between them as it seemed from the way they were acting, she could see why the mud-slinging had begun and why the father was in the line of fire.

'Let's concentrate on Ben, shall we?'

His father gripped the handrails of the bed. 'I was with him all the time, Doctor—he didn't fall or bang his head anywhere.'

'Was there any time when you weren't watching him? Any chance he could have had an accident without your noticing?'

'No. Apart from when Ben fell asleep for a bit, and I caught forty winks myself. It's been manic recently, getting my new place ready for Christmas. But I woke up before he did and when I checked on him I noticed this lump that had appeared whilst he was still asleep.'

Strange, Eva thought. So if there was no chance of trauma, what else could it be? A sebaceous cyst? Pott's puffy tumour? A cyst was unlikely, as it would have been present for some time before becoming infected.

'Has he had a cold recently?'

The mother answered, 'For over a week. He's had a badly blocked nose.'

Eva bent down to look at her patient. 'Is your head sore, Ben?'

Ben nodded sadly.

She knew she needed a CT scan to confirm her diagnosis, but before she could say anything the parents began again.

'This would never have happened if he'd been with *me*,' the mother sniped.

'Well, you were at work, weren't you? He had to be with me.'

'I should have asked my mother.'

'I can look after my own son!'

'*Can* you? Because we seem to be in hospital—and I don't really think that means you looked after him very well, does it?'

Eva raised her hands. 'Please keep your voices down.' She stepped from the cubicle and sighed. These two parents were obviously struggling to share custody of their child.

Would she and Jacob become like that over time? Would she be ringing him, wherever he was, and yelling at him down the phone for not being there? She hoped not. All she'd ever wanted was for Seb to be happy, and having warring parents wasn't the way. She'd seen too much of that growing up in foster homes. If Seb ended up in hospital ill, she hoped they would pull together for their son and not bash heads like these two parents were doing.

Jacob seemed a reasonable man. So far. He'd promised he would stick around for Seb. But people made promises they couldn't keep all the time. If things got tough and Jacob left...

I hope he doesn't. I hope he can prove me wrong.

He was a very handsome man; she'd be stupid to think he would remain single. What would happen if he fell in love with someone? If his life was filled with someone else? Would Jacob still want to be around her and Seb? She was his past. They'd only shared a bed once. Made a child together. The likelihood of him having feelings for her was small.

She'd always, *always* been the one in control of Seb's life. Both mother and father to him. Now that responsibility was going to be shared and it scared her. What if Jacob did something wrong? Jacob wanted a say in his son's life. What would *that* be like?

She wasn't sure she could see it going well.

We need to get together and talk about this. It's all changing so fast.

But she wanted desperately for it to go smoothly. For

Seb. He was a good kid. Responsible and very mature for his age.

I definitely don't want us to be like Ben's parents.

She set her shoulders and went off to order a CT scan for Ben.

Jacob was there, waiting for a patient of his own. He took her to one side. 'We need to talk.'

'Yes, but not now. I've got a patient.'

'So have I! But I don't want to talk about this at your home, Eva. Not with Seb in earshot.'

'So you do care about what he hears?'

'Of course I care. I'm here for Seb forever. He's part of me. He's part of my life. I've just called my parents. Told them I'm back. Told them about Seb.' He let out a huge sigh. 'Big phone call for them.'

'You did?' Surprise filled her face. She wondered how they'd reacted.

'They were…very happy.'

'They were?' Eva felt a warm feeling in her gut. A small spark of happiness. She could accept that people had rejected *her* in her lifetime, but for Seb she wanted nothing but acceptance and welcoming arms.

'Yes.' Jacob nodded.

Eva looked at him, shocked at this turnaround. She hadn't suspected this. 'Big day for the Dolan family.'

He nodded and smiled. 'Yes, but telling my mum she's a grandmother again tended to make everything all right. When I rang off she was getting excited about shopping for more Christmas presents.'

'But they were thrilled?'

'Very. Although it did make me think that I need to get Seb something for Christmas, so I wondered if you'd do me a favour?'

'Depends what it is.' She smiled to show she was joking. But she did want to hear what it was before she agreed to anything.

'I don't know what he'd like, so I wondered if you'd come Christmas shopping with me? There's only a couple of weeks left till the big day.'

'When?'

'Later today?' Now it was his turn to smile. 'When our shifts are over? Well?'

She couldn't think of any reason why not. She had a good couple of hours before she had to pick Seb up from her neighbour's and she needed to go shopping herself, really. Christmas was looming fast and she didn't know when she might next get some free time. She didn't want to leave it to the last minute. Plus, it would give her an opportunity to talk to him. Learn more about him.

'Okay. I'll meet you after my shift ends.'

He drove them both into town. It wasn't too far from the hospital, but it would have been impossible if they'd tried to walk it. Once he'd found them a parking space, after circling a car park for ten minutes, they got out and headed into the shopping centre.

The first thing they heard, apart from the noise of chattering shoppers, was Christmas music. A beautiful rendition of 'Silent Night' was being sung live by a group of choristers at the base of the elevators.

The interior of the shopping centre was bedecked in beautiful glittering decorations in silver and white and an enormous tree stood at one end, festooned in white fairy lights with an enormous silver star at its apex.

'Wow! That looks amazing!' Eva gasped in wonder, instantly sucked into the atmosphere of the season and forgetting all about the pressures of work—the clock-watching, the reports to write out by hand as well as on the computer, the endless stream of patients, the sickness, the damage that people could do to one another. 'You almost forget there's life outside of the hospital.'

'There's a grotto.' Jacob pointed at a small wintry woodland display, festooned with mechanical bears and a snowy wood cabin. 'We should bring Seb.'

We.

She liked that. It sounded strange after being the only one to think about Seb. That he already seemed to see them as a family unit felt surreal. But good. Seb had loved having his daddy there last night, and Eva had to admit that she had been looking forward to him coming again.

It was nearly Christmas. And here she was, shopping with the father of her child, and it all seemed so simple and so easy—if she would just let it be that way.

'Where do you want to look first?' she asked.

Jacob pulled off his hat and gloves and shoved them into his pocket, running his fingers through his gorgeous hair to straighten it out. 'I don't know. There's just so much!'

'That jigsaw was a hit. And he likes playing football. Maybe a small trampoline?'

'I don't want to get him another jigsaw. I'd like to get him something fun.'

'Shall we just browse?'

He looked about him, overwhelmed by all the places they might have to go. 'Why not?'

They set off into a huge store that specialised in children's toys. It was so noisy in there! Filled with parents doing the same thing, along with children testing out the toys on display, watching robotic dogs and hamsters whizzing about on the floor. They sidestepped those and headed down one of the aisles, where there seemed to be an abundance of educational toys.

'What sort of things did *you* like as a child?' Eva asked.

'I played outside a lot. In the orchard. I made up a lot of my own games. Bits of wood for a sword, made my own bow and arrow—it was useless, but it was fun! You?'

Eva shrugged noncommittally. 'I never really had much. I was hardly ever in a real home for Christmas, and the children's home I kept going back to just got us practical things like clothes or shoes. I got a copy of *Black Beauty* once and I read it over and over until it fell apart.'

'I'm sorry to hear that.'

He looked it, too, but she didn't want his pity. She shrugged it off. 'It's okay. Anyway, this Christmas Seb really has a sense of what's going on and he's excited. I want to make it special for him.'

'Me, too.'

There seemed to be plenty of things to choose from. Games that would teach children about shopping, about telling the time, about learning the days of the week or the months of the year, or what the weather was like. Jacob didn't want to get his son anything like that. He wanted to get Seb something that was really fun.

'Three's a difficult age. What sort of things can he do?'

'He's very active. He likes physical things—going to the park, climbing on the frames, riding on the swings and things. I bet you made yourself a rope swing in that orchard of yours?'

Jacob laughed and nodded. It was good to see him smile so broadly. His face lit up with genuine joy and it felt good to know she'd made him feel that way.

'I did.'

'Was it any good? I've never tried one.'

'Never? We'll have to remedy that one day.'

One day. That implied he was sticking around, didn't it? She hoped so. Because she liked this. Being with him.

Shopping together for Seb. Doing stuff to make their son happy. It was like being united. Wanted...appreciated.

Valued.

It made her feel good. This had to be what everyone else felt.

They headed into another aisle that was filled with cuddly toys of all kinds. A large fuzzy lion was an obvious choice.

'We *have* to get him this.'

Eva nodded. Seb would like that. 'Good choice.'

Jacob tucked it under his arm and they carried on looking, ignoring the aisles full of dolls and anything pink. 'Unless he *wants* any of this?' Jacob asked.

'Er...no. Seb wouldn't be interested.'

'Just checking. Equal opportunities and all that...' He smiled.

She laughed and realised she was enjoying herself. Jacob was turning out to be the nice guy she'd hoped for. She was actually living one of the scenarios she'd once dreamed about. Being in that happy family unit...being that perfect family.

Almost.

She didn't want to spoil it. It felt good. Strangely comfortable. Pleasant.

They stood in the queue and Jacob paid for the lion. They headed back into the shopping centre and he bought them both a hot chocolate. They sat on a bench that suddenly became vacant, quickly slipping onto the seats before anyone else could, and watched the shoppers rushing by.

'This is nice,' Eva said.

'The hot chocolate? Or resting?'

'Resting!' She laughed and took a sip of her drink. 'No—this. All of it. Christmas shopping for our son together.'

Jacob looked at her and smiled.

He really was a handsome man and, looking at him now, she could really see how he and his son shared the same smile.

'I'm glad. You know, you've mentioned your childhood... What was it like?'

She glanced at him. 'You really want to know?'

She didn't mind telling him. It hadn't been a perfect childhood, but she'd made peace with that a long time ago. The past wasn't important now. What mattered was the future. And she didn't think he'd judge her if she told him. Being a doctor, he'd probably be quite understanding.

'I do.'

'The reality of it wasn't that great. I went to ten different foster families. Some of them were okay. One was really nice and I really didn't want to leave them. A young couple—the Martins, they were called...Sue and Peter. I really thought I'd get to stay with them. Be their daughter. But then Sue got pregnant with twins through IVF, and when she was about six months pregnant I suddenly found myself back at the children's home again.'

'That must have been difficult.'

'It was. I didn't understand what I'd done wrong.'

It was an understatement. She'd been incredibly hurt. And it had been a turning point for her. The point at which she'd decided never to rely on other people to make her happy. That she'd just look out for herself. No more performing seal acts to make potential foster carers think she looked cute and adorable. No more behaving well because the staff at the children's home had told her to. She'd behaved well before and look where that had got her!

'How old were you?'

'About nine. It was a tough time. I thought I'd done

something wrong and cried for what seemed like forever. Then I got used to not being wanted.'

'It had to have been a tough decision for Sue and Peter.'

She looked at him, searching his face for hidden meaning, but she didn't see anything. There was no guile there. He genuinely thought it must have been a tough decision for the couple. But she'd never thought of it that way. She'd only seen it from her own—hurt—point of view.

She thought of what they must have gone through now... making the decision to send her back. 'I guess it was.'

'Did you ever learn what happened with your own parents? Your biological parents, I mean?'

She sipped her chocolate. 'Wow. You *really* want to hear a sad story at Christmas time, don't you?'

'No. But I want to hear *your* story.'

He looked steadily at her and she eventually met his gaze.

'I was told that my mother was a young girl. A teenage runaway. She got pregnant, no one knew who the father was and she didn't want to raise a child on the streets. So she gave me up.'

'I'm sorry.' He looked at her with sadness in his eyes.

'It's not your fault.'

'No, but it must have been hard.'

'Not at first. I just sort of accepted the story. I've thought more about it since having Seb. I couldn't imagine giving him up. My mother, whoever she was, must have gone through hell to make that decision.'

'I think you've probably got her spirit and bravery.'

Eva smiled, then they both got up, throwing their polystyrene cups into the bin.

They wandered through a few more stores and she noticed that he kept looking at her when he thought she wasn't watching. She wondered if he pitied her. She didn't want that. She didn't need it. Pity did nothing for anyone. It certainly never made things better.

When they finally got to the last store and saw a beautiful blue-and-silver bike that was the perfect size for Seb, Jacob's face broke out into a broad smile.

'A bike for Christmas! His *first* bike. That'll be perfect.'

Eva beamed, too. 'I agree. But he'll need a helmet, too—and stabilisers.'

'You're happy for me to get it?'

She nodded and looked at him. 'I'm happy.'

Back at Eva's home, they unloaded their shopping and Jacob helped her hide the bike away in her bedroom closet, draping it with clothes for extra camouflage.

It felt odd having him in her bedroom, near her bed. In her most intimate space… With the gifts put away, they stood a few feet apart, just looking at each other.

'Well…I guess I ought to go. Shall I come back later? To read to Seb?'

'Yes. That would be great. He'll enjoy that.'

'So will I.'

She stared at him some more, her fingers fidgeting, unsure of what to do. She started when he took a step towards her. Then another. Tentatively, he reached up and stroked the side of her face.

'I've enjoyed this afternoon. Spending time with you. Being with you. Thank you for telling me your story.'

The feel of his fingers stroking her face sent tingles down her body. Her breath caught in her throat and she became hyperaware. Aware of his solid gaze, of where his hands were, how close he stood, exactly what he was doing.

'I enjoyed it, too.'

'I'd like to…kiss you.'

She breathed in, her chest feeling so full of air, so full

of hope for what he might do next, what it might suggest, she almost wasn't breathing at all.

'You would?'

He came nearer still. They were centimetres apart and she could breathe in his scent. Her body was doing something strange inside, with the excitement of his proximity. It was as if there were tumblers and acrobats in her stomach, and tiny, tiny dancers in each and every blood cell, pirouetting and twirling their way through her system. And their spinning was getting faster and faster the closer Jacob came.

Her lips parted.

She wanted him to kiss her. She wanted him to so much!

'There's something about you, Eva...'

She was hypnotised. His face was so close. His eyes were upon hers, burning her heart with their intensity; his mouth was so near, so tantalisingly near!

Was she doing the right thing? It didn't *feel* wrong... but surely this couldn't end well? Whenever she thought everything was going right for her, the world would pull the rug from under her feet.

She wanted his kiss, though. It was the way she'd felt once before. But this time there wouldn't be anyone jetting off to another continent straight afterwards. This time it wouldn't be a one-night stand. This would be something else. A couple reconnecting. A woman and a man who had already made a child together, who had been parted by geography and mileage, who could now be together. Who could be stepping towards the future together.

'But...' He reached up and threaded his fingers into her hair, his hands gently holding her face.

'But?'

'I don't want to ruin this friendship we're creating. I don't want to ruin it for Seb.'

'You won't.'

She looked deep into his blue eyes and saw his soul. He was a tortured man still. She could see that. Sense that. He carried pain within him, something he still hadn't shared with her, but she knew deep in her heart that if she just gave him some time, gave him some room to feel comfortable with her, then he would share it. And once he shared she could help him. She knew she could.

It was probably the lust talking, telling her it wasn't a problem, but she couldn't help it. Being this close to Jacob was electric.

How bad could it be? It wasn't as if he'd murdered anyone. He wasn't a bad guy. Something had hurt him. Something or someone had taken hold of his heart and crushed it.

Eva wondered if she could help him mend it. But what would happen if she did? If she let him in, if she started to care, then she would be taking a chance on him that she'd never, ever taken with anyone else. She would be opening herself up to being hurt again. There *was* that risk, wasn't there? Every other relationship in her past had failed. What would make this one so special?

But what if *this* was a relationship with the potential for something amazing?

That tantalising thought hypnotised her. Blindsided her doubt for a moment.

Jacob pulled her towards him.

Her body pressed up against his and then her eyes closed as her lips met his. Elation flooded her system with ripples and waves of intoxication as the reality of kissing Jacob again sank in.

Their shared kiss, though tender, opened up something inside her that she hadn't been expecting.

A fervour. A *need* that she'd never experienced with any man before.

She burned for him. Breathed him in. Melted into him as she felt his hands caress her and hold her against him. The solidness, the hardness of his male body against her soft femininity was a beautiful yin and yang.

The last time she'd kissed this man she'd lain naked in his arms and allowed herself to fly through the skies with him, soaring amongst the clouds and the heavens as he'd taken her to fever pitch and back again. Being in his arms again felt so *right*, and strangely so *familiar*—as if it had been seconds since they had last held her and not years. His lips were warm and soft against hers; his body was against hers… It made her come alive…

He pulled back to look at her with glazed eyes.

She had no doubt that she looked the same.

Eva touched her lips. 'Will you be with us at Christmas?'

'I'll need to see my family, too, but, yes… I'll be with you for Christmas.'

His family. The people she hadn't met yet. These strangers she would now have to share Seb with. Leave herself open to inspection from. It didn't seem too scary right now, with Jacob, but she was worried about what would happen later.

What would he be like with them? What did she know about him? Really?

Eva craved for all this to work out, but experience told her not to get her hopes up. She wanted not to be afraid. But she'd been hurt so many times before…

I want to be part of a family so much!

But did she dare hope she could actually have it?

Jacob had come back for the evening. They were sitting together in the lounge, whilst Seb played on the floor between them.

'I spoke to my parents again. Said we'd probably take Seb one day before Christmas.'

She frowned. 'Oh?'

Before Christmas? She only had one weekend free between now and Christmas, and spending it with a family she didn't know didn't sound very appealing. Besides, these people probably wouldn't even like her.

'Don't you want to take him on your own? I'm sure they don't want me hanging around—'

Jacob shook his head. 'It'll be fine!'

'No. It's probably best it's just you and Seb at first.'

'They'll want to meet you. I'd really like it, too, if you came. They're very friendly! If anyone is going to get questioned it'll be me. I'm the one who stayed away.'

She smiled at him. 'I know. It's just…difficult for me. Isn't it hard for you, too? You stayed away for a long time. Aren't you worried about going back?'

Jacob nodded. 'I am. There are lots of memories there.' He thought for a moment, his eyes dark, and then he said, 'Someone I loved…she died.'

'I'm so sorry.'

'It's fine. I've accepted it now. That's the whole thing about going back. I need to face my demons over being there again.'

'And you don't want to go alone?'

'I could go alone…but I'd like you to be there. It's not just Seb who's a part of my family now. You are, too.'

She could feel her cheeks flame with heat. 'Really?'

'Really.' He laid his hand on hers.

'Thank you. Do you…want to tell me about her?'

He looked away. 'She was a childhood friend. Someone who came to mean a great deal to me.'

She nodded. It was understandable that he should have someone like this in his past. And now she could understand some of his reluctance to go back home. It had to be a past love. A love affair that somehow went wrong, perhaps.

A tinge of jealousy announced itself, but she pushed it away. She had no right to feel jealous about this.

But was he over this woman? She wasn't sure. Obviously the pain of loss was still there. She'd seen it in him before. The night they'd met.

They watched Seb play on the floor, silent for a moment, Eva sipping at her tea and Jacob looking back at her darkly, stuck in his memories of the past.

He was hurt. That much was clear. But surely he must have moved on? She didn't want to be his soft place to fall just because he was hurt—she wanted to be his because he wanted to be with *her*. Heart, soul—everything.

Anything less was too risky.

If she suspected he wasn't over this woman then she'd walk away from a relationship with him.

Why did he have to tell me about her? It was all going so well...

Eva needed certainty in her life. Needed security. If Jacob and events in his past somehow threatened that, then she'd separate herself from him immediately. Better to keep him at a distance until she knew for sure. Better to tread carefully.

It wasn't just about *her* anymore.

CHAPTER SIX

A WEEK LATER Jacob took them some Christmas lights. Small white fairy lights to hang outside, around the guttering and over the small fence in the front garden. Eva had told him she hadn't decorated the outside of her house as she hadn't felt safe going up a ladder on her own with just a three-year-old to steady it.

That morning frost had covered everything, making surfaces slippery, and as he worked he could see his breath billowing out around him and his fingertips turning redder and redder as they lost more and more feeling. The little plastic grips that would secure the lights along the guttering were fragile, and he lost more than he used as he tried to force them onto the edge.

But he didn't mind. He felt *useful*. The past few nights when he'd turned up to Eva's home he'd noticed that she was about the only person in the street with no Christmassy outdoor lights so he'd offered to do it, knowing Seb would like it, too.

Eva stood at the bottom of the ladder, holding it, looking up at him and laughing every time he cursed as another clip skittered away from his fingers and fell to the ground.

'Will I need to get you another packet?' she asked, laughing.

He grimaced as he forced another clip into position. 'Maybe. At this rate I might start suturing them on.'

The last clip went into place and he descended the ladder to collect the lights so that he could trail them across the front of the house.

'Can you believe people go through this madness every year?'

'Christmas is a time to make everyone happy, isn't it?'

He nodded. 'Kids, maybe.'

Eva frowned. Surely *he'd* had good Christmases? 'Is Christmas not a happy time for you?'

She seemed genuinely interested in his experiences. But he felt bad about talking about them. His childhood Christmas memories were great, and he knew hers weren't. She was the one who'd been in foster care—not him. It was that one Christmas Eve he'd experienced five years ago that really bothered him.

'It wasn't for you.'

'My Christmases were...different. I ended up in so many places I lost track of all the varying traditions people had.'

'But were you happy?'

She shrugged. 'I never belonged. I always felt I was intruding on someone else's memories.'

Someone else's memories... No. He didn't want to mess with those.

'Christmas was just fine for me until a few years ago.'

He picked up the knot of fairy lights and began to untangle them, handing Eva one end so he didn't lose it.

'We made Seb on a Christmas Eve. That's a good memory, isn't it?'

His numb fingers stopped moving as he looked at her. She was bundled up tight in her winter coat, her red hair just peeking out from underneath her woolly hat, and her nose was bright pink over her thick, fluffy scarf. She looked like a model posing for a winter-clothing campaign, and he almost wanted to take a picture of her to capture the image.

'Yes. But Christmas Eve isn't all jolly excitement and meeting hot chicks at parties.'

She stared at him, amused. *'Hot chicks?'*

Jacob managed a smile. 'You *were*! I'd not expected to see anyone like you at that party. I hadn't gone looking for a one-night stand, you know.'

She looked about them to make sure there were no nosy neighbours listening in. 'I'm glad to hear it.'

'I was looking to…escape. Forget for a while.' Jacob pulled at more of the wire. 'What were *you* doing there? That night?'

'Well, I hadn't wanted to go, either, but decided to make the best of it once I got there. From what I remember, your eyes looked…sad.'

Jacob headed back up the ladder, so that she wouldn't see the look on his face. He didn't want to talk about Michelle right now. He didn't want to tell Eva about what had happened. Not yet. Not what he'd done. Because if he did then she might be horrified with him. She wouldn't see Jacob the doctor, father of her baby.

If he told her the truth she'd be appalled.

Because he'd killed a woman.

A woman he'd supposedly loved.

No one got to do that and then be entitled to happiness. This life—this chance with Eva and Seb—he *wanted* it, but he wasn't sure he'd be allowed to keep it if he told her the truth. What if he took *her* for granted, too? Or, worse still, Seb? What if they argued and she ran off? Or drove off and…?

The thought of Michelle's blood in the snow smacked him straight between the eyes.

'That someone special I told you about…she died on Christmas Eve. Each time it rolls around I tend to think about it. That night we met, the party was a great excuse for me to say goodbye to a few friends and hopefully forget for a while.'

'Did it work?'

He looked down at her from his perch atop the ladder. 'It did. I met *you*.'

Eva looked up at him and felt her heart flutter in her chest. He'd met her on the anniversary of this woman's death, and though he'd been hurt, though he'd been pained by the day, she had helped manage to soothe him—if only for a short while.

She'd always known she'd seen something in his gaze that night—before she'd spoken to him, before they'd got close. He'd been grieving! It seemed so obvious now. And they'd made something beautiful out of something painful.

They'd made Seb. And here they were, years later, together. Who knew how it would end?

She hoped it wouldn't.

The days running up to Christmas began to pass much too quickly.

Jacob spent as much time as he could at Eva's—playing with Seb, having dinner with them and then reading Seb his bedtime story. He also took him out for walks on his own.

Eva began to learn more about the father of her child— he liked reading and photography, and had taken loads of photographs in Africa, some of which she thought he should enter into competitions, they were that good. And she learned about the work he'd done in Africa—first in an eye clinic, saving the sight of thousands by performing simple cataract operations, and then he'd helped build a new school.

He was certainly handy around the house. The dripping tap in her kitchen had been fixed, and he'd shaved a few inches off a door that had never shut properly and he'd even offered to help repaint a room.

But she was wary of taking advantage of him. Of letting things move too fast. He was there for Seb, after all, not her—though they were getting along well as a unit, and she couldn't help but notice how attractive he still was to her.

Since that kiss after their shopping expedition she'd felt torn about experiencing it again. She wanted to. Very much! But she was afraid of what would happen if she did. Too many times she'd thought she could have something and keep it forever, and it would always be torn from her grasp.

It was difficult to concentrate sometimes, with him in the house. He'd be reading to her son, lying on Seb's bed with his arm wrapped around him, and she would watch them from the doorway and marvel at how homely it looked and how it made her feel all warm inside and safe. But then he'd come downstairs and put his coat on to leave, and there'd be that awkward moment at the door, when he'd kiss her goodbye on the cheek and then look longingly at her, as if he wanted to do more.

She'd been keeping him at arm's length. Trying not to let herself get carried away by his being there and the thrill of the season. Letting him know, subtly, that she wasn't rushing into anything. Believing that if she kept him at a distance she'd be able to stop the pain before it came if anything went wrong—that somehow it wouldn't hurt as much.

But it didn't stop her yearning for another proper kiss. She could feel the tingle in her lips at the idea each time he came round, wondering if maybe today he might kiss her again, but Jacob seemed determined to respect her boundaries.

And still Eva was determined to crack his exterior. To delve deep inside this man who had fathered her child and find out more about his past. She wanted to understand him. Know the pain that he carried. Because if she did then she would know if she and Seb were safe from being left behind. She wanted to know about Jacob, and the fact that she didn't know him as well as she could frustrated her.

Perhaps if she did go and meet his family then it might provide her with the opportunity she needed.

Jacob was sitting next to her on the couch. Wine had been poured and the fairy lights twinkled outside the window and, in the corner of the room, twisted around the Christmas tree.

The television had been turned off. It was just the two of them. Seb was fast asleep upstairs.

'I'm glad you came back from Africa when you did, Jacob.'

'So am I.'

'I was terrified, you know—at first, when I saw you standing in Minors that day. All I could think of was how was I going to tell you about Seb.'

He smiled at her. 'You managed it.'

Eva laughed and sipped her wine. 'Just about. What was it that made you come back? From Africa? Did something happen? To make you come?'

She watched as his blue eyes darkened.

'Something. *Someone*, actually. You have to understand I met a lot of patients over there. Heard a lot of sad stories. The people there were brave. Proud. Each one touched my heart, day after day, but there was this one story that I just couldn't get out of my head.'

'What was it?'

Jacob poured more wine into their glasses and put the bottle back on the table.

'This man brought his wife into the hospital. His name was Reuben and he was in his seventies. You could see the *life* in his face. The wisdom and the pain etched into every line. But he held himself tall and proud. His wife was dying of malaria and we watched her fade every day for about a week.'

Eva listened intently.

'Reuben told me that he'd met his wife, Zuri, when they were teenagers. They'd fallen in love, but Reuben's family had arranged a marriage for him to another woman and they forbade him from seeing Zuri. It broke his heart, but he had to do what his father ordered. He married this other woman and they had children and he said it was a good life, if not a loving one. His wife died when Reuben turned seventy, and he thought that was it for him. That he would die lonely because his children had all grown up and flown the nest. Until he met Zuri again in the market.'

Jacob smiled.

Eva smiled, too.

'Zuri had lost her husband long before. She had been unable to bear children and he had walked out on her. She'd been alone for years. But Zuri and Reuben got together and married within weeks of meeting each other again. They'd been married only three months when he carried her into my hospital, exhausted and spent. When Zuri died, just a week later, Reuben stood with me at her funeral, and he turned to me and thanked me. He said that life was short and that if I had any loved ones at home then I should return and be with them. Because you never knew when life could take them away from you.'

'Poor Reuben.'

'He told me those three months with Zuri had been the happiest of his entire life. His story stuck with me…eating away at me. I kept thinking about Reuben for months afterwards. The twists and turns of his life. How he'd ended up with the one woman he should have been with from the beginning. How he'd known it was special with her. How the short time he'd had with Zuri was the happiest he'd ever had. I kept thinking of you. Of the night we met. How it had felt…special. How you'd made me feel. I wanted to come back and find you. Tell you. See if there was something we could make of that connection we'd felt.'

Eva nodded. 'Because life is short?'

'Exactly.'

He reached up to stroke her face and she leaned into his hand. His gaze was intense as he focused on his fingers, tracing her jawline and then moving down her neck, over the pulse point there that was throbbing madly and down to the neckline of her top. As her pulse accelerated his hand dropped away and he looked up at her, suddenly uncomfortable.

'What is it?'

'Nothing.'

'There's something, Jacob. Please…please tell me. It could help.'

He still looked at her, uncertainty in his eyes.

She could tell that he wanted to say something but was afraid to. *Why?* Surely he trusted her? Had he done something terrible? Because if he had then she needed to know. Not just for her, but for Seb, too. She had to know who she was getting involved with. It was the only way to protect her own heart.

'I *want* to tell you…'

She reached over and took his hand in hers, cradling his fingers with her own, wrapping her hand over his. 'You can.'

'I've never spoken of this to anyone.'

'Then, it's time. If you keep pain inside it eats you alive, Jacob. You can't live with pain all the time. You know what they say about a problem shared?'

He squeezed her fingers. 'It's a problem halved?'

'That's right.'

He let out a big sigh and then nodded. 'A year to the day before I met you was supposed to be my wedding day.'

Eva tried not to show surprise. 'Okay…'

He let out another breath. It was clearly getting easier to say the more he spoke. 'I was getting married to Michelle. She was a childhood friend. She lived next door to my parents' smallholding and we grew up together…and then we became something more.'

Eva tried to imagine him with someone else. Loving another woman intensely enough to want to marry her. The idea of it made her feel uncomfortable.

'You loved her?'

He nodded. 'Yes. I thought so anyway.'

Eva frowned and took a sip of her drink.

'I proposed and we set a date. December the twenty-fourth. It seemed romantic. We'd hoped for snow and we got it, too. For the first time in years it came down quite thick. It had been raining the previous day, so no one thought it would settle, but it did. It made everything look beautiful.'

She could picture it in her head. 'I can imagine.'

'I was at the church, waiting. You know how brides are meant to be late? Well, I waited outside for her to arrive, thinking I'd head into the church when I saw the bridal car. She was a bit late, but I thought that was because she was getting ready on her own. She didn't have a father or any brothers to give her away. She was going to walk up the aisle alone.'

Eva sipped her wine. It all sounded lovely so far. But she knew something was coming. Something bad. She could tell from the way he was telling the story. The fact that he'd never spoken of this. She could hear it in his voice. See the pain in his eyes. The same look he'd had four years ago, when she'd met him at that party.

He looked away. 'She never made it.'

'How do you mean?'

'She was hit by a heavy-goods vehicle. Side impact on black ice. She wasn't wearing a seat belt and she was thrown from the spinning vehicle. She died on the tarmac, bleeding into the snow.'

Eva covered her face with her hands. How awful! 'Oh, Jacob, I'm *so* sorry!' No wonder he hadn't wanted to speak of this! His bride…? Dying on their wedding day…?

He wouldn't meet her gaze. He just stared at the carpet.

Now she understood. Now she understood the look that had been in his eyes at the party. The most horrific thing had happened to him. Of *course* she could understand it now. Understand why he had kept this in for so long.

But she was glad that he'd felt able to tell her. To confide in her. It meant something. That they were getting closer. That he trusted her with this information.

It all made such sense. His childhood friend, this Michelle, a woman he'd grown up with. A longtime friendship becoming something more, something more intense. Love. Commitment. And he'd lost her on what should have been the happiest day of his life!

She wondered briefly what Michelle had been like. The woman who had been Jacob's friend…who had become his love. What hopes and dreams had she had about their married life together? She would have got ready that morning, ready for church, for her wedding—and how happy she must have been.

Now Eva understood why he didn't look forward to Christmas. Why it held bad memories for him.

'Perhaps now…with us…Christmas can become a good time for you again?'

He looked at her. 'I hope so.'

'Thank you for telling me, Jacob. I know it must have hurt.' She squeezed his fingers. 'I really feel we can move forward now. I'd like to go with you to your parents' place.'

Though she still felt nervous about it—and would continue to until they'd been. Until she'd seen how his family were with her. But if Jacob could make this huge step forward by confiding in her, then she could do this for him. It would help him. Her, too. And it would give her the opportunity to learn more about this man she wanted to trust implicitly.

Jacob focused on her as she spoke, nodding. 'I'd like that. So would they.'

He continued to stare at her and she stared back. They were so close to each other on the couch. Their legs had been touching the entire time Jacob had been speaking and while they'd sipped at their drinks.

She hoped that now he had started to open up about himself he would continue to do so. Perhaps back at his childhood home, confronting old memories, he would do so. She could learn more about him. About Michelle.

What if he still loves her?

The horrible thought impeded on her warm feeling inside and she tried to crush it down. Ignore the fact that she'd thought it. But the more she tried to ignore it, the stronger it seemed to get.

Jacob had had the love of his life ripped from him! It wasn't a love that had slowly died. It hadn't ebbed away with the years. She hadn't cheated on him.

She'd *died*!

He *had* to still love her!

And if he loved a dead woman how could they ever truly be together? She wasn't going to try to compete with a ghost.

She couldn't afford to get involved with him. She couldn't risk her relationship with him. It would end badly.

Perhaps it would be best if she kept her distance from him until he'd sorted out the feelings he still had.

She looked down at his lips, at his smooth mouth amongst the small forest of stubble that grew around his jaw. A small scar marked a brief valley on his chin. How had he got that? Shaving? A boyhood accident?

What if he *wasn't* still in love with Michelle?

Would she be risking ruining their relationship by creating distance between them when she didn't need to? Would she be fulfilling her own prophecy by keeping him at arm's length?

Life is too hard!

Her gaze went back to his lips. Then to his eyes. He was looking at her so intently. All she had to do was lean closer, close the gap, close her eyes and then he would be hers…

Eva stood up abruptly, placing her wine glass on the table. 'It's nearly time for you to go.'

'Of course.'

This was best. To have the distance they both needed.

It's the right thing to do.

So why did it hurt? Why did she want him to stay? Because if he stayed who knew where it might lead?

It was best this way. He was clearly still grieving—he

was the last person she should be letting herself get involved with right now. She knew that.

He nodded and grabbed his jacket, pecked her on the cheek and headed into the hallway. She heard the front door open and close.

She pressed her hand to her cheek. The warmth from his lips was fading away.

It felt awful to create space between them, but it was the best thing to do.

The house was normally quiet when she woke up in the morning, and she could sit and read a newspaper quietly with a cup of coffee before Seb came bouncing down the stairs, full of life and noise.

But this Saturday morning Jacob had arrived early, and the smell of frying bacon filled the house, causing her to salivate. Even though she didn't normally eat fried breakfasts—she was a cereal and half a grapefruit kind of girl—she wolfed down bacon, two sausages, scrambled eggs and toast.

Jacob was a good cook, and Seb was enjoying having his father around for breakfast.

They could talk to each other for hours, and Eva had often found herself having to grab a book and go off and read somewhere while Seb got to know his father. It was only fair after all. They had three years to catch up on, and Eva no longer felt as if she was being left out.

Jacob had learned that Seb enjoyed nursery, loved sport and animals and wanted to be a doctor one day, like his parents. Seb was also hoping for snow on Christmas Day. Lots and lots of snow. And Seb had learned that his dad had gone on safari and met a real-life leopard, seen a lion pride and even been charged at by an elephant.

It was only as they talked, as they chatted, that Eva realised they were so alike in their mannerisms. Why had she not realised that Seb rubbed at his chin when he was thinking, the same way Jacob did? Why had she not noticed that that they both stuck out their tongues slightly when they were concentrating?

Silly things. Inconsequential things. But everything she noticed was amusing and quaint. Familiar. Things *she* didn't do but Seb did. Why had she never wondered if they were traits from his father?

Jacob was clearing away their greasy, tomato ketchup-smeared plates when he asked Seb a question. 'Seb, do you remember I told that you my parents have a small farm with lots of animals?'

'Yeah,' Seb answered.

'Well, your mum and I have been thinking, and we thought you might like to visit there today. Stay the night. Get to know your grandparents and see the animals.'

Eva nodded as Seb looked to her, as if for permission. She was pleased that she'd agreed to take this step. But it was a huge about-turn for her. The idea of meeting Jacob's family had at first been scary. She'd never wanted to stand in front of strangers and be judged again. But since Jacob's revelations about Michelle, and with the way their relationship was developing, she'd begun to accept that this was the right thing to do. Especially for Seb. These people she didn't yet know were his family, and whether she and Jacob became something or not his family would always be there for her son.

This was an opportunity that she had never had. It was an enormous step forward for them both.

'Can we?'

'Course we can.'

Seb beamed a smile at them both. 'Cool!'

'We'll need our wellies!'

Eva was still anxious at the thought of meeting Jacob's parents. Even though he'd told her they were nice and friendly. They would assess her.

But she had to remind herself that she was an adult now—not a child. If Jacob's parents and family didn't like her, it didn't matter too much. What mattered most of all was that they knew Seb and adored him. If they didn't like *him*... Not possible! Of *course* they would love Seb. They *had* to.

So she was off to the Dolan smallholding. Where everyone who had no right to judge her lived. Perhaps Jacob was pleased she was going because then his parents wouldn't be able to have a go at *him*?

This weekend was going to be truly uncomfortable for her. Jacob had apparently already told them that they'd need separate beds...

Going to meet a new family again... How many times had she done *that*? Stood outside on the pavement, by a social worker's car, whilst a new family came out to greet her. Assess her. Judge her worth.

They'd all be looking at her. Deciding if they liked her or not. Deciding if she was worth keeping.

It shouldn't matter what they think. I am part of their family now. Because of Seb.

But it did matter.

It mattered a lot. She *wanted* them to like her. She *wanted* to be accepted. She really wanted to be welcomed into the Dolan family.

It was a two-hour car journey that became nearly four. Everyone was driving slowly and more carefully due to the ice still on the roads.

Eva sat in the front seat as Jacob drove them in his sleek black car, with her stomach knotting with nerves at every

mile. Jolly Christmas music played over the car stereo—
music that she would normally sing along to. But not today.
She was a bag of nerves—as jittery and shaky as a naked
person in the Arctic.

The last time she'd felt this nervous she had been taking the pregnancy test. Her stomach was clenched tight,
her mouth was so dry she could barely speak and she had
to keep stretching out her fingers to prevent cramp as she
was clasping them so tightly.

And to think I thought I was being relaxed about this!

Outside, the world was doing just fine. Only a week to
Christmas and it was a beautiful, crisp winter's day, with
blue skies and bright sunshine. They passed fields of graz-
ing horses and cattle or sheep as Jacob drove them down
winding lanes through the countryside. There were some
flowers growing at the roadside that she'd never seen before. Winter honeysuckle? She wasn't sure. She'd never
been green-fingered.

It all looked so beautiful and serene, but as they passed
a sign for Netherfield Village—the place where his parents' smallholding was meant to be—she could almost
feel her blood pressure rising all by itself. The village was
picture-postcard perfect. Literally, she could have taken a
photo of its village square and used it as a Christmas card.
It was sickeningly beautiful. The type of place you wanted
to move to the second you saw it.

Jacob seemed nervous, too, as he drove. He was going
home to his family, but he seemed edgy. She supposed that
was to be expected. He'd been away from home for years.
And he knew that by going back he'd be facing old, painful
memories. She was proud of him for doing it, and pleased
that he was able to do it with her at his side.

Her stomach rolled as she thought about how she'd kept
his parents' grandson from them. Not deliberately—but

would they readily accept the fact that she'd not been able to find Jacob? If they were going to have a go at her she hoped they'd do so out of Seb's eyeline and earshot.

She hadn't kept their grandson from them on purpose. They'd lost three years of their grandchild's life. Three years that they'd never get back. Three years of memories and photos and home videos that didn't exist because she'd not persevered in finding their son.

Had she given up too easily?

No. I tried my best.

The thought of meeting them filled her with nerves, and though the fried breakfast had seemed a wonderful idea a few hours ago she could feel it sitting heavily in her stomach now, the grease swirling around inside her like an oily whirlpool, making her feel extremely queasy.

'Nearly there now, Seb!' Jacob called over his shoulder to his son.

'Great!'

Seb leaned forward in his booster seat and looked between the two front seats through the windscreen as Jacob steered his car through the quaint village, past a pub called The Three Horseshoes, a post office, a grocery store, some quaint thatched cottages and then down another lane.

'There's the alpacas!'

'Wow!' Seb exclaimed from the backseat.

Jacob laughed. 'We keep them in the fields where we have the chickens and the geese and ducks. They keep away the foxes and my mum uses their fur to make quilts and baby blankets.'

'They keep away foxes? What? Like guard dogs?' Eva enquired.

'Exactly.'

Seb wound down his window for a better look, letting in a blast of cold air. 'They're funny!'

Eva smiled at his amusement. They were close now, and she could feel Jacob's apprehension building.

Just past the alpaca field he turned into a smaller lane, with lots of lumps and bumps. The car jolted them around as its suspension system struggled with the holey road, but then they were pulling up in front of a redbrick farmhouse with window boxes and a border collie dog lying outside, panting heavily, its breath fogging in the chill air.

'That's Lucy,' Jacob said. 'Come on, Seb! I'll introduce you!'

Father and son got out of the car and had gone over to the happy dog, making a big fuss of it, before Eva could even remove her seat belt. The dog wagged its tail madly at Jacob and lasciviously licked at Seb's happy face.

Eva took that moment to look around her.

To the side of the house there was a rotary washing line, empty and frosted, there were plant pots and tubs filled to overflowing with winter bulbs and early crocus and there were blue gingham curtains at the windows, tied back with sashing.

Eva almost expected to see a hot apple pie cooling on a windowsill!

There was a ginger cat curled up on an outdoor chair in the winter sun, and it opened a lazy eye as she closed the car door and blinked in the bright sunshine.

With the rolling fields set as a backdrop to the old red-brick house, the place was beautiful!

Seb and Jacob were still ruffling the dog's fur, Seb beaming, when the front door opened and Jacob's parents emerged from inside the house.

Eva felt her hesitant smile freeze on her face at their appearance. This was it. The moment she'd been worrying about. She looked to Jacob to see how he'd react, and saw him stand back and stare at his parents, a half smile on his face.

They stared at each other for a moment. Eva could see that Jacob's mum was dying for her son to speak, but Jacob seemed incapable of saying anything.

Needing to break the tension, Eva stepped forward, away from the car. 'Mrs Dolan?'

His mother turned.

Her son looked so like her. Jacob's mother was tall and slim and had the same dark colouring, though her hair had a grey streak in the centre, but his father was already grey haired and slightly plumper.

And they were both smiling.

'Eva!' Mrs Dolan stepped towards her and embraced her firmly, pulling her into a bear hug she couldn't escape from. 'You must be tired from your journey. We were expecting you hours ago! Come on in! We've got freshly baked biscuits and mince pies inside, and a fresh pot of tea.'

She released her and beamed a smile at her.

Eva was delighted. 'Er…lovely… Thank you.'

This was more like it! Eva felt instantly accepted! Where had *this* sensation been as a child? Where had the warm bear hugs been then? Where had the home-baked biscuits and the welcome and the *acceptance* been?

'Jacob!'

Jacob's mother pulled him to her, squeezing him tight, as if she never wanted to let him go, and then she kissed him on both cheeks and looked at him for a long time, her hands cradling his face.

'You've come *home*! You've changed…'

Then she turned to Seb and pulled him into a hug.

'And you must be Seb! We've been *so* looking forward to meeting you!'

Jacob looked relieved and managed to smile fully at last.

Jacob's father walked over and gave him a hug and a quick back slap. Then they stepped apart.

'Hi, Dad.'

'Son... Good-looking boy you've got there!'

Once Seb had stopped ruffling the dog's fur and rubbing its belly, they stepped into the farmhouse. The front door took them straight into the kitchen, which was made up of old wooden units, with dried flowers and copper-bottomed pots hanging from a rack above. There were two metallic strips on the walls, holding a line of knives and shiny utensils, and in the centre of the kitchen a huge oak table that had been laid for guests.

Candy-cane bunting decorated the walls and a huge spray of holly erupted from the vast copper pot set in the fireplace. Christmas cards lined every available surface. Clearly the Dolans were very popular people!

A vase in the centre of the table held a beautiful bouquet of pine stems, interspersed with cinnamon sticks and dried orange slices. Unusual, but very aromatic, and around it were the promised plates of pies and biscuits. A hot teapot with a knitted Christmas-bauble cosy sat at one end, where Jacob's mother now stood.

'Do sit down, everyone—and help yourself.'

Seb tucked in with gusto—which was surprising, considering the size of his breakfast—whereas Jacob took nothing, only accepting a mug of tea. Eva noticed that Jacob's gaze kept flicking to a photograph on the mantelpiece that looked like a picture of him with a blonde woman.

Michelle?

In the picture Jacob sat with his arm around the woman's shoulders as they both posed on what looked like an old country stile. She had long honey-coloured hair, almost down to her waist, and they had their heads together, grinning for the camera.

She had clearly been cherished. And was obviously much remembered, with her picture having pride of place in one of the main rooms of this home.

Eva accepted tea and politely took a biscuit, wondering if the Dolans would ever put *her* picture up? She hoped so. It had started well, so far...

'It's so wonderful to meet you at last, Seb,' Mrs Dolan said. 'Your daddy has told us so much about you. Are you looking forward to Christmas?'

Seb nodded, his mouth full of mince pie.

She smiled broadly. 'We hear you like animals?'

Seb nodded again, stuffing in another mouthful.

'We'll take you out later and show you them all, and then you must visit the orchard. It's where your father used to play.'

Seb looked at his dad and grinned.

Jacob smiled back. 'It's also where I first broke my arm, trying to jump the small stream that's there, so try not to be *too* like me. We don't need to take you to A&E again.'

Mrs Dolan took a biscuit for herself. 'Of course! You had an accident, didn't you? Bumped your head? Were you scared, Seb?'

'A bit...'

Mrs Dolan looked up at her son, then at Eva. 'You're both at the same casualty department, aren't you?'

Eva nodded and smiled. This was so *odd*! They were talking to her as if everything was normal. As if she was *wanted* there. It felt great!

'We've been here in this house forever, it seems. Ever since Jacob was a little boy himself. A bit younger than you, Seb. You must get him to show you the tree where he carved his name.'

'If I can still remember which tree it is.'

'Of *course* you remember. You might not have been here for a while, but you know this place like the back of your hand.'

'You mentioned an orchard, Mrs Dolan? What do you grow there?' Eva ventured her first question, feeling her cheeks flame with heat as everyone turned to face her at the table.

'Bits of everything, really. Apples, pears, greengages, plums—you name it, we've got pies made of it in the freezer! In the spring it looks amazing, when it's all in blossom. And you must call me Molly, dear. Mrs Dolan makes me sound like my mother-in-law!'

Molly Dolan smiled and her whole face creased with delight and happiness.

These people were being *nice* to her! It seemed so strange! It wasn't what she'd been expecting from them at all! A childish delight was filling her on the inside as she soaked up their warmth.

'I'll show you around,' Jacob suggested. 'Fancy a walk? Stretch the legs?'

'Oh, finish your tea first!' Molly urged. 'Always in a rush to get away, Jacob. You've only just got in and sat down.'

'We've been sat down for nearly four hours, Mum. In the car.'

'But Eva needs time to absorb everything. This is all new for her.' She turned to Eva. 'He's always the same when he gets here. It's as if he can't wait to shrug off the city—he has to go out and roam around the place and get the country back into his blood. How he got any work done in Africa, I'll never know.'

She'd mentioned Africa. Jacob's bolthole. But she hadn't mentioned it with any discomfort. She'd not said it as a preamble for launching into a round of questions for her son. She looked as if she was comfortable sitting and waiting until Jacob was ready to talk about it.

Eva sipped her tea. It was perfect. Not too strong. And as she looked across the table at Jacob she began to understand him a bit more. He had a lovely family. Warm, welcoming parents. And he was clearly loved.

Maybe she would be, too?

Eva and Jacob were strolling through the orchard. Seb was with his grandfather, learning the whistles that were used to control the sheepdog, and they could hear them faintly in the distance.

The sun was shining down brightly, but there was no warmth in the cold air and Eva was glad she'd chosen a long coat, hat and scarf. She could feel the sun on her face only barely, and her toes were going numb with cold. It was a strange feeling. But it didn't bother her too much.

She loved the winter. The shortening of the days, getting cosy in front of a fire at night, drinking hot cocoa and being warm and dry inside whilst outside the weather was doing its worst. Wondering when it might snow...

This was the first opportunity she'd had in ages to enjoy the season. She'd been working so much just lately, and had been covering extra shifts until Jacob's arrival. It always got busier towards Christmas in A&E. People and alcohol didn't always mix well, and there was a reason it was called the 'silly season'. There weren't often moments when she could feel carefree and relaxed, and this was a bonus.

All those hours spent worrying in the car... Wasted! She could have sung along to those Christmas songs after all. Mr and Mrs Dolan were lovely. And now she was here, at Jacob's home, with him walking alongside her.

It was hard not to keep stealing glances at him, wondering how he was doing being back here, surrounded by memories. She was enjoying the warmth of his family and feeling she belonged.

'It's very beautiful here, Jacob.'

He nodded and smiled at her. They were walking at a slow pace, with no apparent direction. Just ambling together through the trees.

'You have a wonderful family.' It was true. 'The type I used to dream of having.'

'Thank you.'

She looked directly at him and stopped walking. 'Can I ask something?'

He nodded, squinting at her in the winter sunlight. 'Sure.'

'Why did you have no contact with them? They clearly love you. Care for you. I can understand how you didn't want to be facing old memories by *being* here, but why didn't you keep in contact with them?'

He stopped walking and faced her. They were in a bit of a glade, surrounded by bare, knobbly trees. A robin chirped near them, singing its melody to mark its territory for any other robin that might be listening. It was a happy sound.

He sighed, looking about him. 'It's difficult to say. I know they love me—and please don't think that I take that for granted. I don't. It's just…I knew what it would be like after my wedding day. After Michelle died. They'd look at me with pity, and they'd want to support me and look after me, and I just felt that I didn't deserve it.'

'I don't understand. *Why* didn't you deserve it?'

'It was my fault she died.'

'But you weren't driving that truck that hit her. You couldn't have known that would happen.'

'I know, but...' He trailed off and stuck his hands into his pockets, obviously wrestling with telling her more.

Why wouldn't he say it? Did he not trust her enough yet? Or—her heart sank—perhaps he didn't want to say it because he knew the admission would hurt her.

He still loves Michelle.

'I can't tell you.' He shook his head.

Her worst fears were realised. He still had feelings for his dead fiancée! That *had* to be it. It couldn't be anything else. It was the only thing she could think of that would stop him from confiding in her.

The knowledge of what he was hiding pained her like a punch in the gut. Trying to be brave, trying not to show how much the realisation hurt, she decided to be magnanimous. She would still be his friend, and she was here to help him get through his memories.

'You've made a big step forward by coming here today. You should be proud.' Her voice almost broke as she thought about how she would have to step back from him.

'The place reminds me so much of Michelle...'

As he looked about him Eva tried hard not to show how much his words hurt.

'We played here.' He gestured at the ground. 'Right in this spot. That tree over there... We climbed it. Many times. Tried to build a tree house in it. That small stream... That was where we built the rope swing. And inside the house in every room there's a reminder of her.'

Of course there is! I should never have come today. I could never compete with her memory.

'I saw the picture on the mantel. Is that her?'

He nodded.

'She was very beautiful.'

'She was.'

'What happened to you after she died?'

He let out a big sigh. 'I shut down. I couldn't face anyone. I couldn't bear their sympathy and their pity. I headed up north. Went to Scotland. Somehow managed to find a B & B that had a room and spent the New Year there. Then I just wandered around, basically, though I came back for the funeral.'

She swallowed a painful lump in her throat, realising the depth of his feelings for Michelle. She couldn't compete with this kind of love.

'That must have been difficult.'

'It was. I didn't want to see anyone. Didn't want their words of comfort. Michelle was dead because of *me*. Her mother was alone, crying, her heart in pieces, because of *me*.'

'I've told you—it wasn't your fault Michelle's car got hit.'

'Wasn't it?'

His eyes had darkened and the mood had shifted. She could tell he still had a lot of pent-up feelings about what had happened.

'No. It wasn't. Jacob…' She stood in front of him and took his gloved hands in hers. The sun was shining into her eyes and she was having to squint to see, but she could see his tortured face in front of her. 'What happened to Michelle *wasn't* your fault. You've got to let go of that thought. Stop running from it.'

'That's the problem with running. You take your problems with you. They're still in your head.'

'I know. When Seb was born I felt so much guilt. Guilt that he didn't have a father, as I hadn't had a father. Guilt that he didn't have a family around him, the way children should. And even though I did what I could to be a dad as well as a mum, I carried that guilt around with me like a millstone. It's still there. I still feel it even though you're here now. I still worry. What if you leave? What if you're not ready? I've let you in, I've let Seb get to know you and love you, and yet you could still leave. I know what it feels like to lug heavy thoughts around.'

He squeezed her fingers and lifted them to his lips, kissing her hands. 'I won't leave.'

Mesmerised by the action, wanting more than she knew he could give, she looked up into his eyes. 'You won't?'

He shook his head. 'No. I couldn't. Not now.'

'You'll stay for Seb?'

I know he's not staying for me.

He released her hands and stroked her face. 'I'll stay for you both.'

He lowered his head to hers to kiss her, checking her reaction for any sign that she might refuse him—checking that she welcomed his kiss.

Oh, she welcomed it! Wanted it. Wanted *him*! Despite her fears, despite her worries, she embraced the warmth of his soft lips as if it was the last kiss she would ever have from him.

It was bittersweet. Knowing now how he felt about Michelle, she accepted that she would have to take a step back from him. Just let he and Seb be close. There was no room in his heart for *her*, too. Not now. He was a man wrapped up in the past, tethered by his pain to a ghost.

His lips claimed hers, and as his tongue hesitantly entered her mouth and licked her own she almost groaned with wishful yearning and grief for her loss of him.

The orchard was forgotten. Netherfield Village. The house. Jacob's family was forgotten. Here beneath the weak winter sun, in Jacob's arms, was exactly where she should be. But her heart was pained. She knew she couldn't have him. This might be their final kiss. The end of their romance.

'Eva…I'm so glad I met you.'

Eva took a step back—away from his arms, away from what she wanted. Breaking contact, she managed a weak smile. 'I know. Me, too. But…I'm not sure I'm ready for this. And to tell you the truth I'm not sure that *you're* ready for this, either.'

He frowned as the sun shone down on his dark hair, and she couldn't help but notice how delicious he looked in his jeans and boots and a heavy black jacket. Still tanned and healthy from his African adventure.

She sidestepped a snail that had not yet made it into hibernation, unwilling to ruin another life as she moved farther away from Jacob.

'We both made our choices in the past, but it was easier to do so then. It was just us. Me alone. You alone. But now we have Seb, and we have to make the right decisions. The right *choices*. So we'll get it right for *him*.'

He nodded, studying her face, clearly hurt by her words. She watched him look at her, no doubt noticing the smattering of freckles that she could never quite hide with makeup, the way her mouth was curved into a false smile. He'd focused on her lips…

'We should get through Christmas and then…start making some decisions,' she said.

Jacob nodded. 'Okay. I'll ask Dr Clarkson if there's a chance to extend my contract.'

'Right. Okay.'

'And what should we tell Seb? Do we tell him we're together or…? Kids are perceptive. Do we say anything at all?'

She didn't want to tell Seb anything! Why would she risk devastating her son? She would die before she let that happen!

'I think we should keep quiet for a while. We can discuss what's happening later.'

'Later?'

'When you've worked through everything. When you're finally…free.'

He looked at her and slowly nodded. And she knew that he could see she was putting the brakes on their relationship.

Seb was out exploring the farm with Jacob and his dad, and Eva was in the farmhouse kitchen with his mother, helping her to clear up. There was an easy atmosphere between them and they worked well together—Molly wiping down the kitchen surfaces as Eva dried the dishes and put them away.

They'd had a lovely home-made soup for lunch—carrot with coriander that had been grown by the Dolans—accompanied by Molly's rustic bread rolls, filled with sun-dried tomato and onion seeds, which had taken the simple meal to another level. Now she was sated.

If I were a cat, I'd be curled up in front of the Aga.

Eva put the last of the dishes away, folded the tea towel and stood by the kitchen window. Looking out, she could see Seb and Jacob, chasing each other in the grounds, and she smiled.

Molly came to stand next to her. 'I never thought I'd see the day.'

'Me, neither.'

'Jacob…here…back on the farm. With his family. Where he's meant to be. It's going to make this Christmas really special, having him back.'

Eva glanced at the older woman and saw a sadness in her eyes she'd never noticed before. Was it sadness at not having known about Seb? Was this going to be it? The moment Jacob's parents told her how they really felt about missing out on their grandchild? Was this the point when the nice family turned on her?

'I'm so sorry, Molly.'

'What for, dear?'

'For not persevering in trying to find Jacob—or any of you—to tell you about Seb. If you're mad at me, I'll totally understand—'

Molly turned to look at her in shock. 'We're not *mad* at you! Oh, my dear, we couldn't be happier! All right, we missed out on Seb's early years and we'll never get those back, but you've given us the greatest gift in Seb, and because of him we've got our Jacob back.' She patted Eva's arm. 'Sit with me. I want to tell you something.'

They sat down together at the broad oak table.

'We never thought we'd see Jacob again after what happened—' She stopped short, clearly unsure as to whether to say anything more, glancing over to the picture on the mantel.

'I know about Michelle.'

Molly nodded gratefully. 'I didn't want to say anything unless he'd told you. Michelle was a wonderful girl. She was lovely and she and Jacob made a happy couple. She grew up next door and was always in and out of our house. She never had any siblings, and we used to think she enjoyed all the family chaos she found here. It wasn't till later we realised it was all because of her feelings for Jacob. She seemed so carefree and full of life, and we were all surprised when she became a trainee barrister—it all seemed so very serious for such a sweet girl. When they got engaged our Jacob was head over heels in love. It looked like his life was becoming sorted. A doctor…engaged to be married… The future looked great for them both. When they set a date for the wedding we were all so happy for them. Our son was going to be settled and we wouldn't have to worry about him anymore.'

It was painful to listen to, but Eva could picture it all too well. 'But then she died...'

'Then she died,' Molly repeated, nodding her head softly. 'We were all devastated—most especially her mother. I did what I could to help her through it, but Jacob just disappeared. We were *so* worried. Frantic! We didn't know where he'd gone.'

'Grief does strange things to people.'

Her eyes went dark. 'It does. I've seen it. I never thought we'd get back the Jacob that we know and love so much, but here he is, with a son of his own, and he's smiling again. We have *you* to thank for that, Eva. We can never thank you enough.'

Molly took Eva's hands in her own and held them tightly, squeezing hard.

Eva smiled back, and then gave Molly a hug. Was this what it was like to be hugged by a mum? It felt so good, and Molly was so soft and warm and welcoming. A part of her didn't want to let Molly go!

Tears painfully pricked her eyes at this feeling of being so near, yet so far. Of almost having become a part of the only family that had ever welcomed her.

The next day they all sat down to a hearty breakfast together, though Eva didn't eat much after a sleepless night. Molly stood over the cooker, making a full English breakfast, wearing a flowery apron and beaming at them all like the cat that had got the cream.

Eva could see why she was so happy. She not only had her son back within the fold of her family, but a new grandson, too.

Jacob suggested they might go for a walk into the village and have a look around before lunch.

Molly thought that was a great idea. 'We'll come, too! We could have lunch at The Three Horseshoes before you have to go home.'

They all set off, wrapped up in their winter coats, with Seb splashing through ice-covered puddles and making a nice muddy mess of his trousers.

As they got closer to the village of Netherfield, Seb began to complain that his legs were getting tired.

'Come here, champ.' Jacob lifted him up into the air and over his shoulders for a shoulder ride.

'Watch your jacket!' Eva warned, noting the muddy rivulets running down Seb's boots.

'That doesn't matter. The jacket will wash.' He held on to Seb's hands and they walked ahead of the others, Seb giggling happily, perched up high.

Molly fell into step beside Eva and threaded her arm through hers. 'Don't they make a wonderful sight, the two of them?'

She smiled. 'They do.'

'You must be so happy they're getting on well?' Molly asked.

Eva nodded, forcing a smile. 'Oh, I am! Christmas is going to be so special this year for Seb.'

'And for Jacob, too, I suspect. He deserves a happy Christmas again. Things are looking up at last for the Dolans!'

Eva said nothing. Were things looking up for *her*, too?

Jacob stood with his father at the bar of The Three Horseshoes. They'd given their group's food order and were waiting for their drinks to be served so they could take the tray to their table.

His dad patted him on the back. 'It's good to have you back, son. We've missed you.'

Jacob smiled. 'I'm sorry I went AWOL for so long, Dad. It wasn't fair on you and Mum.'

'We understood. We know you felt guilty about Michelle, but so did everyone else. You felt guilty… We felt guilty…'

'Why did *you* feel guilty?'

'Because we couldn't protect you from the pain you were in.'

Jacob could feel his eyes welling up. The burn of tears was being held back from bursting forth by sheer will. He was suddenly overwhelmed. Glad to have come home. Glad to be back with family and glad that they understood him.

Eva had been right from the beginning. About him coming back. She'd known more about family than he had.

He turned and looked at her across the pub. She sat with his mother, was smiling at something Seb was saying. But he could see that she was holding back. She had been ever since that moment in the orchard. They'd kissed and then… something had happened. She'd created distance between them and now she seemed to be…apart from them all.

It was probably for the best, even if he didn't like it. He couldn't be with Eva the way he wanted to be unless he told her the whole truth of what had happened. That was the only way he could fully give her his heart. By being honest. But if he *did* tell her… His heart sank at the thought. She would turn away from him. She would be appalled at what he'd done. She would want nothing to do with him and he couldn't risk that.

But she's already turning away from me and I don't want to lose her!

Their gazes met across the bar. Eva looked at him for a moment and then glanced away.

And he knew, in that moment, that he was already losing her.

CHAPTER SEVEN

LEAVING NETHERFIELD HAD almost made her cry. For the first time in her life she had felt welcomed by another family. Jacob's parents had managed to put right, in a single weekend, the years of hurt and pain she had felt every time she'd been sent back to the children's home. She could remember every occasion of being placed in the back of the car, solemnly refusing to turn back and wave at the family she was leaving.

But that Sunday as they'd left Jacob's parents she *had* turned round. She'd waved, she'd fought back tears, and she'd felt as if she was waving goodbye to them forever.

Being in Jacob's company was becoming more difficult. She *wanted* to be with him! Had developed feelings for him. Wanted to connect with him, physically and emotionally. But she knew she had to hold herself back until his feelings for his dead fiancée had been resolved.

If that were possible.

She'd died in such tragic circumstances…Jacob would probably always feel *something* for her.

Her yearning for him was intense. It was as if her body *craved* him when he was near. She would breathe more heavily, she would tighten her hands into fists to stop herself from reaching out to touch him, she would lick her lips in memory of his sweet kisses…

It was torture...

She felt scared. She'd never wanted a man so much! Never wanted to be with his family so much! To turn up again at Netherfield and know she'd be welcomed. That people would smile and be overjoyed at her arrival.

Eva had never had that before. And she wanted it back. Not just for her, but for Seb, too. For all this time they'd been alone, never knowing what they were missing out on, but now they could be a part of that. A part of his family.

But how much of a part? Even Molly had asked what was going on between her and Jacob.

She knew what she would *like* to be going on. But he wasn't ready. Jacob had shared things with her. Personal things. Thoughts. Emotions. The events of his past, as she had with him. But there was still the ghost of Michelle.

Did Michelle rule Jacob's heart? Would he ever let her go? Was he holding himself back from her because deep down he still loved Michelle?

Was she trying to compete with a ghost?

Because that wasn't a battle that anyone could win.

Jacob was generally happy with the way the visit to his parents' place had gone. He'd really not known how his parents would react. He'd expected his mum to go over the top, to cry a bit, maybe gush about having him back and ask him to promise never to go away again.

But she hadn't. She'd been just fine. Dad, too. They'd been thrilled to have him back, but they'd made the weekend more about Seb—about welcoming him and his mother into the family and making them feel comfortable.

He'd observed, as if from a distance. Letting it all be about them unless his mother had particularly asked his opinion on something or deliberately involved him. It had been so good to be back. He hadn't been overwhelmed by memories, as he'd expected himself to be. It had been bearable.

Because of Eva and Seb.

If it hadn't have been for them he knew he would never have managed the weekend without feeling haunted. But their being there had somehow stopped all of that.

Because of them the visit had been about the future. About how much Seb and Eva could be involved. About how much they were now a *family*.

Of course his mum had fed them all as if they'd never seen food before, and had insisted on packing them off for the journey home with freezer bags full of sausage rolls and pastries and pies.

They'd stood in the doorway and waved him off with tears in their eyes. Eva had looked tearful, too, but she hadn't wanted to talk about it.

He'd promised his parents he would call within a couple of days.

And he had.

They adored Seb, as he had known they would, but they also adored Eva, and that meant a lot to him.

Eva meant a lot to him. Finding her again had turned his life around. He'd known that first night at the party that she was something special, but to have thought that she would bring him this much happiness... He'd not expected that to happen.

He'd hoped that when he found her again she would be his friend, but other things were happening. As he got to know Seb more, and the more time he spent in their home, the more he was getting to know Eva, and he knew she was more special than he'd ever believed. Could feel it in his heart.

He so wanted to be able to tell her the truth. The *real* truth about what had happened on his wedding day and not the sanitised version that everyone else *thought* was the truth.

But how would she react? That was his biggest concern right now. If he told her before Christmas... But he so wanted to spend this precious time with them—he couldn't tell her!

She would view him with horror. Look at him differently. Judge him. And he couldn't bear the idea of not being with Seb over Christmas. It was just a week away— he could keep it inside until after the Yuletide season, couldn't he?

I should have been honest with her from the start. But how exactly do you say that to someone? That you are responsible for someone's death? It's not the kind of thing you drop into conversation with someone new.

And now that he hadn't told her the truth for so long... it would be harder to say anything at all.

He wanted to be with Eva. He wanted to be with her in a *relationship*.

But he knew that if he unburdened himself of his guilt, she might walk away...

Eva had had enough pain in her past. Did he want to cause her more?

Their days at work began to pass quickly. With Christmas-party season in full swing the doctors were rushed off their feet, dealing with what felt like a swarm of drunk and disorderlies they had to keep an eye on, as well as dealing with all the usual illnesses and injuries.

There was a slew of norovirus lockdowns on various wards, so they had to limit who they admitted into hospital and where they sent them, causing the corridors to be filled with patients on trollies, moaning and groaning to their paramedics that they hadn't been seen yet.

It was a heady mix of patients filled with Christmas cheer and patients who were grumpy and angry. Everyone's temper was getting shorter and shorter.

In the evenings Jacob would come round to Eva's to read to Seb, and Eva would cook them all a meal that they would eat together. It all appeared quite domesticated and happy, but there was a palpable tension that they could both feel, and both of them refused to mention it in their fear of ruining Christmas.

At work, it was getting harder and harder for Eva to be normal around him. Their relationship—whatever it was—was confusing. Jacob was being polite, keeping his distance, and she was feeling hurt by it. She sneaked looks at him when she thought he wasn't watching, and yearned for his touch.

But she knew they had to be absolute professionals, who showed no familiarity, no favouritism, who showed no attraction to each other, and this just further reinforced to Eva the wisdom of his pushing her away.

She knew it was for the best.

But that didn't make it any easier when all she truly wanted was to be in his arms.

One night they were both tidying up in the kitchen after their meal.

Eva was loading the dishwasher and Jacob was passing her the dishes after scraping them clean over the bin. Their fingers kept touching as they passed and accepted plates and other items, and tiny frissons would ripple up her arms each time. She tried to ignore them. Tried to tell herself that she *could not* have this man. Not right now. Not whilst his feelings were so confused.

Politely, she thanked him for each item, and then, when it seemed she was saying 'thank you' too much, she just looked at him and smiled a thank-you. But then he'd smile back, and then those smiles and glances became longer and longer, until they were just standing over the open dishwasher, both holding the same plate and just looking at each other.

The way Jacob was looking at her—as if he was hungry for her, as if he wouldn't be able to breathe unless he kissed her—made her feel all giddy inside. How long had it been since that kiss in the orchard? Not long at all. And yet it felt as if decades had passed.

Her lips parted and she looked at him, desperate to tell him how she felt about him.

Suddenly Jacob stepped around the open dishwasher and kicked the door closed with his foot. He grabbed her and pulled her into his arms.

Eva was backed against one of the kitchen units, could feel the edge of the work surface digging into her bottom as Jacob's body pressed up against hers. She could feel *him*. Every wonderful inch of him. He cupped her face in his hands and tilted her lips up to his. Kissing her, devouring her face with the force of his passion.

Oh, yes!

Kissing him felt so good! As if they were meant to be! His soft lips, his stubble gave her a sweet, yet burning sensation that flowed from her lips down through her body and ignited a fire deep within her that made her crave more of him. More than just a kiss. More than just lips touching.

She wanted everything about him. His hands, his mouth, his *body*. She wanted all of him. To be with him the way they had been when they'd conceived Seb. Naked and entwined. Unable to get enough of each other.

As their kiss deepened her hands found their way under his shirt, feeling the burning heat in his skin, the powerful muscles contained within him moving smoothly as he kissed her.

I want you!

She wanted to say it. She wanted to take that step and just *tell* him. That she was here. In his present. A real woman who loved him. Yes, *loved* him—if only he would give her the chance.

Remember he's in love with someone else.

Eva pushed him away and was left gasping from the force of his passion.

He looked confused. Hurt. But then his glazed eyes finally got some sense back in them and he stepped away, out of the kitchen.

She heard the front door open and close with such finality that she couldn't stop the tears. She cried. Cried for the fact that she would never have him the way she wanted to. That until he got over Michelle he would never be hers.

I should have kept him at arm's length. It's too painful.

'He's in cardiac arrest!'

Jacob's patient lay prone on the bed, his eyes closed, his mouth agape. Greg Harper had been brought in by his wife, Ginny. He'd been feeling unwell all day, and after an hour of trying to work the ground in his frost-hardened allotment had come in complaining of being short of breath. Ginny had said that he'd looked extremely pale and had felt clammy. She'd called for an ambulance as her senses had told her it was something serious.

It had been a good decision. Because now Greg was in a hospital setting as his cardiac arrest occurred, and therefore theoretically stood a much higher chance of survival.

Jacob lowered the head of the bed and called for the crash team. This was his first case of leading a resuscitation since he'd joined the department a few weeks ago.

Eva came running over, along with two other doctors and nurses.

'Compressions!' Jacob requested, his voice stern and clear.

Eva stepped forward to do them, clasping one hand above the other and placing them centrally to Greg's chest. She began to compress his chest, maintaining a steady rhythm, as Jacob called out further orders to the rest of the team.

'I want pads on, and venous access. Sarah—you take the airway and get an oropharyngeal airway in.'

Jacob took a step back and oversaw it all. He stood in front of Ginny, who had hidden behind him, not daring to look.

The defibrillator pads were soon attached to Greg's chest and Eva stopped compressions momentarily for the machine to assess Greg's heart rhythm—if any.

'He's in VF. Shocking.'

The doctor in charge of the machine checked to make sure no one was touching the patient and then pressed the button with the little lightning rod on it. Greg's body juddered slightly.

'He's still in VF.' Sarah looked up at him.

Jacob stood firm. 'Continue CPR. Adrenaline.'

The drug was administered into a vein and Eva continued pumping the chest. Her red hair swung back and forth with the force of her compressions and her breathing was becoming heavier. Compressions could be exhausting—especially if resuscitation took a long time—so they liked to rotate staff every two minutes.

'Please don't let him die! Please save him!' pleaded his wife, Ginny.

'Pulse check, please.'

A nurse checked the radial pulse. 'Weak.'

'Continue.'

Jacob's voice rang loud and clear in the department. Cardiac arrests were dramatic, especially to an onlooker, like a family member or friend, but to a doctor they were some of the easiest cases to deal with in A&E, because there was a recognised pattern of treatment. You knew exactly what you had to do and when you had to do it.

Not every case in the department was so clear-cut. People came in with mystery ailments all the time, or didn't tell the doctors all their symptoms, or lied. Cardiac arrests were obvious and they knew how to deal with them.

'Assess rhythm.'

A further shock was given, then oxygen pumped in via a bag valve and mask.

Jacob glanced at the clock. 'Amiodarone. Three hundred milligrams.'

Greg groaned and his wife gasped, peering round Jacob to see if her husband was showing any signs of waking up.

'Pulse check?'

The nurse felt the patient's wrist. 'I have a strong pulse.'

Sarah, managing the airway and monitoring the machines, confirmed that the patient was making respiratory effort and that blood pressure was slowly rising.

'Well done, team. Once Mr Harper is stable I want him transferred to ITU. Until then I want him on fifteen-minute obs.' Jacob turned to Ginny. 'We've got him back, but we need to make sure we keep him with us. He's in for a difficult twenty-four hours.'

Ginny nodded. 'Yes. Can I speak to him?'

He nodded. 'Of course.'

'Thank you, Doctor! If I'd lost him…'

'You didn't.'

She looked shocked at his abrupt tone, then said firmly, 'He's my *life*.'

The look in her eyes softened his mood and Jacob understood. He laid a hand on her arm apologetically. 'I know. Talk to him. Sit with him. When he gets a bed in ITU I'll come and let you know.'

Ginny smiled her thanks.

He turned at the doorway and looked at her, sitting beside her husband's bed. They were lucky. They'd had each other for years, it seemed. The love. The comfort. Why could *he* not have that? Didn't he deserve it?

What he felt for Eva... He'd allowed his physical desires to overwhelm him the other night. He hadn't been able to help it. She was just so beautiful, and the way they were both holding back had been killing him.

I need to tell her the truth.

No one knew the real truth. Except him and Michelle.

Could he wait until after Christmas? He wanted to. Knew it was probably the best thing. But it was so hard! He loved her and he couldn't have her. Not until she knew the truth—only then could they be together.

If she isn't scared away.

And Eva didn't come alone. She came as a package. With Seb.

He couldn't hurt that boy.

That boy was his life now. If she took him away from him... No. No, she wouldn't do that to him.

Then, what have I got to lose?

Those first nights under the vast African sky he'd thought about Michelle and the way he'd treated her. What he'd done to drive her into the arms of another. He hadn't been able to bear to admit the truth. And his thoughts had always come back to Eva. The woman who had briefly brought him back to life. Thoughts of her had pervaded his mind, but he'd tried to dismiss them as the thoughts of a mixed up, grieving man.

Those nights alone in Africa had made Jacob re-evaluate his life. Think about what he wanted. Not only what he could do for others, but what he needed to do for himself. And all he'd been able to think about was his own family, back on the farm, and the woman with red hair...

Eva.

She'd done a great job with Seb. And all alone, too. She was a strong woman. He had to believe that her internal strength would help get them all through this.

He needed her.

Knew it as he knew the sun would rise in the east.

He burned for her. Couldn't think straight around her anymore.

I should just be honest with her. Get it over with. Then we can move forward. Together.

Jacob spotted Eva across the department. As always, she looked gorgeous. Her curtain of red hair fell in a perfect wave and her crystal-blue eyes looked up at him in question as he walked across to her. She'd made a small nod to the season and was wearing tiny dangling Christmas trees in her ears. They might have looked ridiculous on anyone else, but not her.

He stood in front of her. 'Hi.'

'Hello.'

His fingers itched to touch her. To hold her. Since that kiss in the kitchen it had been killing him to keep himself from touching her. From being with her. How he'd managed to walk away from the house the other night he'd never know.

Her reaction to that last kiss the other night hadn't lied. She'd wanted it, and had responded to it in a way that he'd liked. As his lips had trailed over the delicate skin at her neck he'd inhaled her scent and had almost drifted away on a cloud of ecstasy. She'd smelled so good and she'd felt so right and he'd wanted her again.

He could see no reason to keep punishing himself by staying away. Didn't they both deserve more?

'Eva? May I have a word with you?' His voice was thick and gravelly, as if he was finding it difficult to talk.

'What's up?'

'In private.' He made eye contact and enforced it, staring hard at her, making sure she understood him.

But she seemed nervous. 'Talk to me here.'

She stood up and put her hands into the pockets of the long cardigan she wore.

'Well?'

She was looking up at him, and he so wanted to cup her face and bring those sensuous lips to his own, but he controlled himself and took a step back. 'I need to speak with you.'

'You are.'

'Privately. I thought tonight, when I come round, I could cook *you* dinner for a change.'

'Oh. Okay. That would be nice.'

'I need to tell you *everything*.'

She swallowed. 'Everything?'

He nodded. 'You need to hear it all.'

Eva watched him walk away from her.

He was going to tell her tonight. Tell her that he could not give her his heart. Not until he was over his grieving. He would tell her that he would still like to be there for Seb, but that whatever had been happening between the two of them had to be over.

She bit her lip as she felt tears threaten, but then pushed away her grief.

She wouldn't cry over him anymore.

She would get through tonight and she would be strong. For Seb.

This didn't have to ruin his Christmas. It was only a couple of days away.

Eva set her mind on being strong. On keeping a safe distance. On remaining upbeat.

At least she tried.

Eva came home from her long day at work to gentle piano music on the stereo system, fairy lights and candles lit throughout and the most delicious smells emanating from her kitchen.

She hung up her bag and her jacket and kicked off her shoes, padded barefoot into the lounge. There was no one there so she headed into the kitchen, where Jacob stood stirring something on the hob.

'Where's Seb?'

'With Letty. And she said he could sleep over, too.'

Eva raised an eyebrow. Really? He'd sent Seb on a sleepover? Just how upset did Jacob expect her to be?

He passed her a glass of white wine. Whatever he was cooking smelled mouth-wateringly good. Like Jacob himself.

Stop it!

But it was true. Jacob had a wonderful scent, and when she was up close to him and he held her in his arms…

Eva shook her head to clear it. She needed to think straight. But the idea that there was wine, good food and Jacob… It was all muddying the waters!

Only a few weeks ago life had seemed simple. It had been her and Seb against the world. Then Jacob had come back. And since he'd found out he was a father he'd practically moved in and turned her world upside down! She wasn't even sure she was the same person anymore. She knew she'd changed.

Jacob looked particularly delightful this evening. He wore dark trousers and a crisp white shirt, and his tousled dark hair just crept over the edge of the collar. He had broad, powerful shoulders and a neat waist, and she could only try to remember the powerful, muscular legs beneath the cloth…

He was a sight for sore, tired eyes.

And she wanted him.

The knowledge that he also wanted her, that he'd got himself hot because of her, had barely contained himself because of her, was an aphrodisiac she tried to ignore!

'What's cooking?'

Jacob turned, and the beam of his smile lighting up his face brightened her heart. He was trying to put things right. He was trying to give her a good night before he ruined it with whatever news he thought he still had to share.

'An African specialty. Yam and crayfish risotto, inspired by my time in Gabon, followed by a *malva* pudding.'

'What's a *malva* pudding?'

He smiled. 'It's very rich, very buttery, and filled to the brim with syrup. You'll love it.'

She nodded. Sounded good. 'Wow. You really did learn a lot in Africa. When did you go to Gabon?'

'In between my times at the clinic.'

'And what did you discover?'

Her mouth dried as Jacob took a few steps towards her. He was literally millimetres away from her, towering above her and staring down into her eyes as if he'd just discovered the most beautiful jewel in existence and was hypnotised by it.

'I discovered that I'd left behind the one person who could've changed my life.'

Her. He meant *her*.

And, boy, was that electrifying stuff! She felt so alive with him standing right there, looking down at her, devouring her with his gaze. She felt as if she was waiting for him to inch those last few millimetres closer, so that her body could lock into his, like a key in a padlock.

Were they made for each other? She felt that it might be that way. Physically anyway. But what about the other stuff? The boring stuff that grown-ups had to think about. Like trust and reliability and dependability. And love.

Did Jacob love her? She knew he loved Seb. He was definitely there for his son, and it seemed he spent every spare moment he had at her house. But what of his feelings for *her*? There was a definite attraction between them, but was he still in love with his dead fiancée?

'Jacob, I don't know what I am to you.'

He tilted his head, as if questioning her. 'You're very important to me.'

'Important? Is that all?'

Jacob looked shocked and upset. 'You're Seb's mum. You're the woman I can't stop thinking about. You chase every other thought out of my head and, believe me, that's difficult to do.'

She put her wine glass down and turned to face him. '*Every* other thought?'

He smiled. 'Most of them.'

'It's the ones you don't tell me about that worry me.'

'I *will* tell you. But I'd like us to enjoy our evening first. Let's allow ourselves that. Forget the difficulties for a moment. Just enjoy being with each other for now.'

She could do that. She didn't like postponing the pain that she knew was coming, but she wanted to enjoy him whilst she could. If pain was coming, then so be it, but there was no reason why she couldn't just let go and enjoy being with the man she loved for a few moments more.

She smiled. 'So what do we do now?'

Jacob smiled back at her. 'Eat dinner. Start afresh. Can you do that with me?'

Maybe. It was scary still.

But perhaps I'm tired of being alone?

She stood up and grabbed her wine glass. 'Let's eat dinner.'

Jacob nodded, smiling.

The crayfish and yam risotto was divine! The yam was sweet and soft and the crayfish was succulent and melted in her mouth.

Eva glanced at Jacob. 'This is lovely, by the way. You might not have noticed from the way I've gobbled it all up like a hippo.'

Jacob picked his fork up and grinned. 'I had noticed, and I didn't for one minute compare you to a hippo. And thank you. It's a compliment.'

She took another mouthful, and when she'd swallowed it she looked at him across the table. 'Tell me more about Africa. Your work there.'

He met her gaze and nodded slightly, his face thoughtful. 'Well, you know about Reuben. But there were so many people out there who all changed my life in a small way.'

'I'd like to hear about it.'

'Cataract surgery was the first thing I did. There just seemed to be a never-ending line of people with the need for eye surgery. Not just old people, but kids, too. Seeing a child regain his eyesight was amazing, each and every time.'

'I can imagine.'

'There was this one kid who saw his mum for the first time when he was eight years old. The look of happiness on his face afterwards…' Jacob had a faraway look in his eyes and simply smiled.

Eva could only imagine how he must have felt. 'You said you helped build a school?'

'That was much later—but, yes. Again, there were just so many kids who'd never even seen inside a classroom and we could quickly build one in about a week. To see them all go in and meet their teacher, start writing on blackboards… It made me appreciate all that I'd had in my life. All that I'd taken for granted.'

'Sometimes we need reminding.'

'With each patient I met, each story I heard, it just made me realise that I was getting ready to come home. To find *my* happiness again. To believe that I could have it.'

Eva nodded.

'The African people are so noble. And proud. But in a good way. They're honest and heartfelt…and even though most of them hardly have any material things they're intensely happy if they have family.'

'Did you feel alone out there?'

'To begin with. But I ignored it. I've always been headstrong, but being in Africa taught me that sometimes you need to pause and reflect. Think things through.'

'Before you came back?'

He nodded, intense blue eyes staring back at her from across the table.

'And what do you want from life now?' Her breath hitched in her throat as she half hoped he'd say her, but she was half afraid he'd say something else.

'You. And Seb. I came back intent on finding you and I did. I'm going to be really honest now and say it—and hope

I don't sound like some kind of mad stalker. It was no accident that I walked into your A&E. I knew you were there.'

She gasped. Shocked. He'd *known*? Then that meant he'd known exactly where he would find her when he came back! He'd pretended it was a surprise to walk in and find her!

'But you had no idea about what happened after you left. About Seb.'

'No. And once I was over the shock it was a wonderful surprise. Regret, yes, for the lost years…' Eva's eyes were downcast, so he reached out and grasped her hand with his own. 'But joy at having more family. An amazing son with the woman that I…'

She looked up. 'Yes?'

What would he say? That he loved her? She almost couldn't breathe, waiting for him to say it.

He stared at her intently. 'That I have feelings for.'

Eva exhaled. Slowly.

'Feelings? What kind of feelings?' She licked her lips, watching as his eyes tracked the movement, then moved back up to look into her eyes.

'Strong feelings. I want us to try to be together. Properly.' He stood up from his side of the table and came round to hers.

She watched him move, aware that her heart was pounding and her breathing was getting heavier, her mouth drying in anticipation. 'Jacob—'

He took her hand in his and bade her rise from her seat. 'Would you come with me?'

'Where?' she croaked, her voice almost not working at all.

'Upstairs.'

Upstairs. To bed. Sex. That was what he meant.

She wanted to. Physically, her body wanted that very much, as did her heart, but her head was telling her to think twice. Tomorrow was Christmas Eve. The anniversary of his wife-to-be's death. The anniversary of the night they'd slept together for the first time. Did she want to sleep with him knowing that he didn't feel for her the way she felt about him?

She shook her head. 'I can't be anyone's second best, Jacob.'

He stroked her face. 'You could never be second best for me.'

Jacob gazed down at her, his eyes glazed with a sexual hunger that she wanted to satisfy. Feelings be damned! Why *shouldn't* she have him? The last time she'd slept with him had been all those years ago, and though the memories of that night were awe-inspiring, she wanted to be with him one last time—no matter what happened afterwards.

Jacob scooped her up into his arms and carried her easily up the stairs and into her bedroom, closing the door softly behind them.

Eva, laughing, allowed Jacob to set her down on the edge of the bed. She looked at him, watching as he stood before her, undoing the buttons of his shirt from top to bottom.

It was mesmerising.

He pulled his shirt from his trousers, and as soon as she saw the smattering of dark hair that dipped beneath his belt buckle she quickly stood up, unable to stay away from him a moment longer, and helped him off with his clothes.

To have him before her, totally naked, as she slowly slipped off her own clothes, was magical. The memory she had of him, of a younger, less muscular Jacob, was stunning enough, but to see him now—more heavily set, broader, stronger—was a powerful aphrodisiac.

And he wanted *her*.

Eva slowly reached out to touch him. Her doubts silenced.

* * *

Eva blinked and opened her eyes. Frosty sunlight was streaming in through the open curtains at her bedroom window and her body felt deliciously exhausted.

Christmas Eve!

What time was it?

She felt as if something had woken her, but she couldn't think what. Had there been a sound? Her alarm clock?

Blinking, she turned and glanced at it. Ten minutes past seven. Still early. Yawning, she turned back to look at Jacob, asleep in the bed beside her. His dark hair was all tousled and wavy. From sleep? Or from her fingers? It could easily be both. There'd been moments last night when she'd held his head in her hands as his tongue had worked its magic and she'd grabbed hold of him, her fingers splaying in his hair as he'd brought her to ecstasy.

What a night!

His face looked so relaxed this morning, and he had a five-o'clock shadow darkening his jaw. She'd felt that stubble last night and it had been delicious, tickling her skin and her tender places. Her inner thighs felt roughened and sore. But in a good way.

He was lying on his stomach, his head resting on his hands, and he looked so peaceful, his suntanned skin set healthily against the white of her sheets. His muscled arms and powerful shoulders a delightful addition to her bedroom. And farther beneath the sheets... *Oh, my!*

Last night had been even better than the night she'd spent with him four years ago. She wanted to reach out and touch him just once more, to prove that this was real. As she did so, and her fingers touched his jawline, his eyes opened and he smiled slowly.

'Morning.'

'Good morning.'

He was blinking at the half-light coming through the bedroom curtains. 'The night got away from us.'

'It did.' Swinging her legs out of bed, she grabbed her robe.

'Where are you going?'

'To make some tea. Want one?'

He pulled himself into an upright position, the sheets just barely covering his modesty. 'Sounds great.'

Smiling, she headed downstairs and into her kitchen. The remains of their meal last night were still there, and she smiled at the memory of the food and what had come after...

Then her thoughts darkened. They hadn't talked. They hadn't discussed what they'd meant to. Should she raise it now? Was this a good time to remind him of her doubts?

Look at what had happened last night! It had been amazing! Skin tingling, electrifying. The passion that had been between them...

That's how it could be between us if we let it. If we refuse to face what we don't want to face.

She wasn't sure if they could do that. Surely the lies they were telling themselves would soon creep to the surface and ruin what they had?

No. They *had* to talk. It was the only way.

She couldn't quite believe it. Everything was going right in her world. She'd gained the family she'd always dreamed of. They could be a unit. They were both striving for the same goals. They were both there for Seb.

They were there for each other.

Mostly.

She laid her hand on her heart as she looked out of the kitchen window, waiting for the kettle to boil. She could feel it beating. *Dum-dum. Dum-dum.* It didn't have to beat alone anymore. She'd lain her head on Jacob's chest last night as they'd fallen asleep together and it had beat with the same rhythm. *Dum-dum. Dum-dum.*

She was no longer alone!

Eva wasn't sure what she'd done to deserve so much happiness. Perhaps after all her years of suffering as a child, of being alone, being the outsider, this was her reward now? This sense of belonging that she felt being with both Seb *and* Jacob?

Whatever it was, it was amazing.

She made the tea, and some toast, and prepared a tray to take upstairs. For the first time in her life she would have breakfast in bed, and then *she* would be the one to cause her life to come crashing down around her ears.

She'd let him have a shower. Then she'd had one and now they were both dressed.

As he pushed his belt into its buckle, he looked at her. 'What's wrong?'

She looked up at him from her seat on the bed, nerves racing through her body, causing her heart to pound like a jackhammer as the possibility of abandonment crept ever nearer.

'We never did talk last night.'

His eyes darkened. 'No, we didn't.'

'I think we ought to.'

Jacob stared at her. 'But last night... We...we were so good together! I'm not sure I want to taint that with what I have to say.'

Eva wrapped her cardigan tightly around herself. Neither was she. But she couldn't move forward in a relationship with him if she was lying to herself and allowing him to lie to her.

'Nor do I. But I think we both need to be truthful. For Seb as much as for ourselves.'

He sighed and settled down on the bed across from her. 'You're right.'

She sucked in a breath. Okay. She was ready.

'Tell me.'

He nodded, thinking, his eyes downcast. Then he looked up at her.

'On my wedding day something happened that...that no one knows about.'

Okay. That wasn't the direction she'd thought this would start, but she'd go with it.

'What?'

'Michelle made it to the church. She didn't die on her way to the service like I told everyone. She made it there.'

Eva was confused. 'She *made* it?'

'Remember I told you that I was outside, waiting for the first glimpse of the wedding car? I'd been too fidgety inside, so I was walking around to rid myself of the nerves. Then suddenly she pulled up in her car.'

'You *saw* her?'

He nodded. 'She wanted to speak to me before the service. She told me that she'd cheated on me. With my best friend Marcus. She said that I hadn't loved her the way I ought to and so she'd looked elsewhere.'

Eva hadn't expected this! 'She *cheated* on you?'

'She said she still loved me, that she wanted to go on with the wedding but wanted to enter our marriage honestly.'

He paused for a moment, then stood and began to pace the room.

'I was furious! Furious that she'd cheated on me, but furious with myself, too—because I'd *known* something wasn't right and I'd ignored it. I knew there was no way I could marry her still. We argued. I said some things...*horrible* things. I don't know what came over me, but I ripped into her verbally. I couldn't bear to look at her. The more I looked at her, the more I hated her. I ordered her to go away. Told her I never wanted to see her again for as long as I lived. She was crying, mascara all over the place, begging for my forgiveness, but I told her to—'

'What?'

'Something *horrible*. She ran from me. Ran back to her car and screeched off. I knew she was driving recklessly, but I was so angry I didn't care!'

Eva covered her mouth with her hand. They'd argued and then she'd died? No wonder he felt awful!

'Jacob…'

'I stood outside the church for ages. Trying to think of how I was going to go inside and face everyone. Tell them the wedding was off.'

'So what happened then?'

'The police arrived.'

She knew what was coming.

'They said that Michelle had died. That she'd been in a car crash, had been thrown from the vehicle. Everyone assumed that she'd died on her way to the church. They were all crying and weeping and dabbing at their eyes with tissues and I just couldn't bear it! It was all so false! None of them knew the truth and all of them wanted to pity me. Wanted to see me collapse in a heap of tears.'

'You must have been in shock.'

'I didn't know *what* to feel. I'd been furious with her and sent her away and she'd got killed. *My* fault. If I hadn't sent her away… If I'd given us a chance…'

Eva couldn't believe it! She could see now how difficult that must have been. For him to have known the truth— that Michelle had cheated—and yet for absolutely everyone else to think they'd been so in love. As she had. But if this was what he'd been hiding, then perhaps he *wasn't* still in love with Michelle!

'*This* is what you've been keeping from me?'

He stood in front of her. 'I'll understand if you don't want anything to do with me,' he said.

She stared at his face. At the pain in his eyes. Seeing the way he was so bowed down by the guilt he'd been carrying all these years.

She was about to say something when there was a furious banging on her front door.

'Eva! *Eva?* It's Letty! Hurry—it's Seb!'

Letty…? Seb…?

She flew down the stairs, Jacob following close behind, watching helplessly as she fumbled over her keys to unlock the front door. Then she flung the door wide.

Letty stood there, with Seb draped in her arms, pale and unconscious.

'Oh, my God!'

'I can't wake him!'

Eva stared at her almost lifeless son and felt her legs give way.

'*Seb?*' She shook his shoulders gently, then with more force. When he didn't respond she pinched his earlobe. Nothing. She placed her ear over his mouth.

He was still breathing!

The doctor inside her started to analyse, and her gut filled with a nasty sensation as she just knew that something bad had happened.

'Call an ambulance.' She turned to Jacob, but he was already on his mobile.

This was wrong. So very badly wrong.

She kept trying to rouse her son as Jacob spoke on the phone to ambulance control.

'He won't wake up. Not responding to voice commands. Not responding to pain. He's unconscious.'

Eva looked up at him. 'Wouldn't it be quicker to drive him in ourselves?'

'In rush hour? No. Let's wait for the ambulance.'

It was agonising just to sit and wait. To know what they knew and think of all the horrible things it might be. Meningitis? Encephalitis? An infection? Something caused by the earlier accident?

It took an age, it seemed, before the ambulance arrived outside her house.

The paramedics, at least, were familiar to her. Friendly faces. People she trusted. Letty quickly relayed how she'd found him that morning and told them that he'd seemed okay the night before, except for saying he had a headache.

'What?' Eva frowned. 'He had a headache? Why didn't you tell me?'

Letty looked upset. 'I'm so sorry. I didn't think it was that bad.'

The headache could be vital. Different diagnoses flashed through her mind…all the things it could be. But her brain kept telling her just one thing.

Meningitis.

She knew it in her heart, but didn't want to admit it. Not Seb. Not her boy. *No.* It was Christmas. This couldn't be happening at *Christmas.* It was wrong. He shouldn't be like this. He should be getting excited about presents under the tree and Christmas carolling, or looking out for snow…

The paramedics quickly gave him oxygen and bundled him into the ambulance in double-quick time. They allowed Eva in, but held their hands up at Jacob.

'Sorry—only room for one. Can you get to the hospital under your own steam?' And they set off with lights and siren going.

Eva sat in the back with her son, reeling as they went around corners and bollards and through traffic lights, knowing that Jacob would be trying to travel separately behind them in his own car. But he wouldn't be allowed to speed, or to go on the wrong side of the road, and would be delayed in getting to the hospital by traffic lights that they could just speed through.

Briefly she thought about what he'd just told her. About his wedding day. About what had really happened with Michelle. But she pushed it away. That didn't matter now! She needed to focus on Seb.

They got to the hospital fast, and yet it also seemed to take an age. Seb still wasn't responding, but the ECG leads told them he had a good heart rate. That was good. *Something* had to be good in all this.

She was feeling incredibly sick. And guilty. Her son had been dreadfully ill next door, deteriorating, and she'd not known because she'd been sleeping with Jacob!

Eva exhaled heavily and stared at her son. Willing him to read her mind.

Stay strong. I need you, Seb. I need you.

Jacob gripped the steering wheel tightly as the ambulance sped away from him, its lights turning the street blue, then black, in an ever-flickering wail of pain that seared straight to his gut.

What was wrong with Seb? He was no paediatrician— the headache could be anything. But it was the only clue to this whole mess.

Everyone had headaches at some point in their lives— it didn't necessarily mean anything. What did it mean for Seb? He was pale, unconscious. There were a variety of things it could be. An infection...something wrong with his brain. A blood disorder. It could be anything. Something to do with the bang on the head he'd received during that accident on the day he'd found out about his son.

He was a doctor, and all those possibilities were popping into his brain and then out again as he dismissed the thought that it could be any of those things.

He couldn't lose Seb. Not now. He'd only just got to know him. He'd only just begun to appreciate what it was like to have such a wonderful son. To lose him now would be life's cruel trick...

Christmas Eve! It's Christmas Eve again! I'm not going to lose him!

He'd only just found his son... What man wouldn't be thrilled to find out that he had a handsome, strapping young boy? And he was so clever, too—and popular at nursery. Everyone wanted to be Seb's friend. Everyone wanted to sit next to him. He was a good kid. Diligent. They didn't want to know him because he was the class clown. He was a good friend. A nice boy.

The best.

Only now he was lying in the back of an ambulance, speeding to A&E. How had that happened? How had two doctors—two *accident and emergency* doctors—not noticed that their child was ill? Sickening for something?

Had there been earlier signs? Had they missed them? Jacob cursed.

His stomach roiled with nausea and he rubbed at his forehead as a sharp pain shot across his brow.

The ambulance was way ahead of him now. There was no chance he could keep up. Not safely anyway. He wasn't trained to drive like that, and if he wanted to get to the hospital in one piece himself he knew he had to be patient. Had to be careful.

The traffic lights ahead of him turned red and he cursed them out loud in Afrikaans.

The lights took an age. Or so it seemed. It was probably only twenty seconds or so that he waited, but for Jacob, watching the ambulance disappear in front of him, it was tantamount to torture. His heart was in that ambulance. If he knew anything right now it was that.

His whole life was in that ambulance. Seb. Eva. His future.

What would happen if he lost either one of them? He shook his head, refusing to go down that avenue. It would drive him mad with insanity. He couldn't tolerate the thought—it was just too painful. He felt his heart almost shudder at the thought and bile ran up into his throat.

No. Not that. No. I forbid it.

He couldn't lose them. Not now. He'd only just found them. He'd only just expanded his world to allow them in. And now that he had, his life shone bright. Like a brand-new star in the night sky. He couldn't imagine the future without either one of them.

He'd come back to find Eva. To set things right again. Surely it wasn't all about to go wrong a second time?

The lights turned green and he gunned the engine, shooting forward. He had to remind himself to be careful. He overtook a slow driver and glared at the young man behind the wheel of the car as he passed. Did he not *know* he had to be somewhere? That his son could be *dying*? *Get out of the way!*

Just a mile or two from the hospital now. Not long and he could be back by Seb's side. Standing with Eva to be there for their son. Together. As they always should have been from the start.

He would not be leaving her to fight this fight on her own.

He briefly thought about calling his parents. Then

everyone who loved and cared for Seb could be there at his bedside to support him.

We'll get you through this, Seb. We need you to get through it. I need you to.

There was the exit he needed for the hospital.

Jacob looked out through the windscreen at the bleak landscape. It was all greys and dark browns. The ground was hard and frosted, the trees lifeless and still. He could just see cars and exhaust fumes and frustrated drivers, impatient people hurrying everywhere, trying to get home to their families. To their warm hearths and jolly Christmas jumpers and repeats on the television.

He was frozen in time.

He paused for a moment, pulling over onto the hard shoulder briefly, whilst he fought against nausea and the fear.

He hesitated, took a breath, then pulled back out into the traffic.

CHAPTER EIGHT

THIS WAS SO ALIEN. So strange. To be the one standing back and watching other doctors fuss around her son.

Her son.

This was no random stranger, brought in from the streets. This was no drink-addled unknown blaring out 'Silent Night', or a faltering pensioner with a dodgy ticker. This was *her child*. Her *son*. Her reason for living.

And they were sticking him with needles. Each piercing of his skin pierced her heart, causing her to flinch. She watched him bleed as they searched for venous access and felt her heart breaking into a thousand tiny pieces.

An intravenous drip—a bag of clear fluid—hung by his bedside… Always so innocuous before, but now seeming so threatening. He clearly needed fluids.

How long since he'd last drunk anything? She didn't *know*. She hadn't been with him. She'd been with Jacob!

Machines beeped. Doctors fussed. Vacutainers popped. Voices called out.

'Stat.'

'Do it now!'

She glanced at the readouts on the machines. His pulse was high, his pressure low.

They kept pushing her back. Politely. She was getting

in their way, she knew it, but she *had* to see him. *Had* to keep contact with him. Hold his hand. See his face.

As he lay there she thought back through his whole life. Her pregnancy… Waddling her way through work at the hospital. Those blissful few weeks of maternity leave when she'd been able to put her feet up and rest…

Only she hadn't rested, had she? She'd shopped for baby clothes, for nappies, for equipment—a pushchair, a cot. She'd got the nursery ready, decorating a room for the first time and tipping paint all over her shoes. Then there had been all that palaver with getting the mural on the wall. By the time she'd finished it she'd hated all the characters, only loving them again when she'd taken a step back to marvel at the finished room.

She'd wanted the world perfect for her son. Fatherless, she'd wanted him to have everything else.

The day he was born… Hours and hours of labour, during which she'd been determined to give birth naturally, in her longed-for water birth. The pain had been intense. She'd almost caved and asked for pain relief. She'd always thought she was a tough cookie. But then Seb had been laid in her arms… His chubby arms and legs, his scrunched up fingers and toes and his button nose. His shock of dark hair… He'd looked so much like Jacob she'd almost dropped him.

Almost.

But she'd never let him go. How could she? He'd been perfect. Gazing up at her with eyes so blue she'd thought that the whole world's supply of the colour had gone into his eyes and she would never see a blue thing ever again. Kingfishers would be dull. Bluebells would be just…bells. So blue his eyes had been…

Then there'd been the first time he'd said *mama*. He'd been on the verge of saying it for a long time. Sound-

ing out the *m* for ages, saliva dribbling down his chin as
he chomped his lips together over and over, and then…
'Mama.' Heavenly. Perfect. She'd scooped him up and
smiled at him so broadly, and he'd smiled back, giggling,
and she'd known then, as she knew now, that the perfect
little boy she held in her arms would hold all the power
over her heart for the rest of her life.

His first attempt at walking—toddling on his chubby
legs. Each new day in his short life had given him more
and more independence, taking him further and further
away from her as he learned what he could do for himself.
And still her love for him had grown and grown…

Only he looked lifeless now.

Sleeping, but worse. Pale and unresponsive. Not how
he'd ever been and not how a three-year-old should be.

He should be awake, getting excited about Christmas
Day tomorrow, sitting in front of the television set or playing outside. Doing a final bit of Christmas shopping with
her, perhaps. Helping her make biscuits. Licking out the
bowl when she made the icing…

Not here.

Not in a hospital bed with needles and cannulas and IV
drips and heart monitors and ventilators and all manner of
other things going on.

I can't do this. I can't see him like this.

'He needs a CT.'

She glanced at the doctor and felt alone. *So alone!*
Where was Jacob? She *needed* him. Needed him more than
she'd ever needed anyone. She shouldn't have to face this
alone. Whatever was happening to her son. Whatever the
CT might reveal. This wasn't the sort of thing she should
do by herself. Hadn't she put herself through hell so she
could rely on him? Hadn't she let him in so she could share
this responsibility with someone else?

She'd always thought herself strong. Independent. Looking out for herself and Seb in the best way she knew how. And she'd done well at that. But this…? This was something else. This was a torment and a cruelty that she couldn't face alone.

I need you, Jacob!

Eva couldn't tear her eyes away. She needed to see what they were doing to her son. What they *weren't* doing.

They were good doctors. The best. She *knew* these people. It wasn't as if she'd put him into the hands of strangers.

She knew what they suspected.

Words wouldn't soothe. Reassurances didn't matter. Not until your child was whole and well again did anything matter.

Eva felt awful for the way she'd always been so detached with everyone else's kids. But she'd had to be. If she'd got attached, or personally involved, allowed her feelings to interfere, then she'd have been a worn-out wreck.

Only now she was on the other side. Not the doctor. The relative. *She* was the grief-stricken mother. *She* was the one with tears staining her cheeks, her eyes red, searching for hope. *She* was the one grasping at straws and hoping beyond anything that today's doctors and today's medicine could save her child.

Eva felt so alone. So isolated.

But deep down she knew she wasn't. There was Jacob. Somewhere…

Where *was* he? Why wasn't he here yet? Was he still driving to the hospital? Madly searching for a parking bay? Who cared about getting a parking ticket? He should be here by now. Perhaps even now he was running to the A&E department?

Her shoulders went back and her chin came up as grim determination strengthened her.

He's coming. I know he's coming!

She looked at Seb's pale face.

She'd never had to face a crisis like this before. And she felt so lonely.

For the first time in years she wanted her mum.

Jacob blew through the doors of his own A&E department, bypassed Reception and, jacket flying, ran into the maze of corridors that had become like a second home. His gaze flicked to the admissions board but he couldn't see Seb's name.

So he wasn't in cubicles. Nor in Minors.

He had to be in Majors.

Or Resus.

Oh, my God.

He tried to swallow, but his mouth had gone dry. People he worked with tried to say, 'Hi, Merry Christmas!' But he brushed past them and rushed into Resus—where he found Eva by their son's bed. Her eyes were swollen and she held Seb's limp hand in her own.

'Where have you *been*?' she demanded.

Jacob looked shocked. 'I couldn't find a place to park. What's going on? What have they said?'

'They don't know.' She turned back to her son and clasped his hand again. 'They've run tests, done a CT. We're awaiting results.'

'How is he?'

'The same. They want to move him to Paediatric ICU.'

'When?'

She shook her head. 'I don't know. When they can.'

She had no energy for Jacob now that he was here. All her focus was on her boy.

It wasn't good enough. How many times had he impotently stood by, waiting for a bed space to become available? How many times had he had to console a relative because the beds manager couldn't sort out a bed backlog? Too many times. He'd not been working here for long and he was already fed up with the bureaucracy of the hospital and the stupid red tape that stopped them being able to discharge patients who didn't need to be there.

Jacob turned and grabbed the wall phone, almost ripping it from its lodging as he punched in the number for the bed manager.

'Rick?'

'Yes?'

'Dr Dolan in A&E. My son is here in Resus, awaiting a paediatric ICU bed. What's the hold-up?'

There was a pause, during which he heard a brief shuffling of papers. 'Paediatric ICU is full at present. I understand there may be a bed free soon—though I believe there's a possibility that your son may need surgery first.'

'Surgery?'

He saw Eva's face blanch.

'That's not good enough, Rick. My son needs the care of the paediatric team and he needs it *now*. Where's Bilby? Surely he's in today?'

William Bilby was the top paediatric doctor in the entire UK, and he happened to work at their hospital. He'd won awards for the work that he'd carried out in neurological medicine, and families came from across the country to consult him.

'He's not here today. He's on Christmas vacation with his family.'

'Call him.'

'That's not in my remit, Dr Dolan.'

'Then, I'll call him myself!'

There was a sigh. 'Look, I'm sorry about your son being

ill, but we all have to stick to what we do best for the efficient running of this hospital. I can't prioritise your son...'

'Well, I will!'

He slammed the phone back onto the wall, almost crushing it beneath his grip, and turned to look at Eva. She was pale and shocked.

What was he thinking? She needed him to be strong—not for him to turn into some angry monster. He'd lost his temper badly once before and look at how *that* had turned out.

'Sorry,' he mumbled. Then he went across to Seb's bed and took his son's other hand, held it to his cheek. 'Come on, champ...' He looked at Eva, determined not to cry.

Her eyes were large and swollen with tears. 'You said surgery?'

'They must have found something on the CT. Why has no one come to see us?'

He hated this. Hated this not knowing. This being left in limbo.

She shook her head and a solitary tear descended her cheek. 'Am I going to lose him? *Am* I? I don't think I could bear it, Jacob.'

'We're not going to lose him.' He squeezed his son's hand, hoping somehow that the force of his will would somehow make it so.

At that moment, the doors to Resus opened and Sarah came in, her face full of concern. She went straight over to Eva and Jacob. 'We've had a good look at the CT and the scan confirms that Seb has a small subdural haematoma. It's probably been bleeding for a while, as these injuries are usually slow leaks—as you know.'

'You think it's from that bus crash a couple of weeks ago? He banged his head then.'

'It's likely.'

Jacob frowned. 'The neurologist said he didn't need a scan. The *idiot*! He *missed* this!'

'We all missed it, Jacob.' Eva laid a hand on his arm.

Sarah looked to her friend. 'We'll be taking Seb in for surgery right away. Once we get in there we'll clip the leak and remove the haematoma. That should relieve the pressure on Seb's brain.'

'And he'll regain consciousness?'

'Hopefully.'

Hopefully...

Eva shrugged. 'What do we do whilst we wait?'

Sarah just looked at her. 'Try to remain calm. We'll look after him, Eva. You know we'll do our best.'

They could only hope the hospital's best was good enough.

Jacob stood up and began to pace the floor, glaring through the glass at people carrying on with their normal lives whilst his was in turmoil.

Of course they all had jobs to do. He knew that. But he couldn't understand how these other people could be so calm whilst he felt...

He could be losing his family here. His precious family! His *son*! His beloved son! The one he hadn't known he had—the one he'd only just got to know, to love, to cherish. He'd thought a few days before that the worst thing in the world would be to tell Eva the truth about what had happened in his past, but he'd been wrong. You had to tell people you loved them because you never knew when they might be taken from you.

This was what was terrible! This was the worst thing *ever*!

'I'm going to call my parents.'

Eva nodded. 'But they'll be upset. So far away, they won't be able to do anything.'

'They'll want to know.'

She acceded, and then turned back to look at the empty space where her son had been.

Eva had thought she was very familiar with the sensations of pain and grief and loss. She'd also thought she was familiar with waiting. Being patient. But she'd had no clue as to the real agony parents went through whilst they waited to hear if their child had made it through lifesaving surgery.

She stared at the doors where the surgeons would emerge, praying, begging, pleading for them to open so that someone would come and tell her that Seb was fine. But the doors stubbornly remained closed. For hours.

When they did finally open—when the surgeon did finally emerge—she almost couldn't bear to hear his words, convinced it had all gone wrong.

The surgeon removed the mask from his face and smiled. 'The surgery went very well. No problems. Seb was stable all the way through. You'll have your little boy back with you in no time.'

Eva sagged with relief at the news. *Thank God!*

The staff in Paediatric ICU had done their best to make it *not* look like a department in a hospital. The walls were painted in a soft cornflower blue, bright and brash with cartoon characters from all kinds of series in a kind of cheery, animated Bayeux Tapestry.

The nurses all wore colourful tabards, with teddy bear name badges edged in tinsel, and there were Christmas trees galore, all surrounded with fake presents—empty boxes wrapped in colourful paper. From the ceilings hung paper chains and the children's snowflakes and snowmen, fat Santas and reindeer.

There was too much effort to make it look jolly.

Fake jolly.

To make the parents as well as the children forget that they were in such a terrible place.

Jacob felt as if he was in hell. The one day he'd hoped would pass without incident and it had turned into the day his nightmares about life came true.

This hurt. He ached. He felt powerless. As both a doctor *and* a father. Now he realised why family was so important. He wanted them here. He wanted their support.

He was glad he'd told Eva the truth.

He still didn't know her reaction. She'd not really had a chance to say. She hadn't looked horrified…but then they'd heard about Seb. She hadn't had a chance to let it sink in.

She might not want anything to do with him. A man who could be so cruel to someone he'd supposedly loved…

If he'd treated Michelle right in the first place—respected her, not taken her for granted once that ring was on her finger—then his happiness now wouldn't be at such great risk!

Eva was the one who had given him Seb. Eva was the one who had cared for and looked after their little boy so well. And then he'd turned up on the day of Seb's accident, distracting her. They'd both been distracted. Both shocked by seeing the other. And they'd missed what had been happening to Seb.

Eva was going to be the one to choose what happened to them all now.

He stared at her, memorising her face. The soft arch of her eyebrows, the laughter lines at her eyes. The gentle slope of her tear-stained cheek. The deep lines across her brow.

'We still need to talk,' he said.

'I can't—not right now.'

He understood. This was the wrong time. She would probably want to wait until Seb was back with them both before she let him down gently.

Hopefully, she would still let him see Seb...

London at dusk was an ethereal place. The sky above was a strange watercolour mix of blue and pink. Purple undertones highlighted the clouds against the dark grey outlines of the buildings. Bright spots of Christmas lights shone out from various streets and windows, and the traffic on the myriad streets below made the place seem alive.

Jacob looked out across the skyline and unclenched his fists. Fear had caused all of this. Fear of losing a boy he'd only just come to love. Fear of losing something, *someone* so precious...

He was calmer now. More sensible now that he knew Seb was going to be okay.

Reaching into his jacket pocket, he pulled out his phone, scrolling through his contacts until he found the number he wanted. William Bilby. The UK's top paediatrician.

It rang a few times, then was answered, the sound fuzzy.

'Hello?'

'Bill? It's Jacob Dolan—'

'No need to say anything, Jacob. I'm on my way in right now. I'm about five minutes from the hospital.'

He was on his way in? But who'd told him about Seb?

'How did you know?'

'Rick told me. He gave me a call. But I've had to drive in from Surrey and the roads are hell.'

Rick. The beds manager. The man he'd yelled at. Jacob closed his eyes in thanks, knowing he would make sure he apologised to the poor man when he got the chance.

'Kids bounce back, Jacob. Much better than adults do.'

'I hope so.'

He rang off, staring out to the horizon. He knew he ought to go back. Knew he shouldn't have left Eva like that. Alone in that horrible empty room. But he'd had to get out. Had to get some fresh air. Be away from other people. The rooftop offered that solace he craved.

His phone bleeped to life.

How's Seb?

His mother had texted. He could only imagine their panic and pain. Could see in his mind's eye his mother's frantic scurrying to get in the car and head from Netherfield Village to London. A place she didn't really like. Today of all days. Leaving her home at Christmastime...

The cold fresh air had done its job, and the chill was now making him tremble and shiver.

And Bilby was coming in, too. He felt sure they could get all this sorted.

Seb had to be out of Recovery soon... Was he already back?

I ought to check. I ought to be there when they bring Seb back to us.

The fresh air had helped. The space. The crispness.

He headed back down.

As Seb was wheeled back into the room a new doctor arrived. Mr Bilby. Eva wasn't sure, but she thought this was the man that Jacob had asked for when he'd rung the beds manager. Whoever he was, he had a kind face with a wide smile, and he did his best to put Eva at her ease.

'I've read the report. The surgery was a great success. We've got Seb's back here—don't you worry.'

Good. He knew they were doing their best.

They all rushed over to Seb's side when his bed wheels had been locked into position.

Jacob grabbed his son's hand and kissed it, then turned around, nodding an acknowledgement of Mr Bilby. 'Bill.'

'Observations are good, Jacob. He should come round soon.'

'Good.'

'Temp's normal. BP's normal. We've just got to wait for the sedation to wear off.'

William Bilby slipped away and left them alone together. Silent beside their son's bed.

Jacob stared into space, his face shockingly white against his dark hair, his once vibrant blue eyes pale and cold.

Eva stood numb beside him as they both stared at their son. Each of them praying in their own special way.

Early on Christmas Day Seb slowly woke up.

Eva woke instantly, as if by some sixth sense, and heard Jacob say his son's name.

She leaped to her feet, blinking rapidly to get the sleep from her eyes so she could see for herself the marvellous result of her son coming back to her.

'Seb? Sebastian? Oh, thank God! You're back!'

Seb blinked slowly, his eyes unfocused, but he gently gripped his mother's fingers and then closed his eyes again.

'He'll be tired. He might sleep more before he wakes again,' Jacob observed.

Eva glanced at him. 'I'm scared to think that this might end well. I've hoped that way before.'

'His observations are good. His intercranial pressure is normal. We *can* hope, Eva.'

She stroked her son's fringe back from his face. 'You wanted to talk earlier?'

He looked up at her and met her gaze, his heart palpitating in his chest. Of course. He'd promised himself— promised them all—that he would face this. Her judgement of his actions.

It was the only way he could set himself free. If she chose to walk, then so be it. He wouldn't blame her. But he *had* to know he would still have Seb! He couldn't lose him.

I don't want to lose her, either. I love her!

He swallowed and looked back at his sleeping son. He didn't want them to break up in front of their son. He believed that Seb might hear them. He wanted this to be private. He wanted the opportunity to talk to her without any chance of interruptions.

'I know where we can talk.'

Giving one final look of love at Seb, he led Eva outside and up onto the hospital roof.

CHAPTER NINE

EVA BEGAN TO SHIVER. And it wasn't just from the cold.
'What is it?'

'It's Michelle.'

Michelle. I knew it! He still carries a torch for her! He still loves her!

'What about her?'

She needed to hear him say it. If he still loved this woman from his past, then fine. She would walk away. She would do the decent thing. Because if the past twenty-four hours had taught her anything, it was that the most important thing in her life was Seb.

'It's *my* fault she's dead. *I* killed her, Eva.'

Eva looked at him, incredulous. 'No, you didn't!'

'Of course I did. Didn't you hear what I said? I didn't treat her right. I got complacent, got stupid. I should have seen what was going on! But I didn't. And because I didn't, I yelled at her. As if it was *her* fault! I upset her so much she couldn't see where she was going and she crashed.'

'I heard you, Jacob. It was terrible, I grant you—tragic—but you weren't to blame.'

He'd been expecting to hear her agree with him. To start blaming him, too. But she didn't. The shock of hearing something else startled him.

'I wasn't?'

'*No!* She chose to have an affair, Jacob. She could have told you how she was feeling—but, no, she cheated on you with your best friend! And, whilst we're at it, *he* should have known better, too! No one forced her into her car that day. She was upset—she should never have driven. She has to take responsibility.'

'I feel so guilty...'

'Of course you do. You're human. *I'd* feel guilty. But don't forget everyone else on that day and how they must have felt.'

'What do you mean?'

'The driver of the heavy-goods vehicle. Do you think *he* felt guilty? Do you think the paramedics felt guilty because they couldn't revive her? The doctors in the hospital? We both work in A&E—you know how we feel when we lose someone.'

Jacob stared at her hard, his eyes glassy with held-back tears. 'I was so afraid of telling you... I thought I would lose you.'

Eva shivered slightly in the cold. 'What? You thought I'd say it was over? You think you're not worth staying for?'

'I've caused so much pain, Eva.'

'The only thing that will cause more will be if you tell me that you still love her!'

Jacob looked at her in shock. As if it was the last thing he'd be feeling. 'I don't love her.' He looked confused by her statement. 'I never loved her *enough*.'

What? What was he saying? Eva didn't understand.

'I don't understand. Are you in love with her or not?'

'No. I love *you*.' He looked down at the pitched felt rooftop. 'You deserved the truth from me. But if you want to walk away from me now you know it...I'll understand.'

'Walk away? Don't you *get* it, Jacob? I *need* you! I never thought I'd be able to say that about anyone. *Ever!* Apart from Seb…but he's part of me… I knew I loved you ages ago. But I felt I couldn't tell you because I thought you still loved Michelle and that hurt! As I stood by Seb's bed, watching the doctors work, watching them trying to fix him, I felt so alone! And I'm done with that feeling. I'm *done*! You and I… We're… We could have something really special. I knew it all those years ago, when we first met. There was something special between us then.'

'What are you saying, Eva?'

'I'm saying I want to be with you. Together. As a family.'

'But what happened to Michelle—'

'Was a tragic accident! Nothing more! I need you to let that go.'

Jacob sucked in a breath. 'Without you and Seb I'm nothing. I can't let *you* go.'

She stepped closer, pulling the warmth of him against her. 'You don't have to.'

'You mean it?' He hesitantly risked a smile.

'I mean it.'

She reached up on tiptoes and kissed him, and she forgot how cold she was, pressed against him. Feeling herself against him.

With him.

'I spent so long standing alone, Jacob. It was just easier for me, I thought, to push you away before you left of your own accord. I thought I was protecting myself. Protecting my heart from being crushed.'

'I'll never hurt your heart. I'll always cherish it. I'll always cherish *you*.'

She reached up and stroked his face, and as she did so snowflakes began to fall. A soft flurry of snow, sweeping in across the capital in the morning light.

They looked about them in wonder, and then back at each other.

'It's snowing! On Christmas Day! Seb will love this!'

Eva snuggled into his chest, feeling safe, feeling *home*.

'So we're going to do this? Together?'

She nodded. 'Together.'

They kissed.

As the snow fell all around them on the rooftop of the hospital, alone in their own special little world they kissed. Their cold noses pressed against the cheek of the other, and their hot breath warmed their mouths and lips as they proved their commitment to the other.

When they broke apart Jacob looked her in the eyes. 'I love you, Eva. From the moment we met I haven't been able to get you out of my head. You've always been there for me. Even in the dark times. Even when you didn't know it.'

Eva let out a big grin. He loved her!

'I love you, too, Jacob.'

'You do?'

She nodded, then shivered. 'But could we go back inside? I hate to be the one to spoil a romantic moment, but I'm freezing!'

Jacob wrapped his arm around her as they hurried back to the rooftop door. There was a bang in the stairwell as it closed behind them, and they ran down the steps, laughing and breathing heavily.

Back in Seb's room, they found he was still sleeping, so they sat beside each other, knowing Seb would get better, that this story would have a happy ending for all of them. And soon, hopefully, Seb would be out and about on his new bike.

Jacob raised her hand to his lips and kissed it.

When Seb woke again he would have the best Christmas present he could ever have wished for.

EPILOGUE

'I'D LIKE TO make a toast!'

Jacob stood in the lounge of his parents' home, in front of the vast fireplace. A small fire was crackling away, keeping them all warm and cosy despite the fresh snowfall outside.

A whole year had passed, and this Christmas Eve had thankfully arrived without incident.

Eva and Jacob had been married for three months. Their September wedding had gone without a hitch, despite his nerves about it being to the contrary, and this last year had been the happiest of their lives.

He raised his glass to his family, looking at all their happy, smiling faces. There were still one or two pieces of Christmas wrapping paper on the carpet that had been missed, but that didn't matter. Seb was sitting on the carpet, surrounded by a big pile of toys and wearing the paper hat from a Christmas cracker. Eva sat between his parents on the couch, feeling very full after his mother's most ambitious Christmas yet.

'I'd like to raise a toast to family,' he said, raising his glass once again before letting his gaze come to rest on Eva. 'Family is the heart of everything. You don't have to be blood relatives to be family. You just need to be surrounded by those you love and those who love you back. Love is the greatest thing we can give one other.'

Eva beamed at him and gave a little nod.

'But most of all I'd like to make a toast to my wife, Eva...'

His parents raised their glasses and looked towards her.

Eva felt excited. Nervous. She'd been dreaming about this moment for a long time. About telling them. Seeing how they reacted. Because this time she was going to share the experience. This time, she wouldn't be going through anything alone.

'And to the baby she's carrying.'

Molly almost dropped her glass. She gasped, her hand covering her mouth in genuine surprise and joy. 'You're *pregnant*?'

Eva nodded happily.

'You're pregnant! Oh, Eva!' Molly burst into tears and hugged her daughter-in-law, and Eva hugged her back.

This was what she'd wanted. For a long time.

Family.

To belong.

To be loved.

'To family!' she said.

They all raised their glasses, and they were just about to clink them together before taking a sip when Molly grinned and swiped Eva's champagne flute, swapping it for her own—non-alcoholic—orange juice.

'To *family*.'

* * * * *

COMING SOON!

We really hope you enjoyed reading this book. If you're looking for more romance, be sure to head to the shops when new books are available on

Thursday 27th December

To see which titles are coming soon, please visit **millsandboon.co.uk**

LET'S TALK
Romance

For exclusive extracts, competitions
and special offers, find us online:

- facebook.com/millsandboon
- @MillsandBoon
- @MillsandBoonUK

Get in touch on 01413 063232

For all the latest titles coming soon, visit
millsandboon.co.uk/nextmonth